Storm Crashers

Storm Crashers

Richard Wickliffe

Oak Tree Press Corcoran, CA

Oak Tree Press
Publishers Since 1998

For information, address Oak Tree Press, 1700 Dairy Avenue #49,
Corcoran, CA 93230.

Oak Tree Press books may be purchased for educational, business, or sales
promotional purposes. Contact Publisher for quantity discounts.

First Edition, June 2016

ISBN-13: 978-0692912492

Dedicated to my kids: Rich, Jack and Cassie.
Their love and existence allows my
ongoing juvenile creativity and fun "what-if" questions

Prologue: Selina

Selina was born on the west coast of the Sahara Desert with no fanfare. In such grueling conditions, her adolescence came quick. She was impatient to cross the Atlantic to seek her destiny as her brothers and sisters had done. Like them, she'd been described as alluring and mysterious –but her aggression became alarming.

She developed faster than most. After a virgin tryst in Barbados, she tramped through the Caribbean with wild disregard. Her followers increased as she matured, but they became troubled at her volatility. Selina had no regard for the people she hurt, or the wounds left in her wake.

With no national allegiance, she stalked victims in Jamaica and Havana before eyeing the vulnerable United States. In the southernmost city of Key West, the eccentric residents ignored her arrival with parties in the streets. As if their lack of respect offended her, Selina snubbed Key West to slither west into the Gulf of Mexico.

As her watchers studied her increasing strength and persistence, they gave her a new name: *Hurricane* Selina.

Miami's National Hurricane Center watched a ridge of high pressure push Selina to a northwest track into the heart of the Gulf. She strengthened from 110 mph to a 145 mph hurricane in less than six hours. When she coiled northeast towards Florida's west coast, she was a Category 4 storm with winds of 150 mph and a possible storm surge of eighteen feet.

Utilizing the letter "S," Selina was the year's nineteenth named storm. The only thing predictable about her was that she'd have more siblings before the end of the season.

1. Uninvited

The security guard peered out the window of his ten-by-ten shack. He'd left a one-inch gap between storm shutters to assess the night. He cupped his hands to see into the darkness. His forearms had blurred tattoos of "Marines" and a Bengal tiger, hinting at wars in exotic lands, numb to any fear. But old Pete's eyes showed alarm as he gazed into the howling night.

His guard station was at the foot of the driveway to an immense oceanfront home. The house was on Millionaire's Row, which faced the Gulf of Mexico, boasting Mediterranean and Cape Cod-style homes. The only thing between the homes and the Gulf was South Seas Lane, already covered in two inches of water. Waves were breaking closer to the road every minute. Palms swayed in the escalating winds. The only illumination came from a flashing yellow light at a corner intersection. The area had been abandoned.

Captiva Island, just offshore of Southwest Florida, was accessible by road to her sister, Sanibel Island to the south. Their connection had been severed years before by a storm, forming a channel between the two islands. A lone causeway linked the islands of Sanibel and Captiva to Florida's mainland. Quiet islands for the wealthy — that they could actually drive to.

From Pete's view of the road, he saw flashing strobes from an approaching police cruiser. As the car crept into view, he saw it shining a spotlight towards each of the estates. The neighbors' vehicles were gone from their driveways. The residents had evacuated, as ordered by Lee County officials. The homes seemed safe and secure.

Pete's shack flickered from a lamp and a small television. The news advised viewers it was 1:35 a.m. A haggard weatherman had his sleeves rolled up. "Folks, even though Selina's landfall could be two hours away, you need to be safe at one of our many shelters…" A satellite image showed a massive cyclone heading towards Florida's west coast. Pete plopped into his chair and took a deep breath.

He flinched at a knock on the door that had the clang of metal on metal. He stood to unbolt the door and squinted one eye like Popeye to see a young officer in rain gear.

"Pete, you shouldn't be here!" The boyish cop shouted over the wind and pelting rain. Pete struggled to hold the door to allow him inside.

"Sorry Randy, but I'm stayin' put!" Pete barked with a smile.

"You need to get over the bridge before the roads flood." Officer Randy inspected Pete's claustrophobic shack. A desk, a fan swirling cigar smoke —and a bottle of cheap rum. "There's a *mandatory* evacuation."

"How do you enforce 'mandatory'? My job's to watch the house!"

"Ms. Larriott's house will be fine." Randy lowered his voice to the old man. "Think about your own safety. You need to be home–"

"–*My* home is a single-wide in Fort Myers," Pete interrupted. "This shack's a cement bunker. I survived Charley *and* Andrew while living in a trailer. I ain't going nowhere."

Randy shook his head and looked at his watch. "I'm the last cop on the island and I got to be over the bridge by 2:00." He looked at the old man. "We'll probably lose phones and cell reception. Will you *promise* to be careful?"

Pete slapped the kid on the shoulder, "I'll be A-okay." He unbolted the door. Randy lifted his hood to dash back into the rain. Pete relocked the door and his smile faded when he turned to the television.

"...The new coordinates show Selina's track to be anywhere between Sanibel and Cape Coral..." Onscreen, satellite animation of the storm looked more daunting than before. A triangular graphic projected the storm's path. Near its center was Fort Myers and Sanibel-Captiva Islands. The fatigued weatherman continued, "She's now a Category 4 hurricane with sustained winds of 150 miles per hour. Fort Myers is already reporting tropical storm-force winds." The man looked ominously into the camera. "If you're on any of the barrier islands, you *must* evacuate immediately."

A crack of deafening thunder. Pete looked up at the ceiling as the bulb flickered. The shriek of the wind sounded like imminent phantoms. He scurried to his window.

From the foot of the driveway, he looked towards Ms. Larriott's home. Lush landscaping and tall palms swayed. The two-story estate was adorned with regal arches, columns and a Spanish-tile roof. The home had several security lights illuminating the front.

Pete jolted at a bolt of lightning and an eruption of thunder. The shack's light went out —as did Ms. Larriott's lights. Pete huddled at the window in complete darkness. As his eyes adjusted, something outside caught his attention.

Levitating across the lawn were small pinpoints of red light. They looked like fireflies, except red. Pete counted five points of light approximately six feet above the ground and two feet apart. They were all moving towards Ms. Larriott's house in a seemingly straight-line formation.

Magnetically drawn to the mystery, Pete cracked open his door. He stepped outside with no regard for the door as it flew open. He shined his flashlight across the lawn and upholstered his .38 caliber.

The hovering points of light descended a few feet as if *ducking*. Pete stepped across the lawn, striving to aim his light in the wind. Simultaneously, the lights froze in midair.

"Who are you? I got a gun!" Pete shouted over the wind's howl.

The five points of light were stationary, now just three feet above the ground —but they did not blow in the wind. *Fireflies can't do that...*

A jagged, triple spear of lightning revealed the sources of the lights: crouched across the lawn were five dark figures. The lights were emanating from the sides of their heads. Though squatting, they appeared to be human. But against the black background, they were indistinguishable shadows.

Pete aimed his light and shouted with authority, "Who are you?"

The closest figure stood, revealing itself in the light's beam. The shape appeared to be a six-foot man. He was covered in black fatigues and body armor. Concealing his head was a helmet and black mask with goggles. The face looked like an angry black insect. The point of light came from an apparent headset. Though the eyes seemed mechanical, the *creature* appeared angry.

Pete's hand shook as he aimed his gun. "*Soldiers?* What are you guys...National Guard?"

The menacing *soldier* lifted a baseball-sized object. Like a professional pitcher, he wound up, stepped forward and hurled the object towards the guard.

Pete dropped to the muddy ground. The object buzzed over his head and exploded with a bright blue pulse on a corner of the guard shack. Pete curled on the ground with his eyes clenched as debris rained down around him.

With another flash of lightning, Pete peered across the lawn to see the mysterious soldiers gone. They'd vanished into the wind like imaginary specters. Pete jumped to his feet and ran, away from the supposed safety of the house. He ran into the night with no regard for the escalating wind or waves submerging South Seas Lane.

In formation, the five soldiers continued towards the estate's backyard. The men wore identical black armor, helmets and gear, yet they carried no evident firearms. In the shelter of the patio, they stopped to face each other. The tallest man lifted two fingers and signaled to two of the others. The two men nodded and moved out, jogging in unison away from the property. The three remaining soldiers turned towards the patio's French doors.

The tall man removed a small, flat mechanism from his belt. It emitted a glowing spectrum through the door's glass. The man's mask crackled with a mechanical voice. "Impact glass." He turned to the smallest man. "LeBeau?"

The diminutive soldier, LeBeau, stepped forward holding a pen-sized device. He inserted its tip into the key hole. Within seconds, six LED lights illuminated as the lock's pins and tumblers were matched. The lock clicked and LeBeau opened the door.

The tall man led the smaller LeBeau and a third stocky soldier into the home's richly-appointed library. The men aimed no weapons and entered the house with no attempt at discretion. They seemed confident no one was home.

Small lights from an emergency power source illuminated a marble foyer and a winding staircase surrounded by opulent fine art. On pedestals were priceless nineteenth-century urns. On the walls were gold-framed oil paintings appearing to be over a hundred years old. Ornate antiques and books adorned the entire room.

The men split into three directions. The tall man proceeded to the staircase. The stocky man turned to the left into a hall leading to bedrooms. The short LeBeau moved to the right into a corridor.

The tall man ascended halfway up the staircase to approach an oil painting. The oil on canvas was an original by French artist Jean-Luc Brulé. It depicted a French general, circa mid-1800s, riding a white stallion. The soldier reached to his helmet to turn on a small light that gleamed forward towards the painting. He methodically inspected the art. As smooth as an archer reaching for an arrow, he reached to his back to retrieve a long, thin tube. The cylindrical tube was attached to his back with hoops and a Velcro material.

Holding the tube with one hand, he lifted a retractable blade and gently cut the painting from its frame. He rolled the art and inserted it into the cylinder, which he returned to his back. He proceeded up the stairs to the next painting.

The stocky man entered the large master bedroom. The room was appointed with a four-poster bed and a sitting area. The back wall had a row of French doors leading to the backyard. The escalating wind was howling against the doors.

The man approached a photograph on the wall. He turned on his helmet light and lifted his goggles to inspect the portrait with his own eyes. The photo was of an exotically-beautiful brunette lady and a pretty five-year-old girl. The woman appeared mid-thirties with high cheekbones and striking almond eyes. She and her identical daughter beamed smiles of undeniable happiness.

"This is your house..?" The stocky man smirked as he studied the lady's face. He moved an inch closer to observe the little girl. The man's face was sweaty and seemed incensed. He narrowed his eyes to observe the jewelry worn by the woman in the photo. He turned to a dresser. Within seconds he located drawers filled with jewelry. In plain view was a ladies two-tone Rolex and diamond bracelets. There had been no attempt to hide or secure the valuables. Either the jewelry meant nothing to the homeowner, or she'd believed her house would be untouched. The man raked the jewelry into black pouches on the thighs of his uniform.

In a dark hall, the smaller LeBeau used night vision to navigate. Within a green glow, he looked at his watch that was counting backward from "0:56:30." He flinched at a crack of thunder and looked up at a shriek of wind. He turned on his helmet light to inspect a security alarm pad on the wall. He lifted his goggles to read the model number. He smiled.

The Lee County Sheriff's Office was a flurry of activity. Officers and employees were stumbling into each other to answer phones. A twenty-year-old Public Service Aide was eating Funyons when something on his monitor captured his attention.

"Sir, several burglar alarms are going crazy," the PSA shouted.

A frazzled deputy clutching a Styrofoam cup of coffee squinted at the computer. "Alarms always go *wacko* with all the power outages. Electrical surges make the alarms go off and on. I've seen a dozen already. You can disregard 'em." The deputy moved on towards a vending machine.

The assistant shrugged. If they didn't care, he didn't care.

At the top of the Larriott staircase, the tall soldier concealed a third painting. He turned to see the stocky man approach from downstairs. They moved to the second-floor corridor to speak.

The thicker man panted as he spoke, "There are cameras. We'll hit 'em on the way out." He leaned closer, "I found the safe, like in the blueprints. Torch proof. We need C4."

The tall man nodded. He lifted a hand to his headset, "LeBeau, bring *the fire.*"

Standing around the corner, paralyzed with fear, was the brunette lady —the once-beautiful homeowner from the portrait. She trembled as she stepped back into the darkness of the corridor.

Alexandra Larriott held her breath and walked backward in slow motion. She didn't blink and her mind raced. *They're in my home!* Her bare feet on Berber were as silent as a cat's paws. The intruders' voices faded as if the men were moving downstairs. In complete darkness, Alexandra felt her way along the hall in search of a door.

"Fire?" Alexandra wondered. The intruder said, "...bring the fire." *What does that mean? Guns? Arson?* Her steps grew quicker the farther she got. In the dark, she slid her hand along a chair rail until she located the door. She clutched the doorknob, struggling to open it without a sound. She slipped into the room and closed the door behind her. Finally taking a breath, she turned on an emergency light. She exhaled a sigh of relief when she looked at the floor. Curled in a Tinkerbell blanket was her angel, five-year-old Cassandra.

The six-by-six foot room had been a laundry room she had reinforced with cement walls. A red logo on the wall read, "Severe-Weather Safe Room." Along with advanced features and security cameras, the safe room had been one of her first priorities when she'd purchased the house. A small power source provided energy to a few lights and the cameras. On the wall, a cabinet contained flashlights, water bottles and a first-aid kit. Above the cabinet, four monitors displayed images of the bedrooms and living area. The unlit bedrooms were barely decipherable.

Alexandra manufactured a weak smile as she crouched beside Cassie. "It's okay, baby." Her voice trembled. Cassie said nothing as she rolled her eyes up to her mother. Their moment was interrupted by an abrupt crack of thunder. They flinched and Cassie's eyes welled with tears.

"*Shhhh...*" Alexandra held a finger to her lips, fearing Cassie might scream. "It's just thunder, sweetie. God's watering the plants." They looked at the ceiling as the wind howled. Alexandra was only wearing a bathrobe as if caught off guard by the intruders. She tightened her robe and ran her fingers through her long hair, unable to calm her trembling hand.

Cassie pulled a thumb out of her mouth. "Are we safe in here?" Her voice was high and gentle.

Alexandra feigned a smile. "Of course, honey." She tried to appear calm by avoiding any erratic motions. She stood nonchalantly to reach for the phone on the wall. Her smile faded to discover the line was dead. She pulled her cellphone out of her robe's pocket. The display read, "No Service." She took a breath, deliberating. Alexandra unlocked and opened a drawer. Under a storm-tracking map was a Smith and Wesson 9mm semi-automatic. With her back to Cassie, she gripped the gun and concealed it in her robe. She huddled in the corner beside her daughter. She said nothing as the smack of rain on the roof intensified. Her eyes darted to each claustrophobic wall of the closet-sized room.

Can I go through with this? Alexandra searched her feelings. She took a deep breath to reconcile any enduring courage. The men were in *her* house, on *her* property. Legally, that changed everything, *right?*

Anything she did –or didn't do– would have to be for Cassie.

2. Lightning and Illusions

The two men who'd been ordered to split from the team jogged inland from the Larriott estate. Ignoring the squalls, they approached an intersection surrounded by lush foliage. They trotted towards the free-standing Captiva Pharmacy.

Though equipped in identical armor and helmets, one was lanky and athletic –the man who'd thrown the grenade like a baseball pitcher. The other was large with thick arms and wide shoulders. He moved with soldier-like discipline, seeming to be the senior of the two.

They approached the small pharmacy. The store's architecture was unrefined 1960s. It stood alone with vacant fields on both sides. All lights for the pharmacy were off. Like the rest of the island, it was without power and had been evacuated.

They jogged to inspect all four walls of the building. The front doors and windows had been shuttered with aluminum panels. The larger man signaled for them to return to the store's rear.

A rear delivery door was not shuttered. The thinner man reached into a pouch and produced a stick of finger-sized putty that he applied to the door's hinges. The larger man inserted a one-inch antenna. They crouched around the corner and engaged a remote detonator. A succinct, compact explosion blew the door from its frame. Through the smoke, they charged into the building like stormtroopers.

Officer Randy flinched in his seat at the sound of the nearby explosion. His cruiser was idling through six inches of water trying to flee the island. He stopped his car and looked in his rearview mirror.

"Dispatch, I got a code-two," Randy shouted into his radio the code for an urgent, but non life-threatening situation. "Probably a transformer hit by lightning."

A reply came through heavy static. "Ten-four. Make it fast. Landfall could be in less than an hour. Over."

Randy made the U-turn towards the Captiva Pharmacy.

Utilizing their night-vision, the two men leaped over the counter to enter the pharmacist's work area. They turned on their helmet lights to inspect the cabinets and bins. They moved fast, breaking cabinet doors until they found what they were looking for: containers of OxyContin and anything with methadone, morphine or codeine. They raked the valuable narcotics into weatherproof pouches. The larger man gestured to his luminescent watch. The other man nodded and they exited the pharmacy.

Alexandra stroked Cassie's head with one hand and gripped her gun with the other. They'd be secure if they just remained in the safe room. But her primitive desire to venture out resumed. She didn't take her eyes off the monitors on the wall. All the rooms appeared empty. *Did the men leave?*

Something caught Alexandra's eyes in a monitor. In her master bedroom, there was movement in the shadows. She narrowed her eyes to discern any shapes in the image. A pulse of lightning illuminated her bedroom, revealing three men. Alexandra stood, needing to confirm what she saw. *Maybe just an illusion in the monitor?* But with another flash of lightning, she saw them again. Three dark figures were in her bedroom. *Do they have weapons?* Her mind raced and she clutched her gun.

She turned off the monitor before Cassie could notice it. After a moment of maternal deliberation, fueled by adrenalin, she stooped to whisper, "Cass, listen to your headphones..." *Maybe it'll drown out the sound*, she hoped. "I'll go downstairs and get some ice cream before it melts. Does that sound good?"

Cassie cautiously smiled and embraced her bunny. Alexandra unbolted the door and looked down. She spoke in a slow, deliberate tone, "I'm going to lock the door behind me. *Do not* open it for anyone. Promise?"

Cassie's smile vanished at the odd request. Her mom exited the room with the clanging of steel as the door was rebolted from the outside.

In the property adjacent to the Captiva Pharmacy, lightning revealed a scrubby field and blowing vegetation. In the center of the field, the two soldiers from the pharmacy stood side by side, gazing in the sky as if looking for something.

Officer Randy's car, flashing its strobes, approached from the street a hundred feet away. The two men turned their heads but didn't attempt to flee.

Randy stepped out of his car in his rain gear. He held a hand over his eyes to block the rain, noticing the men's helmets and armor. "Who are you?" he shouted. "Some...response team?" He looked at the sky trying to see whatever the men were looking at. Gusts of rain made visibility impossible.

The ominous soldiers did not reply. They looked back into the sky.

"What department are you with?" Randy put a hand on his gun and stepped closer.

A mechanical voice emanated from the thinner soldier. "Watch for lightning."

"What?" Randy contorted his face in confusion. He studied the soldier's goggles and mask. The helmets appeared modern, but with flared sides reminiscent of Nazi helmets.

One soldier removed a device from his hip and pointed to the skies. He mechanically growled, "Watch for lightning!"

When Randy looked up, the soldier aimed the device at him. A spark discharged from the weapon, sending two electrified barbs into the cop. Randy dropped his gun and fell to the ground. The barbs emitted sizzling, energized pops as he shrieked on the wet grass, writhing in pain.

The two soldiers resumed their task, moving closer together.

Randy cracked his eyes up at the men. Unable to speak, he emitted unintelligible cries. The two soldiers were fastening something to their uniforms. The thinner man looked down at the cop. The soldier cocked his head as if studying him. He then raised a hand to his helmet and gave an odd salute.

Before Randy's blurred eyes, the two men shot straight up into the sky like missiles. The black figures vanished into the wind and rain without a sound. With only the storm's howl, they disappeared as if they'd never existed.

Convulsing on his side, the cop began hyperventilating in a puddle of rain. He mumbled through gasps, "They weren't... real. Just... lightning." Officer Randy passed out in disbelief.

3. The Assailant

The two armored men hung from the bungee cords that had sprung them from the ground. The MH-68A Stingray helicopter ascended through the mounting storm. Their *terra launch* from the rendezvous had been successful. Though cords were fastened to their vests, the men still had to grasp the lines through gusts as they were winched into the chopper.

Their sleek –and stolen– Stingray helicopter had been designed for Coast Guard interdictions and sea rescues. It had since been painted all-black, making it virtually invisible without any exterior lights. It was reminiscent of a black hornet, with its external guns and forward-mounted sensor. As the soldiers pulled themselves into the chopper's cabin, it took off like a missile, easily piercing the wind and rain.

Alexandra gripped her pistol in front of her with both hands. She stepped from the staircase, praying that her trembling hands would settle. A small emergency light on the ceiling enabled her to navigate the entryway. She paused in the foyer, her breathing audible. She turned towards the dark hall leading to her master bedroom. Bare-foot on marble, she moved without a sound.

As she crept down the thirty-foot hall, she heard voices that sounded like walkie-talkies. With the echo of wind and rain, the content of the men's conversations were garbled. She crouched low the closer she got. She stopped two feet from the threshold. Alexandra took a deep breath and craned her neck to peer into her bedroom.

As her eyes adjusted, she could make out three men standing near her far wall. A green glow from the men's goggles provided subtle illumination. The men were standing with their backs to her. *They can't see me,* she realized. They were able to work in pitch-dark conditions. *They have night-vision,* she guessed —but *she* had an intimate knowledge of her home, even in the dark. Through her French doors, lightning provided sporadic visibility.

The tall man pulled something from his belt as a shorter man removed a painting from the wall. Exposed behind the picture was a wall safe. The tall man's device emitted a radiant x-ray projection. Illuminated on the safe's door like magic was a visible depiction of the locking mechanism. As the man adjusted the green x-ray projection, the contents of her safe became visible. Alexandra cowered in the doorway with a conflicted mix of panic and wonder.

Alexandra lifted her gun. She closed her eyes and took three deep breaths. She said a silent prayer, pleading for the courage she needed. *This is for Cassie...* She opened her eyes and stood. She straightened her arms, standing in a ready stance. The men still had their backs to her twenty feet away. It had to be now.

"Freeze! I have a gun!" Alexandra shouted.

The three burglars flinched. They turned to face their assailant. The tall soldier was the first to react, reaching for his belt.

Alexandra screamed, "I said don't–"

The tall man fired an electroshock weapon. Two barbs struck the door to her right, spewing sparks. Alexandra dropped to her left, escaping the darts, but crushing her shoulder against the doorframe. In doing so, she inadvertently fired her gun.

The tall man shouted in pain, grasping his thigh. Alexandra

peered up to look at the man. For such a nightmarish creature, the man was vulnerable. He turned to the other two and shouted orders, pointing to the glass doors.

Concealed in the shadows, Alexandra fired again. Her bullet grazed the armor of one man, shattering the glass beside him. With the fracture in the storm-proof glass, the door shattered inward, sending rain and wind wailing into the room. Alexandra covered her face from the whirlwind of glass and rain. The air smelled of ozone and salt water. The cyclone of debris stung her skin like a sandstorm.

In their protective gear, the men ran through the shattered doors. They smashed through the glass with their padded forearms and helmets, sending shards to the floor like daggers. Long drapes lashed behind them, helping them disappear like ghosts.

Alexandra got up to run after the men. Gripping her gun, she ran toward the doors at full speed. In that millisecond, she realized it was *she* who had turned the hunters into the prey. *Three armed men against a five-foot-three woman?* It was easier than she could've ever dreamed.

She felt indestructible —until searing pains shot up her leg. Her bare feet sliced through the shards of broken glass. She screamed in anguish, yet unable —or unwilling— to slow her stride. With adrenalin pumping, she continued through the doors and into her backyard. The soggy mud eased some of the pain. She swiped her feet with her hand. Some pieces of glass were too small to remove in the dark. With a limping jog, she scanned her property. She heard the crackle of walkie-talkies to the left, beyond the pool. Oblivious of her injuries, she took off through the garden.

The smaller soldier, LeBeau, stumbled through a jungle of shrubbery. Despite his night-vision, he fumbled and slid through the wet property.

Close behind him, the stocky soldier was shouting into his radio, "Butch! Butch! Are you hit?" He struggled to navigate a maze of palms and garden statues. The men's heavy panting reverberated within their humid masks.

Twenty yards behind the two men was their wounded leader, Butch. He limped with a thigh injury. Butch shouted into his radio, "Keep moving! Make the rendezvous!" He labored through the swelling gusts. He couldn't keep up with his men.

"I called the police!" Alexandra shouted, familiar with the nuances of her yard. She knew a path that led to a dune preserve behind her home. The men were heading in that direction. With the frequent lightning, she could see the wounded soldier trotting thirty yards in front of her. "Stop!" She shouted with no decline in determination.

When the man turned to look back, he slipped in mud. He fell onto his side with a mechanical grunt.

"Do *not* move! I'll shoot!" Alexandra screamed, moving towards the fallen soldier.

The man looked up through his menacing mask. He labored to stand, keeping his eyes on the woman. He outstretched his hands as if surrendering. Palm fronds whipped in the wind beside him, partially concealing his body.

"What do you want?" Alexandra shouted. She stood unyielding, aiming her firearm. She squinted in the rain to observe the man. Wind and sand stung her eyes.

Behind a swaying palm, the man stood static like a mannequin. Alexandra paused at his inaction, using the moment to catch her breath. She narrowed her eyes, trying to see the man. "You think you're bad now?" she taunted. "Take off your mask —coward!"

After three seconds of disarming stillness, the man made a move for his belt. Alexandra fired. The armored man fell to the muddy ground, motionless.

Alexandra was frozen. She scanned the dunes for any sign of the other men. *Did they hear the gunshot?* It was hard to believe the soldiers would leave their man behind. She looked down at the figure on the ground. He didn't move. It was too dark to see if he was breathing. She took a step forward, aiming her gun at his neck —the only spot of unprotected skin. *Is he dead?*

A burst of wind hurled a thirty-foot palm plummeting to the ground beside her. Alexandra screamed, stumbling to dodge the tree. She squatted, looking at the tree and then back to the man. Wind screamed over the dunes. An eruption of thunder made her jump. Transformers on nearby electrical poles exploded with blue light. Alexandra had no choice; she turned to race home. Hurricane Selina was coming ashore.

A rush of endorphins acted as a temporary pain killer for her slashed feet. A Category 4 storm *on top of* shooting a man consumed her mind. Her only goal was to get back to her daughter. She needed the sporadic lightning to find her way home. She dodged whirlwinds of sand and debris until she reached her house. Patio furniture had shattered her back doors.

Alexandra entered her home, limping with her wounds. Rain blew inside, flooding her once-extravagant living room. Sheer drapes blew in the wind. With the ominous lightning, her house looked like a haunted mansion. Saturated in a muddy robe, Alexandra hobbled up her staircase. She felt her way along the second-floor hall to the safe room. She used a key from a chain around her neck to unlock the door.

Alexandra entered the room. One emergency light was still operational. She was shocked by the trail of mud and blood from her feet. But as she turned and looked down, she smiled. Cassie was curled under her Disney blanket, peacefully asleep. Alexandra envied the inexplicable defense mechanisms of children. With a jolt of thunder, her only light went out.

Alexandra illuminated a flashlight towards her feet. She used a bottle of water to wash away dirt and blood. From the first aid kit, she used tweezers to remove the visible slivers of glass. She hissed and her eyes watered as she sprayed alcohol on the open cuts.

Biting her lip with pain, she looked up at the ceiling. Deafening clatter sounded like roof damage. *Or is it footsteps in the attic?* Her eyes darted with paranoia. Was it the sound of men? Could *he* still be alive?

She cowered in the corner with Cassie, still gripping her gun. The storm sounded like an arriving locomotive. Her flashlight's batteries faded and the light flickered out.

Have they come back?

4. Dan Holms: Stormtrooper

Dan Holms' office was his kitchen table. He scratched his three-day growth of beard and took a sip from his third Corona. He wanted to try that LandShark beer from Jimmy Buffett, but it was a dollar more. He alternated between watching the storm on CNN on a fifty-inch in the living room, and on a local channel on a thirty-two inch placed beside it. An ancient black and white emergency TV on the kitchen counter was on yet another channel. He was proud of his poor-man's mission control, but it was 2:45 a.m. and his eyes were blurring.

He rubbed his forehead, aged beyond his mid-thirties, with a perpetual tan and hints of silver at his temples. To focus his eyes elsewhere, he looked out the kitchen window onto the waterway behind his home. With only a slight breeze, coconut palms silhouetted the moon. He loved his simple neighborhood in old Fort Lauderdale. The houses were 1960s ranch-style on an inland waterway that *technically* led to the sea. Affordable paradise, he used to boast. Too bad it was all up for sale.

He checked his laptop on the cluttered table. No new messages from his boss at Insurex. Dan already knew his assignment. He finished his beer and looked at the big screen to see Hurricane Selina devouring the west coast of Florida. The phone rang and he looked at his caller-ID. He grimaced when he saw that it wasn't his boss.

"Hi Liz," his voice was weary. "Yeah, it came ashore around Sanibel. If it continues northeast, Lauderdale should be fine. I'll be fine. 'Til tomorrow, that is."

The woman on the phone was irritated. "You have to go there tomorrow?"

He frowned, "Insurance is my job, you know."

"I thought you only investigate fraud stuff." Her voice was like angry gravel.

"Liz, there's big money for the first storm reps." He was defensive, "The *honest* people need a lot of help. Sadly, the fraud will come later when scam contractors head south or people see all their neighbors getting new roofs–"

"–So you *won't* be showing the house this weekend?" Liz interrupted.

"No," Dan closed his eyes. "This house has been for sale for six months. What's a few more weeks?"

"I could really use the money," she retorted. "When you and I split up, I thought you–"

Dan stood, interrupting louder. "–I'm the guy mailing boxes of your crap to Seattle every week. There's a Cat-4 aiming for South Florida and this is all you care about?"

"You just said it's *not* hitting you now."

He stopped, knowing a no-win argument when he heard one. He took a deep breath and cleared his throat. "I'll probably be living in a tent or a trailer for the next few weeks. Fourteen-hour days, seven days a week. But it'll be big money. I'll send what I can–"

"–Why don't you just sell the house?"

Dan could feel his blood pressure spiking. He turned to the television, choosing to ignore the phone. The news showed incoming footage of inconceivable devastation. He placed the phone on the table, allowing Liz to drone on. He stepped closer to the screen to observe the storm's trail. He shook his head that he'd be in the middle of it in less than eight hours.

Dan tossed his worn leather duffle onto his bed. He filled it with every khaki shirt and pair of cargo pants he owned. In a disaster area with no AC, he'd still need long pants to avoid mosquitoes that inevitably hatch in flood zones. He packed one nice, long-sleeved Columbia fishing shirt in the remote chance of any social outing or fishing. He packed a canvas hat for the inescapable sun and swamp boots for the uncertain terrain. In a leather backpack, he packed a Canon digital SLR to document damage. He grabbed his old-school Dictaphone for the recorded statements he'd need. He packed a Swiss Army knife for everything else.

Liz had mockingly joked about him packing a bullwhip and fedora. He was elated the day she'd announced she was moving to the opposite end of the continental U.S.

He paused to consider any other needs. He raised a brow and pulled his Glock 17 from the bedside drawer. Something his company would never permit. He carefully wrapped the handgun in the center of his duffle.

He looked at his watch and took two ibuprofens. He stretched across his bed like a cat, praying for just four hours of sleep. He wondered if this would be his last bed —or air conditioning— for weeks to come.

As bad as it looked on TV, Dan hoped it'd be a fairly routine storm. Certainly nothing out of the ordinary.

5. Fight or Flight

The two fleeing soldiers were unaware of their leader's fate. After leaping a fence, they hustled through dunes covered with sea grape trees.

They tumbled into a pit on the far side of a ridge. The men crawled to the bottom, between dunes. Breathless, they huddled and lifted their masks.

The smaller LeBeau panted with a slight French accent, "The Stingray's due any second!"

The stocky Curt looked back, shouting for their leader, "Butch! *Butch!*" He was sweating with an angry face. "I'm going back!"

LeBeau grasped Curt's shoulder, "We can't!" He pointed to his watch. "Do not deviate!"

"We're not leaving my brother!" Curt growled.

"He zapped her!" LeBeau speculated. "He'll ride out the storm in her house!"

Curt pushed a finger to LeBeau's chest, "You *want* him gone!" His rage obscured any concern for the storm. "I heard a shot!"

"It was thunder!" With martial arts precision, LeBeau swiped his arm to force Curt's hand away. "He's safer than we are."

LeBeau and Curt huddled to endure a cyclone of debris churning around them. LeBeau pulled a flare from his belt and ignited it.

The Stingray's female pilot was annoyed at the two men she'd airlifted near the pharmacy. Red control lights illuminated her and the two soldiers in the cabin. She shouted over the engines, "You idiots zapped a cop!"

The more athletic man, Pitch, removed his helmet. "Just a stun." The young African-American man added, "He'll think he was hit by lightning —if he survives the storm."

His hulking partner, Tag, removed his helmet and shouted, "They should be finishing the last house —a three-story, due west." Tag was middle-aged with a Marine buzz cut.

The Latina pilot, Dalia, watched an infrared terrain map. "They know the rendezvous! They're six minutes late!" The chopper bucked in the winds. "I can't stay in this shear much longer!"

"We leave *no one* behind!" Tag barked. "Keep scanning for their heat."

The perturbed Dalia was in her late twenties. Her helmet couldn't contain her dark, exotic features. In any other predicament, she'd be attractive. But she scowled as she struggled with the controls.

"I don't see anything!" Pitch shouted at the display. "The cold rain's cloaking their heat —wait!" He looked at Dalia. "I see them. But only two..?" The display showed the red glow of a flare next to the green glow of the two figure's body heat.

The Stingray swayed in the winds as it descended to five feet above the ground. Curt and LeBeau climbed up the embankment towards the chopper. From within the Stingray, Tag and Pitch pulled the men into the cabin. As soon as Dalia got the thumbs-up from Tag, she pulled the chopper straight up, climbing back into the tumultuous sky.

"We gotta' go back for Butch!" Curt lunged towards Dalia. "He's still out there!"

LeBeau pushed Curt aside, struggling to explain. "We encountered the resident. Butch is back at her house. He'll be fine!"

The large Tag pulled the men apart. "How do you know Butch is okay?"

LeBeau was snide. "A ten-year SEAL can handle a hundred-pound woman." Though short, LeBeau spoke with arrogance. "He's safer than we are!"

The chopper banked hard to the right with a squall. Dalia shouted, "This bird ain't designed for a Cat-4. We have to exit —*NOW!*"

Tag looked down at Curt. "Butch is trained to find shelter. He'll radio us tomorrow." Tag's baritone resonated with finality. The men buckled themselves into their tight quarters. The floor's steel panels vibrated as if the craft was being pulled apart by the winds.

Curt sat in resignation, "If you're wrong, I'll kill every one of you!"

Tag, LeBeau and Pitch looked at each other as if more concerned with Curt's mindset than for the welfare of their leader.

The Stingray helicopter flew inland, due east. To avoid wind velocity that increased with altitude, the chopper remained only fifty feet above sea level. At a speed of 140 nautical miles per hour, the effects of the storm diminished every second. Focused and using both hands to navigate, Dalia was confident, flying via night-vision, radar and infrared.

Within twenty minutes they were over the center of the state. There were no lights on any horizon. The darkness was not from power outages, but due to 4,300 square miles of uninhabited Everglades. The expanse of swamp and sawgrass filled the southern interior of the Florida peninsula.

Dalia followed a programmed trajectory that led towards a single point of light in the middle of nowhere. As they got closer, the twinkle became a lone streetlamp beside a steel structure. The building's corrugated half-barrel design was reminiscent of a World War II hangar. Eighty miles from the storm, the area had electricity. The lamp illuminated a weathered sign that read, "Jeb's Mosquito and Crop Dusting."

The Stingray landed in front of the hangar. Two steel doors on the building slowly opened. The chopper rolled into the building and the doors closed behind it.

Within minutes, the team exited the building's rear doors in two identical black SUVs. The trucks followed a dirt road for ten miles through the marshland. When they reached the I-75 interstate, they activated flashing lights on their dashboards. The two trucks turned east —away from the storm— past a sign reading, "Fort Lauderdale 40 Miles."

The trucks appeared to be nothing more than a couple of emergency vehicles from some nondescript state agency. On the four-lane highway, vacant at 3:30 a.m., they drove home.

They kept trying to contact their leader, Butch. All but Curt weren't worried. He was an expert, trained in survival. Nothing to worry about, especially against one frightened single mother.

6. A Pirate's Treasure

At 6:30 a.m., a crimson sunrise fractured the dispersing clouds. On Captiva's western shore, debris was scattered across the swamped roads. Coconut palms were twisted like pipe cleaners. Estates along Millionaire's Row were intact, but most had suffered severe roof damage. Shallow-rooted Australian Pines littered the area like a lumber yard. Seagulls hovered in the winds and squawked as they surveyed their turf.

Across from South Seas Lane, the dune preserve was scattered with garbage washed up by the tide. A beagle mutt chased a clump of twine blowing across the sand like a tumble weed. A scruffy man yanked on his dog's collar. The man was lanky and had the skin of tanned leather. With his beard and frayed clothing, he looked like an old pirate. He walked his mutt through the sea oats and beyond the "Keep Off of Dunes" sign to follow a path of debris.

The man kicked over a few boards, looking for anything of value. He walked his dog deeper into the brush, scanning his path, left to right. He mumbled an inventory of the objects he saw, "Driftwood. Rope. Baby doll head. Sunscreen. Wine bottle." He lifted the bottle to see it was empty. Disgruntled, he threw the bottle against a coral rock twenty feet away.

He raised a brow at the shattered bottle. "Wha's that Buddy?" he grumbled. He led the dog towards the glass. The pirate hunched lower and squinted to look into the shadows beneath a palm. "Is that a...." His eyes widened. "...an arm?" Buddy began to bark.

A human arm was visible under the palm frond. The pirate froze. His dog pulled his leash taut, barking wildly at the body. The man crept forward and lifted the branch. "Oh *geeze*, Buddy..."

The corpse was face down in the sand. It was wearing black fatigues and a helmet. One glove was missing, revealing a swollen gray hand. Strapped to its back were three tubes approximately three feet long. The pirate cocked his head like his dog and leaned closer. He observed the edge of some sort of artwork protruding from a tube.

The dog stopped barking and began sniffing the body. The pirate looked over both shoulders with wild eyes. "Anybody around here, Buddy?" Confirming he was alone, he crouched closer to the body. He slid one of the tubes from the corpse's back.

His bloodshot eyes focused on the man's belt. On it were devices like he'd never seen. Gun-type mechanisms, a walky-talky and gizmos straight from the old *Star Trek*. The pirate's eyes twitched.

As he peeked into the man's thigh pouches, he nearly choked –it was a tangle of gold chains, rings and watches.

He scooped up the loot, stuffing the items into his backpack. He gathered the three tubes and yanked Buddy's collar. "Let's get the hell outta' here."

The door to Alexandra's safe room cracked open. She peeked out to see a shaft of daylight in the hallway. She smiled at Cassie with a singsong, "I see sun-shine!" She kneeled beside her daughter who was nibbling on a Pop Tart. "I'm gonna' take a *look-see* outside. I want to make sure everything's okay."

"You're gonna' leave me alone?" Cassie's voice quivered.

Alexandra turned on a small battery-powered television. She found a fuzzy channel showing the millionth rerun of *Sponge Bob*.

"I'll be right back. We'll get dressed and get out of here." She locked the door behind her. *Just in case.*

Limping with her bandaged feet, Alexandra stepped gingerly through her backyard. The pool and yard were littered with debris and vegetation. She clutched the pistol in her robe's pocket. She paused to look towards her neighbors' houses. There was no one else outside. She took a deep breath. The breeze carried the scent of decaying seaweed.

Alexandra tried to retrace her path from the night before. There was a stench of dead fish, washed up by the storm. In the tall grass before her, she saw something −she gasped, startled. *A body..?* Her pulse increased. She then realized it was a garden statue face down in the grass. The overturned sculpture of Michelangelo's David looked like a nude corpse. She sighed and continued forward, scanning the ground for the body of the man she'd shot.

Alexandra's steps became quicker. *He's got to be here...* She limped beyond a knee-high fence that bordered the preserve behind her home. She grew anxious, unable to locate any sign of the man. She *knew* she'd shot him. *Did he escape? And if so...?*

A leg. Directly in her path, surrounded by sea oats, was a man's leg extending from under a cabbage palm. It was wearing a black boot. It was him.

Her eyes widened, but she didn't pause as she approached the body. She moved the branch to see the corpse, face down. She stopped to absorb what she saw. She gave a slight nod, accepting it was the man −and he was dead.

She crouched, comprehending her predicament. She looked around, *can anyone see me?* She was alone. She reached to turn the man's helmeted face towards her. He wore goggles and a vent-like mask. Her trembling hand lifted the man's mask.

Alexandra gasped. She was revolted by the man's bloated face. It was ashen gray with purple, bulging eyes. Foam spewed from the nostrils like an angry dragon. She sprung back when a sand crab crawled over the man's face. Alexandra's reaction was a mix of disgust and confusion −and then panic. It was not what she'd expected.

What have I done? She looked up at the realization. *What did I do...?*

The pirate hastened his steps, dragging his mutt behind him. He clutched his backpack in his arms. Written in marker on the canvas was his name, "Cap'n Rick."

"We gotta' go, gotta' go..." Cap'n Rick repeated. He had no concern about leaving the body. He knew he hadn't killed the guy. *Takin' from a dead man ain't stealin'*, he reckoned. *He won't need the stuff no more.*

He wondered if the man had been some sort of National Guard troop. *Must've drowned, poor bastard.* Cap'n Rick tried to think if he'd left any fingerprints. *Nope...*

The devices and weapons had to be priceless —especially on the street. *And what about the art?* he wondered. There had to be galleries that would pay top dollar for that stuff. *But where?* He'd have to call some of his old pawn shop buddies.

7. Assessments

Interstate I-75 runs primarily north and south along the west coast of Florida. Near the southern city of Naples, I-75 takes a sharp turn due east, cutting a straight line through the barren Everglades. The road that connects Florida's east and west coasts through the swampland also went by another name, "Alligator Alley."

North of the Alley, I-75 was bumper to bumper with trucks, SUV's and enormous RV's, all heading towards Sanibel-Captiva. The trucks displayed "Catastrophe Team" signs from every insurance company imaginable. Just days before, their respective companies had sent them down the east coast of Florida to avoid the storm evacuees. After the all-clear sign, they'd crossed Alligator Alley to approach ground zero. National Guard troops had been deployed to direct the overwhelming traffic.

Dan Holms' white F-250 Pick-up was stopped in the middle of the chaos. A magnetic sign placed on the door announced: "Don't Fear, Insurex is Here."

Dan was nursing a forty-six ounce black coffee from a Citgo fifty miles back. It was doing little to revive his weary eyes that gazed transfixed at the line of vehicles before him. The rest of him was equally fatigued, in his wrinkled khakis and photographer's vest. He cocked his head as he listened to the radio.

"...Florida Power and Light estimates 800,000 homes are without power this morning. They're working around the clock to restore power to Lee County residents." Dan shook his head. It was going to be a hard storm duty.

He raised an eyebrow as the news continued. "Experts say Selina could've been much worse. A gust of dry air from the northeast weakened the storm before it reached land. The gust transformed a Category 4 monster into a less-threatening Category 3..."

Any hints of optimism were doused as the broadcaster continued, "However, Lee County Sheriffs have confirmed thirteen deaths. They say more bodies may be discovered as their efforts continue..." Dan rubbed his eyes.

After only three and a half hours of sleep, Dan knew he needed to beat the traffic. In the rear of his truck he'd packed his duffels, coolers of water and caffeinated beverages. He'd brought gas cans and camping gear for a worse-case scenario. After Katrina, he had to live in a tent for a month in Biloxi. The storm had destroyed every hotel within 100 miles.

When Dan crossed Alligator Alley, he turned south on rural State Road 29 instead of north towards Captiva. In doing so, he targeted Marco Island, south of Naples. Just as he'd hoped, he found a motel with one room left –but only if he pre-paid for a month. South of the storm zone, the place had electricity and wireless internet. The early bird got the worm, but now he'd have to sit in traffic for untold hours. At least he was sitting with A.C. and a radio.

The reggae ring of his cellphone pulled him out of his daze. He looked at the caller ID and answered. "Hey boss. Yeah, I'm still forty miles from Captiva. Believe it or not, I found a room. But it's in Marco, seventy miles from ground zero. It's old, but it's on the beach. Not a bad place to do paperwork at night."

Dan's face turned solemn. "This storm's *bad.* I can't show up and start looking for fraud. They'd kill us in the press. I figure I'll be holding hands and writing some big checks for a while." He shrugged, "But I don't think there will be much out of the ordinary..."

In urban Fort Lauderdale, a maze of anonymous industrial bays was covered in graffiti. Within the compound, commercial trucks came and went like worker bees. Manufacturers, tire shops and exporters went about their trades with no concern for the business of their neighbors.

The *CAT team* –"Catastrophe-Activated Team" as LeBeau had cleverly devised– had a basic office within one of the warehouses. He and their co-founder, Butch, had convinced the landlord to forgo any paperwork if they pre-paid one year's rent in cash. No background checks, no identifications. They'd filled the 1,000 square feet with tables, desks and office chairs bought with cash from bankruptcy auctions. The prior evicted tenant left a refrigerator and a microwave. The bay had two locking doors between the main entrance and work area.

There were four tables pushed together in the center of the room to serve as a boardroom. The tables were covered with a variety of laptops, purchased through dummy accounts on eBay. Cables and extension cords snaked in every direction. In the rear of the room, a row of flat panel monitors served as their "mission control," with feeds to every news and weather network available via their (illegal) satellite and DSL.

Second-hand school lockers contained basic firearms, but most of their paramilitary technology and weapons were housed at their remote Everglades hangar. Each CAT member had permits for their personal firearms –registered to their countless aliases. If their Lauderdale boardroom were ever raided by neighbor kids or street cops, their computers would be pulsed with a magnetic surge sufficient to erase the hard drives. Duplicate systems in the Everglades were cloud synchronized daily. They posted occupational licenses listing them as public adjusters and "engineering consultants" –just vague enough to explain their storm gear, computers and unintelligible live-feeds.

The weary CAT team sat at their long conference table, littered with coffee cups. They were showered and clean, wearing fatigue pants and t-shirts. But the looks on their faces were less than refreshed.

On one side of the table was the Latina pilot Dalia and the large Tag, who looked like a fifty-year-old Marine. Seated on the other side was the athletic black guy, Pitch. Beside him was the small, middle-aged LeBeau wearing bookish narrow glasses. Off to the side was the eternally-angry Curt, attempting to act as interim boss.

"You didn't want to go back!" Curt shouted at LeBeau. "You *wanted* Butch gone! We coulda' saved him." The team looked at LeBeau for a response.

The diminutive LeBeau had a constant, unsettling grin. "Do you have any rational motive?" He spoke with an effeminate nuance. "Having Butch gone wouldn't make me the boss. You're his brother; you're the boss —for now."

Tag scratched his buzz cut in confusion. "Butch isn't answering his radio. How can we confirm he's safe?"

"How *could* he be safe? The bitch had a gun!" Curt barked.

Tag was skeptical, "This little lady just came out blasting? She wasn't supposed to have any guns."

LeBeau glared at Pitch, accusatory, "*Pitch's* backgrounds showed no record of any firearms. So why would we expect her to have one?" Pitch replied, "Evidently she *did*."

LeBeau enunciated in a flowery, educated manner. "No plan is perfect, evidently. Butch created our no-deadly-weapon rule. So far, our electroshock weapons and PIG grenades have been sufficient diversions."

Tag shook his head. "Butch had all the art and half the jewels. Now he's missing. Pretty convenient."

"What are you insinuating, jarhead?" Curt shouted.

A more diplomatic Pitch raised his voice. "I'm sure Butch is fine. He knows the contingencies. He'll contact us." He paused in reflection. "Radio and cell towers are down. While we wait, I'm okay with Curt making the calls —love it or hate it."

Curt scowled at the comment. He turned to the only quiet member, Dalia. "Can you salvage this, *honey*? This might be the last storm of the season. Any secondary opportunities?"

The darkly-attractive Dalia seemed miffed at the "honey," but ignored it. She'd kept quiet, knowing she was a junior member on the team of former-military alpha males.

Dalia spoke in a polished manner, "I *have* been working on a proposal." She brushed her black hair behind her ear as she operated a remote. A projection of Florida appeared on the wall. "The storm's northeast path makes a straight line towards St. Augustine." She used a laser-pointer showing the storm's diagonal path through Florida. "Though Selina's been downgraded, she's still a lethal storm." There was a hint of a smile with the word *lethal*.

"How fast is it moving?" Tag asked in his baritone.

Dalia smirked as she calculated, "Selina's moving over land at just twenty miles per hour. St. Augustine's 275 miles away." She pointed to the map. "That puts the storm here, over the east coast at...18:00 hours."

LeBeau nodded with a finger to his cheek. "With the storm it'll be dark at six o'clock. St. Augustine has a barrier island that'll certainly be evacuated."

Pitch added with interest. "I'll search our databank for targets. How fast can we get there?"

Dalia smiled at her intrigued teammates. "The Stingray can maintain 140 knots, so we can get there within...two hours?" She zoomed-in on the map to display the coast of St. Augustine.

The hulking Tag stood to approach the projection. "If we can locate a small bridge, we can take it out." He looked at Dalia. "You can drop us off and pick up before the storm's outer bands brush the coast."

Pitch interjected with enthusiasm, "I can take out a bridge with a PIG grenade. The magnetic pulse will show on detector grids as nothing but lightning. We'll be gone before they know what hit 'em."

Tag, Pitch and LeBeau nodded in unanimous agreement.

Curt threw his hands up. "You guys just decided *everything*? You know I'm sitting right here!" He shouted like a child.

LeBeau looked at Curt and mocked, "We're sorry. Does this meet with your approval, *Commandant?*"

8. Victim or Suspect

The corpse was taped off among the sea oats. Lee County Sheriff's deputies formed a perimeter around the debris-covered dune preserve. Local cops struggled to direct traffic on the adjacent beach road. Curious neighbors drifted closer, pretending to clean up trash as they tried to catch a glimpse at whatever was going on.

Alexandra Larriott's arms were crossed tight as if she were cold. Her long dark hair blew in the breeze as she stared at the body, six feet away. The corpse was face-down, left untouched until the coroner could arrive. The body was covered with a yellow plastic tarp.

Alexandra saw a cop shrug, saying it was the fourteenth body of the day. It was still the first man she had ever killed. She thought she might throw up again.

After Alexandra found the body that morning, she'd limped back to Cassie for a long hug. Before contacting any authorities, she and Cassie had taken a bath together. She'd felt a need to be clean when she made the report.

The house was still without power, but the bathroom's skylight provided light and the water heater still contained warm water. Alexandra had a long talk with Cassie about the unpredictability of life. Nature had sent the storm, and outside might look messy. But not to worry, policemen will come to help. In a few days, they'll find a nice place to stay, far, far away. Alexandra didn't discuss the burglars. She knew what it was like to have nightmares.

Alexandra put on a fresh pair of jeans and a designer t-shirt. She picked out a sundress for Cassie. She instinctively chose bright colors to liven the mood that loomed in the air. She knew when Cassie saw the devastation outside it would be upsetting —in addition to the sight of police officers.

After procrastinating, Alexandra took a deep breath and strolled out the front door. She hoped that police might be in the area, or at least a neighbor that could help report the shooting. She knew that after reporting the incident, she'd feel an enormous weight lift. The police could then investigate and possibly catch the other burglars. Maybe her neighbors were burglarized as well. Then it dawned on Alexandra —she might be some sort of local *hero*.

As she hobbled down her driveway, she was shocked to see the damage to Pete's guard station. Hopefully he was home, safe. If he'd been there and seen anyone, he surely would've warned her.

"Are you okay ma'am?" A voice called from her right.

She turned to see a young Captiva Police officer. Unable to drive a car on the road, the officer was surveying the damage from a golf cart. He steered around branches to approach her. "Can I help you?"

"Yes." Her eyes watered and her voice trembled. "I need to report a shooting."

Two plain-clothes detectives approached Alexandra on the dunes beside the body. The female detective was mid-thirties and attractive with long blonde hair. The other was a dour, balding, mid-fifties man. Due to conditions, they wore Lee County polo's and jeans. They appeared exhausted.

The pretty blonde detective smiled and extended a hand. "Ms. Larriott, I'm Detective Nadine Stratton with Lee County Sheriffs.

This is Detective Al Rodka." The humorless older detective nodded. Nadine Stratton had a natural Nordic look, without any hint of make-up.

Alexandra shook their hands and re-crossed her arms.

"Your daughter's beautiful," Stratton spoke with sincerity. "We have a PSA inside keeping her busy with Barbie dolls."

"Thank you," Alexandra was grateful. "I don't want her to see...all this."

Detective Rodka remained somber, plowing ahead with the cliché, "Ma'am, I know it's been a rough day, but can you tell me what happened here?"

Alexandra had diminishing patience. "I've already explained it to two officers—"

"—That was the Captiva cops," Rodka interrupted. *"We're* the Sheriffs."

Alexandra gritted her teeth at the unpleasant man. She took a breath and proceeded, "Like I said before, this was self defense. I caught these...*men* robbing my house. They had weapons. They were in my bedroom when I startled them." She pointed to the rear of her house. "They ran out the back doors. I chased them out and shot—"

"—So you *admit* you shot this man?" Rodka interrupted in his Brooklyn accent.

Alexandra frowned in thought. "Well, yes. The men were armed and looked like...*soldiers.*" She realized it sounded outrageous. "They had helmets and armor."

"The armor didn't help much." Rodka was sarcastic. "You're quite the sharpshooter." He pointed to the corpse. "You hit the only inch of exposed neck."

Alexandra narrowed her eyes. "I've had handgun courses, sir." She raised her voice. "I am a single mother who's cursed with money." She pointed to the body. "These soldiers were robbing me!"

Rodka shook his head. "Technically it's not robbery. Unlawful entry of a home to commit a felony is a *burglary.* And you're telling us some sort of 'Delta Force' targeted your home?"

Detective Nadine Stratton remained quiet, as if subordinate to

Rodka.

Alexandra put her hands on her hips. "Okay, they were *burglarizing* my home, endangering my daughter. I don't know who they were. I had the right to shoot!"

The more amiable Nadine Stratton finally spoke, "Ms. Larriott, you may be correct. A homeowner can use reasonable force to protect themselves or to prevent a crime."

Rodka glared at Stratton as if she'd spoken out of place. He kneeled beside the corpse and lifted the plastic sheet to reveal the man, face-down in fatigues. "I don't see stolen art or *Seal Team-6* weapons." He looked at Alexandra, "Your actions went from self-defense to *assault* the minute this man tried to exit your property."

"*I'm* the homeowner," Alexandra pointed to herself. "I can protect my property!"

Rodka motioned to the ground. "You shot him here on *your* land?"

"No." Alexandra surveyed the area. "I shot him closer to the path. My yard ends twenty feet from the pool. Why?"

Rodka and Stratton looked at each other. Rodka stepped towards Alexandra and lowered his voice. "Ms. Larriott, why don't we go down to the station? We can talk more privately."

Unnerved, Alexandra shouted, "Am I under arrest or something?" She looked over her shoulder to see neighbors craning their necks from their backyards.

Nadine Stratton spoke up to soften the blow. "Ms. Larriott, this isn't an arrest." Her voice was calming. "We just have questions. Your story is extremely..." She searched for the right word. "...unique."

Alexandra said nothing. Her lip quivered.

Stratton placed a hand on her shoulder. "The PSA can drive you in an unmarked car. It won't be embarrassing. Aides at the station would love to watch your daughter." She exuded an insistent smile. "Will you please come with us willingly?"

Alexandra's tough exterior cracked. She closed her eyes and cried.

Detective Rodka drove the Lee County SUV as workers moved branches out of their way. Nadine Stratton gave grins and little waves of gratitude to the county workers for their efforts.

Stratton turned to the stone-faced Rodka. "Weren't you a little rough with her? This isn't the Bronx, and she isn't some...first-degree killer."

Rodka remained somber. "With all due respect, I know your little stint in homicide is to shine you up for promotion, but some jobs still need to be tackled like a—"

"—Like a what? Like a *man*?" Stratton interrupted. Attractive and feminine, she easily held her own. "Al, get out of the '70s. I've had the same bad day as you. I haven't slept in twenty-four hours. I haven't even checked my condo to see if my roof —or cat— survived."

Rodka scrunched his face at her outburst. "Nadine, we're not even supposed to be handling murders today. This island's been blown to crap, people missing. Our entire office is supposed to help with civil order and search-rescue. *Not* a new homicide with a rich lady shooting looters like it's the Wild West." He looked at Stratton. "Maybe girl cops from Michigan should teach us about compassion—"

Nadine interrupted, ripping into her partner. "—I heard what you said at that happy hour, *Al*." She looked him in the eye. "You joked I was just your female *token* down here." She let the remark sink in. "I didn't transfer all the way down here to deal with the same low IQ's." She edged closer, "And this isn't just some 'stint' in homicide for promotion. Believe it or not, I thought I could learn from you." She grinned through her teeth. "Especially since you've been doing the same job since before I was born!"

Rodka navigated the road and finally mumbled, "Touché." There was nothing more to say. Two miles later, he added, "I guess I should be careful. You could be my boss one day."

Stratton had no reply. She turned towards her window with a slight grin of victory.

9. Car Talk

Dalia drove the team's black SUV, snaking its way out of Fort Lauderdale. The afternoon rush hour thinned as they headed west on Alligator Alley. The CAT team would have forty minutes of light traffic to debate any mission concerns. Then the Stingray chopper would be off, back into the perilous arms of Selina.

The team's founder, Butch, had originally chosen the Hummer as their primary transportation. In Iraq, he and Tag had fallen in love with the military's High Mobility Multipurpose Wheeled Vehicle – "HMMWV' or the more common "Humvee." The trucks were built solid with plenty of space for equipment and a low profile for wind resistance. Butch loved the trucks, but was hesitant to drive such a conspicuous vehicle back in the states.

Then the Humvee went public under the name "Hummer," including GM's smaller H2 and H3 sports utility vehicles. With their ostentatious popularity, Butch saw their elite vehicles being driven by soccer moms cradling phones on their shoulders while sipping Starbucks. The trucks' reputation waned with their gluttonous gas consumption, but Butch believed their proliferation would help with anonymity, especially on the congested roads of South Florida.

To avoid irritating U.S. titling laws, Butch had purchased their first truck with cash from the plant in Port Elizabeth, South Africa. He'd been amazed how easy it was to grease the palms of South African officials to get the truck out of the country. However, he'd underestimated the security precautions in smuggling the truck into Florida through Port Everglades. After all payoffs, it had been one expensive truck.

With the expansion of the CAT team, they'd needed a second vehicle. Tag found a simpler way to get their next truck: just buy it stolen from a traditional thief in Miami. First, he'd purchased a demolished Hummer from a salvage yard in Hialeah. He'd taken that truck's Vehicle Identification Number, and installed it on the dash of his pristine stolen truck. In the event of any inspections, his new truck would appear to be legally registered to one of his many identities.

Both trucks had been painted black, with their windows covered with impenetrable limo tint. No gaudy chrome or aftermarket items had been installed. There were no cliché James Bond weapons. The trucks would pass any routine traffic stop. However, the trucks had been coated with a Radar Absorbing Material −RAM− which absorbed high energy microwaves and reemitted the energy at altering wave lengths, making radar detection virtually impossible. The vehicle would be practically invisible if driven at night with all lights off. They'd simply have to use infrared night vision in order to drive. It couldn't get any easier.

As the newest member, pilot and gopher, Dalia was the designated driver. She chewed Dentyne as she drove west through the Everglades' Big Cypress Swamp. Beside her sat Curt, enjoying hearing himself shout orders, *"Turn here. Go straight. Speed up!"* LeBeau was in the rear next to Pitch and Tag, who were geared in their fatigues.

LeBeau adjusted his small glasses. "We'll use an airfield in Jax for refueling while you two are busy," he informed Pitch and Tag as they secured their uniforms' straps and zippers.

"Sounds good." Tag looked at Pitch, "You got the PIGs?"

Pitch smiled and patted his torso. "Four grenades."

LeBeau spoke in his ornate manner. "I'll confirm your targets while you're *en route*." He gave a coy smile, "I'm also checking backgrounds on a new recruit."

"Really?" Tag's brow went up. "I like the profile on that 'Lex' guy. He'd be a nice catch."

Pitch nodded. "Yeah —we need a new hacker. Especially with Butch gone–"

Curt shouted, "–Don't say that! We don't know–"

LeBeau's eyes fluttered as he interrupted. "–I assure you Butch is fine. He'll probably contact us today."

The imposing Tag looked down at LeBeau. "Humor us: call our contacts in Lee County in case they...*found* him."

LeBeau sighed. "I'll make the calls. You two return in one piece and maybe Butch will be here to toast a new member of our team."

The truck turned north on a gravel road that lead past barricades and through a wooded area. Dalia announced, "Hangar in fifteen."

LeBeau leaned forward to speak to Dalia, "Tell us your flight plan." The men looked at her, also curious about her plan to fly the Stingray without detection.

She rolled her eyes but replied, "The Miccosukees have 128 miles of unmonitored Indian Reservation. That'll cover me 'til I head east to Vero. The storm will be approaching mid-state, which will create heavy radar clutter. The Dopplers will have their eyes on the storm, not unidentified news choppers. To play it safe, I'll maintain a hundred feet. With our lights out and the RAM, we'll be invisible."

LeBeau smirked and looked at the men. "You should bow and thank me for hiring her."

10. Let the Claims Begin

Dan Holms' weary eyes tried to appear pleasant as he looked at the hundreds of residents waiting for help. In a two-acre field in Captiva, people were lined up in rows based on their insurance carrier. The national companies like Allstate and Liberty Mutual had the longest lines. Dan's company, Insurex, had the shortest.

Regardless of company, Dan's fellow claims adjusters wore identifying polo shirts. Dan, of course, had on his khaki photographer's vest and cargo pants. He figured he might as well be comfortable during twelve hour stints in non-air-conditioned humidity. After paying Mrs. Rosenbaum to re-screen her patio, he stretched, got a bottle of water and observed the impressive storm operation.

Most companies had immense recreational vehicles, dispatched by their corporate offices in the Midwest. They were parked in all four corners of a large field and the adjacent parking lot of a closed restaurant. The RV's came with built-in offices, computers, televisions and restrooms. Extension cords stretched in every direction to humming generators. Satellite dishes provided signals for laptops. NASA would be impressed.

Dan had a laptop, but not an air-conditioned RV. He had a folding table, a thick book of blank checks and a sign that read, "Don't Fear, Insurex is Here." The red-polo reps from the big companies looked down at him as if he were a parasitic public adjuster. Dan was used to it. He was no longer one of *them*.

It never ceased to amaze him how fast the companies could arrange a storm operation. The large carriers had teams who only planned for catastrophes. They'd scope storm-prone areas to procure rental and hotel agreements. A minimum of 30,000 square feet of shelter, such as vacant stores or strip malls, would be needed for induction centers and claim handling. They'd snatched up motel rooms and long-term housing –sometimes traveling a hundred miles from ground zero. Phone systems, generators, fuel and cellphones needed to be ready. Office furniture had been leased. Rental car agreements were obtained for entire fleets. Post Office boxes needed to be established for incoming mail. All the things no one thinks about.

Dan volunteered to be a part of the first wave. The initial reps made the most money, but under inhospitable conditions. They were the people who arrived immediately after a catastrophe. The areas usually had no electricity or running water. Roads were obstructed with debris. The reps had to be prepared to work from vacant lots, fields or tents. Lodging was left up to them. A seasoned rep would pack camping gear, a chain saw, canned goods and clothes that could be washed in a sink.

To reward their hard work and long days, catastrophe reps were paid handsomely. They also received hefty per diems, which they could either save or spend on meals. In devastated areas, there were usually no dining options. With seven-day work schedules, and the need to arrive immediately, most catastrophe reps were single and without young children. Dan was newly single, had no children and undeniably broke. The perfect stormtrooper.

A pudgy Captiva Police officer kicked Dan's boot as he stretched. "Hey, it's Danny, the Indiana Jones of insurance fraud." The redhead cop gave a wise-ass smile.

Dan didn't look up from his laptop. "Officer Sully..." He shifted in his uncomfortable lawn chair. "I see your humor's undamaged."

The cop chuckled. "You working at *Insurex* now? I never heard of 'em."

Dan was unfazed at the jab as he pecked at his keyboard. "They're the state's new startup, but they're solid."

Disappointed that he hadn't upset Dan, the cop tried again. "You don't look as busy as us real cops." He was sarcastic with the words *real cops*. "Are you here to 'investigate' our poor folks for fraud?" He shook his head in disbelief. "The worse storm in years and you guys are already looking for ways to not pay."

Dan blinked with tolerance. "I'm here to write as many checks as possible." He yawned, not threatened by the harmless cop. "You'll be glad I'm here when gypsy contractors arrive to rip-off your neighbors. Or worse..." He looked at the cop as if he should know what he was referring to.

Sully reluctantly nodded. "That *was* good when you busted those alien smugglers stealing boats. That saved a lot of Cubans." His tone softened. "My sister was working the ER when that pregnant refugee came in. That saved that gal's life. I guess you helped us big time." He looked at Dan with brief sincerity.

"We're all on the same team." Dan smiled, "That's why I need friends in the Coast Guard, Customs, Sheriff's Office..." He jabbed back at Sully, "Even your little shop."

The cop scoffed, "You never want to see us! You're always asking about that pretty blonde deputy." He squinted to recall, "What's her name...?"

"Stratton, Nadine Stratton," he replied without pause. "Being pretty's a bonus, but she's a good cop. Smart and experienced." Though Nadine had crossed his mind in the past few months, he hadn't rallied the courage to call her. But now, after all, he was on her turf.

Sully sighed, "She's better than our klutz recruits who nearly got themselves killed last night."

"Someone hurt?" Dan perked up.

Sully nodded. "We have a new kid, Randy. He was passed out in a field. He said lightning hit him." He leaned closer. "You ready for this? He said *space men* zapped him and flew off into the sky." He slapped Dan on the shoulder and laughed, "Imagine that! Space men finally decide to visit earth and they pick a hurricane!"

"Was he one of you typical alcoholics?"

"Maybe," Sully shrugged. "Doctors said it was delusions brought on by a lightning strike." He chuckled, "He wasn't the only whacko. An old security guard showed up at our substation, screaming at our window to let him in."

"What was his deal?"

Sully paused for drama, "He wanted to report that military troops were attacking our island." Sully grinned, "Pete thinks the troops were using the storm as cover." Sully cackled again. "Top that!"

Dan smiled. The stories were actually raising his spirits. "One of your insane locals?"

"No." Sully's smile faded. "Pete's a war veteran and a smart guy." He shrugged as he conceded, "But also a notorious drunk." Sully turned to go on about his duties. "So I guess that explains that."

"Colorful characters in your little paradise," Dan shouted before returning to his customers.

"Hello ma'am, can I help you?" Dan asked the next policyholder with a smile. An elderly four-foot-ten woman stepped forward and took a seat at Dan's table. She appeared about ninety and wore a 70s-era lime pantsuit.

"Bless you for coming out so fast." She smiled with crooked lipstick. "I finished these for you." She handed him several completed forms.

Dan made a cursory review of the papers. He turned to his laptop, "Alrighty, Ms. Goldman," he tapped a button on his keyboard and a portable printer came to life. "I'm issuing you a $5,000 advance."

The woman held her hands to her face with joy. "*Advance?* What for?"

Dan took the check off the printer and signed it. "You might have to wait for contractors. You can use this money for small repairs, hiring folks to move branches, or even get yourself a hotel." He handed her the check with a smile.

"What if I stay with my sister in Boca for free?" Ms. Goldman asked.

Dan flashed a smile. "Keep the money; our secret." He winked.

She gushed. "Bless you, Mr. Holms." She noticed several forms still in her hand. "Is this where I can also make the burglary claim for my jewelry?"

Dan was confused. "You lost jewelry in the storm? Or are you talking about a prior burglary?"

Ms. Goldman looked up to speculate. "No. It's a new burglary. My safe was broken into *during* the storm. I had an heirloom diamond from my fifth husband."

Dan squinted, "Is it possible you might find it when we get electricity back? Maybe you hid the jewelry *before* the storm?"

The woman turned visibly irate. "Young man, I am not senile. Why would I move jewelry from a steel vault in a cement wall?" She stood, not much taller. "My neighbor had priceless art stolen. Do you think all of us seniors are insane?"

"No ma'am, I'm not saying that." He lifted his hands. "But if you're submitting a *burglary* claim, we may need to open an investigation. That would be a separate loss from your *hurricane* claim."

"So what?" Ms. Goldman pruned her face.

Dan tried to explain, "You would then have a burglary deductible, in addition to any deductible for the storm. It's two separate losses."

Ms. Goldman raised her shrill voice, "The hurricane and burglary happened at the *same time!*" Her eyes narrowed, "The big insurance company's not so fast with the money now!"

Dan swallowed. This much-needed escape from Liz might not be the island getaway he'd imagined.

11. A Crack in the Veneer

"Is Detective Stratton going to join us?" Alexandra timidly asked Detective Al Rodka.

"She can't make it," Rodka grumbled as he led her down a hall within the Lee County Sheriff's office. "It's just going to be you and me, Ms. Larriott." He looked at her. "Is there a problem with that?"

Alexandra swallowed and shook her head.

Alexandra and Cassie had been driven to the sheriff's headquarters in Fort Myers, fifteen miles inland. A Public Service Aide, a heavyset intern named Isabel, drove them in an unmarked Bronco. Isabel was quiet and seemed to have no knowledge of Alexandra's predicament. She was genuinely sweet to Cassie, which Alexandra appreciated.

The three spoke little when they departed Captiva. Isabel was busy steering around debris into the neighboring Sanibel Island. They had to wait for road crews to flag them over the causeway that led to the mainland.

Alexandra held Cassie tight in the backseat. As the oblivious child hummed to her Barbie, Alexandra gazed at the devastation. Up-rooted trees, downed power lines and shattered windows. The up-side-down world seemed parallel to her own. In the last twenty-four hours, her life had become uprooted and shattered. At the exact moment the morning before, she'd been enjoying coffee and braiding Cassie's hair. She was now being driven to the sheriff's office for confessing to killing a man.

She took a deep breath to stall another crying episode. She didn't want Cassie to see her crying –again. The child had seen too much in her five short years.

Alexandra used the time to rationally focus on her dilemma. She knew people could defend themselves if attacked, especially intruders who trespass into a home. She had both defenses. *I shot an armed intruder who was aiming a weapon.* But why didn't the body possess any weapons? He did try to shoot her *–right?*

Alexandra was confident it'd be a clear case of self defense. She might even be considered a hero in her community. Alexandra sat upright, determined to have faith the sheriff's investigation would substantiate her story. Surely they'd review the security video, find evidence of breaking and entering. Alexandra decided to remain strong and would staunchly stick to her story.

But she didn't like Detective Rodka. He was a wrinkled cliché from a TV crime drama. At least Nadine Stratton seemed sympathetic. Her face was compassionate. And it was Detective Stratton who'd mentioned a citizen's right to protect their property. But which of the two was the senior detective? Rodka appeared angry every time Stratton spoke. Rodka seemed to be the boss, and that was bad.

When they'd arrived at the Lee County Sheriff's office, the building was busy with squad cars, utility vehicles and cops directing traffic. Isabel said they were at the main headquarters since most of the satellite offices were without power. She explained the jurisdiction was divided into six districts to cover Lee County. Each district had its own headquarters, similar to small departments, handling all crimes. When Isabel mentioned "homicide," Alexandra's heart skipped a beat.

As Isabel led them into the building, Rodka was waiting for them with folded arms. He told Isabel to play with Cassie in a break room. Isabel assured Alexandra there'd be plenty of snacks and a box filled with Legos. It wasn't a courtesy extended by Rodka; Isabel was *ordered* to watch Cassie while Alexandra was being questioned.

Questioned... Alexandra repeated to herself. Isn't that what they do to suspects before being arrested? She amassed all her strength and kissed her daughter goodbye. Cassie seemed apprehensive when she waved goodbye to her mom.

Rodka guided Alexandra by the shoulder. Busy officers rushed through the halls with local emergencies. The floor vibrated from the incessant humming of generators.

"Let's go in here," Rodka said as he opened the door to a small office. "Have a seat."

Alexandra sat in a metal chair in front of a small desk. She looked at the bare walls of the claustrophobic room. Rodka closed the door behind them. There was barely enough room for the desk, chairs and the two of them. The light above them flickered with the irregular electricity.

"Where's Detective Stratton?" Alexandra asked. She was uneasy being alone with Rodka. She prayed for the more pleasant Nadine Stratton to swoop in any minute.

"She can't make it." Rodka had a grim smile as he sat at the desk. "I need her to visit the storm morgue. I want her to observe the coroner's assessment of your 'mystery soldier.'"

Alexandra had a sudden chill. "Where's the storm morgue?"

Rodka shook his head as if reminded of a sad truth. "Our hospitals are prioritizing the living. With the death toll, we're using a closed-down hotel for the bodies. You know the old Sanibel Lodge?"

Alexandra shook her head. She only knew her safe world on Millionaire's Row.

"The hotel's been abandoned for years. It's got the square footage, but barely any power until they get more generators."

She crossed her arms, disturbed by the vision of her victim lying in a dilapidated hotel.

Rodka turned on a handheld recorder. "Ms. Alexandra Larriott, as you know, I'm Detective Albert Rodka." He spoke louder and more formal. "I'm recording our little chat so I don't have to *fiddle* with notes. Do I have your permission, ma'am?"

Alexandra nodded, unnerved.

Rodka appeared annoyed. "Ms. Larriott, the recorder can't hear you nod. Can you speak up? Do I have your permission to make this recording?"

"Yeah, yes you do," Alexandra cleared her throat.

"Okay, your name is Alexandra Louise Larriott," Rodka flipped through his notes. "Your address is 573 South Seas Lane, Captiva Island, Florida, correct?"

"Yes."

"How long you been there?"

"About six months."

Rodka looked up, rolling his hand at the brief response. "And..? Where did you live before that? What brought you to our community?" He emphasized *'our'* community.

She tried not to let his condescending tone affect her. "I lived in Canada, Montreal. I moved down here..." She paused. "...after my husband passed away. He was an art dealer."

"I'm sorry for your loss, ma'am." His sympathy vanished as he sucker-punched her with his next question. "Earlier today, you confessed to shooting –and killing– an unidentified male. Correct?"

Her eyes bulged at the sudden question. She stammered, "He was a burglar... I just–"

"–Just yes or no, ma'am?" Rodka interrupted.

Alexandra's eyes glistened with tears. "Yes."

"Ma'am, do you have a concealed weapons permit?"

She recoiled, "No –I don't need one in Florida..." Her voice quivered, "I just–"

"–You were just off your property when you shot a man and he died," Rodka interrupted again.

"Yes. But he was robbing my house!" Alexandra retorted with surprising strength. "I know I can shoot *criminals* that are trespassing into my home! He was trying to get away!"

Rodka had a menacing smile. "So, he *was* fleeing?"

"Yes!" she barked.

Rodka grinned as if she'd fallen into a trap. "He was *off* your property when you shot him?"

Alexandra froze, calculating the implication.

Rodka leaned in, his voice prominent. "Ma'am, you shot him off your property, as he was attempting to *flee* your property. Isn't that true, Ms. Larriott?"

Her voice trembled. "But he tried to shoot me first."

"There were no weapons." Rodka snapped, "You saw the body."

Alexandra couldn't hold it any longer. She openly cried.

Rodka watched her sob as if gaining satisfaction from her humility.

"I think I need an attorney now." Her cry became more emotional. "And I want my daughter."

12. One Path to Respect

Within the CAT team's urban Fort Lauderdale office, Curt and Le-Beau were seated side by side at their workstations. Their control panels had large plasma monitors and the men wore radio headsets, each remaining focused on their own console.

LeBeau narrowed his eyes through his glasses at a satellite image of Hurricane Selina cutting a northeast path through Florida. "Stingray, what's your position?"

"East of Okeechobee," Dalia's voice crackled through the speakers. "Flying VFR, 130 knots. Not much wind –yet. Over."

"You'll have wind soon," LeBeau replied. On his monitor, a red blip to the right of the storm's edge signified the Stingray. "The storm's eye is 100 miles southwest. Watch your tail."

"Copy," Dalia's response had heavy static. "I'll check-in at 17:00. *Two CATs* are ready. Over." She used "Two CATs" to indicate Tag and Pitch they were ready for their drop.

LeBeau looked at Curt, who was huddled close to his monitor. "You don't seem too *engaged.*"

Curt looked defiantly over his shoulder at LeBeau. "You can baby-sit Dalia without me."

LeBeau craned his neck to see Curt's monitor. It displayed a large cover of a magazine called *Island Life*. Displayed on the cover was Alexandra Larriott. In the image, she was beautiful and smiling, wearing a black cocktail dress in front of her home's staircase. The magazine's cover headline read, "Captiva's Newest Art Collector."

"Mind you own business," Curt grumbled like a child.

LeBeau replied with showy sarcasm, "I'm wondering why you're studying a target we already hit. We have two men about to reenter Selina. We should be thinking about them."

Curt swiveled his chair to face LeBeau. "I once knew a cop in Newark who worked organized crime." His eyes became intense, "Do you know why the Russian mob is more feared than the Italians? Why even cops are terrified of them?"

LeBeau rolled his eyes and turned back to his monitor. "Enlighten me."

"Because if you upset the *Waps*, they simply kill you. But if you piss off the Russians, they kill you. Then they kill your wife. Then your kids." He had a vacant grin. "It's *that* kind of fear that gets you respect."

LeBeau furled his brow, troubled with Curt's words. "Perhaps we should move on, and look *forward* to our task at hand."

Curt's face contorted into a devilish scowl. "Move on?" He shouted, pointing to Larriott's image on his screen. "This bitch either captured or killed Butch. It's been over twelve hours and there's been no contact. This bitch is my 'task at hand.'"

LeBeau swallowed, allowing a second for the mood to calm. "Let's settle this. I'll place a call to Lee County." He began typing on his keyboard. "I'm sure I can confirm that your brother hasn't been detained or...found."

Curt paused, "What do you mean, *found*?" He rolled his chair closer. He asked like a child, "You mean 'found' like he could be dead?"

LeBeau didn't reply. On his monitor, the screen filled with a spreadsheet of Lee County phone numbers labeled, "Non-Published

Backlines." LeBeau ran his finger to a column that read, "Dispatch Backline: (888) 555-7645, HOMICIDE x545, DOMESTIC x547..." He entered a number on a keypad and there was an audible dial tone. Curt watched with unease.

On the speakerphone, a female voice answered abruptly, "Sheriff's Dispatch."

Curt watched LeBeau switch to a flawless southern accent. "Hello ma'am, I'm Major Wyatt with the National Guard. Who can I speak to regarding a missing guardsman?"

"Is he missing or possibly deceased from the storm, Major?" the woman asked.

Curt clenched his teeth at the looming admission.

"Possibly deceased, ma'am," LeBeau looked at the floor as he spoke.

"The coroners have a Mortuary Response Team at the old Sanibel Lodge. Would you like me to transfer you to the Chief Coroner?"

"Please, ma'am." LeBeau replied. Curt had wide eyes but remained quiet.

After an eternal transfer of dial tones, a man's voice answered. "Chief Coroner Garfield."

"Hello, I'm Major Wyatt with the National Guard." LeBeau spoke with a perfect southern drawl. "I'm calling about any unidentified casualties you might have."

"Son, they're almost all unidentified." The coroner spoke fast as if rushed.

"Our man was in full gear near the coast of Captiva when we lost contact," LeBeau said. "So the body I'm looking for might be in protective body armor."

The heavy, sixty-year-old Coroner Garfield wore scrubs as he held his phone. "Major, I'm sorry to say we do have a male casualty in gear like you're describing."

The shuttered Sanibel lodge was dark with minimal power. Several lights flickered from a humming generator, revealing a dilapidated ballroom. The large room, built decades before for festive affairs, now had rows of gurneys holding corpses covered in translucent plastic sheets.

Garfield stroked his walrus mustache as he scanned a clipboard. "Major, the man I have was expired when they found him." He scratched his bald head. "But nothing on his uniform said 'National Guard..?'" He looked at the caller ID screen. It displayed, "BLOCKED NUMBER."

"Where are you calling from, Major? Hello?" Garfield was bewildered as the caller hung up. "Major...Hello..?" He shrugged and moved on to his grim duties.

Curt threw his headset across the room. "I told you he was dead!" He screamed and his eyes blazed. "We should've gone back for him!" He kicked a filing cabinet.

One of LeBeau's eyes twitched. "I'm very sorry..." He stammered for words. "Butch was a hero..."

Curt glared at LeBeau. "*You* didn't want to go back. *My* brother!" He pointed towards his computer at the image of Alexandra on the magazine cover. "I will kill her!" He screamed, "In front of her daughter!"

LeBeau said nothing. He knew what Curt was capable of. But was it a juvenile need for respect —or just pure revenge?

Curt stomped towards the exit and slammed the door behind him.

LeBeau was ashamed that he was still paralyzed. *But not with fear,* he convinced himself. He never tried to pacify Curt, but nor did he try to stop him. *Curt's a liability,* he knew. They couldn't afford for Curt to get caught doing something irrational.

LeBeau rolled his eyes with a new thought: What if Curt *could* neutralize the Larriott woman? *That would solve a lot of problems...* LeBeau knew that "Alexandra Larriott" had more knowledge than any law enforcement would ever believe. And more power than they could possibly foresee.

Maybe he would just let Curt do whatever he was scheming to do.

13. G.I. John Doe

Detective Nadine Stratton asked, "The caller knew the soldier?" Surrounded by rows of corpses, she stood rigid in the ghostly ballroom as if one of the bodies might jump up at her. The dead had been covered in plastic sheets, most soiled with blood. Everyone in the sheriff's office knew Stratton had a weak stomach –which was precisely why Rodka had sent her to the abandoned hotel.

The Sanibel Lodge had been built in 1968 to resemble a southern plantation. In its heyday, it had 200 rooms, an upscale restaurant and a lavish ballroom to attract conferences and weddings. The hotel went bankrupt in the late 70s after a dispute over irreparable damage from Hurricane Anthea. The owners defaulted on their mortgage and had deserted the property. The city fenced-off the land, deeming the building a hazard.

Unable to collect property taxes, the city of Sanibel Island *and* Lee County both claimed a legal right to take possession of the land. Years of litigation increased the accruing liens and clean-up costs – ironically decreasing the value of the property. For every year that went by, the land became less attractive to any bank or investor. The city and county's stalemate forced the building to sit and decay.

The derelict, three-story hotel was now in a complete state of disrepair. Windows had been boarded and the property was overrun with tropical growth. Tall plantation columns in the front were covered in thorny, dead bougainvillea. Several windows had been shattered, and signs warned "Keep Out." Over the decades, local kids spun tales that the place was haunted.

The morning after Hurricane Selina, Lee County parked a letterboard sign in the front of the hotel that read, "Emergency OP Center Only." With the local school gymnasiums used as shelters, the lodge's ballroom was the only vacant room large enough to create a temporary morgue. With the fatalities, the area was needed immediately as the coroner waited for national assistance.

As part of the National Disaster Medical System, the Disaster Mortuary Operations Response Teams –DMORT– provided emergency services in catastrophe areas. Their staff helped to identify the dead using x-rays and DNA samples. They had to endure extreme conditions and intermittent power. In addition to identifying those killed by the storms, they had to tackle bodies unearthed from cemeteries. Their job required technical expertise and empathy to converse with the families –as well as strong stomachs.

When a corpse was found, its location was marked and another team would deliver it to the morgue. Its first stop would be a HazMat station to decontaminate the corpses with a bleach solution. The body would then go to pathology to determine cause of death and any identifying anomalies, such as prosthetics, hip replacements, etcetera. The body's personal effects were logged, photographed and sealed in bags.

Unfortunately, it was too soon for any of the prescribed procedures. Since it was merely hours since the storm, Coroner Garfield would have to wait for the DMORT teams to begin work on any of the bodies. Until then, he and his small staff would watch the bodies accumulate, with no air conditioning or proper sanitation. Such luxuries were rarely found the first day after a catastrophe. Generators provided partial power to fans and the hotel's substandard lighting. Garfield knew he'd have to be sympathetic and patient until the national help arrived.

When Detective Stratton entered the hotel, she saw writing on the wall by the Coroner's staff. In permanent marker on ancient wallpaper, the words said, "Let the dead teach the living." It was a promise to help families find closure in the tragedy of Selina.

As she hesitantly approached the ballroom, she smelled the decay. A Coroner's staff person stopped to ask for ID. Stratton had to put on a thin Tyvek –a white protective jumpsuit– gloves and a face mask. Her name was written with a marker on the front of her suit. When Stratton focused in the dark room, she was surprised by the number of people in white Tyveks walking around. She couldn't tell their race, if they were male or female, brunette or blonde. They looked like clones in some future society. With only the sound of fans blowing, the human silence was unnerving.

"That's the only call I've received on G.I. John Doe." Coroner Garfield said to Stratton. They lifted their masks to speak. "The caller said he was with the National Guard, but I lost the signal."

Stratton folded her arms, disturbed by the atmosphere. "The county did request National Guard, but not *before* the storm." The musty room smelled like a combination of mildew, decay and chemicals like alcohol or formaldehyde. She shivered.

Garfield led her to a large body. "Here's your mystery soldier." He lifted the plastic sheet. "We kept on his uniform and armor, but it's got no ID." The dead man was dressed in black fatigues that had protective pads on the chest, arms and thighs. "No personal items were found."

"Oh God..." Stratton covered her mouth, revolted by the bloated corpse. It had a gray face with open, purple eyes and a thick tongue protruding from its cracked lips.

Coroner Garfield seemed puzzled by her discomfort. "How long you been in homicide?"

"Six days," she replied. "I'm cross training before a sergeant's interview." Stratton could feel clammy beads of perspiration growing on her face. As part of her police training, four weeks of the program required ride-alongs with every department. This included homicide and a trip to the medical examiners. She still remembered the examiner had been eating a sloppy Joe as he cut open a body. The scent was unforgettable. It would stick to your clothing. She was proud then that she'd never puked, as many of her fellow cadets had done.

Focusing on the present, she brushed her hair away from her face and shaded her eyes. It was her job to observe the victim —she just didn't want to. She knew she could still be a successful detective —or sergeant— and yet be squeamish. Stratton was determined to get through this, much to Rodka's chagrin.

Garfield swooshed at a buzzing fly as he read from a clipboard. "Male, six-four, two hundred forty pounds —with the armor." He reached to gently lift the man's clenched hand. "His fingerprints are covered in scar tissue as if purposely burned off. Impossible to ID."

Stratton covered her mouth with a surge of nausea.

"Sorry we don't have AC." He chuckled, "If we don't get power soon, this place will be *ripe*."

Stratton turned and dry-heaved. She put her hands on her knees and took a deep breath —*of formaldehyde air*. She looked at Garfield, struggling to appear unfazed by changing the subject. "The suspect who confessed to shooting him said the man was with a team of burglars. What do you think?"

Garfield shrugged. "I'm not trained to tell you what he did for a living. What do you think?"

"The suspect makes a good witness that he was *some* sort of intruder. Rodka thinks he was some survivalist wacko who ventured out during the eye." Stratton squinted at the body as she speculated. "Maybe he was looting and startled the suspect. Got himself shot."

The Coroner put on his glasses and tried to turn the corpse's stiff neck. "Look here."

Stratton bent forward and wrinkled her nose to see what Garfield was pointing at. It was a small purple hole on the man's neck. Expecting a large gunshot wound, Stratton was surprised it was no larger than a pencil hole. "Is that where the bullet entered?"

"Yep. G.I. John Doe expired from an evident gunshot wound exiting the C5-C6 vertebrae, severing the spinal cord." Garfield poked the hole with a pen knife. "He either died instantly or had immediate paraplegia and possibly drowned."

Stratton was confused. "Drowned?"

"If the bullet paralyzed him, he may have drowned on the ground with the storm surge. It could explain the violet blood vessels and foam in the mucous areas." He looked at Stratton. "We'll know if his lungs contain salt water. Either way, no man deserves to die like this."

For an instant, Stratton thought the soldier's purple eyes were staring at her. The buzz of flies increased. The room's ancient chandeliers flickered from the generators. With a rush of anxiety, Stratton turned away, only to face another corpse on a gurney. An old woman's skull was completely caved-in with pink brain matter. Stratton squeezed her eyes shut and covered her mouth with both hands.

"She was hit by a coconut." Garfield said, glancing at the dead woman. "A common hurricane fatality. In the winds, coconuts fly like cannonballs. Even a piece of wood can be a missile, and *splat!*" He mimicked a head exploding.

Speechless, Stratton spun back to the lesser-evil, the soldier. She audibly inhaled.

"Don't worry," Garfield offered a sympathetic smile. "These odors are a natural process."

She's wasn't comforted by this. She closed her eyes, trying to calm her churning stomach.

"I'll x-ray for dental records," Garfield said. "If he's military, they have a dental database—"

Before he could finish, Stratton turned to run, covering her mouth. In the dim room, she stumbled to find a clear path towards an exit. At every turn, she confronted a dead-end of bloody corpses. In the gloomy ballroom, their pale skin seemed to glow from under the plastic sheets.

Clutching her hands over her mouth, she emitted a shrill warning as in *get out of my way!* Stratton pushed her way through clone-like beings in white jumpsuits. She struggled to exit through a panic-inducing maze of gurneys. She finally gripped two gurneys and pulled them apart, slipping her waist past the dead. She raced through the front doors and vomited on the polished shoes of a sheriff's deputy.

One simple assignment in homicide, and she'd failed in grand form.

14. A Second Date with Selina

Though only 5:00 p.m., the skies were dark enough to provide cover for the Stingray. One mile offshore of St. Augustine Beach, the chopper flew fifty feet above sea level. St. Augustine was on the northeast coast of Florida, only eighty-five miles from the Georgia border —precisely where Hurricane Selina planned to escape the state.

Dalia flew to the coordinates for Anastasia Island, a barrier island adjacent to St. Augustine. The chopper descended over a stretch of beachfront property. It wasn't raining yet, but there were already forty mile-per-hour gusts. The Stingray hovered five feet over swirling sand as two men disembarked. They jogged away and the Stingray climbed back into the sky.

Tag and Pitch, in masks and gear, jogged towards large estates. They passed a sign for an upscale community, *Castillos de Ponce De Leon,* boasting immense Spanish-style homes. Operational streetlights meant the area still had power, but it was evident the place had been evacuated —as planned.

Fifty yards from a deserted guard gate, the community had a

drawbridge stretching to the mainland —the route authorities would use. The next closest bridge was five miles away. The drawbridge had been set to an automatic mode, probably programmed for fifteen-minute intervals. Currently, the bridge was open for boat traffic. Pitch and Tag rushed to the seawall beside the bridge.

The thinner, athletic Pitch, reached into his vest to remove a small grenade. He then removed his right glove. "I need to *feel* the ball," he said playfully into his headset.

The larger and stoic Tag said nothing, allowing Pitch to do what he did best.

Pitch gripped the E-PIG grenade and focused on his target. He wound-up like a baseball player and threw the orb towards the exposed gears of the upright bridge.

With a sudden gust, the grenade dipped, missing its target. It skidded across a grassy embankment below the bridge. Tag and Pitch dropped to the ground and covered their heads —but the grenade failed to explode.

"We've never had a dud..?" Tag said in a deep voice. "Try again."

Pitch took a second grenade, aimed and threw it. The E-PIG detonated with a blue explosion, demolishing the bridge's gears. Bright tendrils of electricity flashed with the magnetic pulse. Pitch stood proud and looked at Tag. "Cameras now disabled as well."

Tag said nothing, allowing Pitch his glory. They huddled in the wind and jogged towards the large *Castillos*.

Tall, oak doors were kicked in. Tag and Pitch stormed into their first house with their electroshock weapons drawn. Considering the events from the night before, they boldly announced their arrival.

"*National Guard!* Is anyone home?" Tag shouted with an echoing, electronic voice.

Pitch ran up the marble staircase, "Emergency! Come out at once!" After several warnings and a quick scan of infrared, they knew they were alone.

Though the homes still had power, they utilized their night-vision. If they turned on the lights, they might alert a passerby. If residents were hiding in the house, Tag and Pitch would have the advantage of seeing in the dark —and Pitch thought it made them look scarier.

House by house, they checked the customary places for hidden safes. Tag and Pitch arrogantly chuckled when homeowners thought they'd invented clever new hiding spots. The men's x-ray spectrums made finding the safes simple. Directed explosives and their safe-cracking talents could beat almost any vault. The men were smug that they could defeat anything.

Pitch's specialty was creating dossiers for each homeowner prior to invasion. During the CAT team's seven-month "off season" – primarily November through May– Pitch researched and created databases for wealthy waterfront communities in the southeastern United States. They targeted affluent homeowners that were, preferably, older or female.

Offended, Dalia once asked, "Why *female* targets?"

LeBeau gave a straightforward reply, "They're smaller, more easily frightened, with 50% less upper-body strength."

Dalia scoffed that they'd never met any of her friends in Miami. No one mentioned the irony that LeBeau was five-foot-three and a hundred-thirty pounds.

Pitch would run corporate, courthouse and property appraisal checks to evaluate the financial strength of their targets. He obtained a bogus insurance license that permitted him to run credit reports, allegedly for underwriting purposes. If any of the homeowners ever filed for building permits, he could obtain the house's blueprints. The team never entered a home without knowing precisely what they were doing, and who they were doing it to.

One of the team's favorite methods of finding targets was through newspapers and magazine articles. *Social* columns boasted of wedding and honeymoon plans, and which zillionaire was new to the community. Regional magazines such as *Palm Beach's Brightest* and *Island Life* profiled residents with full-color spreads showing every room of their ostentatious mansions. The photos provided vivid layouts of the rooms, and the owners were usually adorned with their finest jewelry. They bragged about everything, ironically providing roadmaps for the CAT team to take it all away.

In their final St. Augustine house, Tag radioed Dalia to confirm their rendezvous. She'd refueled at a private airfield in Jacksonville that accepted cash gratuities with no questions. With nineteen minutes to go –and one hour until the Selina's arrival– Pitch ransacked a dresser overflowing with gold, jewels and designer watches. He then rummaged through their medicine cabinets for any narcotics with a worthwhile street value.

Tag located the last wall safe behind –surprise– a painting. On its ten-digit keypad, he shined an ultraviolet light. Only three buttons revealed fingerprints: the numbers three, seven and nine. Knowing that only *those* three digits were in the combination –on a ten-number combination– meant there'd only be 10,000 different combinations versus 10 million. Tag's algorithmic descrambler would only need seconds to decipher the combination. *Piece o' cake.*

With their pouches full of loot, the men jogged out of the community. They huddled low through the escalating wind. Two hundred yards away, in the exact spot Dalia dropped them off, the Stingray appeared like clockwork. The chopper descended low enough for Pitch and Tag to climb aboard. The men grasped handles to the cabin and pulled themselves in. When Tag gave the thumbs-up, Dalia sped due east. She flew out over the Atlantic, circling south to skirt the storm.

Strapped in their seats, the men lifted their masks and gave heavy sighs. They winked at each other for another job well done. Then they noticed Dalia turning to them with a look of dread.

Her voice was grave, "Bad news from base."

Concerned, the men leaned closer.

"Butch is dead." She turned back to her controls.

The men stared out at the Atlantic without a word. After a moment of disbelief, Pitch asked the questions on all of their minds. "The *woman* did it? Does Curt know yet?"

Dalia said nothing as she raced south.

15. Tireless and Sleepless

Nightfall was ironically quiet on the west coast of Florida. Just twenty-four hours earlier, anxious residents had evacuated the island in a frenzy. Now, Captiva –though scarred– seemed at peace with a sunset over the Gulf.

Dan Holms walked along South Seas Lane with his leather backpack, a Canon digital around his neck and a clipboard in his hand. He'd driven to the entrance of the neighborhood, but had parked when he saw the road obstructed with branches. He'd decided it'd be nicer to walk along the beach to inspect his list of homes. One particular claim –another burglary *during* the hurricane– seemed peculiar. People usually waited a few weeks before submitting any type of insurance fraud.

Dan squinted at the crimson sun and scanned the ocean. It was common on the west coast to see dolphins playing in the shallow water. *Not in the mood to play yet,* he supposed. He looked at his watch and shook his head. He'd be busy until well after 10:00, and it would take another ninety minutes to get to his motel in Marco. So much for night swimming, he sighed. He just wanted to go to bed. Another

7:00 a.m. day tomorrow.

The big insurance carriers probably had their adjusters in decent resorts, he guessed. Their reps would be frolicking in pools by nine o'clock. *I was once one of them*, Dan groaned.

If it hadn't been for the upstart, Insurex, no one would've hired him. Insurex was a government-subsidized company to provide coverage for homeowners who couldn't get insurance anywhere else. With the increasing number of hurricanes in the past decade, more insurance companies had gone bankrupt or pulled out of Florida entirely. Insurex was called the "insurer of last resort" for many Floridians. As a quasi-government entity, the pay was less than the big corporations, but Dan had little choice. *After just one stupid mistake,* he knew.

Insurex agreed to hire him only if he'd be an SIU adjuster –and a full-time storm volunteer. The SIU –Special Investigation Unit– handled claims that appeared in any way suspicious. Policyholders committing insurance fraud were a rapidly growing problem.

With the inordinate problem of fraud in Florida, the legislature required companies to file anti-fraud plans with the Division of Insurance Fraud, basically asking the companies, "What are you going to do about it?" Insurance companies were ordered to create SIUs to investigate suspicious claims. The carriers needed to staff the teams with experienced adjusters trained to investigate, take statements and frequently knock on doors in unsavory areas. The reps couldn't be easily intimidated, and had to work professionally with attorneys and law enforcement. To Dan, his relationships with police, including the Coast Guard and Border Patrol, were his most valuable assets.

But there were also the cops who teased him, calling him a "wannabe cop." They mocked him when he called himself an "investigator" without a badge. *They wouldn't hire me either.* Dan kicked a coconut and looked at the ocean.

He smelled the air and smiled. *How can I complain?* Over the years he'd worked in the floods of Louisiana and tornado-ravaged trailer parks in the Midwest. He could be in worse places than an affluent island off the coast of Florida. He inhaled with renewed optimism. *I even got a motel on the beach for a month —away from Liz!* But he still wished he had a Corona. *Just two more houses today...*

Dan located the house for his insured, Alexandra Larriott. He looked at a guard station at the foot of the driveway. He noticed extensive damage to a corner of the shack. With the fading sun, he reached into his backpack for a flashlight. He stepped closer to the shack to look at burn marks near the ravaged cement.

"What are you doing?" a gruff voice shouted.

"Whoa!" Startled, Dan put his hands up. He turned to see an elderly security guard armed with a gun. "I'm from the insurance company."

"Let me see ID!" The guard looked like he'd slept in his uniform.

Dan pulled out a badge identifying him as an adjuster licensed by the Department of Financial Services. "I'm Daniel Holms with Insurex. We insure Ms. Larriott's home."

The guard, Pete, squinted at the badge. "Look what he did to my station."

Dan smelled rum and body odor from the old man. "*He?* You mean '*she*' the storm?"

"No I mean 'he' the soldier!" Pete snapped.

Dan raised a brow at the obviously-confused man. "I was just inspecting your damage." He lifted his camera and photographed the shack. "A bad lightning strike. I think it hit your AC and superheated the masonry. The weakened area was ripped away by the wind."

Pete cocked his head. "It wasn't no lightning. It was a *grenade!*"

Dan turned to the guard, realizing the poor guy was drunk or insane. He spoke as if to a child. "Sir, I'm here to investigate several reported burglaries. Have you seen any looters?"

Pete narrowed his eyes in frustration. "They weren't looters. They were *soldiers!*"

Dan humored the man. "Are you talking about the National Guard today?"

Pete's stammered as he struggled for words. He pointed to the ocean. "A team of soldiers arrived *last night*. They came from the beach —just like D-Day. They were using the storm for cover. That's when they tried to *kill* me! Because I *saw* 'em."

Dan looked over to see a lawn chair and a bottle of Captain Morgan's rum. He changed the subject with tact. "Sir, is Ms. Larriott at home? I need to talk to her."

"She's still with the cops."

Dan was now entirely baffled by the disheveled man. "Why is she with the police? About the burglary?"

"No!" The old man stomped. "She *shot* one of the soldiers! Don't you know anything?"

As if dealing with an escaped mental patient, Dan calmly reached for a business card. "Sir, when Ms. Larriott returns, can you please give her my card?" Dan smiled and stepped backwards to escape the drunk and armed madman.

If that's just the guard, Dan wondered, *how old and senile is Ms. Larriott?*

In a dark back office of the Lee County Sheriff's headquarters, Alexandra Larriott was trying to sleep. She and Cassie were curled in a fetal position on a couch belonging to a Lieutenant Coffey. The oblivious child held her blanket, snuggling close to her mom.

When Detective Rodka suggested they stay overnight, Alexandra had been apprehensive. She'd brazenly asked if she was in custody. Rodka said no, promising she and Cassie could have privacy in a back office. He reminded her that her home had no electricity. A handful of other victims —mostly family members of officers— were also staying in the building. In the morning, she'd be free to leave after questioning.

Rodka told her to not leave the county. Calling his bluff, she snapped that she had no duty to remain anywhere. She was never read any rights and was never arrested. Rodka was taken aback as if he respected her resilience. He confessed she had no duty to remain in the state —yet. He then reminded her she *had* to sit for more questions in the morning —if she could ever find her attorney.

At the time of his offer to stay overnight, Alexandra knew her house had shattered windows and no electricity. She also knew it'd be impossible to sleep in the house. The home would contain the nightmare of *those men* —one of which she'd killed.

The lieutenant's office was vacant and the couch looked comfortable. The office had air conditioning and a clean bathroom. A deputy gave her blankets and a throw pillow. Alexandra agreed to stay and Cassie fell asleep in her arms.

A pleasant female deputy opened the door to the office. She cleared her throat to get Alexandra's attention.

Alexandra looked up with a twinge of anxiety. "Yes..?"

"Ms. Larriott, your attorney's phone is still not working." She had a sympathetic Jamaican accent. "Lines are probably down. Maybe better luck tomorrow."

"Thank you," Alexandra whispered so she wouldn't wake Cassie.

The deputy gave a faint smile and closed the door.

For an instant, it sounded like the deputy locked the door from the other side. Alexandra felt trapped. She pulled Cassie closer. *Better luck tomorrow?* She scoffed, *I've got to get our passports and get out of the country.*

16. Lex

A cloudless morning showcased the exotic Miami skyline. The fusion of Spanish architecture, pastel art deco and glistening towers reflected in Biscayne Bay like a mirror.

International tourists and model types made up the brunch crowd at Bayside Marketplace. The outdoor mall, with its marina and upscale café tables on the bay, was still as sexy as it was during its *Miami Vice* heyday.

At the center of the marketplace, wagon-type kiosks sold expensive perfumes, sunglasses and designer watches. South American and cruise ship tourists filled the courtyard. Bayside was a bustling destination for the beautiful to browse —as well as to be seen.

A pale mid-thirties man with dyed black hair stood out among the jovial shoppers. He was handsome, but appeared almost Goth. Spider web tattoos ran up his wiry arms all the way to his neck. He wore a black t-shirt, black jeans and multiple silver earrings. Though he contrasted with the tan, happy crowd, he quietly mingled among them.

The Goth man approached a crowded table selling sunglasses. He tried on several pairs, replacing the ones he didn't like. When a group of Colombian tourists bumped him, he slid a pair of *Roberto Cavalli* sunglasses in his pocket with an almost slight of hand. He then drifted to a booth selling expensive watches.

The keen eyes of a mall security guard watched the man. He observed the black-haired man ask a clerk to see a Presidential Rolex. The man tried on the watch, making small-talk to the sexy Latina clerk. As sly as a magician, the man pretended to polish the watch with his t-shirt, switching the Rolex with a replica from his pocket. After more chitchat, he returned the *replica* to the clerk —with the real Rolex concealed in his pocket. The man winked at the clerk and turned to exit the courtyard.

The mall security guard reached to stop the man. "Sir, I can't let you leave."

The man turned his head without slowing his stride. "Sorry pal, I have an appointment."

"That appointment is with me," LeBeau replied with his disturbing grin. He wore a generic mall security uniform and his narrow glasses. He clutched the man's shoulder. "You *really* don't want a scene here, do you?" LeBeau gave a mock pout.

LeBeau and the black-haired man sat at a café table overlooking Biscayne Bay. Around them, attractive and scantily-clad *chicas* passed by. At a nearby table, a group of twenty-something Cuban girls giggled in bikinis while sipping *mojitos*. Oblivious to their surroundings, LeBeau and the man glared at each other as unflinching as poker players.

A gleeful Latino server with a wide smile interrupted their gaze. "May I bring you gentlemen something?"

"Absolutely," LeBeau crooned. *"Uno café Cubano por favor."*

The black-haired man rolled his eyes. "I'll have a Bud."

LeBeau was appalled with a hand to his chest. "A *Budweiser*? It's 10:00 a.m."

The man frowned at LeBeau and the server walked away. After a moment of silence, the man nodded. "I know who you are. You're from the mercenary chat room. You're 'LEBO-007.'"

"*Very* good!" LeBeau glowed. "Just call me *LeBeau*. And you're the crass 'CoolLEX-69' –or can I call you *Lex*?"

Lex was not cheerful. He scowled, "If you're FBI, I'd already be in cuffs. If you're with Scorpano, my brains would be splattered all over those *chicas* sipping the *mojitos*. Whose sandbox do you play in?"

"I'm just a mall cop," LeBeau shrugged in his security uniform, "– who just so happens to know you're *the* Alex Lee Summers." He added impishly, "The latest contestant on the FBI's top ten."

The server returned with their drinks. Lex kept his eyes on LeBeau and glugged his beer. With the awkward silence, the server walked away.

Lex wiped his mouth, "What's keeping me from getting up and breezing out of here?"

"Peek under the table." LeBeau's mouth curled into a half grin.

Lex glanced under the tablecloth to see a thin silver rod protruding from LeBeau's sleeve.

"I think a six-million-volt prod could cause *serious* arrhythmia." LeBeau took a dainty sip of his espresso. "Your autopsy will confirm a massive heart attack. Then I collect half-a-mill' for catching a real-live most-wanted!"

Lex appeared calm, "You got the wrong man, Waldo." He sipped his beer. "I'm just a guy who runs a shitty tattoo shop."

LeBeau leaned forward and spoke in a hushed tone. "You know that pretty boy in Hialeah who made your new passport, driver's license and credit cards? He's one of *our* subcontractors. Fingerprints don't lie."

Lex's eyes narrowed. "Is this a sad attempt at a shakedown?" He growled through his teeth, "You don't know who you're dealing with. What do you want?"

"Oh, we want *you*," LeBeau replied sharply. "And I do know a *little* about you. There aren't many Army Rangers who've hacked FBI computers *and* robbed banks. You were indicted for use of an AK-47 in the furtherance of a crime, conspiracy to commit armed robbery, and possession of a grenade. You have convalescent training including basic EMT–"

"–I get it!" Lex shouted. "You know how to Google." Several patrons glanced at his outburst.

LeBeau sipped his coffee, allowing a moment of silence. He seemed more civil. "Aren't you tired of running, Lex? Praying every day that some mom in Starbucks doesn't identify you? Look at you – resorting to childish shoplifting." He chuckled, "Though I enjoyed the Rolex switcheroo."

Lex took a chug of his beer and sighed as if acknowledging his predicament. "I'm my own boss right now. No women, no officers, no wardens. I'm not loaded. I come and go as I please." He turned smug, "What's your game? A washed-up mercenary trying to build the 'B-Team?'"

LeBeau touched his fingertips together with a bizarre smile. "We actually call ourselves a 'CAT' team –a 'Catastrophe-Activated Team.'" He looked up at a paddle fan to assemble his words. "We sort of work...hand in hand with natural disasters."

Lex smirked in disbelief. "All this for some...hurricane *Peace Corps*?" He mocked, "That sounds really fulfilling!" He began to stand.

"–We know of your debt to Scorpano," LeBeau exclaimed. "What I'm offering is better than a winning lottery ticket."

Lex stopped. He said nothing and sat back down.

"I assure you we're no Peace Corps," LeBeau smiled. "Think of me as a corporate recruiter. You come highly recommended through our fencing network. You have the military background we prefer, and an *aversion* for the law that aligns with our goals." He folded his hands on the table. "At least let me show you our business model and tactical arms." He grinned, "And, of course, our full benefits package."

Lex squinted in utter confusion. "Who in the hell *are* you?"

17. Fencing for Dummies

The scruffy pirate, Captain Rick, peered over both shoulders like a ferret. Before entering the South Beach bar, he looked in his duffle to inspect the goodies he'd stolen from a dead man.

He'd wasted two hours driving to his favorite Tampa pawnshop, only to learn they had a strict policy of recording the IDs of sellers. Since when did pawn shops have morals?

He'd seen enough movies to know how to fence merchandise. You just sell off a little here, pawn a little there. Rick thought he might even try the Internet to sell some pieces on that Craigslist. At least the Tampa shop referred him to an address in Miami Beach that *might* look at jewelry. *This better work,* he cursed, since he had to drive two hours south, then another two hours east to Miami Beach.

The directions led to a bar on glitzy South Beach. It was only 11:00 a.m., so the club had been closed for only four hours. Would the guy *Jorge* still be there? Rick observed the "Closed" sign from his "84 Buick Regal. He took one more inventory of the items in his bag. There were two gun-like devices that looked like Tasers. Rick knew what Tasers looked like because he hadn't missed an episode of

COPS in eighteen years. There were two small metallic balls the size of oranges. They didn't look like any type of grenade he'd ever seen, but he was careful with them anyway. There were three graphite dive knives and some sort of flashlight. The jewelry consisted of seven rings that appeared to be diamonds, multiple gold chains and ladies' watches. In the trunk of his car were the rolled canvases of art that appeared fancy —though he was no expert of art, except for his black velvet Elvis paintings he'd once won in Vegas.

Rick tapped on the glass door three times. A young, bleach-blond man with a broom came to the door. "Can I *helps* you?" he shouted in a thick Spanish accent.

"Are you Jorge?" Rick asked, pointing to his bag. "Jesse Byrd in Tampa sent me."

The boy unlocked the door.

On a bar that looked like onyx, Rick carefully laid out the bag's contents. Jorge said he only dealt in jewelry, so Rick left the three paintings in the trunk.

Jorge ran his finger over the jewelry, sighing, "Yes, yes, yes, no, no..." He lifted an enormous diamond ring and his eyes twinkled. He pulled out a jeweler's loupe to inspect the gem. *"Dios mio..!"*

Rick smiled. "That's the real deal, ain't it?"

"It has to be three carats," Jorge fanned himself. "But I have to use a *chemicals* test to rule out *moissonite.*"

Rick didn't know what that meant, so he kept a poker face. "How much for the lot —if you paid today?"

Jorge looked up through his bangs. "Patience, patience... I need to talk to many *peoples.* And I don't want your hideous weapons or flashlights."

Rick was getting squirrelly again. "But how much if you had to pay *right now*?"

Sensing his impatience, Jorge eyed Captain Rick head to toe. "If you *gots* somewhere to be, I can't pay you more than..." He frowned, "...ten thousand."

Rick's eyes bugged. "I'll take it!" He didn't want to wait for chemical tests or meetings with more strangers. *Ten grand tax-free was like fifteen thousand before taxes!*

Jorge led Rick to a janitor's closet beside the ladies room. He counted out $10,000 from a banded stack of bills hidden in a tampon box. "Here you go. Now *you* fly away."

"Much obliged," Rick smiled like a tomcat as he shoved the money into his bag. "By the way, do you know anyone who deals in fine art?"

Jorge raised a brow, "I don't, but I know a lady I call *the Queen.*"

"Gimme her digits. I'll get you a finder's fee," Rick chuckled with an emphysemic cough.

After jotting a name and number on a Maxi-pad, Jorge gave Rick the bum's rush out the door. The pirate grinned, waved and marched away.

Jorge dialed a number on a cellphone. *"Hola* your highness! It's South Beach *Jorgy."* He peeked out the window to see if the scruffy man was gone. "You were looking for newbie sellers who suddenly have jewels *and* fine art...?" He paused. "I'm sending someone your way."

18. Dog Tag of a Mutt

"I'm Lieutenant Colonel Sturges." The striking, silver-haired man smiled, "You have a John Doe I'd like to see." The man was handsome and in his late-fifties. He seemed warm, not the square-jawed stereotype of an Army Colonel.

"Glad to have you, Colonel." Coroner Garfield was polite, though protective of his turf. *Why's the Army here?* Garfield wondered. The man refused to wear a jumpsuit and Garfield thought his Army Blue uniform seemed odd for a routine visit. Usually when the Army accompanied National Guard, they wore their field camouflage. "Got your dress blues on, huh? I used to hate formalwear." Garfield attempted small talk as they walked through the dim Sanibel Lodge morgue. "I had my med training in the Army."

Colonel Sturges looked down at his uniform. "I'm escorting 200 Reserves and they want a photo-op for broadcast. National Guard usually handles disasters, but you need all the help you can get down here."

They entered the dark, cavernous ballroom and Garfield motioned with his hand. "Welcome to our nightmare." The morning sun couldn't pierce the shutters covering the windows. A few generated lights flickered on ancient chandeliers that hung over the twenty corpses.

"Show me the man I saw in the bulletin," Sturges said as if giving an order.

The night before, Garfield had placed a photo of the mystery soldier online in hopes of identifying the man. Garfield had been on a Katrina task force in Louisiana when he got the idea of using the web to identify the dead. Though effective, the concept didn't come without criticism. Ethical questions had arisen about posting photographs of dead bodies, especially considering family members. To avoid being viewed by perverted eyes, the photos were made exclusive to law enforcement and the medical community. Software allowed wounds to be blurred with no decomposing visible skin. The department's goal was to identify the dead in a respectful manner. Garfield needed to be creative with the daunting task of identifying the victims.

Garfield knew that storm casualties came with a unique set of challenges. At least in a plane crash he'd have a list of passengers and he could start calling the families. With hurricane victims, their next of kin may be displaced by the storm as well. They might be in shelters, trailers or in other states, not realizing their loved ones were even missing. Tracing their phone numbers and addresses would be impossible.

To make matters worse, the corpses defied the usual rules for forensic identification. Many flood and storm victims had no ID, fingerprints or recognizable features. They might've been washed up on property with no link to its closest home. In some instances, animals –in this case crabs– have damaged the bodies. Depending on timeframe, decomposition could make the job even more complex.

In the worst cases of decay, DNA testing would be required to determine identity. But just like creating his temporary morgue, Garfield knew obtaining DNA testing would be slow and frustrating. During Katrina, the Louisiana State Police lab was supposed to handle DNA testing, but FEMA refused funding because of bureaucratic rules limiting "who" the agency could pay. With Hurricane Selina, Garfield would ask the Department of Health to contribute to the testing, but that would be an equally cumbersome process.

Garfield prayed that DNA testing would be a last resort. In the meantime, he'd post the photos on his online bulletin board and hope for the best. He owed it to the families.

But now he wondered why the U.S. Army was suddenly interested in a civilian casualty.

Colonel Sturges scanned the ghostly ballroom of corpses. "I haven't seen such a sinister morgue since the slums of Katrina."

"It is sad," Garfield nodded as they walked to the back row of bodies. "A Mortuary Response Team is supposed to get us 'frigeration by Monday." He approached a gurney containing the mystery soldier. "Until then, here lies our *G.I. John Doe*." He removed the plastic sheet from the bloated corpse. "One of your boys?"

The Colonel paused and his eyes widened. "No, sir." He leaned over with his hands behind his back to study the body. "We deployed no one here *before* the storm." The Colonel wasn't repelled by the grotesque face. He focused on the man's attire. "No ID of any branch..."

"So where'd he get the uniform? Army-Navy store?"

"No way!" The Colonel touched the uniform's material. "This is state-of-the-art Core-Tex. Weatherproof. Expensive."

"What about the armor?" Garfield speculated, "Maybe SWAT or bomb squad stuff?"

Sturges tapped the outer shell of the uniform. He smiled in disbelief. "It's the new *T-Rex Skin*." He pointed to three-inch disks in the breastplate. "Overlapping scales for range of motion. Silicon carbide that can take more hits than any other combat armor." He shook his head and rhetorically asked the dead man, "How'd you get your hands on this?"

Garfield squatted to lift the helmet from under the gurney. "When they found him, he was wearing this."

The Colonel tried to contain a gasp. He reached to take the helmet and attached goggles. "A prototype Advanced Combat Helmet with protective face mask." He touched the triangular front, "A windscreen with elective oxygen feed." He seemed puzzled as he looked into the mechanical goggles. "*Built-in* PVS Night Vision..?" He shook his head and whispered under his breath, "*Impossible...*"

"So who does he belong to?"

The Colonel stepped back to assess the question. "He's a mutt."

Garfield was offended. "You calling a dead man a dog?"

"A mutt of Specials Ops," Sturges explained. "His equipment is a mix of Navy SEAL, Marine Force Recon, even Army Rangers." He narrowed his eyes and huffed, "No *single* soldier has stuff combined like this. He'd be a hybrid of every classified technology from every branch."

"Don't all 'Special Ops' have the same equipment?"

Sturges scowled like Garfield was a fool. "Do you have brothers and sisters? Didn't you fight over each other's toys?" He stepped closer and recited like a rehearsed soldier, "We may have the same parents –the Commander-in-Chief and the Secretary of Defense– but we love, hate and envy each other. We don't share homework. Some steal it. This man somehow got the latest gear from every department."

Garfield was quieted by the outburst. After a pause, he meekly suggested, "It's ironic a single bullet killed him. You should see his vertebrae."

"His neck..?" The Colonel's eyes flashed with a thought. He reached under the dead man's head to feel the wound. He looked at Garfield. "Do you have an x-ray in your dungeon?"

The Sanibel Lodge's dank kitchen was crammed with every piece of portable medical equipment imaginable. The mildewed, burgundy floor contrasted with the chrome machines placed in the room by the coroners.

With the incessant echo of a dripping sink, Dr. Garfield unfolded a portable x-ray unit. The yellow machine was the size of a toolbox and attached to a rolling tripod. He positioned it above the soldier to capture multiple exposures of the neck and head, per the Colonel's request.

"Don't you have one of those x-ray light boxes?" Colonel Sturges asked. He seemed rattled by the dark and clammy room.

"All x-rays are digital." On a counter beside the filthy sink, the doctor had a laptop. He connected a cable and the screen filled with crystal-clear images from the x-ray.

Colonel Sturges hunched over to squint at the screen. He used a pen to study the area around the soldier's shattered vertebrae. "Look —right here."

Garfield leaned in to observe the spine just below the skull. "The fifth and sixth cervical vertebrae. Splintered by the exiting bullet."

"No —this." Sturges pointed to a perfect square shape no larger than a flake of confetti.

Garfield put on his glasses and leaned closer. "Is that part of the slug or bone fragment?"

"Neither," Colonel Sturges replied. "It's an RFID chip. Probably one of ours."

"A what?" Garfield wrinkled his nose.

"Radio Frequency Identification chip," Sturges replied. He crossed his arms. "Tested, never approved for field use."

"Use for what?"

"It was supposed to replace dog tags. The *plan* was to insert it in our servicemen and women. When scanned, it would give the person's name and medical history in case of emergencies. At the proper frequency, a sixteen-digit code links to information on our database." He looked over his shoulder, then back to Garfield, "In addition, the chips verified rank and were tested for GPS tracking."

"It was never used? Sounds like a good idea."

"The ACLU cried 'Big Brother.'" Sturges grumbled. "There were also concerns of the enemy hacking our frequencies to locate our troops."

Garfield motioned to the dead man. "If this guy's some AWOL soldier, why wouldn't he just cut it out himself?"

The Colonel shook his head. "The men were guinea pigs. They didn't know it was there." He sighed, "That was a fatal error. The program was shut down; all records raked up and classified." After a pause, the Colonel's eyes widened. He turned to Garfield, "Who else knows about this man?"

"The Sheriffs brought him in," Garfield shrugged. "One of the detectives was trying to ID him–"

"–Which detective?" Sturges interrupted.

"Nadine Stratton. A real sweetheart. She's investigating the case of the woman who shot this man."

"A *civilian woman* shot him?" The Colonel asked, shocked that a commoner female could've slayed such an armored warrior. "Do you have the shooter's name?"

"No. She told the cops he was a burglar." Garfield squinted to recall, "She said there was a whole team of them."

The Colonel's jaw dropped. "A whole *team*?" His eyes darted in deliberation. He peered at the doctor. "I need you to slice out that chip ASAP."

Garfield grimaced, "All bodies need to be intact until the autopsies–"

"–I need you to remove that chip *now*," Sturges ordered like the commanding officer he was. "Then I then need you to give me the helmet and uniform, and report this to *no one*." He stepped uncomfortably close to Garfield. "Can you help me with that?"

Coroner Garfield swallowed and nodded, "Yes sir."

19. Make My Day

Detective Al Rodka led Alexandra Larriott to a conference room for questioning. Cassie was taken to a break room to watch the Disney Channel with Rice Crispy treats that'd been brought in by a receptionist.

As Alexandra walked down the narrow hall, she wondered if Detective Nadine Stratton would be present. She couldn't stomach another session alone with Rodka. Then Alexandra hoped her attorney would show up on time. She desperately needed someone to explain that this was an unfortunate misunderstanding.

She entered the windowless conference room and was instantly relieved to see Nadine Stratton seated at the table. Her smile was warm and appealing. She exuded fairness, Alexandra thought. It felt good to have another woman in the room. Rodka simply grunted, "Have-a-seat."

"Good morning Ms. Larriott," Nadine stood to shake her hand. "We won't take any longer than we need to." She motioned to a pathetic tray of thawed bagels. "Something to eat? Coffee? Not exactly Starbucks."

"No thanks," Alexandra was quiet. When she turned, she sighed with relief. *He finally showed up.* She gave a faint smile to a casual man seated across the table. "Hello, Mr. King."

The handsome man was mid-forties with a dark tan. "Hi-ya Alex," he smiled with white teeth. His hair was slicked back and he wore a $150 Tommy Bahama shirt and linen shorts. "Why don't you sit right here." He patted the chair beside him.

Alexandra sat beside the man. He touched her hand and winked as in *I got you covered.*

Rodka closed the door and sat at the table beside Detective Stratton. He looked at the casual man. "Thanks for coming this morning, Mr. King." Despite the ninety-degree humidity outside, Rodka was dressed in polyester and a tie like a rumpled detective. The appealing and casual Nadine Stratton remained quiet, almost distancing herself from her gruff partner.

Mr. King nodded, "Happy to help." He folded his hands behind his head.

Rodka continued, "But as Ms. Larriott's *family* attorney, you should know that your client may require more of a legal *expert.*"

Attorney King gave a charming smile, allowing Rodka to drone on.

"Ms. Larriott has some unique problems, sir." Rodka peered over his glasses at King. "As we mentioned, your client *confessed* to shooting a man as he was fleeing her property. She's admitted that much."

Alexandra perked up to protest, but King placed a hand on her arm. *"Shhhh...* I got this."

Rodka continued, "I don't know where you come from, but around here we can't have citizens shooting anyone who walks by their window like some gangland. This is a peaceful community. Regardless of your client's social status, she's subject to the same laws as everyone else."

Alexandra gritted her teeth. As Rodka babbled on, she watched a spot of cream cheese on his lip that was disgusting. She then looked at the suave and smug King, praying he was as half as good as he thought he was.

The entire night before, Alexandra had tossed and turned, hoping attorney Sheldon King would call her back. He was the only attorney she'd met in the states. *God Knows* she knew attorneys in Canada, but in her short six months in Florida, she'd only met one —at a wine tasting happy hour.

Attorney Sheldon "Shelley" King was a notorious plaintiff's attorney out of Tampa. He specialized in everything from slip-n-falls to large class-action tort cases. He defended the accused and stood up for the little guy. He bragged that when he graduated law school, he put all his money into television commercials instead of investing in an office, expensive suits or vast libraries of law books. He'd made commercials targeted for low-income audiences. He hired ethnic actors for his ads and made sure his staff could *hablar Espanol*. His commercials ran at 3:00 a.m. after reruns of *The People's Court* and on weekdays during *Jerry Springer*.

King knew that, over time, lavish offices and expensive suits would come. And he was right. He targeted deep-pocket insurance companies, threatening bad faith every time. He had almost as many billboards in Central Florida as Walt Disney. He confessed that his first, true love was a podium and a microphone. After just a brief discussion with Alexandra, she wondered if he'd ever turned down a case.

At a charity wine tasting, King had bought Alexandra a glass of a rare 2005 *Miguel Burse* Chardonnay. She'd attended the tasting when she moved to Florida with hopes of making much-needed new friends. Ironically, she'd met King —a toothy shark like the man she'd just escaped in Montreal.

Alexandra appreciated his charisma and arrogant courtroom stories, but she deflected every attempt for a date. With a daughter and new life in Florida, she wasn't looking for a new man, no matter how successful. An obsessive man was precisely what made her run away to Florida. Cassie needed a calm, quiet new life.

As a consolation prize, however, Alexandra vaguely agreed to call King if she ever needed an attorney. It was tragic fate that such a turn of events forced her to call him. After leaving five panicked voicemails, he finally called her at the sheriff's office at 7:00 a.m., promising to be in Fort Myers by 11:00.

Now she needed patience and courage to let him do what he did best. It would have to be King versus Rodka.

Rodka put away his notes as if it were an open-and-shut case. "Mr. King, this case isn't rocket surgery. She already confessed to killing the man. He was unarmed and trying to exit her property when she *murdered* him. The only reason we haven't arrested her is because we were waiting for you —and we have her daughter to think about. There are no local relatives." He shook his head with drama, "I just pray we can find the victim's next of kin."

Attorney King cleared his throat, smiled courteously at the quiet Stratton, and then sneered at Rodka. He was succinct and clear. "Detectives, my client was attacked. Period. The culprit was a *thief* dressed as a soldier, who attempted to flee the scene. I trust you are *fervently* working that case." He looked directly at Rodka, "Your department has a duty to concurrently and diligently investigate *that* crime as well as any other."

Rodka narrowed his eyes. "I only do homicide." He raised his voice, "The man was fleeing because he was running for his life. He was *murdered* by your client. She already confessed on tape." He matched King's smug grin. "I assure you there were no roving gangs of 'soldiers' terrorizing the land."

Alexandra watched King, who seemed to be holding his own against the horrible Rodka. She noticed Detective Stratton gazing at her with almost sympathetic eyes.

"Before I say any more," Rodka grabbed a small recorder from his briefcase, "—and since this is a non-confidential, *voluntary* meeting, you won't mind if I record it so I don't have to fiddle with notes?"

Instead of replying, Attorney King lifted his phone. "Hi Cindy, it's Shelley. Come on back." He lowered his phone and smiled. "Detective Rodka, we're weeks away from any *feasible* arraignment. My client —a single mother— needs to go home and resume her life with her young daughter."

They all turned to see a cute, young court reporter with bobbed hair enter the room. She tiptoed, carrying her own stenograph machine.

"Hey Cindy," King said to the reporter. "Have a seat right here. I believe there's a plug on this wall."

Rodka's jaw dropped. "What the hell is this?"

King steepled his fingers in front of him. "Just so I don't have to *fiddle* with notes, I'm using a court reporter. You admitted this is a non-confidential pow-wow, so I can legally have her here." He leaned in, "Or we can postpone this meeting until we schedule a hearing to ask the judge himself."

Rodka stammered, "Fine..." He scanned his legal pad with uncertainty. "It...doesn't change the facts." He raised his voice in an effort to regain authority, "Mr. King, *here's* how things work down here–"

"–Can you please slow down," King interrupted. "Cindy needs to be able to type this." He winked at the reporter and looked at Rodka. "For the record, can you tell us how long you've been a detective in homicide?"

Nadine Stratton gave a subtle grin that King was turning the tables.

"I've been a detective for twenty-six years," he shouted. "But I'm not the one here to answer questions!"

King tossed his hands into the air. "You never made sergeant?"

Stratton covered her eyes.

Rodka half-stood at his seat, "This is *my* investigation! *I* will be asking the questions!" He sat back down. "Here's how it's gonna' work: the State's Attorney will be–"

"–No, *here's* how it works," King interrupted. "This is an informal meeting; not an interrogation. Your county's up to their elbows in utility outages and displaced residents. The Governor's already declared it a disaster area." He looked derisively at Rodka, "I *assure* you the State Attorney's priorities will *not* be a sympathetic single mother protecting her home and daughter."

Rodka turned visibly red. "Your client doesn't have a concealed weapons permit!"

King replied with a calm grin, "As a Florida resident, my client doesn't need a permit to have a gun in her home for self-defense. *Nonetheless*, she has applied for a concealed permit. Her Florida app is being processed–"

"–She shot and killed a man!" Rodka shouted with fists on the table.

King leaned forward, "Detective, are you aware of the Governor's 'Make my Day' law? If a citizen feels threatened, they can meet 'force with force,' defending themselves without *any* fear of prosecution. It even shields the defender from lawsuits by the attackers or their families."

Alexandra lifted an eyebrow with a slight grin.

"You're missing something!" Rodka fumed. "She shot him *off* of her property!" He screamed, "–By her own admission!"

King spoke as if addressing a jury. "My client was scared. It was dark outside. With the wind and rain, my client's unsure *where* she shot her *attacker*."

"The body was ten yards from her land!" Rodka pounded the table.

King cocked his head, "Hurricane Selina hit the coast with a ten-foot storm surge. Do you think that could *possibly* shift a body?"

Alexandra and Stratton unintentionally nodded at the logic.

King paused, seeming more civil. "Detectives, I really don't care what happened. All I have to do is convince a jury, who was just as frightened as my attractive, appealing single mother." He scowled at Rodka, then smiled at Stratton, as he spoke. "It's a small island where everyone knows everyone. As a community, they're *all* victims of the same catastrophe. Any potential jury would be sympathetic." He perked up as if an idea just popped into his head. "*Maybe* I'll call my cousin at Channel Seven News! They'd *love* to hear my client and her beautiful daughter discussing your department's malicious treatment just to improve your closed-case rate." He placed his hands on the table and looked at Rodka, "*That's* how it works down here."

Alexandra didn't know whether to applaud or stare at the floor. Stratton kept a straight face, avoiding eye contact with her furious senior partner.

King gathered his notes and helped Alexandra stand.

"Where do you think you're going?" Rodka shouted. "I intend to request a bail hearing!"

King looked down at Rodka as if he were an idiot. "You never even arrested her. My traumatized client needs to take care of her five-year-old daughter. With no record, she'd be released on her own recognizance." He lifted his cellphone. "Or do you want to call Judge Negroni right now, who's raking through his own devastated home?"

As Rodka gnashed his teeth, attorney King, Alexandra and the court reporter gathered their belongings and walked towards the door. King looked back at Rodka and shook his head like a disappointed parent. They exited the room and the door closed.

After an awkward moment of silence, Detective Stratton finally spoke, "So, I guess he wasn't just a tax attorney, huh?"

Rodka's eyes blazed. "As your Field Training Detective, I'm ordering you to *drop* any mention of the 'secret soldier' stories. That order's directly from Lieutenant Coffey himself."

"Why? People need to know."

Rodka winced that she questioned his words. "Because I said so. And because he's the Lieutenant. We can't have chaos as people sit outside, guarding their homes from looters. During the last storm, people had shotguns." He stood and looked at Stratton. "And another thing, Coffey wants me to report to him *daily* about your performance."

She was troubled that Rodka had such influence.

"Lieutenant Coffey's going to base any promotions on whatever I tell him." He walked towards the door. "I recommend you don't ruin your pretty little career before it even starts."

Nadine Stratton's large blue eyes watched Rodka leave the room. The old network from her father's day was alive and well.

Then it's decided, Stratton concluded as she returned to her miserable cubicle. She wanted out of the shadow of her unpopular, dinosaur of a partner. She sensed something in the eyes of Alexandra Larriott. There was an unspecified tremble in Larriott's voice and gestures. She was a woman who had been undeniably terrorized.

Though Detective Nadine Stratton was thirty-seven, unmarried and childless, she tried to envision herself in Ms. Larriott's shoes. *Would I have done the same thing?* Was it self-defense? What if others saw looters dressed as soldiers?

Nadine's old sergeant in Michigan used to say, "To decide if something's right or wrong, think of how it would play on the front page of the Times." If a promotion amid a clan of ancient pigs got delayed due to helping a frightened mother, she could live with that.

The first thing she was going to do was dig deeper on Larriott's "mystery soldiers." From her experience in property crimes and burglaries, they could have been amateur looters using the fear of the storm to their advantage. Certainly not *Special Ops* troops that target vulnerable residents. She was almost sure of it.

20. The Orb

The green van belonged to the Army Corps of Engineers. It parked beside the Anastasia drawbridge near St. Augustine Beach. A chubby, balding man in khaki slacks and an olive polo exited the vehicle with a clipboard and camera. He squinted at the destroyed gears of the upright bridge. Engineer Hank Lafferty loved mysteries, which was why the Corps had him assigned to the case.

The Jacksonville District Army Corps of Engineers was responsible for providing engineering and construction to meet the needs of the Armed Forces as well as civilians. The system of waterways was maintained by the Corps since they were part of the nation's transportation system. The 12,000 miles of waterways maintained by the Corps carried one sixth of the country's inter-city cargo. The design and construction of the associated bridges, channels and dams were equally vital.

Lafferty grinned like a Jack-o'-Lantern as he tackled his new challenge. He asked the bridge, "What happened to you?" He zoomed-in and photographed the bridge's gears. They appeared melted or fused together. "Never seen lightnin' do that..."

He checked his notes. According to the National Lightning Detection Network —NLDN— a significant lightning strike was detected via their reporting system. The NLDN used sensors to triangulate lightning strikes on a nationwide detection grid. The grid confirmed a strike at the bridge precisely an hour before Selina hit. *But how'd lightning do all that damage?*

Lafferty stepped down onto a seawall below the bridge's ramp to get closer photos. He'd eventually test for carbon on the gears or fuel residue in case a watercraft exploded beneath the bridge. The security cameras were useless since they'd failed at the time of the strike.

Lafferty crawled down a grassy incline beneath the bridge to search for evidence. He scanned the ground and turned —but something caught his eye. The glint of silver in the thick grass got his attention. It was round and looked like chrome. *Maybe just the bottom of a beer can?*

He stepped closer with enthusiasm about his new puzzle. He focused the lens of his camera on the metallic object. It appeared to be a silver globe the size of a...*baseball.* Before he could click another image, his smile vanished. His jaw dropped with instant recognition —and then terror.

Lafferty flung his clipboard and stumbled up the embankment as if fleeing a rattlesnake. He lifted his two-way radio. "This is Hank! At the Anastasia bridge!" He panted as he kept running, "Get the bomb squad —*NOW!*"

"Greetings, this is Special Agent Hugh Riker," the neat middle-aged man with flawlessly-parted hair stated into his phone. He gazed out the window of his retro-modern office at the Tampa FBI, Counterterrorism Division.

The voice on the other line exuded authority, "This is Army Lieutenant Colonel Sturges, Special Ops Command." He paused to let his rank sink in. "I just got back. The corpse was wearing gear from *three* of my branches."

"I knew it!" Agent Riker slapped his desk and sat upright. He straightened his narrow black tie. "Colonel, I just got a report of a possible E-PIG used to blast a bridge in St. Augustine. That *technically* qualifies this as an act of terrorism."

"An *E-PIG*?" Colonel Sturges chuckled with doubt. "Those grenades never went into production. It can't be."

"Oh, it *be*." Riker smiled into his phone. "If I can confirm, will you *then* work with me on a joint fusion team?"

Sturges sighed, "I need a heap of convincing before I unleash my big dogs."

Riker nodded, not surprised. "I'll get you the evidence –but you should know, as potential *terrorism*, I have a duty to pursue this with or without your help." He paused before playing his next card, "I just thought you'd be interested in recovering some of your AWOL men..."

There was a moment of silence. "Are you suggesting the suspects were *my* former troops..?"

Agent Riker smiled that his hook was set. The much-theorized and elusive suspects would have some very big dogs on their trail.

21. Victimless Crimes

Lex was driven to an urban industrial park in Fort Lauderdale. The weird *recruiter*, LeBeau, drove them in an atrocious and passé black Hummer. LeBeau spoke little once they were in the truck. He opted to tap his fingers on the steering wheel to Mozart. He was vague, mentioning their leader had been "lost," and they were "retooling for an ongoing project."

Lex knew, in theory, he could just run. LeBeau no longer had any weapon pointed at him. Lex could just open the passenger door and jump. *Unless this guy locked the doors.* Then he'd only anger the odd little man. Lex couldn't take that chance.

Like a cliché mob movie, if this guy was going to kill him, he would've already done it. Lex knew he'd have to go along for the ride to see what "offer" the man was talking about. LeBeau had done his homework about his past and nefarious debts. He'd said there were no obligations. If he wasn't interested, he'd be free to leave. *Yeah, right*, Lex knew.

In an unremarkable industrial bay, Lex and LeBeau entered two sets of locking doors that required slider ID cards –the type of system that could be installed quickly with little investment. Once inside, it was cool and quieter than the neighboring body shops. Lex was immediately impressed to see the room full of monitors, laptops and televisions. It looked like a television studio in some third-world country. It would've seemed like a "headquarters" if it hadn't been so...messy. There were wads of duct tape holding down cables and discarded Styrofoam cups everywhere.

Lex's eyes were drawn to a conference table in the center of the room. Seated at the table were two men and a lady wearing t-shirts and cargos. They appeared solemn. They looked up as if they had no idea why he was there. On one side was a large, middle-age man seated next to a lean black guy. Across from them was an attractive Latina.

"*Lady* and Gentlemen," LeBeau announced. "I know we're still mourning, but I want you to meet Lex, the candidate we've been watching."

Watching? Lex wondered.

"Lex..." The big man with the buzz cut tried to place the name. "*Alex* Summers? Your profile's impressive."

They have a profile? Lex knew he shouldn't be surprised. "Thanks." He tried to appear tough. Whatever these people were up to, it was illegal. They probably had weapons like LeBeau. Lex knew it'd be unwise to appear intimidated. He looked at LeBeau, "They know me, so who are they?"

"You're amongst friends," LeBeau touched his shoulder as he motioned to each member. "Over here we have our gentle giant, Tag. He was a twenty-year Marine in Force Recon."

The stone-faced Tag nodded.

"Beside him is Pitch," LeBeau said like an emcee. "He was Army Special Forces. He determines our targets and is our arms expert."

"Pitch?" Lex chuckled like a tough guy, "Because he's black?"

Pitch frowned at the tattooed, wise-ass recruit.

"No," LeBeau replied. "He was a star pitcher for West Point's baseball team." He smiled, "Which has come in handy with some of our unique arms."

Lex gave a sly grin to the quiet lady.

"This is Dalia, our newest member," LeBeau said as he walked behind her chair and touched her shoulders. "In her past life, she was a Coast Guard rescue pilot and logistics expert."

Dalia flashed a smile, but cringed at LeBeau's touch. She was petite with shiny black hair.

"Aren't we missing someone?" LeBeau asked the group.

The team exchanged glances. Dalia spoke first. "Curt's gone. After hearing about Butch, he left for the hangar."

"He's not answering his radio," Tag added.

The smile faded from LeBeau's face. He turned to Lex. "I told you we lost our leader, Butch. He was Curt's brother."

"He took a truck," Pitch added. "He disengaged the GPS. The hangar's camera has him heading west." He paused for the inference. "... Back towards Captiva."

LeBeau sighed and shook his head.

Lex didn't understand the implication. He strutted around the table, studying the computer equipment. The monitors displayed everything from CNN to the Weather Channel. *What are these guys up to?* He bobbed his head and plopped in a seat next to Dalia. "Tell me: how does someone 'lose' a leader?"

"Killed in the line of duty." Dalia had a wicked smile that didn't match her statement. She gave a snide nod towards the men. "*They* misjudged a homeowner with a firearm."

Tag and Pitch glared at her like she'd spoken out of line.

"A civilian?" Lex asked with disbelief, "Didn't *you* have guns?"

"We are not killers," LeBeau spoke as if lecturing. "We are simple thieves. Under Butch's leadership, we agreed to never wield firearms. He was a visionary and we'll miss him."

The men nodded. Tag wiped a discreet tear with the back of his large hand.

LeBeau tipped his head, "We...do carry some non-lethal weaponry. But only for emergencies."

"Emergencies for *what*?" Lex lifted his palms, perplexed.

"I apologize," LeBeau put a hand to his chest. "I haven't fully explained. We transfer the ownership of property during storm evacuations."

"Transfer the ownership of property?" Lex repeated, struggling to seem undaunted. These people were former military, who were technologically skilled —but didn't use guns— to *steal? During storms?* He looked at the group, "Let me get this right: you're a Special Ops team that robs without hurting a fly? Very noble, like a... *Robin Hood* of storms?"

"Robin Hood gave to the poor," Pitch corrected. "We give to ourselves. Old fashioned greed." He put a finger up. "But, *we* found a way to make it victimless."

"Victimless?" Lex exclaimed. "These *storms* are some of the worst tragedies in American history!" Lex caught himself preaching. Using disasters for financial gain? Lex altered his tone to seem less affected. "How is this victimless?"

"It's property that would get lost or destroyed in the storm anyway," Pitch replied. "The homeowners report it to their insurance. The companies don't rake through the rubble to look for the stuff. They just pay it and move on."

"*We* take it instead of the storms," Tag stated simply.

"The homeowners get paid. Then *we* get paid after we fence the merchandise," Pitch explained. "We simply take ownership moments before the storm."

"Moments before a storm?" Lex echoed in disbelief. "The most hazardous time... *conceivable.*"

"The *best* time conceivable," Dalia replied, passionate. "We target barrier islands with mandatory evacuations. Oceanfront property with unoccupied mansions. Cops even vacate. Burglar alarms are ignored. Wealthy ghost towns with zero security."

Lex paused to absorb the concept. To appear cool, he pulled a cigarette from a pack in his jeans and ignited a silver skull lighter.

"No smoking in here!" Tag boomed.

Lex froze. "Explosives?" He should've known better.

"No," LeBeau replied sarcastically. "We're allergic to lung cancer."

Lex dropped the cigarette and crossed his tattooed arms. *These guys are insane,* he thought. They didn't believe in killing, but had zero respect for the most catastrophic storms imaginable. They were concerned about the dangers of smoking, but weren't overly grieving about their dead leader. Lex almost chuckled, "What happened to your leader's body?"

"The authorities have Butch," Dalia motioned to the men. *"They left him behind."*

"Aren't you worried the cops will ID him?"

"Impossible," LeBeau replied without turning from his monitor. "We carry no ID on missions. We've removed all identifying marks and have altered our dental characteristics."

Lex shook his head, "Are *any* of you concerned about reclaiming his body?"

The team looked at each other and shrugged.

"Of course," LeBeau turned away from the monitor. "In fact, Tag and I need to discuss a few developments."

The stoic Tag raised a brow, seeming unsure what LeBeau was talking about.

LeBeau placed a hand on Dalia's shoulder. "Perhaps you can explain to Lex your vital role. "He looked at the team, "There's *already* a new tropical wave off the coast of Africa."

"Happy to." Dalia smiled with perfect teeth.

LeBeau and Tag exited to the rear of the facility. Pitch watched the senior men walk by, seeming offended he wasn't included.

Dalia slid a laptop between her and Lex. "If our plans are followed *precisely,* our missions are as simple as..." She puckered her lips to consider an analogy. "Picking up shells on a deserted beach."

Lex was enthralled by the bizarre presentation —as well as by Dalia. These people had created a burglary loophole with no notions of guilt or remorse. *And they don't hurt anyone?* He didn't believe that.

Lex was curious about the goods they burglarized, but it wasn't his main interest. What kind of *intelligence* had they stolen from their respective pasts? Government secrets? Security programs? Lex wondered. *That stuff would be priceless.*

All Lex *was* sure about, was that he wanted to know more.

22. Breakdown Palace

County workers flagged the convertible BMW through South Seas Lane. Attorney Sheldon King smiled and waved to each worker as he drove. "Future clients," he mumbled under his breath. The car stopped at the driveway to the Larriott estate. In the back seat, Alexandra held Cassie.

King looked back at Alexandra. "You know, you really shouldn't stay here." He flipped his white Oakley's onto his head. "What about my place? My kids will be at my ex's." He lifted two fingers in a *scout's honor.* "No strings attached." He grinned.

"I don't think so," she scoffed under her breath. How could King make a pass during a tragic situation? She unfastened Cassie's seatbelt to flee.

"Sorry." King seemed apologetic. "I just know you don't have electricity... It's unsafe."

"We'll be fine," Alexandra replied as she lifted Cassie. "I have a generator and the sheriffs are sending someone to sit outside. I'll be gone tomorrow."

King scratched his chin. "You know, you *may* have a real problem.

I did some bluffing back there. I've used the *Stand Your Ground* defense before, but they could have a point about you shooting him in the back as he was trying to flee."

"I was the victim!" she barked. "I really appreciate your confidence." She stepped towards her house. "I'm packing tonight and I'll be *far away* tomorrow." She carried Cassie towards the front door.

King shouted, "I promised Rodka you wouldn't leave the state!" He watched her walk away. "Call me..." he pled like a snubbed date.

Though it was only afternoon, her house was dark. Long, sheer drapes blew through the shattered windows. The living room was in disarray, with broken glass across the marble floor. Pedestals and collectables were scattered across the room. Alexandra took a deep breath with a surge of emotion.

She ascended the staircase holding an exhausted Cassie. Near the top, she stopped, noticing the empty picture frames where her paintings had been. She looked at Cassie's face. She had to be appreciative for the things she still had.

She carried Cassie to her canopied bed in her pink mermaid bedroom. She tucked her in for an overdue nap. With glistening eyes, Alexandra watched her daughter fall into a deep sleep. She envied her daughter's peaceful, oblivious face. She was in awe. *How do children forget so quickly?*

Alexandra proceeded to the door of her bedroom –*where it all happened*. Wind blew the shredded drapes. The floor was carpeted in glass. Her lip quivered at her bleak reality.

She looked in the corner of the ceiling to see a single security camera. She'd had the cameras installed in the house immediately after moving in. Four weatherproof cameras, all feeding to a single digital video recorder. The DVR had a 500 GB hard drive with continuous recording for 448 hours at fifteen frames per second. The four-camera DVR had been installed in a safe location in the attic, impossible to locate by intruders. It was supposed to assure unconditional security.

When the first cop had arrived at the scene, Alexandra told him about the system. It *should have* provided exonerating evidence, proving there'd been intruders. It would've shown multiple angles of the men illegally entering her home. But she became instantly nauseous when Rodka told her the DVR had been destroyed. The recorder in the attic had been flooded with the roof damage. Video from all four cameras –her key evidence– was gone.

Alexandra delicately crunched through the glass. She approached the wall safe concealed on the wall. It had never been opened by the men; she'd startled them before they could've defeated it. She entered the combination and opened the safe. Everything was intact: countless banded stacks of hundred-dollar bills and four passports – two U.S. and two Canadian– for her and Cassie. They'd been created with two *new* names. *So many details to memorize.* Under the passports was a gun, another 9mm semi-automatic.

Alexandra sat on the corner of the bed and gripped the gun, but uneasily this time. She shook her head that such a small piece of steel could cause so much turmoil. Regardless, she'd keep it at her side if she was going to stay in the house another night. She had to surrender her original firearm to the sheriffs. She'd almost fainted when they asked for the "murder weapon."

As she stood and walked towards the door, she noticed the portrait of her and Cassie. Her spine surged with goose bumps at seeing the picture. In it, they were clean and happy. She remembered the day in Naples when she and Cassie attended a tea party at the Ritz Carlton. She'd hired a professional photographer for the photo. Like the true *permanence of art,* the portrait captured a perfect moment of pure bliss between a mother and daughter. *It had been so overdue...* Now, the photo only reminded her of how they used to be.

Alexandra's knees involuntarily weakened. Thirty-six hours of no sleep and unimaginable stress finally gave way. With her back to the wall, she slouched to the floor. She wept, clutching her gun in one hand and the passports in the other. Her body fell asleep.

Though she physically slumbered, her brain refused to rest. Nightmares of pitch black, the sound of pelting rain and the wolf-like howl of the wind. The darkness of her subconscious suddenly flashed with a glimpse of a figure. The shape had its back to her and was jittery like an insect. As if the creature heard her approach, it abruptly turned, revealing its monstrous face. The sharp, angular head was cross between a black wasp and a mechanical skull in a helmet. It was the face of the soldiers. Alexandra felt her heartbeat throb in her sleep. The monster raised a hand as if to strike her. It opened its crab-like mouth and screamed. Its shriek sounded like a... *doorbell.*

Dan Holms rang the echoing doorbell again. He looked up at the carved oak doors. He checked his clipboard. It was the correct address for his policyholder, Alexandra Larriott.

As he was about to turn away, a woman's voice groaned from behind the door, "Who are you?" She sounded agitated.

"Daniel Holms, an investigator with Insurex." He replied, "I'm looking for Ms. Larriott..?" He assumed the woman was looking at him through the peephole so he gave a corny smile.

After nearly ten seconds, the door cracked open four inches. A woman peeked out, squinting in the afternoon sun. "Can I see some identification?" she asked in a hoarse voice.

Dan felt bad that he'd disturbed the woman. He patted his chest to locate his badge. The lady took the ID and studied it, allowing the door to open two more inches. Her face softened and she handed his badge back.

"Is it a bad time? I can come back," Dan offered.

"No," the woman replied. "I'm glad you're here." She opened the door to allow him inside.

He was able to observe the lady as he stepped into the foyer. She seemed more fragile and feminine than her initial growl through the door. She had long, tousled brown hair and was wearing a robe as if she'd been in bed. Though she had no makeup, Dan was taken aback by the lady's beauty. She appeared mid-thirties and had high cheekbones and exotic green eyes.

The woman brushed hair from her face. "I'm sorry; I've had a lot of cops here today." She smiled, "I've been waiting for you guys."

Dan looked up at the thirty foot ceiling and was awed by the room's architecture and antique furniture. "You *are* the homeowner, correct?"

She seemed puzzled, "Of course..?"

"I'm sorry," Dan chuckled, "Most homeowners I've met out here are ninety-year-old widows. I guess that's what I was expecting."

She appeared hurt, "I am a widow."

Dan's eyes bulged. "I am *so* sorry. I just meant–"

"–It's not your fault," Alexandra covered her eyes, noting his discomfort. "You're right; I am younger than most of my neighbors."

Dan wanted to kick himself. He'd been there only ten seconds and he'd already offended his customer. He fidgeted with his file. "Ms. Larriott, I'm here to document your storm damage. But I'm also here because you reported a burglary that occurred the same time as the storm?"

"That's right," she replied as if it wasn't unusual. "Please call me Alex." She turned to stroll across the living room. "I'll show you where the jewelry was. Be careful of the glass."

Dan followed the woman. He decided to shut-up to avoid saying anything else wrong. As his eyes adjusted to the dim room, he saw priceless books and antiques strewn across the floor. This was going to be a sizeable loss, in addition to whatever *burglary* she was claiming.

"My room's down here." The woman sauntered, seeming unhurried in her robe.

Dan unintentionally watched her walk from behind. At first, she seemed slow and soft like a cat. Then he realized she had a slight limp –and he also observed her curvy figure. He looked away towards a bookshelf. *Keep your eyes in your head!* He'd been alone too long.

Alexandra gingerly stepped into the master bedroom. "This is where it all happened. The jewelry was in the dresser. They weren't able to open the safe."

Dan gave a meek smile, trying to regain the lady's favor. "Ms. Larriott, I know you don't want to hear this, but it could've been *much* worse. I've seen homes today with entire roofs blown off. You're lucky."

She turned and her eyes blazed. "I'm *lucky*?" Her voice trembled, "Are you joking?"

Dan froze, having upset the woman again.

"These have been the *worst* two days of my entire life!" She shouted and her eyes watered. "Watching cancer destroy my husband was *nothing* compared to killing a man who was robbing me!"

Dan's jaw fell open and his blood pressure spiked. "You...*killed* a man?" He stammered, "That story was true...?"

She cocked her head and looked at him as if he were a fool. "What kind of investigator are you?" She crossed her arms. "What do you *think* happened here?" She pulled a tissue out of her robe's pocket and held it to her eyes.

Dan was silenced. The woman was hysterical because of something he'd said. He wanted to excuse himself with some phony call and then run. Instead, he blurted a dimwitted attempt to pacify the lady. "Alex, why don't you tell me what happened..?"

She looked at him with her red glistening eyes.

23. Fans of Global Warming

LeBeau led Tag out the rear door of their industrial bay. On a loading dock, Tag lit a cigar and leaned on the rail overlooking a used tire shop. Grease-stained workers were shouting in Spanish, chasing a filthy lunch truck.

"Am I the only one alarmed about Curt?" LeBeau asked as he fanned Tag's cigar smoke. "I fear he's very *eye for an eye*."

The unemotional Tag shrugged, "What are you worried about him doing?"

LeBeau removed his glasses and rubbed his eyes. Unlike his erudite pep speeches, he sounded vulnerable. "We *know* what Curt's capable of. We've always preached the cliché never 'return to the scene.' It'd be very bad if he returns to Captiva."

"Butch *was* his brother."

LeBeau put his glasses back on. "Curt's irrational and stupid. He'll try either of two things."

Tag raised an eyebrow.

"He'll try to get Butch's body back or..." LeBeau paused, "He'll try to kill this *Ms. Larriott*." He shrugged, "Or he'll attempt both."

"He's unqualified for either task." Tag took another puff of his cigar.

LeBeau stepped closer, his words quicker. "It might help us if he kills the woman. She has *seen* us..." He let the notion sink in. "But Curt's impatient and clumsy. We can't trust him if he got arrested."

Tag nodded. "He'd cry like a school girl."

LeBeau stared at Tag as if they both knew what they had to do. "Why don't we show Lex our hangar?" He suggested casually, "From there, I'll head to Captiva to find Curt."

Tag recoiled, "You *alone*? I don't think so." He placed a beefy hand on LeBeau's shoulder. "*I'll* go with you."

LeBeau pursed his lips. Tag flicked his cigar at the tire workers.

At the conference table, Dalia and Pitch were taking turns explaining mission details. Lex sat back in his swivel chair, looking back and forth at them like a tennis match.

"We calculate *to the second* our exits." Dalia pointed to a projection on the wall of an animated storm. "I fly in; the team boards; then we fly out." Onscreen, a red blip depicted the chopper heading inland as a cyclone brushed the coast. "If all goes right, we're gone before the outer bands come ashore."

Pitch interjected, "Even though winds might be over 150 miles per hour, the *storm* may travel less than twenty miles an hour —easy to outrun."

Lex leaned back and nodded at his industrial setting. "So, this is your lair?"

Dalia and Pitch paused, puzzled.

"You know, *lair* —a villain's hideout," Lex explained with a smirk. "Usually a forgotten subway station or an old volcano..? You guys picked a garage?"

Pitch frowned at his levity. "This ain't a comic book."

Lex continued to tease. "Your recruiter called you the '*CAT Team*' —A 'Catastrophe-Activated Team.'" He grinned, "Isn't that just a little *X-men*-ish?"

"—We take our jobs seriously," Tag's baritone interrupted from behind them.

LeBeau added from beside Tag, "And we're rewarded *sizably* for five months' work."

Lex swiveled around to see the two men approach. "Why just five months?"

"The heaviest months of hurricane season are June through October," Pitch replied. "That gives us seven months of free time. Travel, time with our families, or planning the next season."

Tag seemed incensed at Lex's frivolity. "We work *hard* those five months. Two years in a row, *four* separate storms made landfall in Florida alone. Last season was a record number of consecutive storms striking the U.S. The most active season in sixty-five years–"

LeBeau put a hand up to calm Tag. "Let's just say we're *fans* of global warming."

Lex said nothing, overwhelmed by the avalanche of information.

Dalia rolled her chair closer. "But every storm could be the season's last, so we double-dipped on Selina."

Lex looked at the four strangers. They stared back with grim faces. He shrugged, "So what do you want from me?"

LeBeau reverted to his corporate recruiter tone. "Our vacancy is for a hacker with a military background and an *aversion* for the law." He stepped closer. "Know anyone who fits that description?"

Dalia moved even closer, her mouth three inches from Lex's ear. She cooed, "There's a fresh tropical depression brewing in the Atlantic..."

Her minty breath on his neck felt like electricity, hazardous but energizing. Lex couldn't contain a slight grin.

"I want to show you our hangar," Dalia teased in a whisper. "Would you like to see my toys?"

24. Tall Tales

Alexandra sat on the only clean corner of her bed. She crossed her arms in her robe as if chilled by her own story. Dan stood with his back to the wall, engrossed by her odd account.

"I did what any parent would do," Alexandra concluded. "There was no time to think. I did it all for my daughter."

Dan shook his head, overwhelmed. What had begun as an insurance claim for an unusual burglary had turned into an emotional tale of self-defense. *But is it true?* The report of the burglary was suspicious. Now an invasion by mysterious soldiers? And she supposedly killed one of them? If Larriott had been a ninety-year-old widow, he would've dismissed her as senile *—but this lady could win an Oscar!*

It seemed easy to prove. According to Larriott, the sheriffs were involved. There would be a dead body. But there hadn't been any mention of it on the news. The police should have all the reports. Dan knew he had contacts at the sheriff's office. *I can call Nadine Stratton —if she can ever forgive me.*

"Are you listening?" Alexandra asked, pulling him out of his daze.

He looked up from his notes. "Just wondering if this is similar to other burglaries I have." He pushed for further shreds of proof. "Do you have...an attorney?"

She blew her nose. "The only one I could reach is a shark I met at a wine tasting. He's one of those TV types. He mentioned some 'Make My Day' law that Florida has where homeowners can use force to defend themselves..?" Her voice trailed as if unsure of the implications.

Dan looked up at a corner of the ceiling to see a small surveillance camera. Suddenly eager, he asked, "Can I see the video?" Such evidence would make his job easy.

"No. All cameras fed to a DVR in the attic. It got wet, destroyed. The police took it."

Dan exhaled, *there's a big surprise.* Any evidence of her mystery men was gone. And the woman's story had inconvenient gaps. Dan pulled a binder out of his backpack and produced a stack of forms. "Ms. Larriott–"

"–*Please* call me Alex," she interrupted with a faint smile.

"Okay, Alex." He tried to return to business. "For the *burglary* claim, I need you to complete these forms. Unfortunately, we can't address the storm damage until the burglary questions are resolved."

She frowned, "What do you mean you can't until the burglary is *'resolved'?*"

He looked at her cautiously, "Based on what you're reporting, the burglary occurred *before* the storm. *That* claim comes first. I have questions on that claim before we can move on. "

"Questions?" Alexandra's voice swelled with emotion. "You don't believe me? You might not cover my hurricane claim?"

"That's not necessarily the case." Dan didn't want to admit she was right. Typically, if someone committed fraud, it could jeopardize coverage for any subsequent claims. Her report of a burglary *during* a storm was odd. He'd investigated similar cases where the homeowners padded their claims with laundry lists of expensive items. But Dan knew his greatest weakness was giving bad news to anyone vulnerable.

He took a breath. "*Alex*, I have a job to do. I can't pay a claim until

I carefully round all the bases." He attempted to switch gears. "Why don't you tell me about the stolen art?"

She narrowed her eyes with growing distrust. "Three were stolen. They were original Brulé's." She seemed guarded. "My husband bought them overseas. They were appraised in Montreal at over $500,000 apiece."

"Do you have receipts, paperwork, appraisals..?"

Alexandra shrugged, "I don't know. My husband did all that. I'm sorry you can't interrogate my *dead* husband."

Dan looked at her. She was becoming irritable and less forthright. He'd evidently struck a chord and she was getting defensive. He closed his file and decided to be frank. "Ms. Larriott, I'm a rep for Insurex's Special Investigation Unit. It's my job to investigate and confirm your version of your loss. Some claims contain what we call 'suspicious loss indicators.' It's my job to resolve those indicators."

"Are you accusing me of *fraud*?" Alexandra shouted.

He held a hand up. "Alex, many claims turn out just fine. Sometimes claims seem odd, but everything can be explained. My job is to work with you to clarify these *unique* facts." He looked at her with pleading eyes. "It would really help me if I had your full cooperation."

Alexandra stood and looked him in the eye. "I've already been locked-up, interrogated and destroyed over this! Why don't you find the *thieves* who did it?"

"It's law enforcement's job to find suspects," Dan was firm. "It's my job to verify the facts of your loss, such as these...'mystery soldiers.'"

Alexandra rocked her jaw in a furious struggle for words. She shouted, "Just *forget* the art! Forget the jewelry! Those are all just material *things*. I'm going to take my daughter far away. Somewhere where people are actually sympathetic and *want* to help victims!" She pointed at the door. "Please leave."

Dan was flabbergasted. He'd never been thrown out of an insured's house before. Mrs. Silver even gave him cookies and a warm Coke when he told her he was investigating her claim. Ms. Larriott seemed very...*fanatical* about her story.

Dan's mind was made up: he would swallow his pride and make the call. If Detective Nadine Stratton would take his call, maybe she could confirm or refute Ms. Larriott's wild story. If she refused to speak to him, he'd be back on his own. As usual.

He timidly dialed the number jotted on his cherished cocktail napkin he'd kept in his wallet —assuming she'd given him her real phone number.

25. Rebuilding Bridges

Nadine Stratton squinted ten inches from her monitor in her cubicle. Her desk was a chaotic jumble of paperwork and files. The walls were filled with photos of her academy girlfriends in Michigan, and a pretty cadet who'd been killed in the line of duty. Rather than pictures of boyfriends or children, she had seven photos of her cat.

There was one portrait of her father and three brothers, all uniformed cops, posing in front of a Christmas tree. She wasn't in the photo because her dad had asked her to take the picture.

Nadine munched on microwave popcorn served in a coffee filter as she typed one record search after another. It was her first warm meal in twenty-four hours.

On the NCIC –National Crime Information Center– she entered the words, "Burglary, soldiers." The index of criminal justice records came back with, "No Matches." She then tried, "Soldiers, larceny." Again, no recent matches. Nadine rubbed her forehead. She needed to find *any* rationalization for Ms. Larriott's story, especially after being reprimanded for believing her at all.

Nadine looked in her makeup mirror to see a few new lines

around her thirty-seven year-old eyes. Her co-workers were heading home to their families. She didn't even have girlfriends in the department to have a drink with. She flinched as her phone rang.

"Detective Stratton."

"Nadine? Hi, it's Dan Holms," the voice said. "The insurance investigator..? At the fraud conference in July you and I... *hung out*..?"

Nadine covered her eyes in humiliation. "Oh God... Hi Dan," she replied. "I guess we did...*hang out*." She squeezed her eyes shut —but smiled. *How embarrassing...*

Three months earlier, Nadine Stratton had attended an insurance crime conference in Orlando. At one of the inevitable hospitality suites, an SIU investigator brought her a martini when he'd heard she worked for Lee County. Dan Holms was tall, tan and rugged. He had a nice smile and a humble demeanor. Best of all, he didn't make any tacky passes at her. He was interested in her work and opinions. She'd been investigating a stolen car concurrently with his company. Dan was the opposite of every one of her male coworkers.

Many of the attendees abused the conference to schmooze with clients, network for better jobs, or play grab ass with inebriated coworkers. But not Dan. He had an endless fascination with Nadine's property cases. And she found his unique approach to investigation just as interesting. Like her, he believed there was no excuse for not being cordial and respectful to people —even if they were suspects.

She also agreed with Dan that it could be easier to prosecute the guilty for insurance fraud than to obtain an indictment for a harder-to-prove crime. After several more cocktails, Dan and Nadine came to the groundbreaking conclusion that insurance investigators and law enforcement could benefit from being nice to each other.

When tuxedoed janitors brushed them out of the reception room at midnight, guests either went to bed or carried on their antics elsewhere. Nadine invited Dan back to her suite —purportedly to show him photos of a recovered Lamborghini. He accepted, with no assumptions. Dan seemed thrilled to look at work photos at 12:30 a.m.

In her suite, as Dan and Nadine leaned-in to view her laptop, their heads touched. When he looked at her, she kissed him. The spontaneous urge came from the absence of male companionship since her ex in Michigan nine months earlier. Her duties in Lee County consumed sixty hours a week, surrounded by zero prospects.

As Nadine recoiled with a timid apology, Dan returned her kiss with increased passion. He slid his hands under her silk blouse. Rather than stopping him, she helped him undo her bra. She paused with a coy grin and excused herself to the bathroom. Dan said nothing and smiled. He hopped into bed wearing only Banana Republic boxers.

When Nadine stepped out of the bathroom, the glow of the television revealed she was nude. Her inhibitions had been doused by the martinis and Dan's charisma. She hadn't done anything remotely as brazen since college. Her blonde hair covered her breasts, but her toned stomach, bottom and slender legs were entirely revealed. Making no effort to cover herself, she slipped onto the bed with poise.

Though she'd known the man for only four hours, his passion for everything had charged her thoughts. Something told her she could trust this *Danny Holms*. He was one of the last, true nice guys. And he was close enough to law enforcement to offer stimulating conversation without being a cop –the only profession she'd vowed to never date.

Nadine stretched her curvy, lean body on top of the sheets, secure in her exhibition –until she saw the expression on Dan's face. "What's wrong..?" she exclaimed.

He eyed her body and sighed. "I *sort of* have a girlfriend in Lauderdale..."

"A girlfriend?" She pulled the sheets up to cover as much skin as possible.

Dan covered his eyes and sat up. "We're *sort of* separated, but we've been together for four years." He handed Nadine a pillow to help cover up.

"But you're... *separated?*" Nadine blurted as if finding a loophole in remaining together.

"She wants to chase a job to Seattle," Dan shrugged. "I told her I wouldn't move. She now wants time to 'think about us.'"

Nadine looked down with mixed emotions. Sure, she was disappointed. But it wasn't as if he was married with kids. In fact, his honesty about his girlfriend –before any sex could've occurred– was almost a...*turn on.* A lot of men would've fired before aiming. His girlfriend, wherever she was, was a lucky lady. "You don't have to leave yet..." she whispered.

Dan sat on the corner of the bed, pretending to not look at her body. "I'm sorry if I embarrassed you. I should've said something earlier, but I was *really into* your discussion."

'Really into' my discussion? Nadine marveled. She'd never heard anyone say that before.

They remained in bed in an unspoken stalemate. She grabbed the remote and found a rerun of Jimmy Kimmel. Within seconds, they found themselves laughing. Nadine forgot she was naked under the sheets. Probably influenced by the drinks, they stayed in bed until they slipped into a deep, contented sleep.

When Nadine's alarm blared Beck's *Dreams* at 6:00 a.m., Dan was gone. There was no trite note on the bedside table. She knew he was embarrassed. She looked down at her naked body and covered her eyes. *I'm an idiot!* Dan would surely think she's some tramp who lures men to her room. Strutting naked out of the bathroom like a pole dancer, she kicked herself. It was too late to sulk. She looked at her stomach and thighs and shrugged. Thanks to morning laps in her condo's pool, she was in decent shape and had a tan. If she was going to foolishly stand naked three feet from a stranger, she might as well look okay. *Oh well, that's that,* she'd decided. She'd never see him again.

Nadine had returned to Lee County that day without attending her final class at the conference. She would never know if Dan had planned to awkwardly avoid her. *Maybe we'll have another case together one day...*

"I'm sorry, Nadine," Dan said on the phone. "Is this awkward? I can call someone else..?"

She found his discomfort cute. "In that hotel, I exposed myself as a test. I guess there was no temptation, so you passed." She played with her earring as she spoke. "So, I will talk to you." In her desperate desire to speak to *anyone*, Dan Holms was the last person she'd expected to hear from.

He stammered, "Oh, there *was* a temptation...I mean, sorry about..."

She decided to let the guy off the hook. "So, are you calling about the hot-pink Lamborghini we found burned in the Everglades?"

"No," Dan sounded somewhat relieved. "We won that case, thanks to your help."

"What happened in the trial?"

Dan replied from his poolside lounger at his retro motel. "We convinced a jury that thieves don't steal a $250,000 car just to burn it." He shielded his laptop as three screaming German kids cannonballed into the pool beside him.

"Where are you, Disney?" Nadine chuckled.

"I'm actually working the storm in your neck of the coast," Dan replied. "I got the last room in Marco." He breathed a sigh of relief that Nadine seemed cordial. His ex, Liz, would've scolded him if he prematurely saw her naked.

"A pool in Marco sounds nice..." Nadine sighed. "I'm stuck at ground zero. I've slept four hours in the last twenty."

"Don't be envious. I'm working fourteen-hour days. I just figured I'd do paperwork from here." He smiled at his surroundings, "After all the devastation, I needed a break for happier scenery." He asked, "How'd you make out?"

"I was safe at headquarters. My condo still doesn't have power." She added with a grin, "So are you calling for *me*, or do you have another sports car-arson case you need me to solve?"

"Oh, I'm calling you," he beamed. "You still working property?"

"Sorry... cross-training in homicide. Why?"

"I'm hearing wild stories I haven't heard on any news. Burglaries that allegedly occurred *during* the storm." He smiled at his notes.

"Three people reported seeing a team of *–now get this–*'soldiers.'"

"*Soldiers?*" Nadine bolted upright.

"Yeah," Dan chuckled. "A Captiva rookie made a report he saw men who looked like *Darth Vader* who, quote, 'zapped him with lightning and vanished into the sky.'"

She didn't laugh. "Who else saw them?"

"A security guard said soldiers attacked him. Then the home-owner told me she shot and *killed* one of them." Dan laughed, "How'd the local news miss that?"

"*–What* homeowner?" Nadine exclaimed.

"Ms. Alexandra Larriott..?" Dan replied. "She didn't *look* insane."

Nadine huddled over her phone and whispered into the receiver, "I need to meet you. I have information."

"But you're in homicide..?"

She looked over her shoulder, "I also need a change of scenery. Do you know the Snook Inn on Marco?"

"Of course," Dan gave a crooked grin. "I know every raw bar in the state."

Nadine asked in a hushed tone, "Can you meet me there at 7:00?"

Dan raised a brow and the corners of his mouth curled. "Yeah...?"

"I'll see you there. Gotta' go, bye." She hung up.

Dan scanned the pool and beach in a daze. He tried to rationalize Nadine's request. "A smart, pretty cop orders me to a Tiki bar happy hour?" He blinked as if solving an equation in his head, and then smiled.

Nadine looked up in thought. An insurance investigator like Dan Holms should have access to numerous databases. He'd already found witnesses. Her eyes darted with renewed enthusiasm. *How else can I prove this?* Glancing at the ceiling, she noticed a security camera. It gave her an idea. She speed-dialed a number. "Toby, this is Nadine."

"Nadine *Stratton?*" Toby replied, surrounded by monitors, video equipment and Star Wars posters. "What bids you to call my humble lab?" The twenty-something bald kid sat alone in the sheriff department's audio/video lab.

She continued in a quiet tone, "You know the *Larriott* recorder we brought in from the scene? Can it be dried out?"

He sighed. "You don't simply *dry* a wet DVR hard drive. It can cause contaminants to bond with the media," Toby corrected. "And if water penetrated the *drive seal*, dirt may've spread onto the platters where the data's stored–"

"–Can you fix the video?" Nadine interrupted.

Toby glanced at a monitor showing black and white fuzz as he speculated. "It's tedious, but if I dismount the platters and chemically dry it, I might *eventually* get an image." He paused, "If the price is right..."

Nadine knew what that meant, "Yes, I'll go with you to the next local Comic-Con." She became serious. "Toby, can you promise me something?"

He noted her shift in tone, "Certainly..?"

"If you're able to get an image, and anything resembles a team of burglars –or *soldiers*," Nadine pled, "Can you *please* call only me?"

"You have my word, *M'lady.*" Toby sighed; he'd do anything for Nadine Stratton.

"What'd you just ask Toby to do?" Detective Rodka's voice boomed from behind Stratton.

Nadine turned and her eyes locked onto Rodka's. "I asked Toby to..." She stammered for a response, "...see if we had footage for a media request."

Rodka narrowed his eyes, "I didn't hear the word, 'soldiers,' did I?"

26. Repossession

Captain Rick scratched his beard as he double-checked the Pompano Beach address. The woman on the phone had said she was the "queen" of art laundering. He parked his dilapidated Buick across from the small house. The one-story, 1950s-era home had rust stains and was overrun with shrubbery. In the driveway was a white van that read, "Popcorn Ceiling Removal."

Rick carried the three paintings rolled in their tubes. He approached the home's screen door and knocked. He'd never fenced stolen art before. It was just like in the movies, *people who knew people; secret addresses...* And they promised all-cash. *Sweet.*

A large, seventy-year-old woman answered the door. She had curlers in her hair and wore a tent-like floral gown.

"Hello, ma'am," Rick gave a yellowed smile. "I'm the...*gentleman* who called..?"

The woman's face lit up. "Are you James?" She stressed *James* with a southern drawl. "Hi, James!" She opened the screen door. "I'm Hattie."

Rick was relieved Hattie wasn't a 300-pound mobster with gold chains. He was also proud of inventing a phony name *—like an international art thief!* He stepped inside and observed the décor which was gaudy even by his standards. The room was filled with Jesus and Elvis memorabilia that looked like it'd been ordered from back of *The Enquirer.* The room smelled like fried spam. He looked down to see the floors covered with plastic sheeting.

"We're having the popcorn removed from our ceiling," Hattie pointed up. "Those little balls get *everywhere!*" Her cackle turned into a cough. "Follow me, sweetie."

Rick followed her to a small bedroom covered in plastic sheets. The walls were filled with velvet paintings of hobo clowns and teary-eyed dogs. He wondered, *this is an art expert?*

She closed the door and put her hands on her hips. "Well, James, let's see whatcha' got."

Rick handed her one of the tubes. Hattie put on reading glasses and slid the canvas out of the tube. She gingerly unfurled it and held it three inches from her eyes.

"My, my," she exclaimed, studying the painting like an aficionado. "Jean-Luc Brulé. I'd say 'round about 1890..." She looked up in amazement, "Is this an original..?"

Rick grinned. "I only deal in originals," he bluffed with a cough.

Hattie's jaw dropped. "You got more like this one, hon'?"

He smiled with dollar-signs in his eyes. He handed her the other two tubes. "Do you...have an offer you'd like to...offer?"

"Most certainly!" Hattie turned to open a small lockbox in the closet. "Do you have any other goodies?"

"I got some self-defense items in the car—" Rick's eyes bugged when Hattie turned.

With both hands, she steadily aimed a .57 Magnum at his scrawny chest. "I'm so sorry, baby," she lied. Without any maniacal monologues, she squeezed the trigger. An explosive pop spewed blood across the plastic-covered floor. Captain Rick's spindly body collapsed like a clipped marionette.

Hattie put down the gun and labored to bend over to lift a corner of the plastic sheeting. She folded the four corners of the plastic over

Rick's bloody mess. She then shouted across the house in flawless Spanish, *"Paco, necesito tu ayuda!"*

The quiet and stout Paco wore painter's coveralls. He stepped outside to open the rear of the popcorn-removal van. Paco and Hattie easily lifted Rick's scraggy corpse, which had been rolled in plastic without spilling a drop. They shuffled through the gravel driveway and rolled the body into the van.

"*Gracias,* punkin'," Hattie winked at Paco before he mutely returned inside. She lit a cigarette and lifted a cellphone from her robe.

Wedged in a line of insufferable traffic, Curt pounded on the truck's steering wheel. His phone rang and he looked at the ID. His voice became almost childlike, "Hi, Momma."

"Hey baby," Hattie said. "I got your fancy art back." Her voice cracked with an emotional quiver. "Now, can you please bring your big brother's body home?"

Curt inhaled with contained rage. "Yes ma'am. I'm almost there." He sniffed, "And I'm gonna' chop up the bitch who did it."

"You were always my good boy."

On northbound I-75, Curt finally reached the exit that would take him to Captiva. The traffic was being flagged through by National Guard troops. The incoming roads were barricaded. Residents were being allowed to re-enter on a case-by-case basis.

On the side of his truck, Curt had placed a magnetic sign stating the generic, "Catastrophe Services." His patience was dwindling as he waited in line to speak to a guardsman.

Curt looked at his bloodshot eyes in the mirror. He rehearsed, attempting a southern accent as realistic as LeBeau's, "Hi. I've been hired to get into the damaged area." He frowned, frustrated that he wasn't as convincing as LeBeau. He *had* to get into Captiva. If the guardsman didn't let him in, he couldn't just shoot and barge through. He'd have only one chance.

Curt rolled up to a National Guard troop. The soldier was wearing protective gear and was armed. Curt lowered his window.

The young guardsman barked, "Are you a resident, sir?"

"No, sir," Curt replied in a pathetic twang. "I've been contracted by FEMA. They ordered me to get in by 6:00 p.m. sharp." He held his breath for a response.

The troop blinked in deliberation. He then moved the barricade aside. "Good to have you. Follow the signs."

27. Stray Electronic Pigs

Deep within the St. Johns County Sheriff's Office –the department responsible for St. Augustine– a steel door warned, "Arson/Bomb Squad Laboratory."

Covered in protective coveralls and goggles, an egghead technician pointed to the small damaged orb. "This little piggy's far from home."

Army Corps Engineer Hank Lafferty's eyes smiled, "What the hell is it?"

When the sheriffs arrived at the Anastasia drawbridge, they'd taped-off an entire city block around the strange silver ball. The Bomb Squad arrived in their mobile-unit truck. The entire team decided to come, including one lieutenant, three sergeants and nine officers. Their jobs typically involved false alarms, homemade fireworks or kids playing Mr. Science with pool chemicals. But this time, since the Corps made the report, the call seemed a little more intriguing.

Their technicians were certified through the FBI, with six weeks of training courtesy of the U.S. Army. They arrived in navy-blue *EOD-9* Bomb Squad suits, complete with blast-protected jackets and groin protectors. Like astronauts, their helmets had voice controls and internal cooling systems to mitigate the risk of heat stress. The bomb techs had to be masters of not only explosives, but x-rays, robotics, chemistry, electronics and HazMat investigations –all while being a cop at the same time.

Their senior tech, the bald, bearded and humorless Van Pelt, noticed a major challenge at the scene. The silver orb was resting on a grassy incline below the drawbridge ramp. The slant appeared to be a 45 degree angle. Only a small tuft of grass kept the ball in place. It appeared that –at any second– the ball could roll down the hill and strike the cement seawall. If it was indeed a grenade, it could be disastrous. Approaching the orb would be like a caffeinated kid playing a game of *Operation* on a bipolar clown.

The grassy hill made the squad's remote-control robot impossible. Members of the Explosive Disposal Team agreed the orb needed to be remotely detonated. But any application of explosive would need to be small enough to avoid further damage to the bridge. If the object *was* a bomb, there was a chance the overpass could be damaged. Hank Lafferty, representing the Corps like a union delegate, was not happy about any threats to his precious bridge.

It was ultimately agreed that the least of all evils would be to detonate the object. The blast could be engineered to discharge downward towards the water, rather than up towards the bridge.

Van Pelt crawled like an inchworm to apply a thumb-size clump of C-4. It was imperative to place it close to the orb –but without touching it. Any minor vibration could send the ball rolling. *Please no breezes,* Van Pelt prayed. Two feet from the ball, he held his breath and hoped his pulse would subside while applying the C-4. He then unspooled a detonation line a hundred feet away to a cement guardrail beside the bridge.

The blast was anticlimactic, considering everyone's assumption the ball was some new terrorist weapon. There was a smattering of applause from officers who'd watched the drama unfold from across the San Sebastian River. The mysterious orb was ripped into several pieces, which were collected for analysis.

The egghead tech, Van Pelt, and the Army Corps Engineer, Lafferty, wore goggles as they peered at a chunk of the orb. The piece was almost an entire half of the four-inch diameter ball. The exterior was silver with numerous spherical patterns.

"It's called an *E-PIG*." The somber Van Pelt added, "We learned it was a dud after deactivating."

"E-PIG?" Lafferty chuckled. "An *electronic pig*?"

Van Pelt blinked, not sharing the humor. "Electromagnetic-Pulse Impact Grenade." He turned to the orb. "Unlike a grenade where you pull a *pin*, you just throw this and it explodes on impact."

"That sounds...*unstable* for a weapon."

Van Pelt shrugged, baffled. "The only impact grenades I've seen are shot from a launcher. This one's larger, as if to be thrown by hand."

Lafferty pointed to the grenade's many dime-sized circles. "What are these little things?"

"*Theoretically*, they're sensors that trigger the weapon over a certain speed —such as thirty miles per hour. That way, it doesn't detonate if you simply drop it."

"Why do you say *theoretically?*"

Van Pelt crossed his arms, bewildered, "E-PIGS are *supposed* to exist only in chat rooms and conspiracy websites."

Lafferty looked up, curious. "What does the *electromagnetic* part mean?"

"*In theory* it means the impact emits a magnetic pulse that causes voltage surges." Van Pelt noticed the confused look on Lafferty's face. "It disables electronics within forty or fifty feet," he simplified. "And the pulse would mimic something as natural as...lightning."

"Geeze..." Lafferty's jaw dropped, "*That's* what destroyed the bridge!" He added with incredulous eyes, "Imagine if terrorists had these things..."

Van Pelt nodded, continuing to speculate, "Supposedly, these were never put into production because they're only as good as the man who throws it." He lifted the metal with his gloved hand. "These weapons aren't supposed to exist —but here we are looking at one."

Lafferty paused and asked innocently, "Did I hear you say you found fingerprints on it?"

Van Pelt froze, unnerved that Lafferty had this information. He removed his goggles. "The U.S. Army and FBI ordered me to say nothing more."

"The Army *and* FBI?" Lafferty asked. "What's going on?"

Van Pelt put on his horn-rimmed glasses. "We have here a... *fictional* weapon, discarded by the military, and found on public property. It was used to destroy a means of transportation. I had a *duty* to report this immediately to Homeland Security."

Lafferty nodded, considering the possibilities. "What if it's just some ex-military vandal who isn't a...terrorist?"

"If that's the case," Van Pelt cracked a cynical smile, "They're going to have some very big boys breathing down their necks." He turned to exit. "And those big boys are on the way."

The anally-neat Agent Riker sat upright to take the call he'd been waiting for. "This is *Senior* Special Agent Riker, Counterterrorism." He smiled with anticipation.

"Colonel Sturges, Special Ops Command," the brusque voice announced with competing authority. "You were correct. We believe the E-PIG is linked to the storm corpse."

Riker blinked with excitement. "We believe they have stolen intelligence *in addition* to weapons." He smoothed his hair with his palm and fidgeted with his tie. "Who are your suspects?"

"Hold your horses, G-Man," Colonel Sturges replied. "I still have big questions. You wanted a basis for a *fusion center*. Now you got one."

Riker beamed like a kid, "A fusion center?" He'd been praying for a multi-department task force. "So, you'll give me men and access to your—"

"—Whoa! I'm not gonna' hand over the keys to my entire department," Sturges scoffed. "But our interests do overlap. And I could use some of your sneaky suits as well."

"You got it," Riker replied. "I have four agents who can do anything."

"*Anything?* Is that right?" Sturges laughed. "Can they decode an RFID chip, and then reinsert it in a two-day old corpse?"

Riker's smirk faded. "*Um*...sure. Anything else?"

"I'll need your best analyst, and someone on a local level to keep things quiet."

Riker's conceit returned. "I have a lieutenant at the sheriff's office keeping a lid on it."

"*County cops?*" the Colonel barked. "We can't have rookies stumbling over each other with national intelligence!"

"Don't worry," Riker assured. "I'll keep an eye on any *radical* street cops who can't follow orders." He wanted to reveal the extent of the groundwork he'd already established, but he stopped himself.

Special Agent Hugh Riker didn't just want this victory, he *needed* it –alone.

28. The Lair

Dalia drove Lex and the CAT team onto a dirt road, north off Alligator Alley. The access road led past a pump station to a canal that ran parallel to I-75. The forgotten trail snaked its way behind a thick hammock of Cypress trees. Concealed from the highway, the truck proceeded on its nine-mile trek through the Everglades.

"There's the hangar," Dalia motioned to a lone structure in the distance.

Seated beside her, Lex studied his surroundings on the jarring road. The landscape was growing more savage as they drove. He saw two ten-foot gators swim off a bank at the roar of the truck.

"Uncomfortable in the front?" LeBeau asked, seated directly behind Lex.

Lex chuckled, trying to appear cool. "I've seen *The Godfather* too many times."

"We want you to have the best seat," Pitch replied from the back.

"We're hoping to *dazzle* you with our operation," LeBeau added.

Tag remained quiet from his uncomfortable position between the two men.

"Why keep your equipment way out here?"

Dalia spoke up, "128 miles of Miccosukee Indian Reservation. Police have no jurisdiction. We pay the Indians *very* high rent for a crop dusting operation. The tribe leaves us alone." She grinned, "And they actually think we're spraying for mosquitoes to help their camping trade."

Lex looked ahead at the approaching structure. The rusted, corrugated building stood alone among cypress trees and sawgrass. The arched metal roof appeared forty feet high and at least sixty years old. Dalia referred to the building as their hangar and it looked like one.

A hundred feet from the hangar, the road was blocked by a razor-wire fence and mechanical gate. Dalia pressed a remote without slowing the truck. The gate rolled open and the truck proceeded towards the building.

Lex turned to see the gate close behind them. "To keep out gators?" He knew he was in the absolute middle of nowhere. If he vanished, his bones wouldn't be found for decades. He also knew he had to convert any anxiety into curiosity.

Dalia stopped the truck twenty feet from the hangar's rusted doors. She engaged another remote and the doors screeched open. Behind them were two additional doors that looked like modern steel. This was a more secure compound than Lex had envisioned.

When the second set of doors opened, Lex's eyes widened. Visible in the shadows was an ominous black helicopter.

Dalia and the men exited the truck. Lex couldn't take his eyes off of the chopper. From his days in the service, he was familiar with a lot of air equipment. This one looked like a Coast Guard interdiction chopper, but it was jet black. With its modified sensors and guns, it looked like an angry wasp. *How'd they get this?* Lex wondered.

He decided to just smack his gum and bob his head as he followed the four inside. When his eyes adjusted to the dark, he saw two black high-performance motorcycles parked beside the helicopter. Each side of the room had cage-like lockers filled with weapons and military gear. The rear of the hangar had workstations that ran the length of the wall, filled with keyboards and hardware. Above it was a row of fifty inch flat-panel monitors.

The five stopped in the center of the room. "So what do you think?" Pitch asked.

Lex smiled, "Now *this* is a lair!"

LeBeau said nothing, almost brooding. He tapped Tag on the shoulder to follow him to the rear. Pitch and Dalia remained with Lex beside the Stingray.

Dalia took the reins as tour guide. "This is our hangar for vehicles, equipment and tactical arms." Her voice echoed as the doors closed, sealing them inside.

Lex looked up, admiring the helicopter. He slid his hand along its slick, black exterior. "The *Bat-copter*?"

"*He's* my baby." Dalia licked her lips almost erotically as she touched the craft. "He's a modified MH-68A Stingray interdiction chopper." She strutted around the craft like a showroom model as she spoke. "His old job included Coast Guard sea rescues."

Lex and Pitch followed Dalia as she described her "male" helicopter. Lex couldn't help but notice Dalia's hips swaying in her fatigues with each step.

She cupped her hand under a ball hanging beneath the chopper. "This is his *radome*." She stroked the geometric ball. "He has forward-looking infrared and night vision, originally used for pursuing smugglers at night." Dalia pointed to the rotors. "To slice through anything hurled at us, the rotors were retrofitted with titanium and a carbon fiber. Like razor blades, they'll slash through branches, debris, hail..." She turned with an orgasmic smile. "Isn't he gorgeous?"

Lex didn't know whether to be aroused or intimidated. He cleared his throat and pointed to the Stingray's external weapons. "I thought you frown on guns."

"Standard issue." Pitch competed for the spotlight. "They're M60 and M240 machine guns, with laser-sighted sniper rifles."

"Jesus..." Lex shook his head at the lethal aircraft. "Can't people see this thing coming?"

Dalia answered the aeronautical questions. "I try to avoid controlled airspace. At night, without lights, she's invisible."

Lex was skeptical. "What about on radar?"

"Air traffic control monitors controlled airspace. U.S. Customs looks for aircraft trying to *enter* our borders, usually not traveling within them."

"Just in case," Pitch spoke up, tapping the Stingray's black enamel. "We covered it in RAM –Radar Absorbent Material. It's a stealth technology that absorbs radar. Between that and the storms we travel in, we're just a blip of clutter."

Dalia brushed hair from her face and puckered. "It'd be a fun ride, huh?"

Lex locked eyes with her. He was drawn to her twisted passion. With his covert lifestyle, moving city to city, it had been years since any emotional or physical attraction to anyone.

"You like these?" Pitch disrupted Lex's daze. He pointed to the two black motorcycles parked side by side. "We also painted these with RAM."

Lex turned and was equally enthralled by the bikes. The ultra-modern cycles were glistening black. He asked in disbelief, "These are some sort of...*Hayabusas?*"

"Modified." Pitch smiled. "Hayabusas are the fastest hyper-sports bike in production. *Easily* over 200 miles per hour. Several years ago, the company had to reduce their power. A timing retard was added to the sixth gear." He shrugged, "They only go about 198 now."

Dalia placed a hand on Lex's tattooed arm. "Like what you see?"

Lex had a leering grin.

LeBeau and Tag exited the hangar's rear door. They faced the horizon to see an orange sunset reflecting in the endless marshes.

"I like Lex's profile. I just don't like Lex." Tag lit a Cuban *Macanudo*.

LeBeau crossed his arms, defensive of his recruit. "You don't *like* him?"

"I dunno'." Tag shrugged. "He's immature."

"We can't all be fifty-year-old Marines," LeBeau snapped. "My sources are *impeccable*. This guy was able to hack the FBI's encrypted email! If he turns down our protection and got caught, he'd be court-martialed for life."

"What if he tries to take our plan and go solo?" Tag asked.

"By *himself?*" LeBeau scoffed. "I found him once. I can certainly do it again."

Tag exhaled smoke. "I don't want you alone in Captiva. I don't trust what you'll do to Curt if you find him."

"I'm not the killer here –remember?" He narrowed his eyes. "And it *might* help us if he does kill the woman."

Tag paused at the concept. "*Kill* her?"

"She has *seen* us."

"If she describes us to the cops, her story will sound insane!"

LeBeau glared at Tag as if he were an imbecile. "Scary soldiers in the night *do* sound insane –until you leave a dead one behind!"

Tag blinked. "Point taken. What do you think Curt will do?"

"He's as predictable as a drunken uncle at Thanksgiving," LeBeau replied. "He wants revenge *and* Butch's body."

Tag looked down at LeBeau. "You won't mind if I go with you?" He stepped closer.

"Fine," LeBeau forced a smile. "Then what do we do with the woman and her kid?"

Lex looked up at the hangar's fluorescent lighting. The enormous room was shadowy, with faraway glints from vehicles and equipment. Ionic air handlers filtered any outside musty odors, providing clean, cool air. The only scents were from the new-car smell of rubber –and a trace of whatever spicy perfume Dalia was wearing.

He stayed close to her as she and Pitch walked to a rack of black uniforms. "So, these are your costumes?"

"Uniforms, Pitch corrected. "Waterproof and breathable Core-Tex." He tapped the outer shell. "Silicon carbide for debris flying at you at a hundred miles an hour."

Dalia reached into a locker. "For your skull, we have Kevlar." She lifted a helmet with attached mask and goggles. "The eyes amplify ambient light, so we can work in total darkness. Same ones used by Marine Ops."

Lex gazed in disbelief at the menacing mask. "How'd you get someone *inside* the Marines to snag these?"

"We did better," Pitch grinned. "We found a weak link inside the lowest-bidding contractor that makes them in Dubuque. We cut out the middleman."

Dalia pointed to the vent-like mask. "The screen allows breathing in fifty mile-an-hour rain. It has an elective oxygen feed for extreme conditions."

Extreme conditions? Lex mused. These people could walk into Niagara Falls unscathed. They were as if every dark faction of a government's Special Ops went AWOL and turned to crime. Or *–God forbid–* some sort of terrorist activities. *But these guys only do home burglaries?* How much cash were they making? Lex had an irresistible goal to know more.

Lex lifted a large flashlight device from a locker. "Cool flashlight."

"Don't turn it on!" Dalia shouted as she pushed his arm down. "It's a *puke saber*."

Pitch took the device from Lex like a razor from a baby. "It's an *LED Incapacitator*!"

"What's it do?"

Dalia took the Incapacitator from Pitch. "It confuses the brain with fluctuating light pulses causing instant nausea and disorientation." She stroked the shaft of the cylinder as she explained, "It also causes temporary blindness. With improper use, it's been known to cause cerebral hemorrhages."

"The Army scrapped it when it killed a test subject with epilepsy." Pitch took it from Dalia and placed it back in the locker. "Now, the nasty little *puke saber's* all ours."

Pitch and Dalia turned to see Lex trying on the helmet and mask. He then grabbed a puke saber. He made a fist and spoke in a deep voice, *"Luke, I am your father–"*

Tag's beefy hand landed on Lex's shoulder. "These aren't toys, jokeboy."

Lex removed the helmet. Pitch and Dalia looked at the stone-faced Tag and LeBeau.

LeBeau announced, "Tag and I are going to Captiva."

Pitch was alarmed, "We're *never* supposed to return to the scene!"

Tag gazed down at the men. "We need to take care of an unraveling thread." His voice invited no debate.

LeBeau looked at Dalia. "Why don't you show Lex the new tropical depression approaching Cape Verde?" He grinned impishly, "This season may be far from over."

29. The Fusion Center

FBI Agent Riker peered across his desk at the young analyst. "Can you tell me what a *fusion center* is?" He patted his hair as he gazed at his hand-picked candidate.

Jenkins replied without pause, "A 'fusion center' is a collaborative effort between two or more agencies." The young man was an African American clone of Riker —the same parted hair, dark suit and narrow tie. "A task force of multiple departments to maximize resources to detect, prevent and respond to criminal or terrorist activity. Fusions might include law enforcement, Homeland, even military."

"Have you ever been part of a fusion center?" Riker already knew the answer.

Jenkins nodded. "I helped Orange County Sheriffs get an $850,000 Homeland grant to start their own fusion center. In addition to terrorism, they've had huge success with gun-trafficking." Jenkins smiled, "A win-win for everyone."

Riker narrowed his eyes to gauge the man. "What do you think about the FBI working closer with the military?"

"Our greatest weapon against terrorism is unity." Jenkins spoke like a brochure. "Since 9/11, we're smarter and stronger than when the Bureau stood alone."

Riker's tone abruptly shifted to play devil's advocate. "What if I dropped you on a team to chase only house burglars?"

Jenkins paused at the question. "Last year, we studied a gang engaged in a series of gas robberies in Kissimmee. On the surface, it looked like kids hitting a tourist area. But our fusion team followed the trail and discovered they helped finance a larger terrorist plot to attack military and religious facilities." He looked at Riker with confidence, "It proved that no line divides criminal and terrorist activities."

It was the right answer. "What are your thoughts on a *covert* fusion team with just the FBI and the military? And to perhaps keep things *off the books* until we can confirm the threats?"

Jenkins sat up tall. "Sir, I see no need to unnecessarily alarm the public or any other parties until I'm ordered to do so."

Again, it was the right answer. Their team *had* to be acutely covert —with their targets kept way off the books.

30. Larriott's Biggest Mistake

What does Nadine Stratton want to see me about? Dan wondered. Was it a plot for revenge for seeing her naked several months earlier? She seemed too cool for that. *This is just a meeting with a cop,* he decided. He'd had numerous exchange-of-information meetings with law enforcement —but never at any outdoor, oyster-shucking Tiki bars.

Seventy-five miles south of Captiva, Marco Island had been spared by Hurricane Selina. Aside from enhanced surf waves, the white-sand island was back to its quiet self. The laidback residents watched news of the storm on televisions, many from raw bars that overlooked the *Ten Thousand Islands* off the coast of Southwest Florida.

"Do you have Bures Brues Lager?" Dan asked the pretty, cinnamon-skinned server.

"Of course, with lime." She smiled with dimples. "Be right back."

Dan, in his "fancy clothes" —a white Columbia fishing shirt and *ironed* khakis— observed the crowd at the Snook Inn. The thatched-roofed bar was as festive as the summer dusk. Unlike Captiva, the crowd was smiling with their feet in the sand. They toasted margaritas to their good fortune —and in respect to their neighbors at ground zero. On a small stage, a mustached guy with an acoustic guitar sang Jimmy Buffett's "Tryin' to Reason with Hurricane Season."

Dan was fifteen minutes early. He knew Nadine might be late driving from Fort Myers. He wanted to assure a waterside table with a view of the sunset. Nothing wrong with conducting business comfortably, he figured.

Dan speculated as he squeezed lime into his icy beer. Nadine had said she was working in homicide. Alexandra Larriott claimed she'd killed...*someone*. So Nadine might know about it —or have information that Larriott was a delusional lunatic.

Dan glanced at a young couple singing along to the Buffett. They were happy and tan, with a dusting of sand from the beach. As they sang and laughed, they drizzled Tabasco on raw oysters and lifted them to each other's mouth. *How romantic,* Dan smiled.

The couple made him think of his ex-girlfriend, Liz. Three things immediately occurred to him. For starters, Liz never once had a tan. She wore enormous hats and incessantly preached about wrinkles. Though she was probably right, it still sucked the fun out of a beach day. Second, she'd been the only human that ever claimed to *hate* Jimmy Buffett songs. *How's that possible?* Dan would ask. *All he sings about is having fun with cocktails on islands.* And finally, she would never, *ever* eat a raw oyster. Liz said she'd never put anything disgusting in her mouth. "No comment," he'd reply.

Dan wondered how he'd lasted four years with her. But he knew the reason: because he was handling claims across America and mailing checks home the entire time.

"Dan..?" The voice of an angel called out.

He turned to see a blonde in a floral top and white shorts. It was Detective Nadine Stratton. "Nadine? Hi..." Dan stood to offer an awkward cheek kiss.

"How've you been?" Her voice affected him like a tranquilizer dart.

"Great. Have a seat." Dan's stutter diminished, "I really...hope this isn't awkward."

Nadine sat across from him and plopped a stack of files on the table. "Not at all." She exhaled as if she hadn't relaxed in days.

When Dan saw her files, he remembered this wasn't a date. He'd also brought documents and photos in his backpack. He motioned to the server for two more beers.

Nadine smiled. "At the conference we did enjoy each other's," she paused. "...work stories."

"*Enjoyed*. Good word," Dan blushed. "I certainly enjoyed." He wanted to compliment Nadine without seeming distasteful. "You look fantastic –for someone working the storm."

"I wish!" Nadine chuckled, "Without power, I took a *cold* shower."

"I'm used to those."

"No one keeping you warm at home?"

He wanted to practice full disclosure this time. "My *EX*-girlfriend went to Seattle for a promotion. I told her I was allergic to 'no palm trees.'"

Nadine laughed, "You're like *E.T.* You get sick away from your planet?"

"Right!" Dan laughed at the analogy. "Take me away from beaches and palm trees and I might dry up and die."

The server dropped off two beers and lit a lantern in the center of the table. He was amused to see Nadine take the beer, squeeze the lime and enjoy a long, overdue slug topped with an *"Ahh..."*

"Looks like you needed a break," he smiled.

"It was a mental and physical necessity." Nadine pulled her long hair into a ponytail.

Dan admired her. She didn't fit any unfair stereotype of a cop. She was feminine, pretty and sweet. A trained photographer could probably turn her into a supermodel. But she didn't seem the type to use her looks to gain anything. Dan liked that she wasn't a twenty-three-year-old kid. In her mid-thirties, she was mature and confident.

The only criticism from Dan's police friends was they described her as an over-achieving workaholic. She did seem to be committed to satisfy *something*.

"You're on your way to being sergeant?" Dan nodded, "In record time, I hear."

"I don't know," she blushed. "I passed my sergeant's exam. There's an opening next month. My Lieutenant recommended I cross train in homicide to help with the interview." She cocked her head, "Who told you?"

"The same cop who told me about a rookie attacked by flying *mystery soldiers.*"

Nadine's smile faded as she was pulled back to the business at hand. "So how are you involved in this case?"

Dan cursed his timing. "My company thought burglaries reported *during* a storm could be suspicious."

"What'd be the motive for fraud? People can claim the items lost in the storm anyway."

Dan was in his element. "An insurance policy might have a burglary deductible of, say, $1,000. But a *hurricane deductible* can be 10% of the home's value. Imagine a homeowner having a $500,000 deductible. People have to find that money somewhere. So priceless rings, jewelry and antiques suddenly go missing." He wasn't sure if it was boring insurance talk. Nadine suddenly seemed preoccupied.

She looked over her shoulder and leaned in. "Listen: my boss ordered me to bury the 'secret soldier' reports. The Lieutenant's threatening firings with a gag order. He says to 'avoid panic.'"

Before Dan could reply, the server returned.

"Would you and your wife like to order?" The girl waited with her pen.

Dan locked eyes with Nadine who had a coy grin. He stammered, "What... about some smoked fish dip? And conch fritters?" He looked at Nadine. "You *are* staying for dinner, right?" The server scribbled the information and breezed away.

Nadine had a mischievous grin. "Dan, is this an information exchange —or a date?"

He smiled, "SIU investigators *are* supposed to maintain relationships with law enforcement."

"Very true," she agreed. "Sometimes it's easier to help you prove fraud than for us to fight for an indictment."

"Tell me, homicide detective," Dan leaned in, "Did Alexandra Larriott really shoot someone? One of these...'*secret soldiers*'?"

"Yes." Her tone shifted, more like a cop, "Ms. Larriott shot a suspect exiting her home. He was wearing some sort of uniform. We haven't found any weapons or ID."

Dan clapped his hands together, "I thought Larriott was insane!" He shook his head. "She told me she has an attorney. Is she in trouble?"

Nadine shrugged, "My supervisor thinks so. I called my *ex* for his opinion—"

"—Your '*ex?*'" Dan interrupted. "What does he do?"

They paused as the server dropped off a platter of fish dip and golden-brown fritters.

"He's with Michigan's Attorney General," Nadine replied. "They also have a 'Make My Day' law similar to ours. A person can use deadly force during break-ins or in self-defense."

"Florida has the same law?" Dan crunched into a fritter. "Sounds like a good defense."

She nodded, "But there has to be proof of intruders or an attack." Nadine was passionate with her opinion. "I know the State Attorney in Lee County. He'll *never* pursue a case against Larriott if there's evidence of a break-in."

Dan recoiled, skeptical. "But her only witnesses are a drunken security guard and a cop who was 'zapped by space men'?"

"Yep," she chuckled at the grim reality. "And her security video got conveniently wet."

Dan slid his plate aside and produced a folder. "Larriott may not be a complete angel." He pulled out color printouts of the oil paintings. "Her claim includes priceless paintings by French artist Jean-Luc Brulé."

Nadine focused on the prints, but shrugged at the significance.

"*These* paintings were reported missing in Iraq after looters raided the Baghdad National Museum."

Nadine almost choked on a cracker, "She's in possession of stolen art?"

"We don't know that," Dan shrugged. "Iraq blamed our soldiers for looting. Reproductions of these paintings are rampant. So, she's either lying about having originals —which is fraud— or she had stolen paintings. Ms. Larriott said her *late husband* bought them."

"Her husband..." Nadine blurted as she dug through a file. "I can't find *any* public records on him. I can't even find records on Alexandra."

"Maybe delays with international records?"

Nadine shrugged, "My ex has ties in Canada. He's going to check."

"Insurex has very little on Larriott. We've only insured her for six months." Dan shook his head at the sparse information. "If the burglars were real, how'd *they* know so much about her?"

Nadine's eyes lit up and she exclaimed, "I think figured that part out!" From a folder, she pulled out a magazine. The name of the publication was *Island Life*. The cover was a photograph of Alexandra Larriott in front of her staircase. Her lavish home was visible around her. The headline read, "Captiva's Newest Art Collector."

Dan took the magazine. In the photo, Alexandra was stunning in a black cocktail dress and appeared much happier than earlier that day.

"It's a local publication for the high society of Southwest Florida."

"I think I get it," Dan nodded, "I've heard stories about burglars who read 'Society' pages in newspapers to find targets. Newlyweds brag about their honeymoon plans. Then the burglars know their homes will be vacant and full of unopened wedding gifts."

Nadine pointed to the full-color spread. "Look: in the background you can see the art. She's even wearing all her jewelry." She flipped to another page. "The photos even show the layout of the rooms."

Dan's eyes widened, "Doing this cover was Larriott's biggest mistake."

They paused to sip their drinks. Though they ate and nodded to the music, it was evident their investigative gears were spinning with synergy.

Dan looked up, "What if your boss wanted her locked up for her own safety?"

She looked at him, puzzled.

"Think about it: if she killed one of a *team* –and she can describe them– shouldn't she be worried about..." he paused, "...them coming back?"

Nadine stopped chewing, "Why would Alexandra return to her *house*?"

"That's where I met her today. Her home has one generator and they're sending a cop to sit out front tonight."

Nadine's eyes locked onto his. She blinked. "Phones are out, so we can't call her." She paused, "And I can't radio the deputy or I'll get fired for just *suggesting* the 'mystery burglars' again."

"So what can we do?"

"I remember something you told me."

He raised a brow.

"Do you still carry a gun you're not supposed to have?"

"I told you that?" Dan smirked like a buccaneer, "A Glock. One of the reasons the big companies won't hire me."

"Good," Nadine stood. "You'll be my back-up."

It took him a second. "You want to go check on Larriott..?" His voice cracked like a teen, "*Now?*"

"I'll read one more story," Alexandra cooed to her daughter. "Then it's lights-out."

"I don't like it dark," Cassie pouted. "I want another mermaid story." She wrapped herself in her covers like a cocoon. Her pink room glowed from a bedside lamp.

Alexandra tried to smile. "Maybe I'll read–" She stopped as the lamp flickered.

"Why'd the light blink?" Cassie asked, her voice trembling.

Alexandra remained calm, "It's just the generator. It can't stay on all night."

They looked at the lamp as it blinked again. Alexandra tried to appear cool as she peered out the window into the darkness.

31. The Monster

Curt ducked in his seat as he looked out the window. His SUV was parked in a discreet spot across the street behind a Florida holly tree. The black truck was invisible as the night grew darker. It was a struggle to remain patient; it was too early to strike.

He used the time to put on his uniform. The only thing on his mind was his self-appointed mission. When he put on the night-vision goggles, his view became as clear as day. He could feel the adrenalin pumping through his veins.

Across the street, the sign read, "Emergency Op Center Only." The building was the dilapidated Sanibel Lodge. Curt cursed as he spied three sheriffs' cars still in the parking lot. Beside the entrance, a single generator was humming. *Just minimal lights.*

Curt traded his goggles for binoculars. He saw no security cameras at the entrance to the hotel, the building was too old. The front doors were slightly ajar to allow extension cords from the generator. *The doors aren't locked* —which meant at least one cop would remain on the nightshift.

He instinctively ducked as two deputies exited the lodge's front doors. Realizing they couldn't see him, he watched them through his binoculars. "You pigs got my brother?" Curt growled. The cops chatted a few seconds and then left the premises in their cars. The parking lot now had only one sheriff's car remaining.

Curt was conflicted how this was going to be almost fun. He adjusted his mask and goggles and opened the door. "Butch, I'm bringin' you home."

Two black Suzuki Hayabusas entered Alligator Alley from a gravel road. Tag and LeBeau accelerated their sleek bikes well beyond 100 mph as they headed west. At that speed, they could be at Captiva in less than an hour —then they saw the backed-up traffic.

In the off chance they were stopped by police, they wore thin jumpsuits over their uniforms. They each wore regular motorcycle helmets. Their combat helmets were concealed on their bikes. They slowed their bikes to assess the traffic.

"Too early for stealth," LeBeau spoke into a voice-activated mic.

Tag accelerated around LeBeau's bike. "Try to keep up, Froggy."

The Hayabusas shot forward like missiles into the congested highway. The two motorcycles split apart, weaving in and out of traffic like a choreographed dance. LeBeau swerved in and out of cars, accelerating beyond 120 mph.

Tag glanced at his teammate and rocketed forward. The two men crisscrossed through obstacles like ribbons curling through the maze of vehicles. The men nodded at each other in their high-speed rivalry of skill.

Old Roy Jessup was just trying to get home on I-75. As he was about to doze in his pick-up, two deafening black streaks screamed by his window.

"*Aaahh!*" Roy screamed and his entire body jerked. He darted his head in search of the clamor. He looked ahead and in his rearview. There was nothing there. He looked down at his empty can of *Electro-Shock* energy drink and shook his head. *No more of that!*

The hotel's ghostly hallway had French provincial furniture and burgundy carpet that had been molding for decades. Tarnished chandeliers flickered like candles. The wallpaper was gray and curled with mildew. A lone deputy sat in an armchair, struggling to read a novel with a flashlight.

Curt's night vision illuminated his view of the corridor with a green glow. Concealed twenty yards away in the shadows, he examined the deputy who was sitting in front of doors leading to the ballroom. The cop appeared fat and slow, but armed with a 9mm and a flashlight. *He'll die of a heart attack before I even shoot him,* Curt chuckled.

Deputy Garcia looked up from his book at a faint sound down the hall. The place looked like a real-life haunted mansion. It gave him the creeps when the day shift reported seeing rats the size of Chihuahuas. The entire place smelled like fungus. A slight, indistinguishable *clicking* sound occurred again. It sounded like a doorknob turning – or the patter of feet from some enormous cockroach.

Garcia stood and aimed his flashlight down the corridor. The beam couldn't reach the end of the eternal hallway. He saw nothing in the blackness. A sudden faraway noise sounded like a door. Garcia stepped from the safety of his musty chair.

"Hello?" Garcia called out. He stepped towards the doors to the ballroom. With a sudden sound to his left, he aimed his flashlight. A ten-inch centipede scurried into a hole in the wall. Though unsettling, Garcia breathed a sigh of relief. He thought he'd do a quick glance into the ballroom, call his daughter, and then return to his book.

Garcia was aware of *what* was being kept in the ballroom. But his sergeant would not reveal how many bodies were there. Garcia's job was to guard the dead's personal belongings. His boss had joked, "The bodies aren't going anywhere..." Garcia took a deep breath and entered the ballroom.

He immediately noticed a sour, chemical scent. He looked up at the twenty-foot-high ceiling. Spider webs hung on the garish chandeliers that barely glowed. Garcia gazed down across the rows of gurneys. There were five rows with four corpses per row. His Maglite skimmed across an old man, a young woman and a little boy. Some were severely wounded; others looked as if they were peacefully sleeping. Garcia religiously crossed himself. He began to well with emotion. *I'm outta' here*, he decided.

As he was about to turn, he heard a crinkling sound from the rear. Like movement of a plastic sheet.

"Doc? You still here?" Garcia shouted, praying for an explanation. He unholstered his Glock and shined his light across the bodies. In a dark corner, he was relieved when he saw a fan blowing the edge of a plastic sheet on a gurney. He exhaled and turned.

Garcia knew he was thirty pounds overweight and forty years old –but he still had 20/20 vision. As he stepped towards the door, his peripheral vision made him intuitively look. He shined his light at a large corpse in the rear of the room. Its skin reflected white through the plastic. It was the corpse of the mysterious *soldier* found in Captiva. He scanned the body, praying he wouldn't see a rat nibbling the flesh. All seemed normal –until the dead man's hand dropped, hanging from the table.

"*Dios mio!*" Garcia shouted as he sprung back. The corpse's hand had moved! Had a rat moved it? Maybe just gravity? His mind raced. He looked up as the chandeliers began to erratically flicker. With one hand, he gripped his gun. In the other, he aimed his light at the dead soldier. What he saw next paralyzed him with horror.

The corpse began to sit up. The sheet fell down to reveal its monstrous, bloated face.

Impossible! Garcia was frozen, but he couldn't look away.

The corpse was nude with a jagged, autopsied Y-incision down its torso. Its black mouth was locked open. Like Frankenstein, the dead awkwardly sat upright on the metal bed. Then it screamed.

Garcia shrieked and fired his gun. The bullet hit the corpse's purple, bruised torso. Its red eyes were open. The *thing* began to unnaturally stand on its feet, emitting a grotesque cry.

"*Madre de Dios!*" Garcia dropped his gun and turned to run. The zombie's cry gurgled louder behind him.

A black, uniformed arm then emerged from beside the corpse and shot the deputy in the back. Garcia clutched his throat, spewing blood as he fell. He was dead.

Butch's lifeless corpse swayed on its unstable feet, and then collapsed to the ground. Behind it stood its puppeteer, Curt, in his black uniform and mask.

Curt's heart pulsed like a jackhammer. Manipulating his brother's dead body had not been part of the plan, but he had to improvise. His black uniform, against the dark background, made him invisible – and he thought Butch would've gotten a kick out of his creativity in killing the cowardly cop.

Curt closed his eyes as he rolled his brother's body in a plastic sheet. "I'm so sorry, bro..." He then strained to lift the fat cop onto the empty gurney and covered him with plastic. Grasping Butch by his feet, he dragged his brother out to his truck and hoisted him into the rear compartment.

He brushed off his hands and took a breath of both relief and exhilaration. He entered the truck and looked in his rearview mirror. His voice quivered, "Now let's get the bitch who did this."

LeBeau and Tag's bikes exited I-75 and raced towards Summerlin Road to Sanibel. They zigzagged through the line of traffic waiting to reenter the islands.

"We're approaching the causeway," LeBeau said into his radio. "ETA fifteen."

"Copy," Dalia's voice replied. "I'll stand by. Over."

Tag and LeBeau slowed their Hayabusas as they neared the front of the line. They stopped in front of a young, agitated National Guard troop.

"Where's the fire, fellas?" the guardsman asked.

LeBeau lifted his helmet. "I'm hoping you can help us." He spoke with mock panic, "My partner and I are veterinarians in Captiva. Our office has been locked since the storm." He added with pleading eyes,

Richard Wickliffe

"There are fifty puppies and kittens *trapped* inside..."

The exhausted guardsman sighed and shook his head. He moved the barricade aside.

32. Ten-Twenty-Four

"We're over the bridge," LeBeau's voice announced through the speaker. "Proceeding to target."

"Copy," Dalia replied with her feet up on the controls. "Check back in fifteen." She and Lex sat beside each other at the hangar's wall of computer feeds.

She gave a coy smile to Lex. "See what I see?" She stretched like a cat.

Distracted between Dalia and looking at the monitor, Lex stammered, "What do you see?"

She motioned to a satellite image of a storm in the Atlantic. "Storm number twenty–."

"–Three more cold ones!" Pitch interrupted, returning with his hands full of beers. He handed bottles to Dalia and Lex and then toasted, "To another active season." He chugged half his beer in one gulp.

Lex watched Pitch grow somewhat disheveled with his third beer within thirty minutes. After LeBeau and Tag had left the hangar, Pitch raided a small fridge in the rear. Dalia's drinking made her giggly —and more flirtatious.

"Thanks, *mon*." Dalia said, closing her eyes as she sipped from her bottle.

Lex enjoyed his beer as well. It was some sort of trendy IPA. It was cold and it had been a long day —and the mood was loosening every-one's lips. He still had many questions.

Pitch pointed to the feed. "We haven't had two storms within one week since..." He frowned to think. "Since last year."

Dalia pulled Lex's chair closer with her foot. "The cycle started in '04. Four storms —Charley, Francis, Ivan and Jeanne— swept through the state within a *six-week period*. The state was hit four times *again* the next year." She became solemn, "And it's only getting worse."

Lex looked at the screen. "You think this new one's coming our way?"

Dalia pointed at the image. "See this ridge of high pressure? It's pulling the storm west pretty fast. At this rate, it could be anywhere on the eastern seaboard in...four days." She gazed at the spiral cy-clone. "In a way, it's almost...*beautiful*, don't you think?"

He looked at her like she was a masochist. "A beautiful monster. How do you fly even *near* something like that?"

Pitch pulled up a chair. "The rendezvous is the hardest part. Dalia invented a way to anchor the Stingray using expandable cords."

Lex turned to Dalia, curious.

She pulled an elastic band from her ponytail and lifted a cell-phone. "Pretend this phone's the chopper. I anchor to the ground us-ing bungee ropes that allow me to drift in the winds." She demon-strated by stretching the band from the phone to the desk. "See? The *anchored* chopper can stretch in any direction. I'm able to hover at the rendezvous, regardless of the winds."

Pitch interjected, "When we're ready, we cut the lines and off we go. We call it *terra launching*." He beamed, "You should see people's faces when we shoot into the sky. *Poof,* and we're gone."

Lex shook his head in amazement. He took a slug of beer, debat-ing what to ask next. He decided to have fun with Dalia's slight ine-briation. "So how does a hundred-ten pound lady steal her very own two-ton Coast Guard chopper?"

She almost spewed beer with a nasal laugh. She covered her mouth, "Oh my God –it was *so* easy!"

Lex was stunned at her flippant reaction. "How's *that* easy?"

"Okay," Dalia spread her hands with playful drama. "When I was in the Guard out of Key West, I took the Stingray on a midnight run. I was *supposedly* pursuing a smuggler. Butch faked an informant tip about a boat running from the Bahamas –short notice, enough to justify me making a solo recon."

"Twenty miles out in the Atlantic," Dalia gestured with her hands to illustrate, "I sent a distress call, citing engine failure. I then made a *rapid* descent. I turned off the transponder when I located Butch. He had a barge disguised as a dredging boat. I landed, and he covered the Stingray in tarps. Then he dumped heavy debris into the water: seat cushions, life preservers and oil. I let the ELT –the emergency locator– give off a few *'pings'* before turning it off." Dalia clapped and grinned, "And I was *gone!*"

Lex was astounded, "Didn't they look for you?"

"We fled the scene with quadruple Yamaha 350's. We used the Atlantic instead of the Gulf –too deep for a recovery, and it explained the ELT fading. We left nothing behind but an oil slick and debris."

Lex sat stunned. He stood and motioned to the entire hangar in awe, "Who thought of doing all...*this*?"

Pitch spoke up, "Butch invented the scam in Iraq during air-raid evacs. He realized emergencies made people leave everything behind." He finished his beer and shrugged, "He figured he was already a world criminal by being part of an illegal war. What harm could it do?"

"He was arrested in Canada for robbing a bank," Dalia continued. "When the U.S. tried to extradite him, he said he witnessed abuse of Iraqi Nationals at the hands of U.S. troops. Canadian authorities refused to extradite because it suggested a 'political' crime. It was a crazy defense, but enough to buy him time. He was allowed house arrest." Dalia shrugged, "That's when his brother Curt helped him escape. He hooked up with Tag and LeBeau, who then recruited Pitch and then me."

"Did he really witness war crimes?" Lex was amused.

Dalia smiled as she recalled. "Remember the *Abu Ghraib* scandal? When Butch went underground, he released photos to fifty news outlets."

Pitch interjected as if competing, "I was discharged for desertion!"

Lex shook his head, "I know why I did it, but why did you all go AWOL? The usual: 'killing of innocents?' The 'horrors of war?'"

Pitch replied. "There are two types that run: One is the kid who never wanted to sign up in the first place. Maybe they ran from a bad home or went off to prove their manhood. The others are the ones who survived some horrible incident, and they feel they didn't deserve to live." Pitch seemed sober. "For me, it was nothing but old-fashioned financial freedom."

Dalia interjected, "After Iraq, soldiers came home to a different world. The security industry wanted armed and experienced personnel. Security firms were burdened with expensive training. Suddenly soldiers were coming home, fully trained and needing jobs."

"Sounds like a great opportunity," Lex shrugged.

"Yeah, lavish jobs as security guards," Dalia scoffed. "Call me crazy, but when LeBeau found me, I thought making seven-figures for five-month's work sounded better than being an airport cop or a bodyguard for a Kardashian."

"It's like a teacher's schedule," Pitch chuckled, "–except for the money part."

Lex smiled, "Speaking of money, how do launder? Pawn shops? Offshore?"

Pitch lifted a hand to halt Dalia from replying. "You know what I'm noticing?"

Lex looked at Pitch, unsure.

"You ask a lot of questions," Pitch's smile was gone. "Are you *truly* interested in us?" He paused, "...Or interested in starting your own game?"

Lex paused. Their attention was abruptly diverted by a voice from a speaker, "...*All units respond...*"

"Who's that?" Lex looked at both of them.

"The cops! *Shhh!*" Pitch snapped. "It's the police scanner." He turned up the volume.

The voice continued through static, "*...Repeat, we have a ten-twenty-four...*"

Pitch and Dalia locked eyes with a look of dread.

"What's that code mean?" Lex asked, frustrated.

Nadine Stratton drove Dan Holms in her unmarked Crown Vic. With blue lights flashing from her grill, she accelerated north on I-75, swerving around slower cars.

"Shouldn't you call for back-up?" Dan sat rigid in the passenger's seat.

"I can't call in saying there could be *soldiers* returning to Larriott's." Nadine cussed under her breath at the slower cars ahead of her. If anything happened to Alexandra, it'd be her fault for not believing her instincts. All because of Rodka's threats —and not getting her precious promotion.

"Everything's fine." Dan turned down the volume on the police radio. "A deputy's at her house. Any criminal would be an idiot to return."

Nadine loosened her grip. "We'll just check. I'll call it a 'public service visit.'"

"After, we can resume our 'information meeting.'"

She smiled. He was the polar opposite of Al Rodka: pleasant, respectful —and attractive. "This is still more exciting than working with the guys in my office."

"Not a fun place?"

Nadine's smile faded. "No one includes me in the sports pools. I'm the one sent out for coffee. The exact attitude I'd escaped up north. Constant reminders that I shouldn't be here."

Dan looked at her with kind eyes, "Nadine, your co-workers love you. And I know —I've worked with them." He smiled when she turned. "You have guts *and* empathy —a rare mix. You connect the dots on a case faster than anyone I've ever met. You're a great detective."

She paused with a bittersweet smile. "Why can't you be my part-ner?" She covered her eyes at her Freudian slip. "At work, I mean."

He blushed, "No one will take me. Cops call me a 'wannabe cop.'"

"Why wouldn't we 'take' you?"

Dan paused as if weighing how much to reveal. "Back when I—"

Nadine stopped him with a raised hand. "—Turn that up!" She pointed to the police radio.

He turned up the volume. "...*Repeat*," the voice said. *"We have a ten-twenty-four..."*

"What's that mean?"

"Officer Down!" Nadine clutched the wheel and stepped on the gas.

"...All-county broadcast. Ten-twenty-four at 632 Seahorse in Sanibel—"

"That's the Sanibel Lodge —the morgue!" Thoughts of the place were almost panic inducing. She had to remain calm.

"...All units respond: Unknown suspect at large. Possible stolen body..."

"Why would someone *steal* a body?"

Nadine had a sudden look of dread. "The dead soldier's at that morgue!"

Dan clutched the armrest when Nadine accelerated.

Time was of the essence. The lives of a mother and child could be in jeopardy. Having Dan with her —with his own gun— gave her the extra courage she needed. Had the offenders already been to Alexan-dra's —or were they on the way?

"Are we going to the morgue like your department ordered?"

"No. We're going to the bad guys' next stop." She stepped on the gas. "Unless they're already there."

33. The Ghost

The deputy outside of Alexandra's home heard a twig snap. Parked beside the guard station, the cop looked out his open window. It was too dark to see anything beyond the damaged shack. Probably just a cat, he shrugged.

Without electricity, the road in front of the estate was dark. Several lights emanated from the house, courtesy of a humming generator. In the driveway, the officer remained in his car, lit by the glow of his laptop.

Deputy Burckhardt was on secondary duty, watching the house for overtime. When he'd heard the news about the slain deputy at the morgue, he'd been ordered to stay put. From the safety of the driveway, Burckhardt said a prayer for his fallen comrade.

Burckhardt didn't take his assignment for granted. It was a safe gig and he could do homework for his Master's Degree. The rustling noise outside happened again. He aimed his car's spotlight to the left towards the sound —it was a man. Standing in the light's beam was Pete, the security guard who wouldn't shut up.

"Hi-ya Fred," Pete waved. "I'll help you keep an eye out for looters."

Crouching twenty yards away in the shadows, Curt checked his weapons. With the one cop busy talking to the old guard, he knew his task would be effortless. Curt took five fast, deep breaths to *pump up.* He was ready.

Alexandra whispered to Cassie, "It's time to go to sleep." In her exhausted state, Alexandra caught herself dozing in Cassie's bed. Cassie was wide awake.

"Can you sleep here?" Cassie asked, clutching her bunny.

Alexandra hadn't thought about her own bed. "Sure, honey." Snuggling close with her daughter would be nicer than sleeping in a bedroom carpeted with glass.

"Mommy, why are we flying away tomorrow? Do I have to change my name again?"

Alexandra was thrown by the question. Her daughter was growing up. It was getting difficult to shield the child from the truth. *But it's to protect her,* Cassie didn't realize. Alexandra cleared her throat, "Sometimes it can be fun to be like... *different* people. Fun to have new names. Like pretending."

Cassie blinked at her mom's explanation.

Alexandra reached below Cassie's bed to make sure her gun was still there. She gripped it and whispered, "Would you like me to keep the lamp on?"

"Yeah." Cassie's voice quivered, "I don't like the dark."

The glow of Curt's night vision confirmed only one cop sitting in his cruiser and an elderly guard standing at the car's window. No other threats. Curt looked up at the house to see a lit bedroom window facing the lawn. *Her pink little bedroom,* he knew. The generator would muffle any noises he'd make while killing the two men outside. The ease of the night was laughable.

Lying flat to the ground like a serpent, Curt was in full gear and mask. He'd parked his truck facing out in the neighbor's side yard with zero witnesses. *I'll be back at the hangar with both bodies by midnight,* he figured. He was undecided what to do with the child. He didn't know if he'd keep her or not.

Curt reached to his belt for the Incapacitator –the *Puke Saber.* He grasped the device, stood, and then glided across the lawn like a shadow.

"I was a Marine MP for twenty years," Pete boasted to the bored cop.

"Is that right?" Burckhardt rubbed his eyes.

"Kids today have *no–*" Pete paused. In the darkness, he gazed at a point of light speeding towards them. He shouted, "The fireflies!" He turned and ran, stumbling towards the street.

Burckhardt turned to see what he was raving about. He flinched to see a figure standing at his open passenger window. It was a black, masked...*thing.*

Before he could react, Curt aimed his Incapacitator. The device emitted pulses of blue light directly into Burckhardt's pupils. He instantly doubled over, sick with a guttural, vomiting cough. He clutched his head and shrieked.

As concise as a machine, Curt lifted his gun and shot the defused cop in his forehead. The silencer emitted three faint pops. The cop slouched over, dead.

Curt marched to the generator beside the house and unplugged the outgoing cord. The house was now dark –except through night vision. He smiled inside his mask. *Here I come.*

"Mommy, it's dark!" Cassie screamed.

"It's okay," Alexandra fumbled to locate a candle and lighter on the bedside table. The lit candle filled the room with a warm glow. "See? Everything's fine." Alexandra knew she had to remain calm.

Cassie pulled the covers up to her mouth. "Why'd the lights go off?" She trembled, on the verge of tears.

Alexandra whispered, "It's just the generator. I'll go check. I'll bring the nice policeman a snack, okay?"

Cassie watched her light a second candle for herself.

When Alexandra turned her back to Cassie, she gripped her gun in front of her, out of view. "I'll be back in two minutes." Cassie pulled the covers over her head as her mommy walked out of the room.

Alexandra crept down the hall with a candle in one hand and her pistol in the other. She tried to remain quiet so she could listen for any unusual sounds. The farther she moved down the corridor, she could hear the breeze shrilling through the broken windows. She didn't hear the generator. *Maybe it's out of gas,* she guessed. *Thank God the deputy's here.*

Using her feet to feel her way in the dark, Alexandra counted the banisters until she reached the stairs. She delicately stepped down, pausing with each step to listen.

Something moved! There was a glimmer in her peripheral vision. She turned and aimed her gun at...*the mirror on the wall.* She saw her reflection, holding the candle. She sighed and continued descending the stairs.

At the base of the staircase, Alexandra stopped. She was unable to see beyond several feet in front of her. The living room walls were too far to be illuminated by her candle. If she was going to move forward, she needed faith that she was alone. She took a step forward.

Unseen by Alexandra, he stood motionless in the corner like a statue. Curt turned off his radio so there was no light. His night vision perfectly illuminated Alexandra. He observed her; long bare legs, her shorts –and her gun. She unknowingly stepped forward and stopped, standing two feet in front of him. Curt leered at her as he struggled to hold his breath.

Alexandra then turned her back to him. As she stepped towards the foyer, he deliberated. *Do I kill her now?* It was so tempting. After all the hostility and planning, she was finally standing three feet away with her back to him. *I can stab her in the spine with a knife!* He reached for his belt.

No, it'd be too artless and quick, he decided. He wanted her alive –for a while. He wanted to show her what she'd done to his brother.

He would shove her face into his corpse.

Should I get the girl first? Curt debated. He could use her to get her mommy to cooperate. He looked at Alexandra, now eight feet away. Curt made his decision; he glided up the stairs like a spirit.

Cassie kept her head covered. Through the blanket, she could still see the subtle glow from the candle. She hummed, *Twinkle, twinkle, little star*...to mask any frightening thoughts until her mom returned. She stopped humming when she heard the creak of her bedroom door.

"Mommy?" Her high voice pled, "...Is it you..?"

The candle's flame was pinched out. The room was black again.

"Mommy...?"

Using his night vision, Curt observed the child trembling under the covers. He leaned closer. The sightless child lowered the sheets to peek into the darkness. Curt froze, but from her vacant gaze, it was obvious she couldn't see him. He could hear her panicked breathing. Like a game, Curt moved closer to see how near her face he could get.

Evidently hearing his animal-like breathing, the girl said something unexpected. *"Daddy..?"* She began to whimper, "Have you come back?"

Curt watched a tear roll down the girl's cheek.

Alexandra recoiled at Cassie's blood-curdling scream. She dropped her candle and raced up the stairs, gun drawn. *"Baby..!"* Her instincts took over, helping her navigate the stairs in the dark. "Cassie..?" She rushed down the hall towards her daughter's room.

As she charged through Cassie's door, Curt stood in her path. He ignited his Incapacitator and pushed it towards her dilated eyes.

"Ahhh...!" Alexandra shrieked. She doubled over, hacking with instant nausea. Curt kicked the gun out of her hand. He leaned over, pushing the unyielding light into her face. Cassie impulsively ran into the far closet, hidden in the dark.

Curt lifted his mask to reveal his angry, sweaty face. "You didn't think I'd come back?" The Incapacitator gave his face a demonic glow. Perspiration dripped from his nose.

"Why...?" Alexandra cried with agony. "What did you do to Cass–" She started to dry-heave, curled into a ball with pain.

Curt lifted her head by her hair. "I want you to see what you did to my brother!"

Alexandra fought to pull herself towards the open window. She screamed, "Help! Officer..!"

Curt tugged her hair harder. "I blew that pig's brains out!" He laughed. "Like I'm gonna' do to you in front of your daughter!" He looked at Cassie's empty bed, "Where did she go?"

Alexandra fell limp, crying and on the verge of fainting. Her defensive hostility drained from her body. She couldn't fight any longer.

34. The Watchers

"This is it! Turn here!" Dan shouted.

Nadine swerved and sped all the way to South Seas Lane. She'd flashed her badge at three stops to get through. When she made a screeching right into Larriott's driveway, there was a sense of relief when she saw the parked sheriff's car.

She haphazardly parked to the right of the cruiser. Nadine grabbed a flashlight; Dan took one from his backpack. They exited the vehicle aiming their lights across the property. Nadine pulled out her badge and trotted to side of the sheriff's car.

Dan surveyed the front of house. "No lights. Maybe she left."

Nadine panted as she approached, "Deputy! I'm Stratton..." She aimed her light in the car and froze. The dash and windshield were spattered with fresh red blood. The cop was hunched on his steering wheel. Congealed blood hung from a cavity in his forehead.

"*No!*" Nadine screamed, "Oh God, no..." She covered her eyes. It was Deputy Fred Burckhardt. A single father who used to bring her Starbucks every Friday. *I never once reciprocated.* Nadine stepped back and instinctively pulled a gun from her waistband and turned

360 degrees.

Dan rushed to her side. "What is it..?" He pulled out his Glock from a pocket in his cargos. He stopped in his tracks when he saw the dead cop. His breathing hastened and he scanned the yard. "Okay... okay," he repeated, struggling to grasp their situation.

"They were already here!" Nadine huffed, "What if they're *still* here?"

As if a natural instinct was emerging, Dan stood tall. He pointed to the generator, "Get the power back on and check the perimeter!" He jogged towards the house, "I'll check inside!"

Curt used both hands to drag Alexandra down the stairs by her feet. "You killed the *wrong* man!" He snarled through his mask as he stepped backwards down the staircase. "I *will* find the kid!" Alexandra's head thumped as it dropped to each step.

"Stop..!" Alexandra cried hysterically. She tried to grab the banisters, but he was too strong. *I'm so sorry Cassie,* she repeated in her mind. *It's my fault...* She had failed.

They could see Curt descending the stairs. With their own night vision, two dark figures stood at the base of the staircase like sentinels. The two soldiers, LeBeau and Tag, remained motionless, cloaked in darkness.

They watched Curt step backwards towards the base of the stairs. He was consumed with dragging and tormenting the hysterical woman. Curt shouted, "I want you to *see* what you did to Butch! You're gonna' *lay* with him!"

The hum of the generator resumed outside. As if someone had flipped a switch, the lights suddenly flickered on. LeBeau and Tag were now exposed.

Curt let go of Alexandra, shielding his goggles from the blinding light. Tag and LeBeau were still unseen by Curt, whose back was to them. LeBeau nodded to Tag; it was now or never.

Tag bolted forward like a football player, taking Curt's feet out from under him. With a grunt, Curt plunged backwards towards the base of the staircase.

LeBeau jumped on Curt, straddling his torso. He shouted, "I've got Curt!" Tag fell onto his legs, pinning him to the ground. As Curt spewed profanities, LeBeau produced a syringe and injected his neck.

In a hysterical panic, Alexandra saw the nightmarish soldiers and screamed. She scurried up the stairs like a crab.

Tag looked at her with his menacing mask and aimed his electro-shock gun.

"FREEZE!" A voice boomed from behind the men.

The soldiers turned to see Dan Holms, standing in a ready-stance with his firearm.

LeBeau dropped Curt's head and dove into the shadows like a panther. When Dan turned to aim, Tag fired his weapon, sending electrified barbs into Dan's torso.

Dan yelped in pain, but lunged to grasp LeBeau's foot. With miraculous strength, Dan swung a punch, landing near LeBeau's unprotected kidneys.

LeBeau hissed with pain, but struck Dan in a Japanese *mawashi geri* side kick. As Dan flew backwards, LeBeau fired his electroshock barbs into his abdomen.

Dan flailed to the ground, clawing at his chest to remove the needle-like spurs. The soldiers dropped their guns, which continued to deliver 300,000-volt surges through attached wires. Dan began to convulse with sizzling pops.

One of the soldiers gazed down at Dan and shook his head. Dan helplessly watched the men lift the sedated third soldier by his arms and feet. With quick precision, the two soldiers carried the man out the door. Dan's mouth foamed and his eyes rolled up into his head.

"Dan!" A female voice shouted through the crunching of glass. Nadine Stratton ran in from the rear doors. She rushed to Dan's trembling body, her firearm ready. "Are they gone?" She swiped the barbs from his skin.

Dan struggled to nod, *"Yesss..."*

Nadine kneeled and stroked his clammy head, "I was checking the rear..." Her voice was compassionate. "Are you okay? Who were they?"

Dan labored to speak, "The soldiers..." He flinched with twinges of pain.

Nadine leaned closer to hear his words.

"They're *real*..."

A hoarse voice shouted from the staircase, "You thought I was *insane!*"

Nadine looked up to see Alexandra holding Cassie. Alexandra was ashen with red eyes. Her face was smeared with tears. Cassie had her face buried into her mom's shirt.

Dan looked at Nadine. "Call for back up *—now!*"

LeBeau and Tag carried Curt across the lawn. They vanished into the foliage that bordered the property. They walked to their Hayabusas parked beside Curt's truck in the neighboring yard. Curt's choice in parking his truck had been foolishly predictable.

"Put him here." Tag opened the rear hatch to the truck. They halted when they saw Butch's corpse wrapped in plastic. A bulb illuminated Butch's face, peering through the plastic with open eyes. Tag dropped Curt on top of the body.

LeBeau winced at the two bodies, "A family reunion."

The men lifted their masks. Tag asked, "Who's driving the truck?"

LeBeau replied, "Take your bike. I have a plan." He dashed to his Hayabusa and rolled it to the center of the street. He dropped the bike onto its side, practically blocking the narrow road. He jogged back to Tag. "I'll drive Curt's truck."

Tag frowned as he mounted his bike, curious what LeBeau was up to. Before he could ask, the silence was pierced by approaching sirens. "Curt won't be out for long." Without waiting for a reply, Tag revved his engine. His bike kicked up gravel as he sped onto the road.

LeBeau started the truck and stepped on the gas. His tires chirped, skidding out to follow Tag's trail.

"I'll scout a path," Tag's voice announced over their radio. "Follow my tail."

"Roger," LeBeau replied into his headset. He glanced in his mirror. In the back of the truck, Curt had ironically shifted to face his brother's bloated face. LeBeau almost laughed.

Dan and Nadine –with their guns drawn– exited Larriott's front doors. They rotated, sweeping the lawn left to right with their flashlights and guns.

"It's clear!" Nadine announced. She motioned to Alexandra, who stepped outside carrying Cassie. "I hear the police. They're almost here."

Dan and Nadine formed a barrier around the mother and daughter. Dan was pale and wet with perspiration. Alexandra had circles around her eyes. The four were wide-eyed and shell-shocked. They darted their heads, awaiting the arrival of the approaching sirens.

Two brown Impalas drove chaotically into the lawn. They had blue lights flashing from their dashes. The cars stopped fifty feet from the house and their doors sprung open. From one car, two men in suits exited, aiming firearms. From the other, a neat, middle-aged man stepped out, aiming his gun with both hands. "FBI! Drop your weapons!"

"It's okay," Nadine declared, lowering her gun. "I'm with Lee Sheriffs!" She pulled her badge from a pocket.

Dan was confused when the agents didn't lower their guns.

"We don't care who you are, Deputy Stratton," replied the grim Agent Riker. "Stand down!" He aimed his gun at both Nadine and Dan. "You *all* will be coming with us."

35. Dirty Laundering

Swerving around debris, Tag's bike led the way for LeBeau's truck. The roads were impeded by branches, sand and puddles. Tag raced fifty yards ahead to scout a path into Sanibel. His bike's deafening engine muffled the approaching sirens.

"Just like as a kid," Tag smiled as he zipped in and out of debris at 80 mph. There was a rare, childlike thrill in his tone. "Try to keep up!" He huddled low and accelerated faster.

"Stay alert!" LeBeau scolded. "Dalia will scan for police chatter."

"Let's get off the island."

Agent Riker shouted to his clone-like agent, "The suspects fled south." He stabbed his finger in the air, "Go *now!*"

The two agents spun their tires in reverse. The car shifted into drive, but then stopped when its headlights revealed the overturned motorcycle blocking the road.

Agent Riker ran his hand over his hair. He looked at Stratton, Holms and Larriott, seated on the sidewalk. The little girl was curled into a ball in her mother's lap. "So what'd you see?" Riker sucked his teeth as if irritated they'd witnessed anything at all.

Before any reply, Riker's radio chirped, "The suspects left a motorcycle behind."

Riker spun to see his agents' car stopped in the road. "Don't touch it," he replied into his radio. "We'll check for prints." He saw his agent exit the car and walk towards the overturned bike. Riker shook his head. "I said forget it! Pursue the targets!"

The agent ignored the order, awestruck by the bike. He spoke into his radio, "It's some sort of...*Hayabusa*–" He stopped mid-sentence when the bike emitted a shrill beeping noise. A piercing, recurring tone like an alarm. As the agent stepped within two feet of the bike, a small red light flashed on its handlebar. The man covered his ears at the excruciating noise.

"Get back!" Riker shouted, "Don't touch–"

The alarm stopped. The agent looked at his boss, "See–" He touched the bike, which detonated in a blinding sphere of flames. The explosion hurled shrapnel, ripping through the cowering agent. Molten steel rained down onto the road. The agent who'd remained in the car ducked to the floor behind the shattered windshield. South Seas Lane was temporarily –and conveniently– blocked by the fiery debris.

Agent Riker threw himself to the ground. Riker's helpless calls to his man were futile. He knew he was dead. Riker stood and dashed around debris to help the surviving agent out of the car. He lifted his radio, "Terminate the rendezvous! Forget the house! Pursue the targets before they get to the bridge!"

Dan and Nadine stood in shock, their faces glowing from the fire. Alexandra huddled with her daughter, shielding her –again– from the relentless chain of nightmarish events.

LeBeau gripped the wheel with both hands. He blinked faster as he struggled to follow Tag's lead. He could feel his pulse throbbing under his armor. *This wasn't in our plans,* he thought. LeBeau prided himself on planning for *any* possible event with the precision of a statistician. He cursed himself for the evening's breakdown.

LeBeau followed Tag onto Sanibel Captiva Road. The bleak straightaway gave him a moment to deliberate. *Who was the man with the gun?* Did Larriott have a boyfriend? Nothing in her dossier suggested any relationships. LeBeau's hands trembled at the possibility that he'd missed something. They'd now been witnessed by two *additional* civilians. That was not good.

As his truck fell slightly behind Tag's bike, LeBeau heard the faraway wail of sirens. His eyes twitched. According to his scanner, neither the Captiva nor Sanibel Police Departments had any units on call. *So who are they?*

He ordered into his headset, "Base: scan *all* frequencies. I hear sirens; I don't think they're local!"

Within the hangar, 120 miles away, Dalia bolted upright with a slight buzz. "Copy that. I'll check any PDs in range." She put on a headset to study multiple frequencies on their digital trunking police scanner.

Lex had been sitting and drinking beside her, attempting to learn details of their operation. Toasting drinks and trading scars with Pitch had also calmed his concerns. Before he would make any career-altering decisions, Lex wanted to know how they liquidate their assets. Burglary and stealing was easy. Turning the loot into cash was an ever-growing challenge.

Thieves in the good ol' days simply laundered goods through pawn shops. Shops were now required to report the names, addresses, and birth dates of anyone hocking merchandise. They logged descriptions and serial numbers, which were matched by law enforcement with stolen items. Priceless paintings and art couldn't just be sold at any gallery.

Despite even *more* beers, Lex was able to learn little from Dalia and Pitch. Even they seemed frustrated at how little they knew. Dalia said the team's founders, LeBeau, Tag and Butch, kept the information offsite, and never shared the details with them, the junior members. Dalia presumed their systems contained encrypted offshore accounts. Most of the high-dollar fencing was done through an enormous network of brokers in countries that had zero pawn laws. Butch used to travel quarterly to the Mid East and Eastern European countries using a slew of aliases.

However, Pitch chuckled at how ridiculously simple it was to liquidate smaller items. Everyday jewelry —especially gold— was sold to any jeweler boasting *"We Buy Gold!"* Gold was currently trading at record highs, and every airport hotel had ballrooms filled with poor schmucks selling off grandma's jewelry. These transactions required zero ID and paid all cash. Any loss in gross value was worth the simplicity.

Dalia said some items without serial numbers were sold right under the nose of authorities through hundreds of aliases on eBay and Craigslist. The nominal income was then transferred to multiple accounts, accumulating into significant sums like rivers feeding into an ocean. The funds were wired offshore —again to accounts that Pitch and Dalia had no access to.

With Butch dead, Lex wondered *who* would take his place. Tag and LeBeau were in an undeclared battle for control. Lex knew that Dalia and Pitch were also lobbying to advance within the ranks. They agreed Curt was the *Fredo* of the team: reckless and stupid. Curt wanted control simply out of nepotism when Butch died. But with this petulant scheme for revenge against Larriott, Curt would be severely punished —if Tag and LeBeau ever found him.

After observing the dynamics of the team, Lex concluded one thing: they all hated each other. They would stab each other in their backs without a second thought. *A fun team to join*, Lex thought with sarcasm.

Lex knew he'd have to wait for LeBeau and Tag to return before any verdicts about this *CAT team*. He needed *all* the details —without arousing any suspicions. He'd keep playing interested.

Dalia replied to LeBeau, "Local PDs are quiet." She smirked, "Did you find Curt?" Lex and Pitch sat close to follow along.

"Later!" LeBeau barked. "Scan channels for Lee Sheriffs!"

Dalia scowled at the microphone and then grinned at Lex. She scanned a spectrum of frequencies. "No activity from the sheriffs. Just drive-by's for looters."

Must be my imagination, LeBeau guessed about the faint sirens in his head.

He stepped on the gas to close the gap between him and Tag. They raced over 70 mph through Sanibel. The island had two main roads running parallel to each other. Tag chose Periwinkle Way, the most direct route to the bridge that led to the mainland. He breathed a sigh of relief.

When he glanced into his rear monitor, he flinched. From a side street, two cars raced out. Blue lights flashing from their grills.

"Someone's on our tail!" LeBeau blurted. "Feds?"

"Go *faster!*" Tag's voice boomed. "We're almost at the bridge!"

LeBeau's hands began to tremble. He could see the cars gaining at a rapid pace. His voice cracked, "Base: do *something!*" His heavy truck, carrying three bodies (one dead) wasn't fast enough.

36. Downsized by Attrition

"I can't check for feds. They're encrypted!" Dalia scolded LeBeau through her headset.

"Isn't that why we got Lex?" LeBeau shouted. "To crack federal codes..?"

Lex looked up, "He wants me to do this *now?*"

Dalia shook her head and replied. "There's no time. Quit crying and use your resources."

LeBeau seethed. The flashing cars were a hundred yards behind him and gaining. It was time to vanish. "Tag: time for stealth!"

"Roger that!"

All lights on the Hayabusa and Hummer were turned off. No headlights, brake or tail lights. On the dark island –on the unlit road– the vehicles disappeared. The men applied their infrared night-vision goggles and accelerated.

"They're gone!" The twenty-eight-year old FBI agent gazed at the road in disbelief. He cautiously accelerated to 60 mph since the two-lane road had a posted speed of 30 mph. "I think they turned off their lights!"

"Impossible —that's suicide!" Agent Riker retorted. "All units: forget the island. Catch 'em on the mainland. All units: block ramps to I-75, north and south."

Tag's favorite nocturnal sport was driving with night vision. His view of the street glowed green with perfect visibility. His infrared display had sidebars that estimated the distance to targets in its center frame. Any potential obstacle was outlined in neon green. Tag zigzagged around debris like a video game.

"*Whoo hoo!* Now *this* is fun!" The burly Tag uncharacteristically squealed like a ten-year old. "Follow my tail, Froggy!"

LeBeau caught up to Tag as they crossed the causeway out of Sanibel. The narrow bridge had only two lanes. Like an unstoppable locomotive, the two vehicles raced across the causeway and onto the mainland of Fort Myers.

Facing out on the side of the road were two government-brown Impalas. With their lights off —and no streetlights for miles— the agents were hidden as they waited for the targets to exit the bridge.

The senior agent looked down, using his teeth to open a bag of Cajun sunflower seeds. He jumped when a blur of deafening sound raced by. Seeds flew all over his lap and he looked up. "What was that?" he radioed to his partner in the next car.

"I'm not sure..." his portly partner replied. "It was like a...flash of...*thunder.*" Both agents craned their necks to look down the road. They couldn't see anything.

"Let's check it out," the older agent decided. The cars turned on their blue strobes and headed east on Summerlin to follow the clamor.

LeBeau saw the flashing lights of two *more* cars in his mirror. He pounded the steering wheel, "Two more tails!"

"Keep cool," Tag replied. "The roads are clearing ahead."

LeBeau tried to recall an aerial view of their route. He couldn't risk turning on the truck's navigation system, as it would create a glow. He'd studied maps of the area prior to Selina. The fastest route to I-75 was east on Summerlin until they crossed Tamiami Trail. Then they could go either north or south to access ramps to I-75.

But LeBeau also knew that anyone pursuing them would predict the same route. "Tag, turn *NOW*," LeBeau shouted, "south on San Carlos to the beach!"

"The *beach*?! That's a tourist road, probably blocked and flooded..?"

"That's why you're scouting a path, Jarhead."

Tag leaned his bike hard to the right to cross into the exit. His kneepad grazed the ground as he made the curve. LeBeau followed in his path with screeching tires. They hoped their maneuver would be invisible to anyone following.

The two FBI cruisers raced east towards *the noise*. Though they didn't see anything, Agent Riker told them to chase anything unusual. The agents agreed that an invisible locomotive echo qualified. If the suspects were racing to I-75, the ramps were already blocked, north and southbound. Like chasing minnows into a net.

Two miles past the exit for San Carlos, the agents rolled down their windows. The rumbling noise had vanished.

"Are they still ahead?" asked the chubby agent.

"They didn't just disappear!"

"We lost 'em!" LeBeau shouted when he saw the two cars continuing east. He accelerated until his truck was ten yards behind Tag. He approached his tail like a NASCAR driver.

"Keep your eyes in your head," Tag said. They zoomed through a tourist area of restaurants and mini golf. "Approaching Matanzas Bridge. It'll take us south along the beach."

When they crested the bridge's summit, they saw a glow from the beach —which meant Fort Myers Beach had electricity. Making the sharp left onto the thoroughfare, they had to abruptly decelerate. In the congested tourist area, streetlamps and traffic lights shined like a poor man's Vegas. Storefronts were lit with the neon of bars and t-shirt shops. With restored power and cleared roads, bored locals were coming out to explore.

"Shit,' Tag grumbled. "People."

LeBeau agreed it was bad. They were traveling too fast to alter their route. The roads had been bulldozed to remove sand and debris. In its place were cars and pedestrians —which meant traffic lights, witnesses and security cams.

"Stay close," Tag said. "Let's fly through this as fast as we can."

LeBeau turned on his nav system. "The tourist zone is only a mile long. Five miles south, Bonita Beach will take us to 75." He smiled, "We'll be twenty miles south of any roadblocks."

"Roger that!" Tag huddled low on his bike as he approached a four-way intersection. He shot through the red light like a bullet. Two crossing cars screeched at the sudden missile. A Camaro and VW Bug collided in Tag's wake. *Whoo hoo!* Tag laughed.

"Idiot!" LeBeau slammed on his brakes, fishtailing on the road to avoid the cars. "You're making a scene!"

LeBeau cringed when he saw locals in tank-tops pointing at his truck. Though their vehicles were black and without lights, he realized they were visible. The sight of a racing Hayabusa and Hummer would certainly cause a commotion. The locals were shouting, "*Your lights ain't on!*" LeBeau dreaded such spectacles, which made him question Tag's intellect. Regardless, he needed to catch up, careful to avoid any rubbernecking riff-raff.

As Tag raced through each intersection —despite the color of the lights— panicked drivers swerved and skidded to avoid collisions. An El Camino stopped suddenly to avoid Tag's bike. The car was hit from the rear and pushed into the window of a pizza shop. Glass rained down on an oblivious teenage couple.

LeBeau had no choice but to follow Tag's irresponsible path. The sound of screeching tires and the *pops* of fender-bender's echoed in their wake.

Fifty-year old FBI Agent Earl Godfrey had taken a gamble by turning south on San Carlos. His hunch paid off when he heard Fort Myers PD report multiple crashes by the beach. Witnesses reported two black vehicles "drag racing" without their lights on.

Godfrey hadn't been told by his superiors *who* they were chasing. From experience, he knew it had to be a suspect under FBI jurisdiction, which could include either bank robbers or kidnappers. When Godfrey heard *drag racing*, he assumed it involved kids. "I've chased a thousand young punks," he grumbled.

Godfrey smirked when he saw people gawking in front of t-shirt shops. They made his job easy by pointing south. When they saw his flashing lights, they shouted, "They went that-a-way! That-a-way!"

Godfrey had to slow to maneuver around crashed cars. Drivers stood beside their vehicles, pointing and exchanging insurance information. But this confirmed he was headed the right way.

"Agent Riker, this is Godfrey. I'm on their trail." The suspects' *trail* was the chain of crashed cars he passed. But the farther he drove, the road started to clear. It was less commercial with fewer lights. The stretch of condos came with darker roads, and that was bad —until he got an idea. As a forty-year local, he knew what was ahead.

He clutched his radio, "Attention: suspects heading south to Bonita Beach." Godfrey flashed a toothy grin, "They have to cross the drawbridge at Carlos Pass. Contact the bridge tender. Raise the drawbridge!"

LeBeau was relieved their surroundings were dark again. He didn't see anyone on their tail. "There's a bridge ahead," he advised Tag, "Cross the bridge, the road will lead to I-75, and then home."

"Copy." Tag's bike slowed and he pulled to the side. "Go ahead of me; I have an idea."

"Like causing a scene with a thousand witnesses?"

Tag remained somber. "I'll follow you over the bridge. I'll hit the ramp with an E-PIG behind me."

Not bad, LeBeau smirked. Let Tag do all the heavy lifting.

"This is base," Dalia's voice interrupted. "Bad news: Lee Sheriffs have been called. They're approaching, two miles to your rear!"

"Take it easy, Froggy," Tag cautioned. "I'll take out the bridge. We can do this."

LeBeau inhaled. He gripped the wheel and sped past Tag's bike. With his night vision, he could see the narrow drawbridge approaching in the distance.

As Tag gave LeBeau a hundred-yard lead, faint sirens filled the air. He looked back to see flashing lights reflecting off the condominiums. He pulled an E-PIG from his vest and revved his engine. His wheels chirped as he sped towards the bridge in LeBeau's path.

LeBeau kept his goggles fixed on the approaching bridge. His eyes suddenly bugged when he saw the guardrail beginning to close. A metal bell clanged. The bridge was preparing to open. He shouted with panic, "It's opening!"

"Accelerate! Accelerate!" Tag bellowed.

LeBeau had no choice; he was speeding too fast. He gripped the wheel and leaned forward. Anxiety provided the adrenalin he needed. He stepped on the gas and aimed at the descending guard arm. The bridge began to open. The ramp's jagged teeth separated and the gears groaned on the forty-year old structure.

His truck snapped the guard arm like Styrofoam. The truck raced at over 80 mph up the incline and LeBeau closed his eyes. At a near 20 degree angle, he jumped the ramp –was briefly airborne– and landed with a jarring rebound on the other side.

"I did it!" LeBeau shrieked into his mic. "I'm over!" He couldn't believe his own bravery. *Wait until I tell the team!* LeBeau slowed the truck and pulled to the side to wait for Tag. Within seconds they'd be homeward bound.

Racing towards the bridge, Tag looked in his mirror. At least two cars were approaching. He gripped the E-PIG in one hand and bent low. The bridge appeared to be climbing towards a 40 degree angle. He pushed the Hayabusa's engines over 100 mph.

Tag's psyche had a sudden flash of 70s daredevil Evil Knievil. He'd been a teenager when Knievil jumped Snake River Canyon on television in 1974 —only two years before a school probation officer tricked him into joining the Marines. Seeing the approaching bridge, Tag knew the jump would be easy. On motocross trails at his off-season home in Georgia, Tag had jumped swells close to fifty degrees. He had to make this work; there was no room for error.

He knew street cops wouldn't attempt the jump. Tag's infrared readout counted down as the bridge approached —a hundred more feet and he'd be launched into freedom. He and LeBeau would then glide to Alligator Alley, and then on to their beloved swamp hangar. Home sweet home.

When Tag entered the bridge's ramp, he threw the E-PIG straight up into the air. He shot forward, climbing the 45 degree incline. Behind him, the grenade rose and then began its descent.

On impact, the E-PIG detonated on a steel grate before the bridge. A blue fireball expanded from the crater. A surge of energy electrified the framework of the bridge. As if in slow-motion, the blast's pulse expanded towards the rear of Tag's soaring bike.

But in his eager race, Tag had made a fatal error: he hadn't considered the Hayabusa's digital fuel injection and microprocessor. The bike used programmed valves to maintain velocity. In short, he forgot the high-tech bike was run by computers —the precise systems the E-PIG was designed to destroy.

In that millisecond, the electromagnetic pulse caused Tag's bike to hiccup. The shockwave threw his rear tire off by a minuscule degree. Tag had thrown the grenade too soon.

When Tag's bike flew into the air, a rare smile was frozen on his face. The deficient speed caused his bike to prematurely drop. With his brain unable to comprehend the crisis, Tag's last sensation was of flying and of being happy. Tag's bike crashed onto the steel teeth of the ramp's other side. On impact, Tag was thrown from his bike as its gas tank exploded. His body flew through debris and fire, and plummeted down the ramp's other side like a ragdoll.

LeBeau watched in disbelief. "Tag –are you okay!" he shouted into his radio. He stood in the road and scanned the base of the bridge with his infrared. The fire and smoke gave off blinding heat readings. Then he saw Tag's lifeless body, twisted in a heap on the side of the road. *"TAG!"*

LeBeau looked up as he heard the bell clanging again. The bridge was attempting to lower. Blue lights and sirens were impatient to cross from the other side. He looked at Tag's body; then at the grinding bridge. There was no time to deliberate.

LeBeau returned to his truck and began hyperventilating with the realization of being alone. He no longer had Tag advising what to do. He stepped on the accelerator, speeding away from the scene.

When no cars followed, it was evident the damage had made the road impassable. Tag had achieved his mission with the valor of a career Marine. LeBeau sped through the quiet community of Bonita Beach and soared onto I-75, south. Approaching midnight, the roads were wide and empty. Within ten minutes the road curved east, changing its name to Alligator Alley, the final leg of his return.

LeBeau breathed five percent easier when he observed no police blocking the eastbound lanes towards Lauderdale. Having to pass through the Alley's toll booth, he knew they no longer had security arms. Thanks to automated toll transponders, LeBeau could race through the Sunpass lane at full speed. A camera might try to photograph his license plate, but it would show as only a blur.

The long Alley provided an overdue break to catch his breath. The forty mile stretch to the hangar allowed time to decompress. The night's events raced in his head. *Tag's dead, Tag's dead...* he repeated, nearly in tears. Having no emotional bond with Tag, his sentiment came from the anxiety of leading a rapidly-diminishing team. He'd been craving leadership, but now feared earning no respect from the remaining players.

Butch had been a true leader. Tag had been the muscle. The impetuous Curt was useful for hazardous missions. *Now what?* LeBeau wondered. Dalia and Pitch were too unpolished. LeBeau knew little about Lex, except he was wanted for multiple crimes and could hack almost any federal system. *We've lost our top players within days!* LeBeau looked back to his truck's rear compartment. Curt was still unconscious. Butch was still dead.

He didn't want to call Dalia –yet. He couldn't bear revealing the night's failure or Tag's demise. *What if they decide to mutiny before I get back?* He began to panic. He turned on his Mozart and practiced deep breathing for the final twenty minutes of his trip.

He crossed the boundary of the Indian reservation and turned at the deserted pump station without slowing less than 50 mph. He spun-out through the gravel, around the hammock of cypress trees, and over the bumpy road towards the hangar. LeBeau needed every ounce of remaining strength to not openly cry.

"Open the bay doors!" Dalia shouted. "He's within a mile, approaching fast."

Pitch hit a switch and the steel doors slowly opened. Outside, the night was black with only the flurry of insects. Pitch engaged a second switch that opened the exterior razor-wire fence.

From the safety of the hangar, Dalia, Lex and Pitch gazed out into the black abyss. Within seconds, the croaks of frogs stopped. The mechanized roar of LeBeau's V-8 grew louder. They stepped back as if a dragon was returning to its hallowed cave.

Bursting from the darkness, the truck charged into the hangar. Its tires screamed and the truck slid to a stop –less than two feet from the wide-eyed trio.

Dalia, Lex and Pitch were silent, waiting for the driver to exit like some heroic astronaut. The door opened and LeBeau stepped out in full, forbidding gear. He was panting, his chest heaving. He pulled off his mask and threw it to the floor. He looked down at his young team.

Pausing for any words of enlightenment, the team saw LeBeau open his mouth to speak.

"Tag is dead." LeBeau stepped down from the truck and marched towards the rear of the room. He pulled off his pads and gear, discarding them to the floor. He stopped and turned. "Can someone *please* get Curt and Butch's body out of the trunk before they begin to stink?"

The remaining team looked at each other and said nothing.

37. And That's What it's all About

The room was stark white with a stainless steel table. Alexandra Larriott guessed it was some sort of interrogation room. She looked down into the somewhat reflective table. The circles around her eyes and her tangled hair made her look like a three-day hostage.

She looked at her two saviors beside her. The insurance investigator, Dan Holms, was seated next to her. On his other side was the deputy, Nadine Stratton, who was usually pretty. She wasn't so pretty now, with mascara running under her eyes —which meant she'd had make-up on. When they'd arrived at her house, they were in casual clothes. Maybe they'd been out socially. *Were they a couple?*

Dan was unshaven and the sleeves were rolled up on his stained cargo shirt. He was handsome, but looked like hell. His hand gently touched Detective Stratton's on the table. There was some sort of connection there. No one spoke. It had to be after 2:00 a.m., and they were all red-eyed and weary.

Frustrated, Alexandra finally asked, "Where are we?"

Dan looked at her and forced a smile. "We didn't go through the main gate, but I think MacDill Air Force Base in Tampa." He put his hand on her shoulder. "I don't know why."

Three hours earlier, the FBI agents had driven them north to Tampa. Dan and Nadine were placed in a car driven by the middle-aged Agent Riker, who'd been shouting all the orders. Alexandra and Cassie sat in the rear of a car driven by a heavy agent. In his suit and narrow tie, the driver looked like a long-lost Blues Brother. The fat agent had a considerate smile, but refused to speak. Alexandra dozed-off before arriving at their destination. Cassie immediately fell asleep in her lap.

They'd been escorted by three unmarked cars; one agent drove Detective Stratton's sedan. Alexandra didn't understand why the senior agent yelled at them as if they'd done something wrong. Was the FBI somehow involved with the man she'd shot? The thought gave her a chill.

The irate Agent Riker had treated Nadine and Dan equally harsh. He kept shouting at them, "What did you see?" From all the radio jabber, it sounded like the FBI had been chasing the suspects. Were they caught? *Would that be good or bad?*

Alexandra withered at a thought: If the feds caught her attackers, what if they flip and testify against *her* —saying *she* murdered their partner in an unprovoked attack? Alexandra swallowed a lump rising in her throat. She was well aware it was illegal to murder people. *I'm a murderer,* she repeated to herself.

Her eyes then widened —where would Cassie go if she went to jail? Her lip quivered at the thought. She had no other family or relatives to help her. Definitely not the poor child's *real* father. She could not, *would not*, let that happen.

Then it hit her like a sledgehammer: they'd already taken Cassie away. When they'd arrived in Tampa, a genial man in a blue uniform took Cassie. He said they had a room where she could sleep. Alexandra trusted the man; she even thanked him. *Where is my daughter now?* Alexandra began to panic. Had she already been whisked off to some anonymous foster home for the children of felons?

The door to the white room opened. The grandfatherly officer in the blue uniform who'd taken Cassie entered. Following him was the terse FBI Agent Riker, carrying several files. They manufactured the weakest smiles imaginable.

The decorated officer spoke first. "Hello. I'm Army Lieutenant Colonel Sturges." He motioned to the man beside him. "This is Special Agent Riker with the FBI, Tampa Division." Though it was the middle of the night, the agent still had slicked-over hair and a firm necktie.

Nadine shouted brazenly, "I'm with law enforcement. I *demand* to know why we're here!"

Colonel Sturges was the warmer of the two. "You're in the headquarters for the U.S. Special Operations Command. We oversee Special Ops for each branch of the military: Army, Air Force, Navy and Marines."

Agent Riker added, "You were attacked by a group that preys on areas evacuated for catastrophes. They're being monitored by the Department of Defense, as well as the FBI."

Dan scoffed, "So, our military's now declared war on *burglars*?"

Riker looked down at Holms. "The FBI certainly cares about interstate burglaries totaling, to-date, over $50,000,000."

Colonel Sturges interjected as if on cue, "Wouldn't you agree that AWOL Special Forces troops are a threat to national security? Civilians can't *fathom* the technology and weapons they've stolen."

"Now they're murderers." Riker looked at Alexandra, "You're lucky to be alive." He turned ominously to Nadine, "Which is why your boss ordered you to *drop* the case." He lifted two fingers an inch apart. "We were *this* close and you decided to play Wonder Woman, jeopardizing the lives of a dozen of my men."

"Good job!" Dan clapped with sarcasm. "You want to catch 'storm burglars?' All you had to do was go to wherever a storm's going."

The Colonel shook his head as in *it's not that simple.* "With any storm's projected path, there are *hundreds* of miles of vulnerable coastline. These suspects are choosing targets for very specific reasons."

Riker straddled a backwards chair next to Alexandra. He did a jerky nod with a sneer, "Ms. Larriott, you and I know the *real* reason they're attracted to you..."

Alexandra gasped with instant emotion. "I don't know why!" She covered her eyes and began sobbing, "I just want my daughter back – and get far away from here!"

Riker pretended to be confused, "You haven't told your pals here why they're after *you*?"

Alexandra buried her face in her hands and cried.

Puzzled, Dan put his arm round her. Nadine also seemed compassionate, but observed the subtle embrace between Dan and Alexandra.

Colonel Sturges stepped forward and extended a hand. "Ms. Larriott, why don't I take you to a nice room with your daughter? We have clean, pretty rooms we use for visiting officers." He had a warm smile and clear blue eyes. "Tomorrow, we'll find you both a safe place. Somewhere that no one can ever touch you again."

Alexandra looked up at the man. Her voice quivered, "You'll take me to my daughter?"

"Absolutely," Sturges helped her stand. He placed his hand on her frail shoulder and guided her towards the door.

Alexandra looked back and flashed a smile of gratitude to Dan. She mouthed *thank you* before exiting the room. He returned the smile and the steel door closed.

Dan and Nadine were now alone with Riker. He faced them across the table. He placed two files in front of him and gazed up at the fluorescent light. "Now, how can I convince you two that you never saw a thing?"

"Why are you gagging this story?" Dan crossed his arms, "Every citizen on the coast needs to know about these killers!"

"They *murdered* a cop I knew!" Nadine shouted. "While sitting in his car, doing his job!"

Riker gritted his teeth with impatience. "Can your brain even *comprehend* the panic? Terrified residents, refusing to leave their homes with impending, deadly storms. Imagine Joe-lunchbox, hiding in his house with a gun, shooting anyone who walks by his window. If people are *conveniently* omitted from knowing the truth, they'll seek shelter instead of being cornered by *terrorists*. That's *my* job."

"So now they're *terrorists*?" Nadine blurted.

Riker recoiled as if she'd spoken out of place. "My apologies; I forget street cops aren't trained in counterterrorism. A 'terrorist' is anyone whose systematic acts are intended to create fear. Did you see Ms. Larriott's face? Do you think she experienced fear?"

"So what now?" Nadine shouted. "Are you going to arrest us because we know about your terrorists? Lock us up, away from the public? How 'bout you read us some rights, or you can let us walk out of here!"

Dan half-smiled, impressed with her outburst.

"I'm not going to keep you here." Riker narrowed one eye in thought. "Because I'm confident that you understand our *direct order* to move on with your duties. No reports of the suspects; no public warnings. Go back to writing speeding tickets and let us do our jobs."

Dan inched forward, matching Riker's glower. "You can bully law enforcement, but I'm not a cop and I'm not a soldier. I'm a civilian who has the job to investigate *any* evidence costing my company millions of dollars."

"Really..?" Riker blossomed with a wide smile. "Insurance boy has a duty!" He opened one of the files on the table and cleared his throat.

Nadine gazed at the files. One folder had her name typed on its cover.

"Daniel Lewis Holms, insurance investigator," Riker mocked the word *investigator*. "Does your *latest* company, Insurex, know about your arrest ten years ago?"

All emotion drained from Dan's face. Nadine looked at him, confused.

Riker kept his eyes on Dan as if he had the details committed to memory. "You know, the arrest from that bar fight that left one man blind? You were drunk at Captain Tony's in Key West. You thought it'd be clever to shove a six-foot biker. When he popped you back, you swung a pool cue like Obi-Wan Kenobi hitting a piñata. The stick punctured the guy's right eyeball. When the cops arrived to pull ten Hell's Angels off you, they found a .38 caliber in your pants —with no concealed weapons permit." Riker closed the file and cocked his head. "Does your company know about that little fiesta?" He lifted a printout of Dan's insurance license. "You're licensed with the Department of Financial Services? How'd the state miss that little nugget? Maybe a social security off by one digit?"

Dan pursed his lips. He didn't blink as he glared at the grinning agent.

"Dan, is all that true?" Nadine asked.

"It's very true, detective," Riker replied. "Mr. Holms applied to be a police officer four times. He's even been rejected for a P.I. license. But you have to admire his passion," Riker smirked. "He's so obsessed with being any sort of *'investigator'* that he now examines fluffed insurance claims." He chuckled, "I guess Dan *Holms* is the *Sherlock* of insurance. Exciting stuff!"

Nadine blinked with doe-like eyes, speechless.

The agent's face softened as he looked at Nadine. "*Miss* Stratton, my heart actually goes out to you. Another disappointing male in your life. It must've been hard being the only daughter in a five-male, police family."

She looked at him, caught off-guard by his comment.

Riker lifted several prints from her folder. "I'm very impressed with the long line of good cops in the Stratton family tree. Your daddy and *three* brothers all made sergeant —or higher. Says here you couldn't climb above being an elementary school cop in Michigan. So you *gave up* there and packed your bags for the Sunshine State." He folded his hands, puzzled. "What I can't determine is: did you join the force as a family tradition, or out of contempt to a daddy who said being a cop is no job for a girl?"

Nadine's face contorted with anger. "Go to hell!"

"Don't get me wrong, detective," Riker raised his hands in surrender. "I have confidence you'll do very well in your department. I have close friends there and I plan to give them a heads-up about your return." He focused his eyes to make a point, "You just need to follow our very easy orders. If you keep your pretty nose clean, you'll have a *very* bright future to brag about at the Thanksgiving table."

Dan and Nadine, seated in their chairs like children, said nothing.

Agent Riker stood. "Oh –and for the legal part– if either of you still feel a need to dig deeper, I'll charge you both with *Misprision of Treason*, a federal offense carrying seven years." He stepped towards the door. "Understood, Nancy Drew and Sherlock?"

They were both pale as they gazed at the floor.

"Do you think they bought it?" Colonel Sturges asked Riker as they walked to see if the base's new Starbucks had opened yet.

Riker paused as he pondered. "We can't detain them without risking serious inquiry. It'd open a giant bucket of eels." He leaned in, "Do you plan to involve the General?"

"Hell no!" Sturges scowled, "He needs to be insulated –for now." He recited like a textbook, "We have a duty to use this fusion team until we have conclusive findings and clear proposals. We're just following some leads."

"Are we going to arrest Larriott, or just make her *vanish* for a while?"

The Colonel shrugged, "I don't care as long as she's gone." He sighed, "But unfortunately we'd then have to deal with her kid."

Riker pursed his lips at the frustrating dilemma. He then flashed a crooked grin, "How's our *other* new witness doing?"

The Colonel beamed, "First thing in the morning, you can see for yourself."

38. The Pyre of Regret

The stars sparkled in the moonless sky over the ink-black Everglades.

The surviving teammates –LeBeau, Pitch, Dalia and Lex– rode three-wheel ATVs a half-mile through the marshes. They remained on a path of high ground to a clearing surrounded by cypress trees. Dalia and Pitch led the way using spotlights. LeBeau stayed to the rear, holding a double-barrel shotgun for any uninvited reptiles. Lex pulled a wagon containing shovels and Butch's wrapped corpse.

Curt had been left unconscious in the hangar. Dalia injected him with another dose of *acepromazine maleate*, a horse tranquilizer they'd purchased from an online pharmacy out of South Africa. Dalia then handcuffed him to the floor of a bathroom.

In a small patch surrounded by swamp, Pitch and Lex dug a hole for Butch. LeBeau avoided any manual labor by volunteering to aim the spotlight, to "look out for coral snakes." The men rolled Butch's corpse into the hole and covered the body with rocks, twigs and brush.

Pitch had fashioned two crosses using lumber at the hangar. In black spray paint, he'd written "Butch" and "Tag" on the crude markers. Pitch placed one cross at the head of Butch's mound. In the soil beside it, he inserted Tag's marker. With no body to honor, Pitch placed a combat helmet on top of Tag's cross.

At LeBeau's direction, Lex sprayed Butch's mound with kerosene. Dalia threw a match on the tomb of rocks and dried palm fronds. The team stepped back, forming a circle around the inferno. Embers danced into the sky and faded among the stars.

Pitch stood closest to Tag's empty helmet –his mission partner. He wiped away a tear as the pyre blazed.

Dalia stood beside Lex. She gently reached to hold his hand. Lex looked into her eyes and smiled.

LeBeau had no tears as he gazed at Tag's empty grave and melting helmet. Though he'd been emotional about Tag's demise, he had more practical thoughts. *Have the cops identified Tag's body?* Did he have any identifying marks or tattoos? The feds might research the origin of the uniform and weapons. It'd be just a matter of time.

He was an imbecile, LeBeau finally decided. *He got himself killed.* Tag had been careless during the chase. *Maybe it's a good thing to have another weak link off the team.* By attrition, LeBeau believed he was now the most intelligent man still standing. Pitch was too envious and simple. Curt would be harshly reprimanded. Lex –if he joined the team– was too new. LeBeau struggled to conceal a smile, *I am the new leader...*

But his erratic emotions circled back to regret. He shouldn't have left Tag behind. He could've collected his body before the cops. If authorities identify him, they could ultimately work backwards to uncover each of their identities –even Curt's *real* motives. It could spell the downfall of them all.

Mentally besieged, LeBeau was now livid that Tag was dead. At least if Tag *had* to be caught, it was better dead than alive.

39. Witness 669-18070

A shaft of morning light illuminated the sterile hospital room. The private room had only one bed, no TV, an outdated cardiac monitor and two vinyl chairs right out of the 1970s.

The room was hidden within the U.S. Air Force Clinic at MacDill. It was on a secured wing, complete with two armed guards at the door. Agent Riker said the guards were a waste of taxpayer money since the patient would be unable to walk for months.

An IV led to the patient's good arm. The large man had one arm in a cast and long-leg casts on both legs. Gauze was wrapped around his bruised, purple head. Despite his inability to move, his good wrist was handcuffed to the bed.

Riker bent over until he was ten inches from the patient's face. He cooed in a singsong, "Donald 'Tag' Taggart, can you hear me?" Unable to rouse him, Riker shrugged at the doctor looming in the doorway.

"Give him time." The bald doctor looked like a frog in a lab coat. He read from a clipboard, "He suffered a severe concussion, a broken right humerus and complete fractures to *both* femurs. He'll have to learn to walk all over again." He looked at Riker, "His helmet and armor did their job."

"How fortunate," Riker replied. "Can you leave us now?" After the doctor frowned and walked away, Riker looked down at Tag's face. He noticed one swollen eye beginning to flutter. He leaned closer, "Are you with us? Wakey, wakey..."

Tag's right eye cracked open. He remained still, but his dilated pupil focused on Riker.

Riker shook his head as if saddened. "Look at you: a Force-Recon Sergeant gone AWOL... I thought *Semper Fi* meant 'Always faithful.' Tell me, Mr. Taggart, are you too stupid to understand Latin?"

Tag said nothing. His bloodshot eye refused to blink.

"I'm going to ask you one simple question," Riker stated in a stern voice. "What *precisely* is your team's next target? I want to know the exact house." He reached for Tag's broken arm and flicked the cast with his finger.

Tag inhaled and his eye watered. His tongue emerged to lick his cracked lips. He made a grunt as if clearing his throat.

"What's that?" Riker lowered his head to Tag's face.

When Riker's ear was three inches from his lips, Tag inhaled and spat into his ear. Bloody saliva spattered across Riker's neck.

Riker bolted upright, eyes blazing, "They'll hang you!" He grabbed a washcloth and wiped his ear. He grinned and shouted, "Congratulations! You'll be the first man executed by court martial in fifty years!"

Tag stared at him, unflinching. A smirk wrinkled across his face.

Riker stomped to the window to compose himself. He straightened his tie and smoothed his hair. He then returned to Tag's bedside. "Did you know your partner saw you dying on the road and chose to leave you behind?"

Tag didn't move.

"That's right. He had *plenty* of time to get you. We weren't able to cross the bridge. But for some reason he just left you there. Lying in a twisted heap."

Tag's eyes slightly fluttered but he did not blink.

Riker stepped closer and raised his voice, "Your *buddy* left you there to *die*! Why would he do that?" He cocked his head, "*That* is who you're protecting?"

After an eternal pause, Tag blinked.

40. Tiberius

On the other side of MacDill AFB, hangar five housed the Hurricane Hunters. Their plane, a Lockheed WP-3D Orion, had just landed. Flown by NOAA –the National Oceanic and Atmospheric Administration– the plane was a flying laboratory, modified to take atmospheric measurements within tropical cyclones. The Hunters were returning home with bad news.

On September 9th –three days before Hurricane Selina– a tropical wave moved off the coast of Africa with little fanfare. With a ridge of high pressure to its north, Selina's young sibling followed westward in her path. As all eyes were on Florida, the new wave passed south of the Cape Verde Islands. On September 14th –two days after Selina's landfall on Florida's west coast– the wave matured into Tropical Depression Twenty Seven, southeast of Barbados.

It was too early to predict its course. The Hurricane Hunters had hoped moderate wind shear would prevent any strengthening. However, their latest flight confirmed what some models predicted: a decrease in shear, with spiral bands developing from the storm's center. With sustained winds now over 39 mph, the storm required the twentieth letter of the alphabet. Tropical Storm *Tiberius* was born.

The Hurricane Hunters would fly again in six hours. If the storm escalated to the critical 74 mph, it would become Hurricane Tiberius, and a hurricane watch would be issued for the eastern Bahamas. It was imperative the Hunters collect enough data for the National Hurricane Center to predict whether the storm would turn south towards Cuba, or be the second storm to target the Florida peninsula in less than a week.

41. Exposed

Dan Holms woke up in the tacky motel room. The room's previous idiot must've set the alarm for 8:00 a.m., as thug rap from Lil Wayne blared. Scowling at the clock, Dan realized he'd slept only four hours. He looked around the room. It was more of a *motel*. Or worse, a motor lodge. The aroma of Marlboros ingrained in the pillowcase wasn't helping his splitting headache.

The room was crappy, even by his standard of living in tents in storm zones. Orange shag carpet and a TV that still had a dial to change the channels. But it was the first place he and Nadine could find at 3:45 a.m.

Dan still had his clothes on from the night before —clothes that started out clean and ironed for their Tiki meeting. Now he looked as if he'd been through a garbage disposal. Nadine was still asleep in her own bed, cocooned in her sheets. She looked a lot better than he did.

He focused on Nadine's face, lit by the glow seeping from behind the vinyl drapes. Despite their tragic evening, her face was beautiful. She'd washed away her makeup before bed, which now accentuated her natural features: a straight, upturned nose; classic cheekbones and natural golden hair. She had a healthy tan that probably came from a few hours a week on the beach *—before Selina.* Dan hoped she'd get another hour of sleep before their trek home.

It had been almost 3:00 a.m. when the FBI finally released Dan and Nadine from MacDill. Agent Riker had reluctantly returned her gun, badge and car keys. He said he was keeping Dan's gun because of his past arrest. Dan countered that he'd obtained his concealed weapons permit after waiting the required five years after pleading 'no contest' to his prior mishap. Riker gave an angry smirk that Dan had called his bluff.

Dan offered to drive and by 3:15 a.m. they were racing south out of Tampa. They were confident their adrenalin would keep them awake for the two-hour ride home.

Within fifteen minutes, Dan caught himself dozing. He agreed to exit I-75 near Parrish to the first motel they could find. At "Rena's Ocean Heir," the woman behind the desk, Viola, was three-hundred pounds and missing an arm. Dan felt bad for the poor souls who seem to work graveyard shifts. In a southern baby-doll voice, Viola offered a room for $49.00 —cash.

Dan took the bed closest to the door and kept his clothes on. Exhausted, neither of them spoke and he turned off the lamp. Nadine took the time to wash up before slipping into her own bed. She said simply, and with a sweet tone, "Goodnight Danny." Mentally and physically depleted, they'd gone to sleep within seconds.

Nadine finally stirred beneath her sheets at 8:30. Her head darted up, eyes skimming across the room. That fleeting moment when people can't remember where they'd gone to bed.

"Good morning," Dan said, propped on an elbow. "Sorry it's not the Ritz."

She faced him and smiled, "You asked for two beds? Quite the gentleman."

He smiled, "I figured you wouldn't sleep with a felon."

Nadine leaned up and grinned, "You underestimated me." The sheet dropped from her shoulder, making it evident she had nothing on underneath. "A bar fight hardly makes you a felon."

Dan tried not to react when he realized she seemed nude under her sheet. A consummate gentleman to a fault, he refused to dip his eyes lower than her mouth. "*So...we probably need to head home..?*"

She squeezed her eyes shut as their predicament haunted her face. "I guess I was *ordered* to go back."

"What are you going to do?" Dan sat up, "Drop the case like the feds want?"

"How can I just *drop* it?" Emotion filled her voice. "I saw a fellow cop murdered. We have *conclusive proof* that Alexandra was attacked by these killers. How can I just ignore everything we saw?"

Dan allowed a second to pass. "Nadine, between the two of us, you have a future. People like you. You'll be sergeant soon." He rubbed his stubble and looked down. "I can always go back to investigating...fluffed insurance claims."

As if sensing his insecurity, Nadine smiled. "Dan, you're incredible at your job. You have more law enforcement contacts than I do." She paused until he met her eye. "I think we should dig deeper. We were attacked by suspects involved in *both* of our investigations."

"You're too young to kill your career." He shrugged, "Maybe I'll keep looking –I've already butchered mine."

Nadine sat upright, scarcely clutching the sheets around her. "You heard Riker. He threatened to call my superiors. The fed's tentacles are so deep in my department, I only have a future if I shut-up and look pretty."

"You're already pretty," he grinned. "I don't think you can shut-up."

She smirked at his levity. "Dan, we're *good* investigators. Riker kept saying there's a reason the burglars are after Larriott. I want to know why."

"Because she killed one of them."

"Not at first." Nadine's passion resurfaced. "There were *hundreds* of evacuated mansions. I want to know why they picked her."

"I can keep searching her background..?"

"What if we can convince some other authority to pursue it? You have contacts in the Coast Guard, Homeland..?" With her enthusiasm, her sheet fell again, innocently revealing her top. She glowed with confidence. "Will you *do it* with me?"

His eyes darted between her eyes and exposed skin. "I'll gladly do you...work with you," Dan covered his face. "I'd love to...help you look into Larriott's past."

"You will?" She was ecstatic. "What if we uncover who these *storm killers* are? We'll make headlines!" She was lively with no regard for her falling cover. "I'll be *swiftly* fired −and then flooded with offers. You and I can open our own investigative firm!"

He laughed, rejuvenated by her enthusiasm. He was no longer uncomfortable that she was half naked in front of him. She was exposing her confidence and trust. Her radiant optimism was contagious.

"Can I ask you something?"

"Sure," he replied to the stunning lady across from him.

"Do you have any attraction to Alexandra? I saw the way she looked at you."

"No." Dan was shocked at her insecurity. "The poor woman was shell shocked. And I did sort of *save her life*." He paused, recalling a slight attraction he sensed when he first met Alexandra. "I suppose there have been cases when insureds flirt when I'm handling their million-dollar claims."

"I'm sorry. It's none of my business−"

"−Nadine," Dan interrupted. He sat beside her and put his arm around her slinky back. "I have no interest in Alexandra." He smiled at the confident yet vulnerable lady beside him.

Her blue eyes sparkled. Their magnetism was abruptly halted by her ringing cellphone. She reached for the bedside table and saw the caller ID. She gasped, "It's Rodka −my boss."

"You going to answer it?"

"What if the feds called him?" The phone kept ringing.

"Answer it! You haven't done anything wrong."

Nadine huffed, frustrated. She answered, "Detective Stratton."

Dan watched her. With the brief silence, he soaked her in; her shoulders and curves. But then he saw alarm splashed across her face.

"How can they?" Nadine shouted into the phone. "Why? What charges?" She stood up, distressed. She barely held the sheets around her. "Hello? Al—"

"What's wrong?"

"He hung up on me!" She looked at Dan and her voice trembled, "Alexandra Larriott was arrested for murder at 7:30 this morning. Locked up, without bail."

"The feds lied!" Dan's brows furled with anger. "They looked her in the eye and promised to help. It was all a lie!"

"Why her? Why do the cops —*and* the bad guys— want *her*?"

"We need to discuss this 'Alexandra Larriott' situation," Agent Riker announced to the two young analysts seated at the table. "We also have basic profiles of the suspects." Riker's FBI analyst, Jenkins, sat at his side like a teacher's pet. At the next table was Engel, a Navy analyst, a ginger with a bad complexion and thick glasses.

Riker turned as Colonel Sturges entered the windowless conference room. Their team was working out of a large room within the Air Force base. The room had two rows of tables facing a presentation area and projection screen. The men bolted upright at attention.

"At ease," Sturges grumbled as he took a seat far from the young men. He seemed wary of their inclusion.

"Gentlemen, we've uncovered a lot in a short time." Riker stood behind a podium in front of the screen and an erasable white board. "Before we start, I want you to hear something."

The analysts glanced at each other, curious at whatever Riker was sneering at.

Riker opened his laptop on the podium and clicked an audio file. He grinned at the Colonel, "We obtained this audio surveillance using your latest parabolic laser mic. I think you'll get a kick out of it." He turned up an audio system.

The men's mouths fell open —not because of the clarity of the audio, but because it was a female voice.

42. (Con) Fusion

The woman's voice playing over the speakers had a subtle Spanish accent.

"...*I was in the Guard out of Key West; I took the Stingray on a midnight run. I was supposedly pursuing a smuggler. Butch faked an informant tip about a boat coming from the Bahamas —short notice, enough to justify me making a solo recon...*"

Astonished, Colonel Sturges cocked his head like a dog as he listened.

The Navy analyst, Engel, scribbled the key words, "Coast Guard," "Key West," "Stingray" and "Butch" on a notepad.

"...*I landed, and he covered the Stingray in tarps. Then he dumped heavy debris into the water: seat cushions, life preservers and oil. I let the ELT —the emergency locator— give off a few 'pings' before turning it off. And I was gone!*"

Riker stopped the playback and smiled with his hands in his pockets. "Maybe we can see if we have any contacts in the Coast Guard."

"I'll check reports for any lost Stingrays," Engel offered, enthusiastic.

"Whoa! No one's calling anyone!" Sturges stood. "Before I move an inch, I need a fast answer." He pointed at Riker, "You located and *bugged* their headquarters? Why in *thee hell* aren't we raiding them right now? I can have Ops there in twenty minutes!"

"No, no, no." Riker shook his head, "You don't want a raid. We didn't 'bug' their headquarters. We used a remote mic, placed on a streetlamp thirty yards from a hangar they're using. There's zero merchandise or cash there. They keep their data elsewhere. We need to keep watching them. Our goal should be to catch these suspects *in the act.*"

Sturges scrunched his face. "Son, I don't give a cat's ass about someone's jewelry or fine china!" He put both fists on the table. "Our government needs the armaments and intelligence they've stolen. This is treason!"

"Sir, hear me out," Riker struggled to soothe the man. "I brought an analyst to explain." He paused until Sturges sat back down. "Engel here is a Navy–"

"–That's another thing," Sturges interrupted. "Before you keep adding people, I want to approve these *boys.*" He pointed at Jenkins in the black suit, "This man's one of yours?"

"Yes," Riker replied. "Agent Jenkins is a counterterrorism analyst. He understands discretion." Riker winked at Jenkins. He turned to the Navy Analyst. "Officer Engel is rated IS –an Intelligence Officer. He was recommended personally by Turnbull. He's already re-searched the dead man's uniform."

Sturges nodded, impressed. "Turnbull's a good man." He stepped towards the gawky analyst and asked like a game show host, "Tell me officer, how could *street crooks* get state-of-the-art uniforms and gear?"

Engel glanced down at a laptop, seeming intimidated. "It's not difficult to get that stuff," he replied in a timid voice. "Recently, our own military –*no offense*– improperly tracked tens of thousands of weapons the Pentagon shipped to Afghan security forces." He clicked a document. "Our own Accountability Office lost track of 87,000 rifles and prototype grenades, one-third of all arms sent to Afghan soldiers between '09 and '13." Even in 2015, the Pentagon couldn't account for $500,000 in equipment given to Yemen, including small arms, ammo and night-vision. It got worse when we closed our embassy in Sanaa and withdrew our advisors." He looked meekly at the Colonel. "Considering the war budgets, it looked bad."

Sturges eyeballed the kid and sat back down.

Engel continued with budding confidence, "The military's had problems monitoring weapons before. We also lost over 190,000 weapons supplied to Iraq's security forces in '11. It was all over CNN—"

"—I get the point," Sturges barked.

In an effort to shift from military blunders, Riker interjected, "What if our suspects were never overseas? How could they get high-tech helmets or night vision?"

Jenkins decided to speak up, "The web: eBay, Craigslist, classifieds." All heads turned to him.

"*What*?" Sturges asked with an expression like he'd sucked a lemon.

Jenkins replied with a mix of confidence and respect, "According to the same Accountability Office, agents, posing as buyers, were able to purchase dozens of prohibited items on the Internet. Combat uniforms, goggles, even light weapons."

Riker interjected as if they'd rehearsed, "From a terror standpoint, our fear is these items could be purchased and sent overseas to be used against our troops, or at home against our own citizens."

Jenkins added, "The U.S. prohibits the sale of uniforms to non-military personnel. But if you recall in "07, Iraqi insurgents used our uniforms to sneak into a base in Karbala. They killed five servicemen. A fast search of the web revealed *numerous* uniforms for sale, despite any sort of bans."

"Jesus..." Sturges exclaimed. "Can't we stop these sales ASAP?"

Jenkins shrugged, "The government asked eBay management the same thing. They showed us that *seven million* listings are added *every day*. That's impossible to monitor completely."

There was a moment of silence. Riker gave a subtle wink to Jenkins for a job well-done. He looked at Sturges, "Colonel, this isn't *all* about the military's gear floating around the globe unaccounted for."

Sturges narrowed his eyes. "Where are you heading with this sermon?"

"The FBI *–and I–* have been on the hotplate as well," Riker proceeded with care. "The Justice Department publicly thrashed the Bureau for improper use of personal data during terror investigations. My agents require access to financial and credit records. The Patriot Act even says *'go right ahead...'*" He stepped closer to the Colonel. "I was told I had to show a 'sound basis' before I can get my agents access to chat rooms to watch for terrorists or how to make bombs." He chuckled at the irony, "I can't get my men access to something that ten-year-old kids do by themselves!"

Riker stepped back to the podium to compose himself. He sipped from a water bottle and straightened his tie. "The farther we get from 9/11, the more they forget. A crime has to practically *already* occur before I can investigate." He thumbed to himself, "I now have to answer to naïve Americans, sprawled in their Lay-Z-Boys?" He threw his hands up, "I can't do my job anymore!" Riker turned away and wiped his brow with a napkin.

The Colonel leaned back. "*Very* good..." He cracked a smile and began to clap. "You two were damn good." He suddenly became serious. "But I've been around a *long* time. I understand what your dog and pony show's all about."

Riker and Jenkins locked eyes with the Colonel. Engel looked up from his notes, puzzled.

Sturges pointed at Riker, "You believe it'll be easier busting these terrorists for something routine like interstate theft and robbery. You're under too big a microscope if you call them 'terror suspects.' But when you catch these burglars in the act, you'll *accidentally* stumble across stolen weapons and technology. You uncover a major threat to public safety *–as well as* millions of dollars in valuables!" Sturges shook his head and chuckled, "Boy, won't you look pretty in the press! I'm surprised you haven't already signed a book deal."

Riker smirked and jabbed back, "You need my help to recover all the weapons and intelligence your department can't seem to keep a grip on."

Jenkins brazenly added, "We also believe your four branches of Special Ops would *love* to get their hands on AWOL former teammates."

The Colonel raised his brows at the reality. "These burglars are our former troops..." He shook his head in disgrace. "How many have we ID'd?"

"Five so far," Jenkins replied. "Sir, there's a new storm that could arrive somewhere on the U. S. coast by Wednesday. Would you like see the suspects we've identified?"

"*See?*" Sturges was skeptical, "You have names and photos?"

Riker smiled. "Colonel, you'll be amazed how much we've pieced together." He pressed a button and a digital projector appeared from the ceiling. He tossed a remote control to Jenkins.

Agent Jenkins stepped to the podium. "We've ID'd five suspects so far. Using the ID of the dead soldier, along with clues from the surveillance, we've deduced a lot by studying relationships, military records, and even speaking with FBI profilers for possible motives."

The room's lights dimmed and the audience gazed towards the screen.

"I'll explain how we derived each name." Jenkins paused with drama and smiled. "Are you ready to meet the *CAT team*?"

The projector came to life and the screen glowed. The men's eyes widened with allure at the first, unexpected, face.

43. The Players

On the sixty-inch screen was the face of an exotically attractive female with raven hair. Expecting only hardened thugs, the men were stunned.

"Gentlemen, this is twenty-three-year old *Dalia Ana Covarrubias*," Jenkins announced. "She's the former Coast Guard pilot we heard on the surveillance. The lady who stole the Stingray."

"How'd you ID her?" Sturges asked with a slack jaw.

"We simply checked for lost Stingrays out of Key West. She was reported missing with the chopper seven months ago." He aimed his laser pointer, "You can see this photo's from an obituary. She was presumed dead."

Engel took a flurry of notes. Sturges was on the edge of his seat.

Jenkins continued, "We can guess at her character and motives based on records." He turned to the screen. "Ms. Covarrubias was raised in a Cuban household in Miami's Little Havana. By age sixteen she already had three arrests: two for shoplifting, one for a controlled substance. At seventeen, her family attempted a Medicaid claim for an induced abortion." He looked at the men, "We're guessing Dalia's hobbies conflicted with her Catholic schooling. A judge recommended the military to straighten her out. She lived on the coast, so her parents probably thought the Coast Guard seemed to be the least hostile option." He looked at the men for any questions.

Officer Engel scanned his notes. "Already, we got her on desertion, theft of military equipment and even insurance fraud if anyone benefitted from her bogus death." He looked up. "And that's *before* interstate theft, burglary or potential terrorism..?"

"Sounds fitting," Jenkins nodded. He aimed his remote and the screen filled with the face of a handsome, young black man —Pitch. "This man is Earl Snipes, formerly with Army Special Forces. We identified him by fingerprints on a dud grenade in St. Augustine when he tried to destroy a bridge." He cocked his head, "For those of you keeping score, destroying a public conveyance qualifies as an act of terrorism."

The men nodded at the shred of leverage.

"Mr. Snipes came from a poor, single-mother home in Louisiana. With impressive scores and abilities, he obtained a scholarship to West Point. He joined the Army, and was hand-picked for Special Forces within four years. His record was commendable."

"He was a *good* soldier?" The Colonel was appalled. "What's his motive?"

Jenkins replied, "Backgrounds reveal he has an elderly mother in Baton Rouge in an upscale assisted-living facility. He has a young brother who's a quadriplegic from diving in a shallow pond five years ago. Both family members have filed for bankruptcy. They both require extensive —and expensive— care. Mr. Snipes' motives may be purely financial."

Riker chuckled as he recalled, "There is one interesting detail: Mr. Snipes used to be a star pitcher for West Point's baseball team."

Sturges shouted at Riker, "What the hell's baseball got to do with any of this?"

Jenkins cleared his throat and proceeded to the next slide. The image was a grainy, ten-year-old photo of Tag. He looked like a bodybuilder, squinting in the desert sun. "This, of course, is our patient-in-custody, Donald 'Tag' Taggart." He looked at the men and smiled, "He was the easiest to ID. When he was waking out of his haze in the clinic, he mumbled his full name, rank and serial number, like the trained Marine he was."

"A *Marine*..." Sturges shook his head with disgust.

"He was a twenty-year soldier in Force-Recon. His career became tarnished four years ago in Iraq. He was being eyeballed for improper relations with a young girl. It would've been the end of his military life –and possible death in the Iraqi legal system. Before any inquest, he vanished." Jenkins lifted a stack of documents. "We located a bank account opened in Dubai. That account wired its balance to an account in the Caymans three years ago. *That* account paid for an annuity in a bank inside a Georgia Wal-Mart."

"Georgia? Is that where he lives?" Sturges asked.

"Off season," Jenkins smiled. "Twenty-year-old *Velma Saucer* of Martin, Georgia, receives income from Tag's Wal-Mart annuity. She's an unemployed beautician with a lake house that she'd never be able to afford."

"Is she his daughter?" Engel asked.

Jenkins almost laughed. "We sent agents to Georgia to find out. It seems Ms. Saucer –thirty years younger than Tag– brags about her Marine *husband*. Tag lives with her November through May, riding dirt bikes and fishing with her six-year-old son. Velma tells neighbors that Tag's away on 'missions' between June and October," Jenkins looked at the men, "–which is coincidentally the height of the storm season."

Sturges and Engel nodded simultaneously.

Jenkins transitioned to the next slide. "Tag was an acquaintance with this man in Iraq." The screen filled with a photo of ruggedly handsome man wearing a scuba suit."

The Colonel's jaw dropped, "The dead soldier I saw in the morgue."

"Yep. Our mystery corpse, James 'Butch' Hulett. A SEAL in Baghdad before being arrested for theft of weapon prototypes. He was on the CIA's 'warrant squad,' busting into suspects' homes in the middle of the night. Their credo, 'surprise and violence of action.'" He looked at the men. "Do the tactics sound familiar? The element of surprise, in the dark."

Jenkins continued, "He was caught in possession of stolen property." He rolled his hand at the men, "You remember: Saddam's palaces, looted for gold, art, jewels..." He turned to the screen. "A stash was hidden in his quarters. Butch was arrested, but escaped during a fake appendicitis. A year later he was a suspect in a robbery in Montreal. The court file's sealed, but he attempted some odd political defense. While the attorneys were busy bickering, he disappeared." Jenkins added with sarcasm, "Canada felt safe that a Navy SEAL could never escape with an ankle monitor during house arrest."

Engel spoke up, "You ID'd him through the chip in his neck?"

"Yes. The code was intact and the Navy confirmed his ID. We then reinserted the chip back into Butch's corpse."

Engel recoiled, "Why?"

Riker stood to reclaim the spotlight. "I believed the suspects would come back for his corpse —and I was correct." He smiled smugly. "We tracked the body to Larriott's last night, which is how we knew to go there." He shrugged, "Unfortunately, we've lost signal."

"Which gives a nice segue to Butch's brother." Jenkins clicked the remote. Onscreen was the sweaty, furious face of Curt. It looked like a mug shot. "This is Curtis Lee Hulett in happier days." Jenkins looked ominously at the men. "As we all know, Curt is the most dangerous."

"No, I don't know," Engel replied as if snubbed. "How's he worse than the others?"

Riker looked at Jenkins and then at the Sturges. "He doesn't know, Colonel."

"I don't know what?" Engel replied, exasperated.

"Curt is a monster." Riker stepped in front of the screen. He took a sip of water, paused, and then continued, "Curt was a sergeant at Parris Island. He drilled recruits through the 'Crucible' endurance test. It's a fifty-four hour exercise, marching forty miles carrying forty pounds plus ammo before a nine-mile run in full gear. It culminates with a climb up a hill called 'The Reaper.'" Riker looked at Engel. "Curt loved to deprive his men of food, water and sleep to simulate battle stress."

Riker glanced at his laptop to locate an image. The screen filled with a picture of a baby-faced teenager. "This is eighteen-year-old recruit Jackie Davies. Jackie threatened to report Curt for decreasing his sleep to three hours and cutting meals to one per day."

Riker paused. Uncharacteristic emotion swept across his face. He cleared his throat, "On his final nine-mile run, Jackie keeled over. Curt screamed for him to get up. He began to repeatedly kick the kid, not knowing he was already dead. Jackie Davies was eighteen; his parents had no other children." He clicked the slide back to the image of Curt.

Silence loomed in the room as the men absorbed Curt's angry, disturbing face.

After a tense silence, Riker added, "That was the same time Curt was beating his pregnant wife."

Colonel Sturges made fists and scowled. "That poor woman waited five years to run from this psycho?"

"What *poor woman*?" Engel raised his hands, not following.

"Yes Colonel," Riker replied, ignoring Engel. "Curt dragged her to Canada. She eventually wised-up, got the hell out of Dodge and changed her name." Riker changed the slide to the face of a familiar woman.

Engel huffed in frustration –until he turned towards the screen. He then understood. "That's..."

"Yep," Jenkins gave a bittersweet smile. "Curt's wife, was –of course– our Ms. 'Alexandra Larriott.'"

The room remained quiet as they gazed upon the face of their new detainee.

44. The Pardon

Astounded, Engel studied the fresh arrest photo. Alexandra's hair was disheveled and she had wide, feral eyes as if she'd been roused from her first sleep in days.

Inspired by the deluge of information, Engel began scribbling notes, drawing arrows to connect the facts. He deduced aloud, "So... Alexandra ran, escaping with all of Curt's assets. She knows his identity..." He looked up. "And he's the father to Ms. Larriott's daughter..."

No one needed to confirm the young analyst's conclusions.

Engel continued with his conjecture, "Curt tracked down and attacked Ms. Larriott, *in addition* to the crimes committed by him and his teammates. So..." He looked up, puzzled, "Why did we arrest her?"

The Colonel replied before Riker could. "Having been married to Curt, we believe Ms. Larriott can provide insight as to how the team operates." He turned to Riker, "Do you believe she knows *how* they choose their targets?"

Riker gave a menacing smile. "With enough thinly-veiled warnings to Ms. Larriott —and enough *sodium thiopental* pumped into Tag, I'm confident we'll know something soon."

The Colonel aimed a finger at Riker, "I don't want you laying a hand on that woman!"

"You have my word," Riker swore. "I have ways that won't require touching her in any *physical* way."

Alexandra was slouched on the floor of her cell like a discarded doll. A female guard had given her an Air Force t-shirt and sweat pants. The tiny cell had a toilet, sink and a small bench. The room reeked of some pine-scented cleanser. The walls were windowless steel as if she were a five-hundred pound gorilla.

Alexandra had finally been arrested. *It was inevitable*, she knew. She'd murdered a man —and it had been the wrong man. She'd never liked her ex brother-in-law Butch, but she never meant to kill him. Curt had found her. He was going to kill her and he'd brought his entire team of thieves to take everything back. In the stormy, raining darkness, she'd shot the wrong man.

She still couldn't get the vision of finding Butch's corpse out of her mind. *The swollen face, the red eyes...* And now she would pay for it. Ironic for a woman who'd been physically abused for so many years.

Alexandra splashed cold water on her face and smoothed back her hair. She had no idea what time it was. There'd been no attempt to give her breakfast or ask if she'd wanted something to drink. The cell was clearly not part of a typical detention center. Since the FBI arrested her, she'd probably be moved to a federal facility. If the sheriffs had arrested her, she would've been thrown in a county jail with whores and drug dealers. *There's a positive*, she thought cynically.

But there was another slight positive: she was now *positively* safe from her ex-husband Curt. She knew he was still alive; she could feel it. She'd witnessed the two masked soldiers carry him away. As long as she'd known Curt, he was unstoppable if he had a goal. He'd already tracked her over 1,600 miles from Montreal, despite her name change.

Alexandra flinched with a rush of memories from the night before.

Curt had been a rabid lunatic in her house. He would've undoubtedly slaughtered her and taken Cassie. Thank God for the insurance guy, Dan and Detective Stratton –yet Curt *still* managed to escape.

With a wisp of optimism, Alexandra knew –despite Curt's determination– he'd never be able to hurt her while she was locked in a steel vault in the center of an Air Force base.

But what about Cassie? Alexandra had slept with Cassie for only a few hours before the feds in suits barged-in to arrest her. They read her Miranda rights, announcing it was 7:32 a.m. Cassie never woke up and Alexandra never said goodbye. They cuffed her and dragged her away from her daughter like she was a calculated killer.

Alexandra prayed that Cassie had been given breakfast or at least entertained by some nice cadet in front of cartoons somewhere.

Her fragile body jerked at the *clank* of steel bolts unlocking. She turned and looked up to see the grim face of Agent Riker standing in her cell.

"Good morning Ms. Larriott," he paused, "–or should I call you *Elizabeth Louise Hulett*?"

She growled like a cornered dog, "Where's my daughter?"

"*Oooh*," Riker cringed. "There's a *teensy* problem with little Cassandra."

Alexandra's mouth fell open and her heart plummeted.

Riker pouted, "Due to your incarceration, your daughter needed to be placed in emergency foster care." He paused, "And the poor thing's taking the *news* very hard."

LeBeau adjusted his glasses and spoke softly in an attempt to appear solemn. "I believe Butch and Tag would've wanted us to remain a democracy."

Within their Lauderdale warehouse, LeBeau sat at the head of the conference table. The remaining team seemed detached. Pitch sat on one side of the table with his feet up. On the other side was Lex and Dalia, sitting close together.

"What's there to vote on?" Pitch asked, devoid of respect. "You've already crowned yourself king."

LeBeau maintained his odd smile and he steepled his fingers. "These have been trying times–" He paused as their next-door neighbor turned on a jackhammer. He blinked patiently at the thundering noise.

Dalia almost laughed watching pompous LeBeau trying to remain cool.

The jackhammer stopped. LeBeau tried again, "These have truly been trying times. Our devastating losses this week have been an enormous setback. We need to–" The jackhammer started again.

Pitch chuckled at LeBeau's attempt at some sort of motivational sermon.

The hammer stopped and LeBeau blurted, "We need to decide two things: Do we readmit Curt? And, in our current state, do we plan to crash the new storm, Tiberius?"

Dalia sat upright, "Did you see the noon update? Tiberius was upgraded to a Cat-3 and growing –and it's three days away. If you want to crash it, we're going to *need* Curt."

"Why do I *need* Curt?" LeBeau challenged in his flowery manner. "I see four of us who are more than knowledgeable."

"It's not just knowledge," Pitch retorted. "It's also physical manpower. Upper body strength and all? If you want to make plans for this storm, we need another man. It's too late to recruit someone new."

Dalia was unconvinced, "Does anyone actually believe Curt's learned his lesson? It's great you put him on a *time-out*, but how else can we possibly threaten him?"

LeBeau smiled, "I warned him. I think he understands."

"*You* scared him?" Pitch laughed. "He already had a wife who left him with all his money and his kid. Then she killed his brother. What else can you threaten him with?"

LeBeau shrugged, "I simply told him I'd inject him with ghetto-grade heroin. I'd then dump him in the Everglades for the gators to fight over. If any body parts are found, the tests would come back he was just a junkie. Then his *momma* in Pompano would find his safety deposit box filled with photos of ten-year old boys." LeBeau gave an icy grin. "He got the message."

The teammates were silenced by LeBeau's unsettling thought process.

"We're not killers," Pitch replied. "And we can't exactly fire Curt. He'd come after us."

"So we're keeping him out of fear?" LeBeau countered. "Ironic for a team that dresses up to scare homeowners."

Dalia spoke up to get the men back on task, "This storm could be *big* financially. It's projected to hit anywhere between Palm Beach and Key West. There's a lot of wealth there."

Pitch and Lex nodded.

"I know Curt's a pig," Dalia looked at the men. "But maybe running away and attacking his wife was some sort of...temporary insanity."

LeBeau sighed, "If the only way to crash this storm is with Curt, we need him on a very *short* leash."

Dalia, LeBeau and Pitch paused at their indecision. They simultaneously looked at Lex, who'd remained quiet with his hands behind his head.

"What?" He dropped the legs of his chair to the ground. "Why are you looking at me? I've never talked to the guy. I don't have a say here..?"

LeBeau smiled and his voice reverted into job-recruiter mode. "Alex, do you even want to be part of our little venture? We need your talents now more than ever."

"I'll be honest," Lex replied, "would you invest in a corporation that lost its CEO and two Vice Presidents in the same week?"

The team looked at each other.

"At this rate, we'll all be dead by Friday." Lex had a cynical smile, "If cops already have Butch *and* Tag's bodies, it's just a matter of time before they come knocking."

LeBeau sat an inch taller, "Both men had zero identifying features. They will *never* identify us. And your skills of hacking federal systems would help us immeasurably."

Dalia leaned close to Lex, "We need you to help balance Curt." She whispered with a flirtatious grin, "Try just one storm." She slid her hand down his inner thigh under the table. "Trust me; it's a *rush* like you've *never* had..."

Lex cracked an involuntary smile at her strange, almost-sexual passion.

LeBeau and Pitch smiled at each other. They knew their new man was onboard.

Pitch unbolted the rusted door to the filthy bathroom. In the dank room, Curt was on the floor, handcuffed to the plumbing.

Pitch didn't say a word until Curt looked up. His pale face was dirty and he squinted in the light like a man jailed in a cave. Curt lifted his brows as if awaiting a verdict.

"It's your lucky day," Pitch announced. "The Governor signed your pardon."

Curt cracked a smile.

Pitch bent closer to his head and whispered, "We also agreed that, if you even *consider* mentioning your ex-wife again, we'll sink bullets into your eyes. Got that, *Curtis*?"

The tranquil Curt said nothing. He nodded, presumably humbled.

"Agent Jenkins!" Navy Analyst Engel shouted, trying to catch up as they walked to the MacDill commissary.

Jenkins turned his head towards the young officer, but didn't slow his stride. "What's up?"

The gangly officer walked at his side. "Riker said you obtained that surveillance recording of Dalia by using a parabolic laser microphone?"

Jenkins nodded as he scanned the cafe's menu board. "The mic was hidden on a streetlamp. Why?"

Engel replied meekly, "*Usually,* microphones can be either parabolic or laser —not both."

Jenkins looked at him.

"If it's parabolic, it'd have a dome hood to capture sounds. It's pretty hard to hide," Engel gave a nervous chuckle. "If it's a *laser* mic, it uses a light beam to interpret sound waves through vibrations on distant windows." He shrugged, "It's two separate technologies."

Jenkins narrowed his eyes at Engel. "What are you suggesting?"

The smile dropped from Engel's face. "It's just that...the recording was so clear..? It just seemed..." His voice faded as his eyes locked onto Jenkins'.

Jenkins gazed at Engel for a beat and eventually smiled. "Probably some new gizmo out of DARPA's tech division."

Engel withered, "Yeah, I guess so."

45. Riddles in the Sand

"I'll take the Country Boy Slam combo," Dan smiled at Brandi, the Cracker Barrel server. "Eggs over easy, with the country ham, hash brown casserole —with cheddar— and surprise me with either corn muffins or biscuits."

Brandi, with her big-hair and dimples, looked at Nadine, "Hon, are you *sure* you just want cottage cheese and peaches?"

"Yes," Nadine smiled. Brandi grinned and waddled off. Nadine lifted her phone. "I guess if I need to call the office, I should get it over with."

That morning, having heard the devastating news that Alexandra had been arrested, Dan and Nadine bolted out of their beds. They took showers and got ready: fifteen minutes for Dan, forty-five for Nadine. Dan was fine with wearing the same shirt from the night before. Nadine recoiled at the thought and bought two counterfeit Mickie *(sic)* Mouse t-shirts at the motel's front desk.

Nadine said she had no appetite, but understood if Dan needed something in his stomach for their two-hour ride home. Dan saw a billboard for Cracker Barrel and the car steered itself.

When Dan opened the door to the restaurant, he was hit with a scent that instantly calmed his stress: potpourri with a hint of cinnamon, laced with the divine aroma of frying bacon. Douse it with coffee, and he'd be ready to strategize with a clear mind.

Nadine clicked off her phone as Brandi dropped off two coffees and corn muffins.

Dan's jaw dropped, "You just called in sick during a disaster?"

She was unashamed, "I worked almost forty hours straight since the storm. I haven't been sick in a year." She sipped her coffee, "Rodka's glad I'm out of his hair."

Dan smiled at her swagger. For a lady who'd been through what they'd experienced, she glowed with confidence. Even in her tacky tourist t-shirt.

"I can work from anywhere," Nadine reasoned. "I have my laptop with access to FDLE and NCIC. I can search criminal records without anyone looking over my shoulder." She leaned in, "With the feds on the case, there has to be preexisting criminal files somewhere."

Dan nodded, "I have access to public records and the National Insurance Crime Bureau. I can search for similar insurance claims across the country. I'm sure other companies have been hit."

Nadine spoke faster as the caffeine hit her bloodstream, "And what about Alexandra? I refuse to believe there are zero records on her —even if she is from Montreal."

"She purchased a house, there has to be property records." Dan sipped his coffee and focused on a nearby fireplace that seemed out of place in Florida. "Some things don't make sense. There has to be a reason the feds —*and* the burglars— are so fascinated with Alexandra."

"I just thought of a slight problem."

"What?"

"My condo has no power or internet. I don't want to huddle in some hectic Starbucks. Do you know anywhere quiet that actually has power and Wi-Fi?"

Dan's eyebrow went up.

"How's this for an office?" Dan waved his hand towards the beach from under their Tiki hut. It was a small picnic table with a palm-thatched roof behind Dan's motel. It was situated on a white-sand beach, fifty feet from the pool of the Marco Island Inn.

Nadine flashed a wide smile, "I'd be a much better person if I worked here every day." She took a seat and gazed at her surroundings as if she hadn't seen a beach in years. She opened her laptop, closed her eyes and took a deep breath of ocean breeze. "Why haven't I tried this before?"

Dan smiled, "The motel has Wi-Fi with a 300-foot range. Two kids helped me drag this table here yesterday until the signal was perfect." He sat across from Nadine, proud of his makeshift office. "If you'll notice, it's the exact midpoint between the bar and the beach. Mike at the bar gave me an extension cord for our laptops." He pulled a stack of files from his backpack and fired-up his computer.

Nadine stretched her neck to each side and began typing on her keyboard. She spread out several files and scribbled information. She looked at her screen. "Yep, I'm online, got my email and cell. Perfect."

Dan logged-in to his company's intranet and opened a thick folder. They breathed audible sighs of relief, with each second sanding away the stress from their prior twenty-four hours. They were unintentionally quiet, engulfed in a symphony of ocean waves, seagulls and faraway children. The motel's hidden speakers played faint steel-drum music. The breeze carried the scent of someone's Coppertone.

Nadine's serenity was disrupted as she focused on her screen. "Oh no."

Dan looked up, snapped out of his reverie.

"This morning, Rodka emailed me about Alexandra's arrest." She looked at Dan, "*He* didn't arrest her –the FBI did." She read from her screen, "The feds leaned on the U.S. Attorneys to arrest Larriott." She looked up, her face flawed by a hurt expression, "The feds have taken away my case *—our* case!"

"How can they just take it?"

She scrolled through the message. "It's not like the movies where the FBI marches in and 'takes over' a case. We usually have good relationships with our local feds. They call us for help and vice versa." She pointed at her screen. "According to this, the Tampa FBI arrested her for *federal* offenses."

"Agent Riker's with Tampa FBI," Dan recalled. He ran his hands through his hair, frustrated. "Why do government agents care about a single mother who shot a damn burglar?"

"The FBI doesn't investigate domestic, self-defense killings. Do they think she knows something?" She shook her head and began typing. "I'm running her name through FDLE. Something's *got* to come up."

Nadine hit enter and she frowned, "Alexandra's lived here six months and never had a driver's license?" She spoke louder with disbelief, "The name 'Alexandra Larriott' has no public records except the property listing for her house. Impossible!"

Dan remained calm in an effort to restore focus. "Okay. Let's think about what we *do* know." He gazed at the clouds as he recited a mental list, "Her married name is Alexandra Larriott. We need to find her maiden name. She bought an enormous house six months ago; there's probably a mortgage." His eyes twinkled with an idea. "It could get me fired, but I can run a credit report. She gave us a social security number, so I–"

"–Dan," Nadine interrupted. "I do have one place I can get her records if she's from Montreal." She paused until he looked at her. "Would it bother you if I called my 'ex' in Michigan? He offered to check Canadian records."

He smiled. "Nadine, why should I care if you call your ex?"

"No reason," she shrugged. "He's with the Attorney General with contacts across the border." She gave a coy smile, "I don't mind if you call your ex –but only if she can help with the case."

"I don't think so," Dan smiled. "She works at Target."

Nadine laughed and they locked eyes until a warm breeze fluttered their papers.

"I'll try the NICB." Dan resumed typing, "The National Insurance Crime Bureau is made up of a thousand carriers that report claims that appear suspicious. They may have bulletins for any crime trends."

"Like burglaries *during* hurricanes," her eyes smiled as she understood.

He pressed enter and his eyes widened. "Bingo." He nodded, "According to this, there's been a spike of thefts reported during hurricanes." He rotated his computer to show Nadine. "I entered the dates for the last three named storms. There are countless wind and flood claims —but I searched for *burglary* claims. To make it significant, I searched for thefts over $25,000." He pointed to a spreadsheet on his screen. "These are spikes in high-dollar burglaries supposedly committed *during* the storms."

Nadine scanned the information, "So these thieves have been busy?"

"I can check by zip code in flood zones." He turned the computer and began to type. After a minute, "The burglaries that seem suspicious are all from coastal areas —from North Carolina to Texas." He looked at Nadine, "Evacuation zones."

Nadine nodded as she followed along, "What *people* are equipped and trained to invade in such severe conditions?"

"Witnesses describe them as 'soldiers.'" Dan kept the ball rolling, "*Soldiers* trained for all-weather, high-danger exposures?"

Nadine continued their stream of thoughts, "...Like Navy SEALS or any special forces."

"Colonel Sturges is with the —"

"—Special Operations Command," they exclaimed together.

Dan nodded, "Sturges oversees Special Operations for each branch of the military."

They paused and turned to grin at nine-year-old twins running after a Frisbee. A breeze caught the disk, sending it into bushes over a fence. The little girl twin shouted in a high voice, "Jack, it got away...!"

Dan's eyes narrowed. "They got away. Trained and equipped with weapons and intelligence. *That's* why a Special Ops Colonel is determined to find them. It'd be a humiliating national scandal to have government-armed thugs terrorizing citizens –who are *already* panicked by approaching storms."

Nadine didn't blink as she scanned the beach, absorbing the concept. "But it doesn't explain why they want Alexandra."

Dan gritted his teeth, "What information does she have that they want?" He shook his head. "Call your ex. There's gotta' be something on Alexandra Larriott."

"What do you want from me?" Alexandra bellowed from the floor of her small cell. "Where'd you put my daughter?"

"Now, that's two very different questions." Agent Riker had a lopsided grin. "Which answer do you want first?"

46. How to T.C.B.

Alexandra's eyes drilled holes into Riker. "I know my rights!" She hissed, "I want my daughter!"

Riker didn't immediately reply. He dusted off his pant legs and sat in front of her on the cell's bench. "Clearly you've seen a lot of movies —when not getting slapped by your ex-hubby. But, in the *real world*, you —the arrestee— can remain in FBI custody until the initial court appearance. The rule is it must occur without 'unnecessary delay.'" He straightened his jacket collar and smiled. "In this state, forty-eight hours has been deemed a reasonable timeframe. So we have you here for two days to think about things."

Alexandra did not blink. She asked more firmly, "*Where* is my daughter?"

Riker replied with mock sympathy, "Unfortunately, I had the *duty* to contact the Florida Department of Children and Families." He fluttered his eyes, "You see, when a single parent is incarcerated, the DCF typically tries to find a local family member or relative to care for the child."

"I don't have any relatives!"

"Therein lies my problem," Riker cringed. "We're not permitted to leave your daughter with just any ole' neighbor or friend. They could be perverts." He chuckled, "And your ex-husband doesn't seem to be up for the task."

Alexandra growled like a protective lioness, "Where is she?"

"The DCF had no choice but to place Cassie in emergency foster care. But don't worry, we have families on waiting lists to accept children at any hour of the day. Especially clean, young, pretty ones with no juvenile records."

Alexandra wiped her eyes and stood. She inhaled with renewed fortitude. Her voice became more composed, "What do you want from me?"

"That's the spirit!" Riker exclaimed. "All we want to know is one teensy thing." He paused for emphasis, "How does your husband and his *Rain Nazis* choose their targets?"

She shook her head, struggling to contain her emotion. "I don't know."

He snapped, "You were married to the guy for seven years and you have *no* idea how they pick their targets?"

"No!"

Riker took a moment to smooth his hair. "Ms. Larriott, I'm worried we may need you here longer than I'd originally anticipated."

"You can't do that!"

Riker shot back, "I can convince any judge that you have knowledge relevant to terrorist activities."

She recoiled, "They're not terrorists and you know it!"

"Oh..." Riker smiled. "So, you *do* know what they're up to?" He stood from the bench and peeked out the small window on the door. He turned back to Alexandra and sighed, "Ms. Larriott —or whatever your name is," he spoke with an unexpected gentle voice. "I *need* you."

Alexandra was surprised at his change in demeanor. Riker was momentarily halting his act of absurd intimidation.

"Between you and me," he whispered, "I need to know their next target so we can be there waiting." Riker displayed a glimmer of sincerity. "I *need* this. This is your chance to do something. And imagine us capturing your scumbag husband. I'll take care of him personally." He furled his brows and smiled.

Alexandra paused and looked at the floor. "What if I *really* don't know?" She stepped closer, "I know what you know: they steal from evacuated houses and businesses. They use the fear of the storm to their advantage." She looked Riker in the eye, "I don't know more than that, and you can't keep me here forever."

Riker conceded with a shrug, "You're right. And little Cassie will eventually be returned to you." He turned towards the door. "It's a shame; her little foster brothers will really miss her."

"Who?" Alexandra winced.

He turned and replied matter-of-factly, "The fifteen-year-old foster brothers she'll be meeting in a few hours. With all those hormones, teenage boys are so..." he paused, "*curious* about girls at that age. Especially young, pretty girls." He pulled the door open to exit.

"Wait!" Alexandra reached for his shoulder.

Riker halted with a grin.

Tag's bruised head was turned towards the blinds of his hospital window. He could see clouds and faraway palms. He could hear the sound of traffic, including the approaching purr of diesels. *Sounds like motorcycles...* he thought as he drifted in and out of a dream.

He imagined being on his dirt bike in Martin, Georgia. Riding a few trails before bass fishing and tubing off his pontoon in Lake Hartwell. A few Jack and Cokes and then sex with his young redneck wife. A perfect summer day.

But he knew he would never go home. Even if he was freed by some miracle, he could never return to his old life. His own team thought he was dead. The feds could fabricate charges to warrant an execution by treason. Tag chuckled despondently that his best-case scenario was to be shackled in some black-site prison for the rest of his life.

Outside, the motorcycle sounds faded. It wasn't his teammates coming to bust him out. Tag was let down, again by the team that had left him for dead.

"Good afternoon, Mr. Taggart," Agent Riker merrily danced into the room. He had a smile plastered across his face like he'd won the lottery.

Tag was reclined in his bed, one arm still cuffed to a rail. He turned his head to see Riker, accompanied by the morose, frog-like doctor. The agent approached Tag. The doctor reached for the hanging drip bag.

"Have you had time to think, Mr. *Traitor*, I mean Taggart?" Riker grinned.

Tag rolled his eyes to the doctor who was injecting the contents of a syringe into his IV. Tag asked in a weak voice, "Meds to make it look like a heart attack?"

"I don't want you dead –yet." Riker watched the doctor finish with the syringe. "Doctor, can you close the door on your way out?"

The doctor frowned at Riker. He exited the room and closed the door.

Riker tapped the IV leading into Tag's free arm. "It's *sodium thiopental*. It decreases higher brain functions. Psychiatrists feel that lying is more complex than telling the truth, so suppression of those higher functions might lead to you actually telling the truth." He chuckled, "But I'm not sure you have any *higher* brain functions."

Tag stared into his eyes and said nothing.

"Mr. Taggart, I'm one for one today, and I hope I'm on a roll," Riker boasted with a cocky grin. "I need to double check some info. I'm just tryin' to T.C.B."

Tag furled his brow.

"You know, T.C.B..? That's what Elvis's belt buckle had on it. It means *Takin' Care of Business*. So just *relax...*" Riker stepped close, "Let the meds work their magic. Just as I promised –and as soon as you're healed– you'll have a brand new, preteen girlfriend in Pattaya, Thailand. You'll have a new life in paradise."

Tag continued to glare, emotionless.

"So let's begin," Riker cleared his throat. "How did Curt locate his wife?"

Tag's eyes dimmed. A single tear rolled down his chiseled cheek. It was time to talk.

Agent Riker whisked past a guard and into Colonel Sturges' office with a ridiculous grin. His shadow, Agent Jenkins, kept up at his side. Riker approached the Colonel's mahogany desk and slapped it with both hands. "I found out how they do it!"

The Colonel looked up with a glower that said *this had better be good.*

"I know how they choose their targets," Riker beamed. "It's the *same* way they found Larriott. It's so mindless, we missed it entirely."

47. The Buried Mole

Riker looked to the right of the Colonel to see a blonde lady in a stylish suit sitting in a chair. "Oh —am I interrupting..?"

"What'd you find?" Sturges asked curtly.

Riker seemed wary of the woman who was mid-thirties and attractive. She looked familiar, "You're with the bureau... Miss..." he couldn't place the name.

"*Agent* Louise Capell," she corrected without offering her hand, "Miami FBI."

Riker looked at the Colonel, annoyed. "You're meeting a fellow agent without me here?"

"She came to us," Sturges replied tersely. "She may have information on the team's leader —which *you've* been unable to identify."

"Their leader?" Riker's eyes lit with skeptical delight. He and Jenkins pulled two chairs from the wall and sat inches from Capell. "We've been trying for weeks..." He stammered, "How do you know their leader? Is his name '*LeBeau*'?"

Colonel Sturges interrupted, "Agent Capell is the head of the bureau's Art Crime Team."

"Art Crimes?" Riker recoiled. "You're asking an expert on *Norman Rockwell* about our terrorist–"

"–Shut up and listen for once!" Sturges barked. Capell smiled at her notes. The Colonel grinned at the lady, "Agent Capell, perhaps you can explain –*again*– what you do."

"Gentlemen," Capell nodded at Riker and Jenkins with poise. "In addition to recovering *Norman Rockwells*," her eyes flashed with sarcasm, "Our department's uncovered more than $225 million in art, to date. Art crime is estimated as high as six billion a year, making it the fourth-highest international crime after drugs, weapons, and money laundering."

The agents seemed impressed as they absorbed the figures.

"Art's an easy way to move stolen assets around the globe," Capell continued. "Laundering cash through banks is too risky. It's unwise to load your car with drugs. But anyone can put a $50 million painting in the back of their car and drive across four countries without questions." She smiled, "Speaking of Norman Rockwell, in 2007 the FBI discovered that Steven Spielberg owned a stolen Rockwell painting, *Russian Schoolroom* he'd innocently purchased in 1989. It had been stolen from a gallery thirty years earlier."

Riker squinted to understand. "So...how is *our* team mixed up in this?"

"One of our agents in Miami was contacted by Canadian intermediaries, saying they knew someone who could get us stolen Jean-Luc Brulé's."

"The French painter?" Agent Jenkins asked.

"Yes," Capell replied. "Brulé's are highly sought after in theft circles." She pulled a color photo of an oil painting from a file. "This painting was stolen during war looting from Baghdad's National Museum." She showed the men the painting of a French general on a white horse. "Our suspect offered to steal it by the end of this month."

Riker gave an animated shrug, "Big deal..?"

She waved the picture in her hand, "The *big deal* is I got this photo yesterday from an insurance adjuster working the storm."

Capell flashed a smile, "This painting was claimed stolen by your detainee, Alexandra Larriott."

Riker scrunched his face with confusion. "How'd you get involved?"

"Insurance companies have a statutory duty to report suspicious claims to authorities," Capell explained. "When a report was submitted involving rare art, the Division of Insurance Fraud contacted me. I plan to meet with the insurance investigator–"

"–Who's the investigator?" Jenkins interrupted.

She looked at her notes, "Daniel Holms with Insurex..?"

The agents smirked at the familiar name. Riker looked at Capell. "How does this relate to the leader of our team?"

"The suspect who met our undercover fits the profile of your team," Capell replied. "And his name fits with the name you just mentioned: *LeBeau*."

Colonel Sturges looked at Riker. "How did *you* know the name 'LeBeau'?"

Riker paused, "I believe it was mentioned on the surveillance tape."

Jenkins interjected, "Is LeBeau ex-military? Maybe a mercenary?"

Capell laughed. "A soldier? Not even close." She cleared her throat, "*Christian LeBeau,* was a French-Canadian antique dealer." She paused, "But he must have some fascination with the military. He applied to the Canadian Army three times. Rejected for ulcers. He fled to America to avoid tax evasion."

Sturges spoke up, "Without any objections, I'd like Agent Capell to be part of our team."

Riker feigned a smile, "Welcome aboard."

"Thank you, gentlemen," Capell smiled. "Maybe you can now share what you know?"

Colonel Sturges looked at Riker. "You barged in here saying you know how the team finds their targets." He paused, "Well?"

Riker leaned on the Colonel's desk with drama. "You won't believe the simplistic way the team finds targets: they constantly review publications, newspapers and magazines. You've seen those fluff stories about narcissistic locals. Stories describing their fortunes, complete with color layouts of their lavish homes. The subjects even wear their jewelry and brag of their vacations to Europe."

"Articles?" Sturges asked. "For all their targets?"

"At least the high-profile ones." Riker explained, "They search the news daily for the entire southeastern seaboard. Vanity stories of charity balls held in homes on Hilton Head. A famous designer's mansion on South Beach." He pivoted towards Capell, "Last year, they hit a wealthy Palm Beach heiress who publicized an Easter egg hunt at her estate. In one magazine, a photo showed a centerpiece boasting her collection of Fabergé eggs. They were stolen two months later. The ninety-year old widow didn't stand a chance."

Capell gasped, "The stolen Palm Beach Faberge's. I know that case!"

Jenkins continued, "Alexandra Larriott was profiled in a magazine, an article titled, '*Captiva's Newest Art Collector.*' The story showed her, her house, her art... That's how the team found her."

"Pretty stupid for someone trying to hide from her husband," Sturges scoffed.

"No one said she's a genius, "Riker nodded. "She figured 1,600 miles away was safe."

Agent Capell interjected, "Maybe we can search publications to predict their next target."

Sturges protested, "We're getting off-task. Who cares about their next target?" He stabbed a finger in the air, "We should arrest them *now* for national security!" He looked at Riker, "You know the location of their hangar. We have more than enough probable cause."

Riker shook his head emphatically. "The financial data isn't there. If we raid their compound, we believe they have safeguards that'll destroy their hard drives. We need to watch them. I want to know where they keep the loot."

"*Loot?*" the Colonel mocked. "What are you, a pirate? This isn't about treasure! It's about stolen military intelligence in the hands of terrorists!"

Jenkins and Louise Capell remained quiet, letting the senior men debate.

Riker replied brazenly, "You don't care about terrorism. We all know the *real* reason you want them." He sharpened his eyes, "For all the stolen classified intelligence from the Navy, Marines, Army *and* Air Force. No *single* department has ever had that much cross-information. If you got your hands on them, you'd be like a coach that has every team's playbook."

Sturges seethed, flustered. He smirked at Riker, "Look at you: the bureau's falling star. You're in panic-mode after two public strikes against you. You've already had your hand slapped for improper investigations. You're praying for redemption, with a final big score before riding off into the sunset. In addition to a fat book deal, I can see your shitty grin on 60 Minutes: '*Fall of the Storm Crashers...*'"

"I have an idea," Agent Capell spoke to break the tension.

The men paused and looked at her.

She gave a calming smile. "If the suspects search for news stories, what if we plant a *fake* article?" She looked at the men. "Maybe we can submit false stories to the cities in the storm's projected path."

The men looked at each other. The Colonel mused aloud, "Putting a worm on a hook..." He looked at Riker. "We could be there waiting."

Capell continued, "Tiberius could hit anywhere between Palm Beach and Key West within three days. We can plant stories to the metro papers in those target areas."

Jenkins blurted, "—We can leak something to our man!"

Riker spun to face Jenkins with flaming eyes. Jenkins froze as if spotted by Medusa.

"Leak something to your *man*?" The Colonel repeated with fists on his hips. He cocked his head in disbelief. "Your man..? Have you had a mole on the team this entire time?"

Riker pursed his lips and looked down. Everyone stared at him, waiting for a response.

The Colonel's eyes danced around the office as he assembled the pieces. "*That's* how you knew the players' names and got such crystal-clear surveillance!" After no reply he barked, "Well..?"

Riker folded his arms. He looked at Agent Jenkins, and then back to Sturges. "Colonel, we do have an agent embedded within the burglary team."

Sturges stated brusquely, "You better have a *goood* reason why I wasn't told."

Riker replied like a politician, "Colonel, I made a deliberate decision to not inform you in order to insulate you and provide plausible deniability. You can deny awareness of any such act, or knowledge of any agents used to carry out such act."

The Colonel sat back down. In doing so, the tension in the room also eased. After a moment he replied, "You should know that, as a career intelligence officer, I cannot be afforded plausible deniability." He looked at Riker and Jenkins, "But you said you're protecting me from something. That means you screwed up somewhere. Start talking."

Riker continued, "I was working Cyber Crimes, monitoring chat rooms. We found a player who fit the profile of a renegade soldier. To seize the moment, I put an agent undercover. It was my opinion that chat rooms were not private enough to be afforded Fourth Amendment protection. I figured someone blabbing on a website was akin to speaking in public.

"My agent's involvement escalated and we were already in too deep. I never received *official* approval for the project from our SAC —our Special Agent in Charge. My agent then received electronic messages that *might've* violated the Communications Assistance for Law Enforcement Act." Riker looked at Capell to clarify his point, "In a *perfect world*, we should've obtained the evidence only by court order after showing probable cause that a crime's being committed. We never had proof of any *specific* crime, so we never pursued any court orders."

The Colonel leaned back in his squeaky leather chair and drummed his fingers on the desk. "So right now, you don't have legally-obtained *cause* to raid their compound. Any of your evidence would be thrown out. *That's* why you want to catch them in the act."

Riker leaned towards the Colonel, insistent. "We all know what they're doing. And we now have Tag and Larriott as witnesses. It'd be *perfect* to catch them committing a crime. You'd get your weapons, intelligence and soldiers back. I'd get the millions in property and a triumph against terror. It's a win-win-win."

Sturges turned to the attentive Louise Capell. "If you helped us create a phony news article to bait the team, how would you do it?"

Capell smiled, honored to be asked. "I can suggest rare valuables that we can photograph and publish." She looked at Jenkins. "Where's the storm's most probable target?"

"On the two o'clock update, the center of the storm's projection is Miami," Jenkins replied. "Regardless if it veers 200 miles north or south, it's a safe bet Key Biscayne will be evacuated. It's a barrier island off the coast of downtown Miami. Only three feet above sea level." He smiled with a thought, "If you're from Miami, I'm sure you have contacts at the Miami Herald."

"I do," Capell smiled with perfect teeth.

"How fast can you submit something?" Sturges asked.

Capell shrugged, "Within an hour..? The Herald won't come out until tomorrow morning, but we can get something on their online edition right away."

For the first time, both Sturges and Riker smiled in harmony.

Jenkins spoke with mounting enthusiasm, "We'll make sure the article has numerous photos and vivid descriptions. As soon as we know it's online, I'll have our informant bring the article to the storm team's attention. That way, they will *absolutely* know about it."

"So whoever suggests the target to the team is the mole..." Colonel Sturges gave an almost envious sneer to Riker, "I gotta' know: which one of those characters is your mole?"

48. The Dresden Red Diamond

At the CAT team's mission control, Dalia and Lex sat side by side at large monitors. Lex was busy typing at his keyboard. Dalia was engrossed in satellite images of the Atlantic.

Lex ran his fingers through his hair and growled.

"Can't crack the federal system?" Dalia asked, focused on her screen.

He typed his keys harder. "Encryption's been modified."

"What about trying a primitive local system like the sheriff's office?"

"Not bad." He gave a charming smirk. "If the feds are communicating with local cops, the same info might be there." Lex smiled at her. "You the only one with brains around here?"

Dalia batted her smoky eyes and smiled. "What do you mean?"

"Why are you the only member who doesn't steal or use weapons?"

Her smile faded, unsure where he was going. "I'm a pilot, so I was hired as a pilot." Her Spanish accent grew more prominent. "My job is to get everyone in and out alive. I'm not a fanatic and I'm not a killer."

"Whoa..." Lex smiled. "*I meant* the others seem like hardened thugs. You're not like them. You're clean, young and actually have a brain."

Her smile returned. "You were also hired for your brain. We all read about your arrests. You hacked some pretty big systems."

Lex squinted at his screen. "I ain't doing so hot right now. I'll try to hack into Lee Sheriffs' less-encrypted email."

"–Hey guys!" Pitch shouted from behind. He approached Dalia and Lex with outstretched arms touching each of their chairs. "What'd I miss?"

"Where have you been?" Dalia asked, annoyed at his absence. "On your phone as usual?"

Pitch looked at her, defensive, "What's that mean? I been speaking to my *real* family. Some of us actually have outside lives." He smiled, "Six more weeks and this season's over!"

"Relax," Dalia snapped. "*Emperor* LeBeau was looking for you."

Pitch seemed concerned. "Our perfumed prince is looking for me?" He looked over his shoulder and lowered his voice. "I realize he's now our CEO, but are either of you concerned about how fast we're losing our men?"

Lex and Dalia stopped typing and looked at him.

Pitch checked over his shoulder again, "After Butch got killed, LeBeau, Tag *and* Curt practically dueled to take over. Now that Tag's dead, I notice that LeBeau–"

"–Someone mention my name?" LeBeau called from behind the three. They turned to see LeBeau standing with his frozen grin. At his side was a pale and expressionless Curt. LeBeau approached and placed a hand on Pitch's shoulder. "Anything I need to hear?"

Pitch blinked, unable to reply. Dalia turned back to her screen.

"Actually, yes." Lex spoke up, filling the awkward silence. He pointed to his screen. "I'm trying something new."

LeBeau adjusted his glasses and leaned towards Lex's monitor. "Really..?"

Lex typed quickly as he replied, "I'm stalking a county system. Today's basic security sometimes misses simple things."

"Like what?" Curt grunted.

Lex explained as he worked, "Governments and businesses spend millions to safeguard their data. But their overly-complex systems require only basic hacking. Their networks have become a jumble of mediocre ideas stitched together like a mismatched quilt, creating security holes I can play with." Lex looked at LeBeau as he typed. "Companies now use Wi-Fi to transmit data from registers, price scanners, etc. because it's cheaper than laying cable. It's child's play grabbing those signals. Businesses forget routine things like texting. Employees text their coworkers, bosses, and straight into their own email. These messages –sent by cellphones– can escape the security of their office systems."

"You just seize the signals in the air." LeBeau smiled as he followed along.

Pitch moved closer to observe. "The sheriffs have just one cell tower."

Lex nodded, "I'm catching signals before they reach their protected systems." After a pause, his screen filled with pages of illegible digital code.

Pitch shook his head. "Looks like Chinese."

"I'll use a word-extractor that'll isolate 'human' words from machine code. It could show any hidden texts."

The team was silent as Lex quietly scanned, inches from his monitor. He shook his head, "A lot of useless info: traffic stops, weather..." He perked up with an idea, "I'll comb the text for key terms like 'burglary,' or 'Larriott.'" He moved closer to his screen.

After three eternal minutes, LeBeau blurted, "Well? Do you see anything?"

Lex ran his finger along the screen as he read to himself. He paused and then turned with a grave expression. "This morning, Alexandra Larriott was arrested by the FBI. Charged for the murder of a James 'Butch' Hulett." He looked at LeBeau, "Wasn't he your leader–"

"–They *finally* arrested her?" Curt shouted with a mix of fury and joy, "The legal system *actually* works?"

"I said drop it!" LeBeau hissed like a cobra, "Enough with your wife!"

Curt matched his glare but said nothing.

Pitch stated the obvious, "They discovered his name..." No one replied, grasping the implication: the feds were getting closer than they'd presumed.

LeBeau raised his voice in a show of control, "We can't worry about the feds. We need to move *fast* with Tiberius!" He looked at the four, "We need potential targets *immediately*. Have any of you found a target?"

No one replied. The four sighed and skimmed their eyes across the monitors.

LeBeau shouted, "You *all* have been researching the entire coast for twelve hours and you've found nothing?"

After a deafening silence, Lex meekly raised his hand. "I'm new at this, but I *may* have found something."

His teammates looked at the new guy, skeptical.

Lex clicked to a news story on his monitor. "I'm not sure if this is what you're looking for, but here's something in the Miami Herald. They profiled a Mrs. Eve Glassburn, some British aristocrat who lives in Miami." He squinted at his screen, "It says she owns the priceless 'Dresden Red Diamond.' It's 26.9 carats, named after the capital of Saxony, Germany. Her insurance company's upset because she insists on keeping it at her estate on Key Biscayne." He looked at his teammates and shrugged. "Is that something we'd be interested in?"

The team was awestruck. A slow grin unfurled on LeBeau's lips. He turned to the others. "I told you this guy would be brilliant!"

Lex's smile appeared to be that of pride. *New guy has a great idea!* Not one of the egocentric thugs had any clue the smile was in disbelief of their gullibility. *A lady would leave a 27 carat diamond in her home? During a hurricane?* Hey, whatever works, Lex smirked.

Lex's acceptance into the team was now complete. His pretend apprehension about joining helped seal the deal. It had gotten to the point they'd begged him to participate. No one was suspicious how an alleged convict could so easily "hack" law enforcement systems. His fictional criminal records, back-dated and uploaded by the bureau, had convinced LeBeau and his fellow teammates. Riker always said ex-soldiers weren't necessarily Mensa candidates.

Lex's next step would be to find a way to avoid being thrown into the storm. Flying into a hurricane with a helicopter full of criminals was not part of the assignment. "Lex" would await his official orders from Agent Riker in the fusion center.

It was comforting that only his federal partners knew about the "CAT team." The local police departments had been effectively suppressed. After LeBeau and Tag's bike chase on Fort Myers Beach, the sheriffs were told it was a national security matter and all records were expunged. The government didn't need competing interests chasing the same prize. Bumbling street cops didn't need to be tripping up Uncle Sam. No one would investigate something they didn't know existed. Even "Alexandra Larriott" had been finally locked up and silenced.

Lex sat back and grinned as his *teammates* fawned over his skills. He was finally convinced that no outsiders were investigating Larriott, her ex-husband, or this arrogant CAT team. No outside parties knew anything about this.

Speechless, Detective Nadine Stratton turned off her phone and gazed across the beach. She repeated the words in disbelief, "Alexandra Larriott is not her name... Her husband's a fugitive soldier..."

Without blinking, she mused under her breath, "Someone needs to know about this!"

49. Witness for the Province Of Quebec

"It's three o'clock somewhere!" Dan sang poorly, carrying two Coronas from the poolside bar.

He'd breezed by his room for a bathing suit and t-shirt. Approaching their Tiki hut on the beach, his smile faded when he saw Nadine's expression. "What's wrong?"

She dropped her phone on the table and looked like she'd seen a ghost. "That was Tom from Michigan."

"He found records on Larriott?"

She shook her head in a daze. "There's a reason we can't find anything."

He put the beers down and stood at her side.

"There is no 'Alexandra Larriott.'" She paused for emphasis, "Her name's 'Elizabeth Hulett.' She's in the Canadian Witness Protection Program."

Dan recoiled, "Protection from what?"

"From *whom*," Nadine corrected. "Her ex-husband. She's not a widow."

Dan looked like he'd been hit by an unseen punch. "Our poor

widow's...not a widow? Is he at least an art dealer?"

"No," her reply was swift. "He's an ex-Marine who was court-martialed for killing a man."

Dan sat as if his knees could take no more. "I think you need to color in a few details."

Nadine skimmed her notes, "Tom couldn't find any record of Larriott —until he ran her by his contacts at the Royal Canadian Police. Canada has a witness relo' program similar to the U.S."

Dan sipped his beer as he followed along.

"The Royal Police administers the 'Witness Protection Program Act.'" She read her scribble, "It provides for the relo of witnesses with information of interest to the police or who fear for their safety. Protection to kids or adults who witness a crime and wish to cooperate with authorities. They helped Alexandra and her daughter move 1,600 miles away. Another Canadian Service —New Identities for Victims of Abuse— provided them new names."

"So she's a victim of abuse," he concluded, "—by her husband?"

She nodded, locating a specific note. "Her ex-husband's name is 'Curtis Hulett.' Tom ran his name for criminal records. Curtis was arrested in Canada after his wife, Elizabeth —aka Alexandra— reported him for physical abuse. Canadian authorities then discovered he was a fugitive from the U.S."

"You said he killed someone?"

"He's an ex-Marine," her tone emphasized the words. "Charged for the murder of a recruit during basic training. Alexandra offered to testify against him in exchange for protection. She was made witness for the Province of Quebec." Nadine looked up from her notes. "That's when 'Elizabeth Hulett' ceased to exist, and 'Alexandra Larriott' was born."

Dan looked at their table littered with notes. "So her husband's finally in jail?"

"No." She leaned forward as if savoring a punch line. "He's missing. As Canadian and U.S. attorneys fought over deporting him to the U.S., he vanished."

Dan needed a moment to digest the barrage of information. He looked at the beach which was a blinding white from the afternoon sun. A few families were strolling in for siestas. He saw a father holding his little daughter's hand. The man lifted the girl and she hugged his neck. Dan smiled at the unrivaled bond between a father and daughter.

He looked at Nadine, "Alexandra took his daughter." He paused, "In addition to his assets." He closed his eyes to sum-up: "Alexandra's husband was abusing her. She wised up and escaped with their daughter. They ran away with new names after testifying against her violent, *soldier* husband..." He looked at Nadine with a shimmer of recognition. "You said his name is *Curtis*..?"

"Yeah..?"

Dan's tone became grim, "Last night at Larriott's —when the burglars attacked— one of them said the name *Curt*."

Nadine mused, "He's one of the burglars..."

"Think about it: he's a fugitive criminal —and a *violent* ex-Marine."

Her eyes widened with a creeping realization. "He came back for her!" She spoke faster as she assembled the jagged pieces. "Curt and his team attacked during Hurricane Selina. He came for her, *as well as* his assets. He would've killed her, and probably taken his daughter." She looked at Dan. "During the storm, Alexandra shot and killed one of his teammates."

"And they're still out there," Dan stated. "Alexandra lied to us about everything she knew."

"She lied to the feds as well," Nadine nodded. "She's scared to death..."

Dan chuckled at the emerging reality, "The feds didn't arrest her for shooting a man. They want information about her husband and their runaway soldiers." He paused with empathy. "They're going to shake that poor woman upside down until something falls out. And God knows where they placed her daughter."

"But she's innocent!" Nadine touched his hand. "We *know* she was attacked —and why."

"And your whole department has been bullied to stay away."

"There has to be a way to get to Alexandra –or *Elizabeth*– and tell her we know. She needs help." Nadine's eyes darted as she brain-stormed. "The FBI can keep suspects in custody until their first court appearance." She huffed, "Riker will keep her in the dark as long as he can."

Though inspired by her passion, Dan reminded her of their primary obstacle, "Nadine, how can we fight the FBI *and* the Colonel of Special Military Operations with zero authority? How could *we* ever get to Larriott in a guarded, reinforced Air Force base?"

She sighed, "We can't." After a sip of her drink, two feathery clouds parted, shining a golden beam across her face. She suddenly glowed, "But I know who can!"

"Who?"

"Hello, attorney Sheldon King's office," the nineteen-year old receptionist with Egyptian mascara answered. "No, Mr. King is busy in a depo–"

"–Then interrupt him!" Nadine shouted with zero tolerance. "Tell him this is Detective Nadine Stratton. His client, Alexandra Larriott, needs his help –*NOW!*"

50. The Nature of the Beast

Attorney Sheldon King, Esquire, spun the tires of his convertible BMW Z4 to make the turn off Dale Mabry. To the right of the entrance to MacDill Air Force Base, he pulled haphazardly into the lot for the Visitor's Reception Facility.

King, with his suntan, smoothed-back hair and beige blazer, barged through the doors of the small office. There was a wall-length desk and a sign-in pad. Behind the desk sat two uniformed Air Force Security Officers.

"Can I help you sir?" a young officer with a red crew cut asked.

"You'd better." King slid his sunglasses onto his head. "I'm attorney Sheldon King and I need to be escorted *immediately* to my client, Ms. Alexandra Larriott."

A tall black officer approached the loud and flashy visitor, "Who?"

King exhaled a frustrated huff and pulled out a scribbled piece of paper to check the names. "My client is being *illegally* held captive by an FBI Agent *Riker* and Lieutenant Colonel *Sturges* with the Special Operations Command."

Redhead squinted, "There's no FBI housed here."

The black officer added in a baritone, "We can only contact Special Operations Command if this is an emergency, or if you know of a threat to national security."

King threw his hands in the air. "The *emergency* is that I have knowledge of your facility detaining a single mother against her will! The *threat* is I'm calling Channel 7 to send ten cameramen for my press conference on your front steps." He took a breath and continued, "Another headline of our esteemed military confining and possibly *torturing* another innocent citizen –*without* allowing her to contact her attorney-of-record!" He put his hands on his hips and looked at the guards. "Thank you, *thank you* for giving me this opportunity to warn the public!"

The guards looked at each other, unsure whether to grasp their firearms or call someone. The redhead mumbled to the other, "Maybe call the Colonel's P. R. Officer?"

King paced the small room for fifteen minutes. Every thirty seconds he huffed, looked at his Rolex, and shook his head.

A skinny Navy officer eventually entered. He wore his Summer White uniform, had a bad complexion and outdated glasses. "Hello sir, I'm Officer Engel," he extended a timid hand. "I work with Colonel Sturges–"

"–I asked to see the Colonel," King interrupted, ignoring the man's hand. "Why are you here?"

The security officers remained quiet. The asshole lawyer was now Engel's problem.

"The Colonel's in an important meeting," Engel replied in a weak voice. "You said you represent Ms. Larriott?"

"Yes, I am her attorney and a dear friend," King shot back. "I was never informed that she was arrested by the FBI. She invoked her right to an attorney, which forbids *anyone* from further questioning without me present." He observed Engel's uniform. "What do you do?"

Engel stammered, "I'm an analyst, sir."

"An analyst?" King kept an abrupt, combative pace, sensing a flaw in Engel's fortitude.

"An analyst in Counterterrorism," Engel blurted.

King paused in confusion. "Then why am I talking to you?" He grew louder, "My client was assaulted by a soldier and she defended herself. Are you saying a *terrorist* attacked my client?" He motioned to Engel's uniform. "Was he a Navy man?" He aggressively pressed into Engel's personal space.

"That's not what I'm saying–" Engel struggled like a flushed goldfish.

King continued hacking at the man like a relentless lumberjack. "–What do you want with a victim of self-defense?"

Engel stepped back. "There's more to this than the murder charge!"

King hesitated and cocked his head. "Really..?" He smirked, "I *order* you to inform me of the *exact* charges against Ms. Larriott immediately!"

Engel froze, trapped in a corner. "I'm unsure of her status–"

"–Status of *what*?" King screamed.

Engel closed his eyes and shouted, "She may've been untruthful about knowledge of a threat to national security!"

King stopped. He nodded and grinned as if he'd exposed the legal gaffe he'd been hoping for. He pointed at the two quiet security officers. "With these two men as my witnesses, did you just call my client a terrorist?"

Engel paused with large eyes and said nothing.

King pointed out the door across Dale Mabry. "See that apartment complex over there?"

The three men craned their necks to look across the street.

"In that parking lot –with your base clear in the background– I'm holding a press conference." King chuckled, "My cousin at Channel Seven News will owe me for a year for the story. I can see it now: '*Terror in Tampa!*'" King exited the jingling door with a slam.

The redheaded officer looked at Engel. "Are you going to tell the Colonel?"

Engel released a warbling sigh of helplessness.

Agent Riker sat across from Colonel Sturges and Agent Louise Capell in the fusion meeting room. "Our man, *Lex*, just communicated with Jenkins. He's on his way to fill us in."

Sturges asked, "I'm curious: how are you communicating with your man?"

"Lex created a secure link on the CAT team's own system. The suspects lack the expertise to know he's texting right under their noses."

The Colonel smiled at the appealing Agent Capell seated next to him. "The bait article was already uploaded?"

"Yes sir," she smiled. "We produced a story of a widow with a twenty-seven carat 'Red Dresden' diamond. It's based on the very real 'Dresden Green Diamond,' one of the rarest gems in the world. Our diamond is reportedly sitting in an unguarded Key Biscayne estate."

"Whose house are we using?" Sturges asked.

Capell was proud to explain, "Our article describes a very specific house on Key Biscayne. I located a government-owned home the FBI seized from a cartel two years ago. The house is vacant and was deeded in a fictitious name in case they do a property check."

The Colonel smiled at the level of detail. "Excellent."

Riker paused at the praise showered on the new girl.

Sturges looked at Riker, "How'd your mole pass their scrutiny? The *Spool*?"

"Yes. His mission name is 'Alex Summers' or 'Lex.' It's a vintage, five-year-old name we took off the Spool."

Capell arched a brow, "the *Spool*?"

"Short for 'Spy Pool.'" Riker paced towards the blonde agent, relishing her interest. "It's literally a pool of names that have fictitious backgrounds. Each 'character' is created years before they're actually needed. Whenever an undercover is needed, we select a character off the Spool database." He smiled, "The older the name, the better. Like a vintage wine."

"Why is older better?" Capell asked.

The Colonel replied, "The point is to slowly fill the names with public and criminal records. With today's technology, your suspects will always check the background of your undercover. You can't just make-up a name on the spot like James Bond. The given name should have *years* of actual, discoverable records. Social Security numbers, property records, criminal, even news articles. Any routine background check will display records planted over a course of years."

Riker continued, "For this project, we needed our man to be a former soldier with a criminal background. Using the *Spool* we found a character created five years ago. The name had been given a past as an Army Ranger with a history of arrests, warrants, complete with phony news stories. Then, we selected an agent who fit the physical profile: six foot, black hair, etc. He studied his character before going in."

All three turned to see Agent Jenkins enter the room. "I just spoke to Lex." He appeared more hesitant than pleased.

Riker rubbed his hands together. "So, what *breed* of terrorists are we crashing?"

Capell interrupted, "I've been limited to Art Crimes for ten years. What types of terrorists are you envisioning?"

Riker was glad to explain. "With this project, we know they're terrorists, but not which kind. God-forbid they're funding an ISIL cell. Probably domestic. Such groups cover a spectrum of views. Right or left-wing groups or some other extremists."

The Colonel remained quiet, allowing Riker to prattle on.

Riker paced as he lectured. "Right-wing extremists fight for racial supremacy and antigovernment beliefs. They cry they're protected by free speech." He looked at Capell, "Left-wing extremists profess a socialist policy, believing they're 'protectors of the people.' They want a revolution instead of using our political process." Riker turned towards Jenkins, "Lastly, there are special interest extremists. These idiots exist on the extreme fringes of animal rights, pro-lifers, antinuclear, bla, bla..." Riker smiled at his junior agent. "Jenkins, tell us what *strain* of terror cell we're dealing with."

Jenkins stared down at a legal pad to choose his words.

Sturges, Riker and Capell were quiet, eager for his reply.

Jenkins cleared his throat, "This is a little unexpected..."

Riker flailed his hands, "What?"

Jenkins replied, "This 'CAT team'—who are remarkably inventive—are..." He looked up at the three, "They're just...*burglars.*"

Riker scowled, "Burglars? Impossible! They must be funneling proceeds offshore to some organization..?"

Jenkins shook his head. "Lex doesn't think so. He's trying to decipher the accounts and caches, but he's 100% convinced they're just thieves. Their sole motive is financial. They only work during storm season, and then enjoy lavish lives the rest of the year."

Sturges shouted in disbelief, "They possess stolen technology from four branches of U.S. military and all they want is goddamn oil paintings?"

Capell frowned at his jab, "Do you know the value of some art?" She turned to Jenkins. "If they have precious art, do we know where they keep it?"

Riker interrupted, "What about money transactions? Maybe they *fund* terrorism..?"

Agent Capell smirked at Riker. "This is starting to look like a case for my department, not Counterterrorism."

Sturges pounded the table, "What's happening with the all stolen intelligence?"

The four paused their uproar at a meek knock on the door. "Who is it?" Sturges shouted.

Officer Engel peeked in. "Colonel..?"

"Yes, what is it?"

Engel sheepishly stepped into the room and closed the door. He took a breath. "You might want to turn on the five o'clock news." He coughed. "Channel seven..."

The Colonel narrowed his eyes at the intrusion. "A storm update?" He fumbled for a remote. He peered over his half-moon glasses and aimed the control at a wall-mounted television. The five gazed intently; such an interruption had to be important.

The screen boomed with the resounding logo for WSDN *Channel Seven Action News*. The channel was the more gratuitous of the local news. Residents joked that the call letters stood for "Women, Sex, Death and News." Sturges turned up the volume.

An attractive Latina news anchor frowned with typical distress. "We have the latest coordinates for Hurricane 'Terrible Tiberius.'" She paused, "But first, we go live to a news conference at MacDill Air Force Base. Local attorney Sheldon King is alleging a possible threat to our community. Our *Action Threat Team* is there."

Sturges and the agents looked at each other. "Who's this shyster?" asked Riker.

The screen filled with a man standing outdoors at a makeshift podium. He was surrounded by a dozen reporters and flashing cameras. Clear in the background, over the man's shoulder, was the entrance sign to MacDill AFB.

"He's outside?" Sturges thumbed to the wall. "What the hell does he want?"

Engel timidly replied, "The situation's not ideal..."

51. Catch and Release

Sheldon King wore an olive Armani suit like the swaggering lead in a television legal drama. He'd had an intern pay the apartment building's manager $500.00 to use their lawn that faced the base. His firm owned a portable stage, complete with risers and a podium that could be transported and erected anywhere in the county within thirty minutes.

Fortunately for King —aside from the busy storm season— it was a slow news day. When he'd contacted his cousin Scott Baker, Associate Producer of Seven Action News, it was easy to entice him with a story promising local scandal and government misappropriation – with a tease of terrorism to lure even the most casual viewer. And the chrome "KING" emblazoned on the podium offered an opportunity for free advertising.

When King received the nod from the cameraman, he looked deep into the lens, "Today, the United States Government conveyed to me information that signifies either of two things. One: there is a terror threat on our coast that our citizens need to be aware of. Or two: military personnel have maliciously labeled my client a 'terrorist' without proof or explanation, exposing the government to charges of slander and defamation, *in addition* to false imprisonment." He paused to let the accusations echo in the audience's ears.

"My client is Ms. Alexandra Larriott." The newsfeed switched to a color photo of Alexandra —a beautiful portrait taken with Cassie. He continued, "A doting single mother and a tragic victim of Hurricane Selina. I am resorting to this forum with a duty to keep the good people of Tampa Bay completely informed." He stressed the words *"completely informed,"* to insinuate some nefarious group wanted to keep certain facts away from the public.

Like a politician, King scanned the small crowd (ten were from his own firm.) "Unless I receive proof of an imminent threat to national security before the courts open at 9:00 a.m. tomorrow, I am filing a lawsuit against the U. S. Government, the Federal Bureau of Investigation and the Justice Department. They have violated Ms Larriott's presumption of innocence, and the consequences have been utterly ruinous. The hunted will drag the hunters into court to expose their blueprint for destroying a defenseless widow. She's been blighted by the allegations, and it's time the authorities acknowledge their part in her undoing."

Cameras clicked and King's face softened. "I understand our nation's need to aggressively protect our borders, but *only* if done truthfully." He then sharpened his eyes like a hawk, "Regrettably, based on their business practice of ongoing buffoonery, we are making the following claims: false imprisonment, false arrest, malicious prosecution, abuse of process, intentional infliction of emotional distress, and negligence in the infliction of emotional distress..."

Colonel Sturges' jaw hung open and he looked away from the screen. His breathing became labored and he turned to Engel with fiery eyes. "You called Larriott a *terrorist?*"

"I don't remember, verbatim..." Engel stammered. He looked back at the television to catch King's final words.

"I leave you with one important plea," King gazed into the camera. "General Lindsey —wherever you are— the taxpayers want to understand why your base would embarrass itself with such reckless attacks against our citizens. Has the 'Well of Terror' gone dry?"

Riker and Jenkins each had twitching blinks. Agent Capell remained quiet, watching the men squirm.

The Colonel pointed at Engel. "Now –because of you– the General will want an explanation from me!"

Capell winced, confused, "General Lindsey isn't part of this team?"

Sturges paused, gulping for words. "We've been... insulating the General. I wanted solid conclusions first. Or better yet, a recovery of military property." He looked at Riker. "Our only saving grace is the General is currently in Fiji with his new bride."

Agent Jenkins spoke up, "As ludicrous as these accusations are, the media *will* want a response from our P.R. rep."

The Colonel looked at Riker. "Your Bureau doesn't need another embarrassing witch hunt."

"*Another*?" Riker mocked. "*Your* Department of Defense has a *stellar* record with terror suspects. Did you visit your Guantánamo cages?"

"Did you forget Richard Jewell and the Olympic bombings?" Sturges fired back, "He won a slew of lawsuits after he was targeted by the FBI." He stepped closer to Riker. "What about Steven Hatfill? *Your* department called him a suspect with the Anthrax attacks. He won nearly six million when he sued your ass." He shouted, "That was all FBI –not us!"

Riker inadvertently stepped backwards. Sturges huffed back to his corner and sat. Engel remained frozen by the door like a mannequin.

With no dog in the fight, Agent Capell spoke up, "Do you even need Larriott anymore?"

The men looked at her. Sturges turned to Riker.

Riker bit his inner cheek in deliberation. "We know how they find their targets. We now know more about Curt than she does. I guess she is worthless."

Jenkins, the voice of reason, interjected, "But she did kill a man..."

Sturges nodded, "She's on the hook for murder. But I'm not sharing any evidence that her intruders exist."

Jenkins nodded. "If we send Larriott back to the State Attorney, the shooting will remain a *state* case, not federal. They'll move her back to Lee County for the murder." He looked at Sturges. "That'll get her off your base –and off our backs."

"They'll probably grant her bail." Agent Riker gave a wicked grin, "Maybe Curt will come back and take care of her for us."

Agent Capell scowled at his comment. No one joined in his gallows humor.

Sturges pounded the table like a gavel. "Then it's settled." He pointed at Engel, "*You're* writing the press response. Tell them: 'The wrong person was briefly detained as a result of a good faith mistake.'" He turned to Riker. "Go ahead and release Larriott to Lee County. When she gets her bail, she can get her daughter back. Hell, give 'em two tickets to Disney."

Riker and Engel looked down in defeat. They mumbled a concurrent, "Yes, Colonel."

An image caught their attention on the television –a satellite feed of an immense, spiraling cyclone. The Colonel turned up the volume.

"...Tiberius is now predicted to make landfall anywhere between Key Largo and Fort Lauderdale," the female meteorologist said. "By tomorrow, the cyclone could attain Category 5 status with sustained winds greater than 155 mph."

The fusion team glanced at each other ominously.

"The storm may weaken across the Bahama Banks, but is expected to intensify as it enters the warmer Gulf Stream." The woman's tone became somber, "Tiberius could strike Florida's east coast within 72 hours. A hurricane watch is expected in the next 36..."

"Mother Nature just set our clock." Sturges looked at the dismayed team, "Remain seated. We're not going anywhere."

Riker looked at Sturges, "Did you finalize the contracts with Onyx?"

"Yep." Sturges nodded and then added cryptically, "They're locked and loaded."

Capell frowned, confused. "What's *Onyx*?"

A corner of the Colonel's mouth smiled at her. "You know I can't use *my own* men on U.S. soil, right?"

52. Black Ink

Almost immediately upon learning he had a team of AWOL thugs running amok, Colonel Sturges had called his contacts at Onyx – using a disposable phone, far from the base's cell towers. The boys at Onyx knew how to keep things quiet, while containing any situation –and they would have all the same toys.

Onyx Risk, Inc., or referred to as Onyx Inc. or "Black Ink," was generically labeled a "private military contractor." They had an elusive P.O. Box somewhere in Langley, Virginia and a 7,000 acre training facility in Moyock, North Carolina. Their one-page website stated that Onyx specialized in "security management consulting." However, the United States' top brass –from the CIA in Langley, to the Special Operations Command in Tampa– knew that Onyx provided many other unique services.

Simply put, Onyx provided armed and trained mercenaries. But the U.S. and most countries avoided using the word "mercenary" within their contracts, and therefore not prohibited as part of the United Nations Mercenary Convention. Onyx's strict contracts de-

manded the same immunity that police and other federal agents enjoyed. Onyx insisted that their ability to provide the highest level of
security required protection from all civil and criminal liability. Since
time was of the essence in most emergencies, the hiring parties usually agreed to immunity requests with little resistance.

What set Onyx apart from other contractors was the pedigree of
their people. Their staff included former Navy SEALs, Marine Anti-
Terror troops, Army Delta Force and Rangers. They could be assembled anywhere on the globe within hours, complete with tier-one
gear. Some men had proudly served in Iraq when Secretary of Defense Donald Rumsfeld confessed to using private military contractors, describing them as cost effective and "not subject to the Uniform Code of Military Justice." Essentially, they were a lethal force
for hire that did not have to obey the same rules as "legitimate" U.S.
troops.

Officer Engel had been given the chore of picking up sandwiches
and coffees for the long night of planning. By the "grace of God," as
Riker had repeated, the Starbucks had finally opened at the MacDill
commissary. Colonel Sturges demanded a hamburger with "real red
meat," but had to settle for cellophane-wrapped sandwiches containing "seaweed."

"I'm curious," Agent Capell asked before sipping her chai. "Why
would an esteemed Special Forces soldier leave the greatest military
on earth to work for a contractor like Onyx?"

Sturges chuckled. "I shouldn't be endorsing this, but I know a former SEAL at Onyx. His annual salary in the Navy was $58,000 for
putting his ass in the crosshairs every day. His first paycheck with
Onyx was for over $50,000 —for his first thirty days of work. I'm
guessin' it was an easy decision."

Engel frowned, wiping hummus from his lips. "I'm having diffi-
culty accepting it, considering the *posse comitatus*."

Riker and the Colonel froze and glared at him as if he'd uttered
profanity at a child's party.

Noting a flash of doubt in Capell's eyes, Jenkins explained. "The

Posse Comitatus Act bans the Army, Navy, Air Force and Marines from participating in any searches, seizures or related activity on U. S. soil. They can't be used as the posse comitatus or 'force of the country.'"

Engel stammered, "Using the military on our own soil can only be approved by an Act of Congress. The penalty for any violation is... imprisonment." He turned to the Colonel. "Even if you use someone like Onyx, doesn't the posse comitatus apply for anyone working under *contract* for our armed forces?"

Riker turned to Sturges, hesitant. The Colonel shifted in his seat. He rocked his jaw to select his words. "Critics tried to open a can of shit after the whole Blackwater fiasco. However, *our* attorneys believed the language of the Act did not prohibit use of a private – *though government-funded–* military to act as a police force." He grinned at the junior members like a car salesman. "Hell, look at the chaos in New Orleans after Katrina. We used contract troops then. Even more recently, did you know that we hired privately-contracted Special Forces troops in Ferguson, Missouri after the Michael Brown ruling in 2014? The National Guard *cannot* handle all the demands." He stared directly into Engel's thick glasses, "Son, Louisiana and Missouri are on *U.S. soil* –and no one complained."

As Engel squirmed for a retort, Riker spoke up. "There are exclusions for 'emergency circumstances.' Even the Patriot Act allows contract troops to provide assistance for any threat of mass destruction within our borders." He huffed and shook his head as if Engel's query had been absurd.

After an awkward silence, Agent Capell gave a sympathetic smile to Engel, sensing every bit of his despair.

53. The Calm Between the Storms

Stars specked the indigo sky over Marco Island beach. A small Tiki hut flickered from a lantern in the center of its table. Nadine and Dan remained huddled behind their laptops. Neither mentioned the fact that their jobs were spoiling such a romantic, storybook setting.

"Here it is," Nadine announced. "The nine o'clock update."

Dan stepped to her side of the table. He peered over her shoulder at a webpage for WSDN News. A "Local" header read: "Attorney King's Client Released; Base Apologizes. No Terror Threat."

Nadine scanned the story aloud, "At 8:45 p.m., Alexandra Larriott was released from *precautionary* questioning at MacDill AFB." She skimmed to herself until she reached the information they wanted. "Ms. Larriott's being transferred to the State's Attorney for the Twentieth Judicial Circuit in Lee County for the alleged shooting of an unidentified male." She looked up at Dan with a faint smile, "I know the ASA in Fort Myers. He'll *never* pursue a murder charge if we can prove there were intruders."

Dan was cautious to be too optimistic. "We have to prove she was attacked. The feds aren't going to admit these guys exist. Too bad we don't have her security video."

Nadine nodded. "I asked an AV tech to try to restore her video. He's trying to chemically dry the *platters* or something. I told him to call me immediately if he sees anything resembling intruders."

Dan handed her a beer and lifted his own. "Here's to a productive day."

She smiled and lifted her Kalik Bahamian beer. They clinked bottles and enjoyed well-earned slugs. She put her bottle down among their four empties and smiled at a stack of notes. "How is it we uncovered more in one day on a beach than three in an office?"

"What does that tell you?" Dan grinned like a buccaneer. "I say we do a quick wrap-up, then go for a night swim."

Her eyes smiled, "Perfect."

Dan was happy. Despite their tribulations, Nadine seemed to be having fun with their task. She was by no means inebriated, but certainly *relaxed*. She giggled more and seemed increasingly at ease. Nadine's joy was infectious during their friendly competition of research.

She lifted a legal pad. "You go first."

Dan placed his post-it notes in a row. "Larriott's ex-husband is 'Curt Hulett.' She and their daughter escaped his abuse, and now he's found them. He's attacked twice so far. He's ex-military. We think all these...storm *crashers* are former soldiers."

"And Curt has a brother, James. The DMV has an old address for him was at Key West's Truman Annex –which is a Navy base. When I called the V.A., they confirmed James 'Butch' Hulett is a former naval officer but wouldn't confirm any further records." She looked at Dan, "That's already two ex-soldiers on the storm team."

"And these AWOL thugs have the feds in a frenzy."

Nadine began to speak faster, "The feds *violated* Alexandra's rights, just because of her ex-husband." She flipped through her notes. "Alexandra ran away six months ago to start a new life. She changed her name and moved over 1,600 miles. Her ex-husband *still* found her."

Dan nodded, "We believe Curt found her from the *Island Life* article. I called the magazine's photographer to see if they were approached by anyone, but I haven't heard back. We think that's how they locate high-profile targets. From Myrtle Beach to Louisiana, I located five articles that profiled people who submitted huge burglary claims *after* the articles were published." He looked at Nadine. "Did you find any articles for the new storm?"

"Online I found a dozen stories involving wealthy residents flaunting their homes. Out of those twelve, only *four* live on beachfront property between Palm Beach and Key Largo. That's a big area." Nadine looked up, "Tomorrow's storm update will narrow the forecast —as well as our list of possible targets."

"Fantastic!" Dan closed his laptop. "Now, if we can just convince *any* authorities that these suspects exist and to take the case." He added with sarcasm, "But only if we don't involve your department, the FBI or the entire U.S. military."

"Dan..." Nadine looked at him wistfully, "Do you know why you're better at your job than I'll ever be? Remember what I said was your biggest asset?"

His unshaven face blushed.

"Your collection of contacts. You go to happy hours with the Coast Guard, Border Patrol and Homeland Security. When you were investigating boat smuggling, all you had to do was call the head of Coast Guard Intelligence. After one lunch in Key West, you had the entire Coast Guard helping you find your boats."

Dan gave a crooked grin. "I guess I am world renowned —in Florida."

She flashed her radiant smile. "You're every police department's loss." She paused, "As well as you ex-girlfriend's."

Dan didn't reply. He leaned towards Nadine's face and planted a soft, gentle kiss. He pulled back and smiled into her stunned eyes.

She closed her eyes and fell towards Dan as she reciprocated the kiss. She grabbed his head with both hands and ran her fingers through his hair. After a full minute of a swirling kiss, she pulled back to see Dan, staggered but composed.

"You know," he had to clear his throat. "My room has ice-cold AC

–but unfortunately only one queen-size bed..."

She widened her blue eyes. "I'm not in any condition to be driving a county car..."

They smiled. Dan stood and took her by the hand. They stepped towards the breaking waves on the starlit beach. They finally realized their perfect storybook setting. An overdue, romantic moment in paradise.

But behind them –east over the Everglades– were slithering pulses of summer lightning and the low growl of thunder.

54. New Toys in the Attic

The tanned meteorologist motioned to the satellite image of the vast storm. "Hurricane Tiberius attained Category 5 status 100 miles north of Nassau at 7:00 a.m. this morning. The track confirms the path to be anywhere between Key Largo and Fort Lauderdale." An animated cone depicting the projected path had Miami in its center.

The weatherman continued, "We're already seeing how stress affects experienced residents with the *second* named storm to hit the state in a one-week period."

At a Miami Publix supermarket, customers were raiding shelves of food like carpenter ants. Women shrieked in Spanish, clawing each other for gallons of water and flattened loaves of bread. A jittery manager spoke into the camera, "We learned from two summers in a row with four storms each. Our customers understand preparation."

The scene switched to a weary Miami City Manager in a loose tie and a polyester shirt addressing the press from a podium. "We've officially declared evacuation zones in Miami-Dade County. *Anyone* on barrier islands from Key Biscayne to North Miami Beach *must* evacuate. If you choose to remain in these areas, help *will not* be available to you."

LeBeau smirked at Lex and Dalia as they watched the news, "Panicked yokels with mandatory evacuations. Textbook."

They turned to see Curt huff into the room with Pitch at his side. Curt grunted towards Lex, "What's the update?"

Seated at Dalia's side, Lex replied nonchalantly, "Larriott's attorney got her released. She's still charged with the murder."

Curt instantly turned purple, enraged. "They *released* her?"

"Forget her!" LeBeau scolded. "She'll be guarded like the First Lady."

"Where's she now?" Pitch asked.

Lex turned to a laptop, "Sifting through e-chatter, looks like they're hiding her in one of those 'Ladies in Distress' safe houses. I don't know where."

LeBeau glared at Curt, "I warned you to *forget* your *EX*-wife..."

"She took *everything*!" Curt shouted with arms tense, "Including my daugh–"

"–Get over it!" Dalia snapped. She stepped within inches of Curt. "We already know the story: your wife took all your shit. Butch is gone. You're a dead dog away from a country song."

Curt made fists at his side to restrain himself. He stared at the four who were equally drilling holes with their eyes back at him.

LeBeau cleared his throat and ruled like a judge, "*We* are dropping all talk of revenge. *We* are focusing on Hurricane Tiberius. *This* is why you are no longer chained to a toilet." He grinned and asked like a robotic second grade teacher, "Do-you-under-stand-Curtis?"

Curt exhaled and said nothing.

The team assembled at the conference table, facing a projection screen. Dalia stood before the men. Using a laser pointer, she motioned at an animated image of Tiberius. "Because of the populated area, I plan to push your rendezvous as close to landfall as possible. Expect gusts up to seventy kilometers per hour."

Lex considered the notion. The others nodded.

"I'll drop you off on the east side of Biscayne, four miles off the coast of downtown Miami. The island will be evacuated. The only bridge from the mainland will be closed. I've located a discreet beach within a residential park to land. There are at least seven high-dollar targets. The 'Red Dresden Diamond' house will be within 200 yards. I'll pick you up after your last target."

"Where you gonna' wait?" Curt asked.

"After drop-off, I'll take the Stingray to a parking garage on the north end of the island." She looked at the men. "When I pick you up, it'll be in the narrowest window we've ever attempted. *Zero* room for error."

LeBeau looked at the silenced men, "Based on the ...*precarious* nature of the drop, we've come up with some new toys. He smiled at Pitch. "Why don't you show us your new prototype, in the event any-one misses their ride home."

All eyes turned to Pitch, alarmed at the notion.

Pitch stood before the men. He lacked the polished demeanor of Dalia and LeBeau, but was an expert at tactical gear. He produced a one-foot diameter nylon fabric disk. It was metallic gray and ap-peared thin and useless. "If you need to endure winds beyond a 'no-return' point, I call this a *Blister Tent*." He flung the disk in front of him. Its wire frame unfolded into a dome-like tent, approximately three-feet high and around.

"For emergency camping?" Curt chuckled like a fool.

Pitch looked at him soberly, "You'll need something if the storm comes ashore and you're caught without shelter. This tent was de-signed by Navy researchers in Antarctica. It can withstand winds in excess of a hundred miles per hour."

The team flexed their brows, intrigued.

Pitch kneeled to the ground. He rotated the tent so the team could see into its opening. He pulled out a lipstick-sized attachment. "This is the trigger. On a hard surface, such as cement or a street, hit this switch. CO_2 will shoot steel barbs into the ground as anchors. The fabric is completely waterproof, windproof and indestructible." He smiled at his teammates, "Just remember your knife, or you'll never cut your way out."

Dalia and the men glanced at each other in awe.

I'm also unveiling another toy," Pitch reached into his vest to produce a chrome sphere the size of a golf ball.

"A compact E-PIG?" Dalia guessed.

"A flash grenade," Curt shouted.

"You're both sorta' right. I call it an *E-bang* grenade." Pitch rolled the shiny ball between his fingers. "Flash-bang grenades emit a bright light and a deafening *bang* to shock the enemy. This E-bang is an *electric*-bang grenade. When thrown to the ground, it explodes," Pitch grinned, "—but it contains a water-based fluid that rapidly expands as steam, engulfing your target."

Curt almost laughed, "It covers your enemy with *steam*?"

Pitch lifted a finger. "*Then,* a pulse of one million volts travels through the expanding water vapor, electrocuting anyone touching the cloud. Of course, the voltage diminishes the farther the cloud dissipates, but you can get a good ten-foot diameter of excruciating distraction."

His teammates gasped like kids at Christmas with a simultaneous *"Wow..."*

Dalia stepped in front of the men and spoke, "As a last escape tactic, we need to discuss the option of 'riding the eye.'"

Pitch, Curt and LeBeau nodded at the suggestion. Frowning, Lex raised a hand. "Okay, I'll bite: what's *riding the eye*?"

Dalia typed on her keyboard and a projection of an animated storm appeared onscreen. "In a hurricane's center, the 'eye' can be roughly twenty miles wide. Within the eye, there are minimal winds and clouds." She used her pointer to highlight the clear blue circle in the center of the cyclone. "If we extend too long, we can remain in the Stingray and find shelter —such as a parking garage. Then we just wait for the eye."

Lex gazed in disbelief at the inference. "And then..?"

"We fly out *inside* of the eye," Dalia replied. Onscreen, the animated chopper remained inside the hurricane's eye, traveling along with the moving storm. "We can casually fly within the eye until we can locate suitable shelter."

LeBeau smiled at the visibly-alarmed Lex. "Don't worry. With all the clutter, we wouldn't show on radar." He chuckled, "And no one would dare follow."

For the first time, Lex seemed unnerved. "We seem to have a lot of emergency plans with this storm."

LeBeau stood. "Thank you, Dalia. Now..." He rubbed his palms together with teasing drama, "Time to vote *yay* or *nay* on the use of heavy firearms."

55. Back to the Real World

"You want to see me Lieutenant?" Nadine Stratton asked from the threshold of her boss's office.

Lieutenant Dale Coffey –Detective Rodka's immediate superior– was sixty-ish and portly with a helmet of dyed chestnut hair. He had a permanent straight face and wore a cheap, shiny gray suit. "*Miss* Stratton..." he looked up from his anally-tidy desk. He emphasized the "Miss," instead of her well-earned "Detective." A corner of his mouth lifted into an almost flirtatious smirk. "Nadine, Nadine...Come on in and take a three-minute break."

Nadine forced a tolerant smile and entered the office. Being five days post Selina, she appeared slightly more "made-up" with stylish hair and a department t-shirt and khakis complimenting her slender figure. However, her once clear and optimistic blue eyes showed the stress of too many hours stuck behind her computer.

Moments earlier, when Al Rodka barked that the Lieutenant wanted to see her, Nadine almost didn't care anymore. She'd been through more in the past week than most cops at their retirement.

On the same day, exactly one week earlier, she'd escorted a Girl Scout troop through the department, and then had helped city workers with plans for Selina. Since then, she'd survived her first Category 3 storm; uncovered corpses; been inexplicably warned to stay away from a helpless victim; she'd puked on a coworker in a haunted morgue; and then she'd seen another coworker murdered. The icing on her shit cake was then being roughed-up and threatened by the FBI *and* the military's Special Op Command. But of course, her senior partner said she needed to "toughen up."

Nadine thanked her lucky stars that she'd reconnected with Dan. The only male in a year who was on the same emotional wavelength. They loved investigation, and had an almost insatiable fervor for their jobs —sprinkled with reprimands from their respective bosses. Considering their dense bureaucracies, it was a miracle they'd found each other. There's a lid for every pot, her mom used to say.

Nadine had remained at Dan's Marco motel for two full nights. The ninety minute commute to Fort Myers was well worth it. They each got back from their duties around 10:00 p.m. They'd visit under the sheets before changing into bathing suits and dipping in the pool to sample Bartender Mike's hand-shaken key lime martinis. She and Dan would then visit their Tiki-on-the-beach for more Larriott strategizing.

While pondering a few loose strands from the Larriott case, one question about the storm crashers kept gnawing at them: how were they getting to and from the burglary sites? They had to zip in and out of residential areas on the fringes of major storms, navigating through insufferable winds and rain. How was it possible?

Dan reasoned aloud through the process of elimination. Cars or trucks were impractical since bridges and roads were either closed or obstructed. It'd be almost impossible escaping once the storms came ashore. Motorcycles could *maybe* navigate blocked roads, but would be impractical for transporting stolen merchandise.

By sea? Since most burglarized properties were on the water, Nadine speculated about the use of watercraft. She and Dan ruled out boats as being too hazardous with the storm surges. The use of a submarine was given low odds since they were too expensive to acquire, despite myths about Colombian drug lords buying former soviet subs.

Which left only one possibility: traveling by air. Nadine pointed out that airplanes –even small private planes– would require lengthy runways. In brainstorming all options, balloons, blimps, hang gliders and the like were ruled out as absurd. This revealed the lone solution: unless the burglars used a vertical take-off (and impossible to obtain) Harrier jet, they were using helicopters. There was no other feasible answer.

Neither Dan nor Nadine knew much about helicopters. There had to be certain models that were designed for high-risk environments such as storms and high winds. Dan promised to call his contacts in the Coast Guard. He'd worked with the USCG while investigating stolen boats used by smugglers. Dan knew they used choppers for interdictions and air-sea rescues. They would know about helicopters that could withstand extreme conditions. Dan and Nadine toasted their plan. It was time to call it a night.

They sprawled nude and exhausted under their room's slow paddle fan, giggling to never-tiring repeats of *Seinfeld* until they drifted asleep. The island atmosphere seemed to rejuvenate their souls. But, unfortunately, the 6:00 a.m. alarm smacked them back to their tedious predicament. It was a mocking contrast to trade their beach office for the demands from their *real* jobs. Nadine felt like a kid who'd run away from home –but still had to go to school.

Nadine prayed that she and Dan's discreet investigation would ultimately succeed. They'd do anything for Alexandra and her poor daughter. Despite threats from authorities, the truth should never *ever* be a bad thing.

Lieutenant Coffey never moved from behind his desk. He just sat facing forward like a bad anchorman. Nadine took a seat in front of his desk. "How can I help you, Lieutenant?"

"I have some *'news'* for you." Coffey sighed, seeming troubled. "I wouldn't call it 'bad' news, just 'news,' because I believe you can make this an *opportunity*."

Nadine wrinkled her forehead trying to decipher his message. "What news?"

"As you can imagine, the storm is really going to suck on our budgets this year." He raised his palms. "We won't know the final tab for years."

"Right..." Nadine leaned forward. "And how can I help you with this?"

Coffey bobbed his head until he finally blurted, "All sergeant exams and promotions are being shelved for a bit."

"*Shelved?*" Nadine's jaw dropped, "How long's a *bit*?"

"I'd say twelve to eighteen months. Then we'll reevaluate." He swooshed air in his cheeks. "Sorry 'bout that."

Nadine's eyes swirled across the room, finding no perches to land. The walls were filled with framed 8 x 10's of Coffey shaking hands with white men in suits around the entire state. *Were the men politicians? Feds? Military?* She scowled, "The sergeant's interview was the only reason I volunteered to do shifts in every department!"

"Just think what great experience it's been," Coffey offered with mock compassion. "You can either stay in homicide or go back to property. I'll let you pick. That's my gift to you."

Your gift to me? Nadine winced, "I want to stay involved with the Larriott case."

The Lieutenant inhaled through his teeth. "Rodka says you two have some...philosophical differences."

"I do have concerns with the case!"

"What concerns?"

"Well, let's see..." Nadine raised her voice, "The corpse was stolen, so we no longer have the victim's body. And Larriott has a strong argument of self-defense."

Coffey narrowed his eyes, "The body is well documented. We have video and photographic evidence. No one's gonna' deny we had a dead man. Our coroner can testify he was shot through the neck." He gave an unpleasant smile, "By the woman who confessed on tape."

Nadine scoffed, "Lieutenant, you and I know Larriott had intruders in her home."

For the first time, Coffey stood. "I know no such thing, *Miss* Stratton." His voice became a low growl, "Show me the evidence. Do you have any video?" He lifted a finger. "Oh yeah —the surveillance was ruined in the storm." He leaned forward, "Be *very* smart about what you claim I do or do not know or you'll be writing speeding tickets for the next twenty years."

Nadine remained in her seat, speechless.

The Lieutenant slowly sat back down. He placed both hands on his desk and cleared his throat. "I've made up my mind. You're going back to property."

"Why?"

Coffey gritted his teeth at being challenged. "Miami-Dade loaned us eighty volunteers after Selina. With Tiberius aiming at Miami, they're calling them back. That's why."

Nadine remained in her chair for nearly a minute. She felt like she'd been punched.

Through the phone's receiver, Nadine's voice was hurried, "Hi Toby, it's Stratton." She whispered, "Any luck with the video?"

Surrounded by towers of audio and video equipment, Toby scratched his light bulb-shaped head. "I'm still running the frames through every digital filter I can. There are still no discernable images that look like burglars or 'soldiers.'" Beside him, his monitor shimmered with indistinct static.

Nadine paused, "Toby: if you get *any* images that fit my description, call me, text me or email me —or all three. I'll contact Negrin."

"The State's Attorney?"

"Yes. If you can do that, I'll take you to this year's Comic-Con myself."

Toby shivered, "And you said you'd dress as any sci-fi icon I wish..?"

Nadine rubbed her eyes, "I guess." She chuckled warily, "What exactly were you thinking?"

"Would it be clichéd if I suggest Princess Leia's golden slave bikini..?"

Nadine replied, "*Only* if you get me those images —I might need a new profession."

56. Broken Arrow

Dan Holms surveyed Captiva's western shore from the third-story roof of a Spanish-style estate. He climbed to the summit to photograph severe roof damage. Balancing on loose terracotta shingles, the roof looked the same as the eleven preceding homes he'd inspected. Storm duty for Insurex was getting pretty boring compared to his prior five days.

His bottle of water was thirty feet down on the ground. "I should invent a holster for water," he grumbled. Dan nearly lost his balance when his phone rang. His poise returned when he recognized the number. "This is Dan."

The man's voice was jovial but abrupt, "Randy Andris, Coast Guard, returning your call."

"Thanks Randy." Dan sat on the roof. He hated interrupting busy men for favors, but as Nadine had said, his laundry list of contacts was a unique asset. It had taken Dan countless years of conferences and cocktails to build such esteemed relationships.

At 7:00 a.m. earlier that morning, Dan had been at the insurance

RV camp in Captiva. He'd made friends with some State Farm guys from Texas who gave him coffee every morning. Though the divine aroma of bacon wafted from the Allstate trailer, Dan graciously accepted Nationwide's day-old Cuban pastries. How nice that competing companies could come together for such priorities. It took a village, he supposed. Once the caffeine cleared his brain's cobwebs, he began his phone calls.

Dan's first call of the day had been to a friend in the U.S. Coast Guard. Though Dan could be at times...*unpopular* with certain types of law enforcement, he somehow had the ability to make contacts with some of their industry partners. After years of attending fraud conferences –as well as vital social mixers– Dan made friends in many fields. Fire Marshalls discussed unique arsons. Agents in the National Insurance Crime Bureau were retired cops who could share information with Dan. It was amazing how rewarding a few parties and jokes could be. Dan would listen to their stories, and they loved hearing his. They were all on the same team, and there was never an excuse for not helping each other.

When Dan worked stolen boat cases in the mid-2000s, he'd made friends in the U.S. Coast Guard. There'd been a surge in stolen boats used for alien smuggling. Refugees paid over $10,000 per person to flee Cuba. Smugglers would steal speedboats and then insure them before making their runs. If their boats got seized, they'd make insurance claims for over $100,000 apiece. When the Coast Guard observed that first-time smugglers rarely got punished, Dan suggested there could be stiffer sentences for insurance crimes. Dan was able to submit his cases to the Division of Insurance Fraud; the smugglers were jailed and the stories made headlines. Dan compared it to Al Capone ultimately getting busted by the IRS. It still got the bad guys off the street.

But this call was for more than helicopter questions. Dan had another reason for involving the Coast Guard: the USCG was not under the Department of Defense. Colonel Sturges' tentacles from his Special Operations Command could not touch the Coast Guard. Sturges' department oversaw missions for the Army, Air Force, Navy and Marines —but *not* the Coast Guard, which was under Homeland Security. Dan had some cool friends that Sturges could not control.

When the feds threatened Nadine to stay away from the storm crasher case, she'd hoped Dan could convince some other authorities to pursue it. Placing a call to the Coast Guard wouldn't be a bad place to start —and by working under Homeland Security, Dan wondered if they'd have a *duty* to examine threats involving turncoat soldiers.

But Dan knew his theory of shadowy soldiers who attacked during storms sounded like schizophrenic hallucinations, so he decided to start the call with easy helicopter queries.

"Randy, you got my message?" Dan smiled into his phone. Randall Andris was the Resident Agent in Charge, Coast Guard Investigative Services in Key West. Dan and Randy had been recently scheduled to present a boat theft class together at the Orlando fraud conference. The day before the presentation, Randy had cancelled, claiming to be sick. After Dan sufficiently browbeat him for leaving him hanging, Randy promised he'd owe him one.

Randy chuckled, "I find it hard to believe you're helping a kid with a book report, but yes, helicopters are my vehicles of choice in high-wind conditions." Randy spoke rapidly, juiced on either high caffeine or a passion for his work.

"What are the best choppers for storms?" Dan pulled a pen and pad from his shirt pocket.

"Well..." Randy paused. "With sea rescues, especially during storms, we might use HH-65 Dolphins, HH-60 Jayhawks, and we still have a few MH-68A Stingrays."

"Are any of those models available to the public?"

"At least the Dolphins are," Randy replied. "My dad flew one as an EMS in Gainesville. If they *are* available, they're stripped down —no guns, no high-tech navigation." He laughed, "But keep in mind, a Dolphin or Stingray starts at over $20 million."

Dan almost choked, "Twenty *million* dollars? For one helicopter?"

"Oh yeah. That's why there's so much paperwork if we ever lose one."

"*Lose one*? Your choppers can just go missing?" Dan's gears sprang to life. Could the burglars have *stolen* one of these helicopters?

"No!" Randy barked, lightheartedly. "I mean if they crash. We had a Stingray go down off Key West seven months ago. That's serious tax-payer money and technology gone."

Dan pondered the information. If the burglars used a high-tech chopper, they probably didn't buy it off the shelf at $20,000,000. Dan wanted to know more about the accounting system for these choppers. Did a crashed helicopter always mean it was inoperable? Do recovered choppers ever get sold as salvage?

"Dan, you there?" Randy asked, "You know I got a Cat-5 heading at us, right? I have real work to do."

Dan snapped out of his daze. "You said you lost a Stingray off Key West. Was it recovered?"

"No, we never found it. The Atlantic's too deep. Are you now working chopper claims?"

"Not exactly," Dan replied. "Did your pilot safely eject, or..."

"Nope," Randy answered solemnly. "We lost her. She was a tough, twenty-three-year old kid and a hell of a pilot. We didn't even have a body to give the family."

Dan's naturally cynical eyes twinkled. "You never found the pilot or the chopper?"

"No..?"

"What was her name?" Dan scribbled notes. "You said it was a *Stingray*?"

"It was in the papers, so it's not classified. She was flying an MH-68A Stingray. Her name was *Dalia*..." Randy paused to recall the name, "*Covarrubias*." He had to spell the name.

Dan's eyes locked with a wave of *déjà vu*. He and Nadine had reviewed hundreds of reports containing *thousands* of names in the past three days. But the names "Dalia," and "Covarrubias" were distinctive. He'd never known anyone with either name, but somehow the words seemed oddly familiar. *Have I seen that name? If so, on which report?*

"Randy, I may have to call you back."

Randy moaned, "Great..."

Dan didn't know why or where his brain stored the names "Dalia" and "Covarrubias." For all he knew, it could've been a waitress's name from five years ago. Or it could be more recent within the plethora of DMV reports. Dan had only saved a few reports that he and Nadine reviewed. If the records didn't fit their case, they were deleted. Dan had to somehow search the reports that he'd viewed and not saved. *How..?*

Dan climbed down from the roof like an ape at feeding time. He drove to a poor-man's Starbucks on Sanibel called Starfish's that had electricity. He ordered an iced coffee and put his earbuds in to block out the rest of the world. From a keychain, he plugged an external drive into the side of his laptop. It contained a program, Zoomba, a search engine out of South Africa that could search *within* a computer as easy as searching the Internet. He could search inside saved and deleted e-mails, documents and websites. It hunted within the computer's cache, the temporary storage where recently accessed data was stored. If Dan recently viewed the name on his computer, it could be found.

Dan typed "Dalia + Covarrubias" into Zoomba. The program searched the trails left by Internet Explorer and Google Chrome, which included data deep within the cache. With any luck, Zoomba would then list all results on an accessible spreadsheet.

To quench his curiosity, Dan hoped at least one of the names would show up. It might just be something like "*Dalia* Greenstein," or some foreign word that looked like "Covarrubias." But Dan was frustratingly sure he'd seen them *somewhere*. He scrolled to the highlighted words on the spreadsheet and his eyes widened. Within minutes he found the Holy Grail: *both* names were there –together. With two such unique names, it *had* to be her.

Dalia Ana Covarrubias showed on a Department of Motor Vehicles report. She'd owned a 2013 Lexus registered to a Miami Beach address eighteen months ago. Based on the DOB, she would've been twenty-three years old –the same age as the pilot who went missing.

Why did she show on a report that he and Nadine viewed three days earlier? What's the connection? Dan re-ran every search imaginable.

On a public records report, Dalia's address in Miami was home to nearly two hundred registered drivers. *How's that possible?* Was it some transient flophouse? Then he saw it —the address was a large apartment complex. The DMV didn't list unit numbers, only the street address. Dan ordered a third coffee to painstakingly review all 197 residents of Ms. Covarrubias's former apartment building. *What's the tie to the Larriott investigation?*

When Dan finally saw it, his hands flinched, knocking his coffee across the table. Two years ago, a Suzuki Hayabusa motorcycle was registered to the same address. Following the tree diagram of information, the motorcycle was once titled to a *James Hulett, Jr.* Dan covered his mouth as he recognized the name. James "Butch" Hulett was the missing Navy soldier. He was Curt's brother —Alexandra Larriott's brother-in-law. And he once lived in the same building as Dalia.

Dan looked up with a vacant expression at the gravity of his discovery. He summarized under his breath, "A former-military fugitive once lived at the same address as a Coast Guard pilot who went missing with a storm-proof helicopter." Dan Holms had just confirmed the storm crasher's mode of transportation —and their pilot.

Coast Guard Agent Randy Andris was no longer jovial. He clutched the phone tight to his ear. He was oblivious to the flurry of activity on the Key West docks behind him. Officers were strapping their boats secure as the gray skies began to pelt rain. Randy huddled into the base to more clearly follow Dan's ominous news.

"Jesus..." Randy's eyes swirled in bewilderment. Any humor in his voice was replaced with distress. "We don't have a 'team' to handle a situation like this... What you're suggesting qualifies this case as..." He paused, "as... *terrorism.*"

"What's the ETA on the first bands of Tiberius hitting Miami?" Dan asked.

"Nine hours—" Randy replied before his cell signal vanished.

57. The Fringe

Dalia lifted off in the Stingray at 7:15 p.m. At 140 knots, the eighty-mile flight would take just over thirty minutes. Onboard, the residual CAT team sat in full gear. Remaining silent over the deafening engines, Lex, Pitch, Curt and LeBeau gazed out the windows with their helmets in their laps. Though he appeared fearless, Lex struggled to keep his eyes from revealing anxiety.

By midday, the news had reported the first waves of "feeder bands," the tentacles of clouds stretching from the outer fringes of Tiberius. The feeder bands pulled moisture up from the Atlantic, feeding the clouds of the storm. This churned periodic bouts of rain, lashing at the coast in waves.

Miami Beach's art deco district felt it first. The chic cafes rolled-in their tables, umbrellas and potted palms. The nightclubs and bars had boarded their windows after last night's patrons finally exited (7:00 a.m.) The luxury resorts dragged in their queen-sized bed loungers from around the pools.

Bumper-to-bumper traffic created a red trail of taillights heading north on I-95 and the turnpike. Miami's residents, hardened by prior storms, were getting the hell out of Dodge. They prayed to get anywhere beyond the forecasters' cynically-named "cone of death."

Some residents would shelter their kids from reality by charging a couple of days in Orlando's theme parks. Some had learned during prior seasons that storms crossing the state could cause more damage in Central Florida than on the coasts. Many drivers would discover that gas stations may give out of fuel by the time their tanks depleted in North Florida. It was a tossup whether it was safer to flee or seek public shelter.

From the Stingray, Lex watched the Miami skyline approach on the horizon. The sunset from the west created a purple tinge across the skyscrapers. Lex reflected back to just five days earlier when he'd met the lunatic LeBeau. At a café table facing Biscayne Bay, LeBeau had sipped his coffee like a fop, offering him a role on the CAT team as if it were Willy Wonka's golden ticket. *How'd I get in this deep?*

Lex's original plan had been to exit the CAT team well before Tiberius and this "Red Diamond" heist. However, Agent Riker was adamant that any abrupt departure would appear suspicious and could jeopardize the entire investigation. Plus, as Riker had reiterated, Lex still hadn't deciphered a heap of information such as the location of valuables and offshore accounts. Riker's relentless badgering pushed Lex into agreeing to stay with the CAT team –but *only* until an actual crime is committed. Lex was assured that something *classified* was supposed to swoop in and save him.

Lex was forced to trust his handlers. But with all his training, nothing prepared him for marching into seventy-mile-per-hour winds with a gang of insane ex-soldiers. He almost resented his government for using him in such a volatile predicament.

If only I had more time, Lex sighed. *Maybe I could've turned Dalia,* he fantasized. He wondered if he could fake an injury. *Then I could stay onboard with Dalia. After dropping off the men, I could convince her to escape with me into the sunset–*

"–LEX!" Curt shouted into his ear. "Wake up!" He grinned as he stuffed a wad of Skoal into his cheek. "Don't be daydreamin,' computer boy."

"ETA fifteen," Dalia announced in their headsets. "Tiberius is on track for North Miami. Projected landfall between 21:00 and midnight."

Lex glanced at his watch; it was only 7:40 p.m. The team's plan was to land before 8:00, then crash homes for precisely forty-five minutes. The Stingray would pick them up at 8:45 —plenty of time to escape the clutches of Tiberius. They'd be hunkered in their compound in time to watch the storm on the live news. The perfect plan.

Lex's plan —or rather *hope*— was to be liberated by his handlers soon after 8:00. Riker said he wanted to catch them in the act. Hopefully the first burglarized house would qualify.

"Approaching Biscayne Bay," Dalia declared. She glanced down to a mile-long bridge stretching to a tree-lined island. "Rickenbacker Causeway to Key Biscayne."

LeBeau added, "Evacuations ended at 6:00. The police exited by 7:00." He grinned with bugged eyes. "There's no one left down there."

To the Stingray's left, Miami's skyscrapers still twinkled. LeBeau frowned; their plans typically relied on their targets being without power. The isolated Key Biscayne was expected to lose electricity before the mainland.

Dalia sliced through the winds towards Key Biscayne. Air traffic had been halted that morning. The air control tower at Miami International had been deserted. In the melee of evacuating the city, no one would notice —or care— about a black helicopter cruising without its lights on. With darkness setting in, Dalia flipped down her night-vision and ordered, "Helmets on!"

Key Biscayne was barely five miles long and one mile wide. The barrier island was an upscale resort community with lush vegetation surrounding immense resorts and residences. Dalia decreased altitude as she skimmed above swaying palms and Australian pines. She proceeded beyond the public beaches to a gated residential neighborhood. The homes a hundred feet below appeared castle-like, with terracotta roofs, bell towers and circular driveways. Lex noticed there were no vehicles anywhere. Everyone was gone. *So how am I supposed to get evacuated?* Lex wondered.

The entire team jolted at a crack of thunder. The streetlights below went black. The island's power was out. Curt and Pitch simultaneously grunted, "*Yeah..!*"

Dalia hovered over a small beach amid Spanish-style mansions. She rotated the craft 360 degrees to scan their surroundings before landing. She checked her infrared monitor, "Nothing warm-blooded within 100 yards −that can stand on two feet anyway." She looked at the men, "Now get out!"

With their helmets engaged, the men disembarked carrying massive M249 machine guns. The M249 SAW −Squad Automatic Weapons− were unanimously voted in by the team. To Lex's chagrin, the team was now heavily armed −no longer unarmed *Robin Hoods* of victimless white-collar crime. At least he was also in full gear and had a weapon.

The four men jogged off as Dalia lifted, creating a cyclone of sand. As the Stingray vanished into sheets of rain, the men studied their surroundings. LeBeau checked his illuminated GPS and turned to a three-story Mediterranean mansion.

"Is that our diamond house?" Lex asked.

"No," LeBeau replied. "We have four others I want to hit first."

Jesus... Lex sighed as the wind howled. *How long is this going to take?*

Dan Holms pulled his truck up to the entrance of the Lee Sheriff's Office. An exhausted Nadine entered the truck and pecked him on the cheek.

"Desk work doesn't flatter you," Dan said as he drove.

"You have no idea." She rubbed her eyes. "Any good news on your end?"

"Seeds are planted. Hopefully in the right garden."

She nodded. "Tiberius is approaching Miami now. With its path, it'll hopefully spare us here. Winds over 155 −she's now a Cat-5."

"*My God...* Miami's first Cat-5 in over twenty years." Dan shook his head ominously.

"You think our burglars would risk going anywhere *near* a monster like that?"

Dan didn't answer. They were silent as she scanned the radio for any updates. He motioned to a folder. "What's that?"

"I got you records for Larriott's concealed weapons training. Why'd you want them?"

"You know, leaving no stone unturned and so on." After a pause, he added, "I'm still playing phone tag with the publisher of *Island Life* that profiled Larriott. I'd like to talk to the photographer who documented her home."

Nadine seemed unsure of the significance. She turned with a demure smile. "Danny..?"

"Yeah..?" Noting her coy expression, he grinned, "What are you up to?"

"What if I told you I got the address for the safe house where they're hiding Alexandra? It's in Naples, less than an hour from here."

He frowned, "The Ladies in Distress place? *Please* don't tell me you want to check on her. You don't think Curt would try–"

"–I'm not thinking anything," Nadine interrupted. "But if Curt wanted to attack her, what better distraction than a storm he's expected to be at?"

Dan's silence turned into a slow shake of his head. "You and I have built a hypothesis that these *killers* are going to show up in the eye of the Tiberius. I've even alerted certain *parties...*" He paused, "Now you think these thieves will *cancel* the storm and attack a house run by social workers –just for revenge?"

Nadine crossed her arms at his tone. "So you admit it: she is only protected by unarmed social workers. She and Cassie are defenseless. As long as she's under arrest, she can't leave that place. There's no better time to snatch her."

Dan bit his tongue and took a breath. "So should I keep my contacts informed, or come up with some eleventh-hour plan-B?"

"Maybe a little of both..?"

The ten-foot double doors were kicked in. The thick oak exploded inwards as the black shapes with the glowing eyes stepped inside. Within the cavernous home, the four soldiers entered with their M249 rifles. Their laser sights sent beams of red crisscrossing within the pitch-black house.

"Anyone home!" Curt shouted with an amplified voice. "It's the CAT team!"

His teammates shook their heads at his foolishness.

Unknown to them, other eyes and ears found his words equally brazen.

58. The Shift

"I can't see 'em, damnit! Where are they?" Colonel Sturges shouted at the monitor.

Deep within the bowels of MacDill's Special Ops Command, Sturges and Agents Riker, Jenkins and Louise Capell sat before a video display. The room's lights were dimmed and the video feed was on a fifty inch monitor. A nameless technician manned the controls.

Though the audio was relatively clear, the monitor displayed shaky, indecipherable images from a concealed camera. The four squinted to make out any shapes.

"They've gone to infrared," Jenkins observed. "Power's out."

Capell frowned, "How can I possibly observe any art?"

"Screw art!" Sturges replied. "If they unlawfully entered a residence, they've already committed their crime!"

"No," Riker retorted. "It isn't the diamond house! We stay put!"

Capell looked at Jenkins, "Where'd you hide the cam?"

"We planted a one-centimeter cam in Lex's helmet." Jenkins grinned, "The smallest in the biz, with 4,800 MHz circuitry to guarantee no interference with his radio."

"But no IR?" Capell had a crooked smile. "You never thought about night vision in homes with no power?" She chuckled at her male counterparts.

Sturges shouted to the tech, "At least tell me you're tracking his GPS."

The tech meekly replied, "Yes sir. Your man's still 200 meters from your primary target."

The Colonel and the agents leaned in, transfixed to the useless monitor.

Walls were x-rayed with technology that focused backscattered photons to reveal objects hidden within the walls. Perfectly viewable holograms showed where the safes were hidden and their contents. Pitch's meticulous financial research paid off. The homeowners had been confident their valuables, cash and bearer bonds were safe in steel vaults within cement walls.

Low-tech approaches paid off as well. Within stucco fortresses, the homeowners presumed their heavily-insured jewelry would be safe inside ordinary furniture. Without the use of any tools, dresser drawers were opened to reveals treasure troves of watches, gold and gems.

House to house, they stuffed their pouches like the Grinch. Art tubes were filled with carefully-rolled masterpieces. Lightning strikes increased as they marched, crashing door after door. No alarms sounded; the residents were probably at their summer homes in the Hamptons. Like picking up shells on a deserted beach.

When Nadine Stratton finished outlining her plan, she asked, "What do you think?"

Dan's eyes darted as they approached I-75. "We have nothing else to do as we watch the storm—"

Her phone halted their discussion. She beamed when she saw the caller's ID. "Hi! You have something?"

At nearly 8:20 p.m., Toby's windowless AV lab was as unchanging as a casino. He smiled into his Bluetooth and said in a singsong, "Hi Nadine, how are you..?"

"—Do you have something or not?"

Toby put his feet up on his desk. "Right now —as I speak— my monitor has an image that you just might like..." He grinned like a cat with a mouthful of canary.

"What?"

On his screen was the black and white surveillance footage from Larriott's damaged camera. It ran at only one frame per second, repeating on a loop. "I was only able to clean a four-second snippet." He adjusted the contrast to minimize static. "After I brightened the clip, I can discern the headboard of Ms. Larriott's bed—"

"—And?" Nadine interrupted with impatience.

"Standing beside the bed are three black silhouettes that appear to be men."

There was silence from Nadine's end of the phone.

Toby scrunched his nose as he moved within inches of the monitor. "Based on their profiles, they're definitely wearing helmets..." He paused, "...like *soldiers*."

In giddy disbelief, Nadine shouted, "You've confirmed three individuals in Larriott's bedroom wearing gear similar to soldiers?"

Dan's eyes widened at the news.

"That proves her story!" Nadine announced so both Toby and Dan could follow along. "These *men* were not invited by Larriott, so that makes them trespassers —intruders." She pulled the phone closer and slowed her voice to a more measured tone. "Toby: can your footage be sent through email or text as an mpeg or whatever?"

"Certainly."

"Then send the images directly to me. I'll forward them to Negrin." She looked at Dan as her mesmerizing smile returned. "He'll release Larriott immediately!"

"Your desire is my delight. *Adieu*." Toby hung up.

Dan smiled and reached for Nadine's hand. "So that's it? This could be over for Alexandra and Cassie?"

She held her head high with satisfaction. "And it'll probably get me fired. Coffey will be livid!" Nadine's smile was unruffled. "But can you imagine the press? A tormented single mother proves her tale. She was attacked and fought off her *assailants* –and the police never believed her!"

"Except for you," he smiled.

She looked at Dan, "I'll call Negrin. Maybe we can get Alexandra and Cassie outta' that house tonight!"

Before Dan could reply, an update on the radio seized their attention. He reached for the volume.

"...Tiberius has made an unexpected turn west-northwest. The prior course projected the landfall in north Miami-Dade. Now, Tiberius is hitting closer to metro Miami. The storm could cross the state, endangering anywhere between Naples and Fort Myers." The newscaster paused, "Can you imagine those poor folks on the west coast hit twice in a week?"

Nadine looked at Dan, "I wonder how fast Negrin can sign-off on Larriott?"

He looked at her with uncertainty, "Can you even reach a State's Attorney at 8:30 at night?"

59. The Soft Cell

"...with this northwestern shift, Tiberius 'could' threaten us again here in Lee County." The fatigued weatherman looked into the camera, "Unfortunately, folks, you know the drill: seek shelter. Let's pray the storm weakens as it crosses land..."

Alexandra quivered at the news. It was *déjà vu*. It was the same weatherman, on the same channel, with the same dire warnings as only five days before.

Holding a sleeping Cassie, she stepped to the room's east-facing window. Gazing into the darkness, she squinted for any sign of lightning on the horizon. *Nothing yet*. There were no storm shutters on home's window.

Alexandra sat back down. With Cassie in her lap, they were cocooned between pillows on the room's queen-sized bed. She observed her surroundings for the umpteenth time in the past seventy-two hours. Her assigned room looked like a romantic bed and breakfast. Pink pillows, doilies and antiques. But Alexandra knew the room was nothing but a cell, designed to hold her captive, yet somehow, ironically, supposed to minimize any stress.

The *Ladies in Distress* safe house was an ordinary home hidden within a gated community in east Naples, practically bordering the Everglades. The state-certified home was designed to offer a safe haven for abused women. It was also used for fragile witnesses or anonymous parties needing protection. A cell adorned with soft colors and pillows instead of steel bars.

Alexandra's bedroom door was not locked. However, the house was governed by sixty-year-old Hilda Campos, a tough Bea Arthur-type who'd boasted that she'd been a prison guard for thirty years. Hilda smiled and exchange pleasantries, but Alexandra was not naïve. She knew *Grandma Hilda* was nothing but a warden, with her finger hovering over a button that could have Alexandra locked up at any time.

Hilda microwaved a couple of Salisbury steak TV dinners for Alexandra and Cassie. She let them rummage through a box of old DVDs and Cassie fell asleep to worn-out repeats of *Full House*. Alexandra then watched news of Tiberius like a hawk. *I gotta' get out of here...*

With mounting stress, Alexandra began to almost hyperventilate. She swiftly hit an intercom button beside the bed. "Hilda!"

After a pause, a ripened voice replied, "What's up, Alex?"

"The news is saying Tiberius could head this way," Alexandra spoke fast. "Shouldn't we go to a shelter?"

"You can relax," Hilda interrupted. "This house was built up to code, and I got impact glass. Solid as a rock."

Alexandra's breathing calmed slightly. "Are there evacuation plans if it heads this way?"

"No!" Hilda scoffed. "It's too late for arrangements like that. You're in *custody*." She stressed the word as a harsh reminder. "I can't just take a *detainee* to some gymnasium."

Like a punch to the gut, a reminder this was no quaint bed and breakfast.

"And remember," Hilda added. "It's lights-out at nine o'clock sharp."

60. Operation: Revelation Fiesta

The CAT team walked in formation through the escalating wind. As the rain began to blow sideways, the men switched to their masks' oxygen feeds.

Lex checked his watch: 8:37 p.m.

"On to the diamond house." There was a smile in LeBeau's mechanical voice, "We can thank Lex for this target."

Dalia's voice crackled through their headsets, *"Attention!"* The men halted at her tone. "Tiberius has turned. Repeat, it has turned on a northwestern path. It'll make landfall closer than projected."

"Does this affect our exit?" LeBeau asked.

"Landfall will be central Dade —exactly where you're standing." Dalia paused at a crack of thunder. "Could be within the hour. Hit your final target and *exit!*"

The men jogged faster towards the end of the cul-de-sac.

LeBeau pointed to an estate fifty yards in front of them. "That's our diamond house."

The Spanish-style three-story mansion had multiple levels, chimneys and a bell tower. Pitch observed iron gates that had security cameras mounted on both sides. There were tiny red lights illuminated on each camera. "They have back-up power." LeBeau nodded to Pitch.

Pitch reached into his vest to produce an E-PIG. Cupping the grenade, he stepped forward. He wound up and hurled the grenade thirty yards. Despite the wind, the orb struck the center of the double gate. A bright blue explosion ripped apart the wrought iron. After the tendrils of electricity faded, the red lights on the cameras went out.

The fusion team's secondary monitor turned to static.

"The perimeter's breached," Jenkins announced to his small audience. "On schedule."

Riker squinted at the blurred feed from Lex's helmet-cam. "Welcome to our little fiesta."

Agent Capell asked the men, "Why did you name this operation *'Revelation Fiesta'*?"

Riker replied, "It was originally supposed to be 'Surprise Party.'"

The home's fortress-like doors smashed inward and wind screamed into the house. The four men entered the tall circular entryway. Using night vision, they paused to evaluate their environment. "My blueprints were right-on," Pitch boasted.

Adjacent to the entrance was a marble foyer. Within the museum-like room, their eyes were drawn to a carved pedestal with a glass case. An emergency spotlight shined down on the glass showcasing an enormous red gem. LeBeau gasped, "The *Dresden Diamond...*"

Pitch cocked his head, "The old lady kept it *there*? Seems stupid." The men stepped into the cavernous room. Three of the walls had arched thresholds to other rooms.

Curt chuckled, "This bitch trusts her security."

Lex stepped back, "Or trusts her guards."

"DON'T MOVE!" the voices roared. A dozen armed troops stepped out of the shadows of the three thresholds. They were equally geared in night vision —and massive guns locked on the four men.

The CAT team was outnumbered, outgunned and surrounded.

61. Deserted on the Island

With almost feline reflexes, Pitch tossed an E-Bang grenade to the floor.

A blinding burst of light. An expanding cloud of steam flashed with a strobe of electricity. Troops within a ten-yard radius shouted with concurrent jolts of searing agony.

Like a magic act, the CAT team was gone. Troops under each of the three thresholds covered their night scopes from the glaring light. Emerging from their blindness, the men aimed at each other from opposite archways.

"FREEZE!" an Onyx troop shouted at the men across from him. His four-man squad wore blue camouflage with scuba hoods identical to those used by Navy SEALs.

In the blurred confusion, the Onyx troops across from them aimed their guns, "*YOU* freeze!" They wore green camo and goggle-like night scopes, same as Delta Force.

"Drop YOUR arms!" The third team of Onyx troops wore black fatigues, ski masks and goggles —same as Marine Anti-Terror troops.

The three teams aimed at each other in a chaotic standoff. As the steam dissipated, they recognized their Onyx peers.

A troop pointed to the staircase, "They went upstairs!"

As the CAT team reached the second floor, Pitch threw an E-PIG towards the base of the stairs. The explosion only partially damaged the marble steps, but he hoped the pulse would disable the troops' electronic night vision. He heard screams and a few errant gunshots from the foyer. "Who are they?" Pitch shouted, "One uniform said National Guard!"

"They ain't guardsmen!" Curt replied as they ran. Following the floor plan, they proceeded towards a master bedroom at the rear of the home.

"Dalia!" LeBeau shouted into his mic, "Come in!" He heard no reply through heavy static.

As the men approached the bedroom, they could hear gunfire and voices rising from the staircase. "They're climbing!" Pitch shouted, "But they don't have vision!" At the far side of the bedroom, French doors led to a veranda overlooking the backyard. As Lex, Pitch and LeBeau entered the balcony, Curt crouched to fire at the approaching men.

"Dalia!" LeBeau tried again, his voice quivering. "We need evac! Repeat–"

An explosion of glass. Bullets shattered the French doors to the balcony.

As Lex and Pitch ducked, they heard LeBeau scream. They looked up to see him grasping the side of his head.

"*Aah*...My helmet's hit!" LeBeau shouted. A bullet had grazed the electronics to his night vision. Sparks shimmered from the side of his mask. He pulled off his helmet and hurled it over the balcony, leaving his headset intact. His chest heaved with panic.

Pitch peered over the balcony. Twenty feet below was a long, narrow swimming pool. The waterfront property was lit by pulses of lightning.

With his head exposed, LeBeau curled into a corner as gunfire intensified. "Who are those troops?"

Curt burst onto the balcony, firing his M249. "A dozen troops – but they can't see!"

Pitch motioned to the pool, "Jump!"

Hesitant to jump, LeBeau looked up at the roof. "I say we climb! Dalia can pick us up on top!" Bullets shattered a window beside them.

Without another second, Pitch and Curt leaped over the rail and into the pool. Lex aimed his rifle towards the approaching troops. As if conflicted –not firing at the men– Lex paused, and then jumped over the rail.

LeBeau was left alone. He looked up at the roof and then down to the pool. With the clamor of approaching men, he stood on a patio chair and pulled himself up to an incline that led to a third-story chimney. He reached the nearest summit as the soldiers poured onto the balcony. Panting behind a chimney, LeBeau could hear the troops' gunshots splashing into the pool.

Lex landed in the pool, feet first. He sank fast with his gear. As he looked towards the surface, he was shocked by oncoming beams of yellow and red. His infrared was picking up the heat trails of slugs narrowly missing him. He prayed his Kevlar could deflect the slowed bullets. At the far end of the pool, he saw Curt and Pitch exiting the water.

With no time to deliberate, Lex crawled along the bottom of the pool like a salamander towards the shallow end. He realized he didn't have his gun; it was too late to turn back. Surfacing at the far end, he looked at the house to see troops on the balcony, shooting blindly into the water. Lex exited the pool and jogged to a patio bar ten yards to the side.

Those troops don't know who I am! Lex panted. He ducked behind the bar to consider his dilemma. His brain spun with adrenalin. The troops were clearly sent by the feds, which was why he didn't shoot them. *Did my CAT teammates notice? Who are they?* Though some uniforms displayed dubious National Guard patches, they had obvious Special Forces training. They had to be contract troops –if so, they were essentially assassins, sent to annihilate the pathetic CAT team.

Lex knew a trigger-happy troop might shoot him the second they saw him. He couldn't just step into the open and wave his hands in the air. And the storm was less than an hour away.

Lex tried to see where Pitch and Curt were hiding. The lawn was long and narrow, showcasing the pool. It ended at a seawall on Biscayne Bay facing the Miami skyline. Both sides of the yard were bordered with thick, tropical properties. At the rear of the lawn was a cabana bathhouse. Using infrared, Lex located Curt and Pitch ducking beside the cabana. They were firing at the unidentified troops.

Lex moaned, perplexed. He was at the midpoint between the troops in the house and his CAT teammates, fifty yards away. *Should I call Riker?* He had to make a decision.

He turned off his headset and pulled out an encrypted FBI satphone. "Command!" Lex shouted, "Your troops are shooting at me!" Lex was ordered to never use his satellite phone except in an extreme crisis. Stuck in the middle of a shootout, without a gun —on the fringe of a Cat-5 hurricane— seemed to be an appropriate crisis.

"Command, come in!" Lex's voice blared through the speakers, mixed with the crackles of gunfire and thunder. *"Requesting Houdini,"* Lex shouted the specified distress code word. *"I need to vanish!"*

Agent Riker, Sturges and the tech huddled close. The fuzzy video showed a massive lawn, sporadically lit by lightning.

Riker was animated with frustration. He pointed to the Colonel, *"Your* hired guns don't know my man!" He reached for the mic to reply to Lex.

The Colonel reached for Riker's hand. *"DO NOT* reply!"

"Why?"

"Because my troops can't see. I have a Chinook arriving with orders to shoot anything that impedes their mission. We got hostiles wearing black —at night— firing at us in fifty mile-an-hour winds!" Sturges leaned closer, "You want them to call a time-out so we can usher your man to the sidelines? Maybe give him some Gatorade?"

"Command —do you read?" Lex's voice roared again. *"Demanding Houdini!"*

The Colonel continued in a more measured tone, "We've achieved step one of our objective. We got your precious CAT team cornered. I have a dozen Black Ink troops on the ground. More on the way. Your man will be fine—"

"—*Tell your men not to shoot!*" Lex's voice was muffled by thunder.

Riker stared at Sturges. After a second, he relented, "Maybe Lex will assume we lost signal. He's a big boy. He can take care of himself." He lifted the mic to his lips.

"Lex, we're losing signal... Hello..?" Riker's voice asked before the satphone went dead.

Lex gazed at his phone in disbelief, enraged. "You're abandoning me?" No one replied. Lex hurled his useless satphone into the air and shouted, "You're deserting me?"

Lex seethed. He *knew* Riker and his handlers could hear him. His satphone was specifically chosen for this mission. It connected to satellites instead of terrestrial networks that could be damaged in disasters. From Mount Everest, to the Sahara, to the South Pole, satphones would *always* work. It was impossible for his signal to be "lost" in high winds. They had lied, and he'd been undeniably abandoned.

Lex closed his eyes and inhaled. With the sputter of gunfire moving closer —and steadily increasing winds— he *had* to make a decision. Run away from the property? *To what shelter?* Run towards the troops with his hands up? *Towards armed men who can't see me?* Or a third option: join Curt and Pitch.

He pulled his mask over his face. Troops were now climbing down from the balcony. Bullets were snapping the palms around him. Lex turned towards his CAT teammates hidden beside the cabana. "Curt, Pitch, I'm approaching from your ten o'clock —don't shoot!"

Through the wind, Lex could hear the drone of a helicopter. *Is Dalia back?* Another fear filled his gut. *Or more federal assassins?*

62. From the Heavens They Came

"Circling, look for me!" Dalia shouted into her headset with both hands on the controls.

"I'm on the roof of the diamond house" LeBeau's voice shrieked. *"Hurry!"*

With the winds approaching fifty knots, Dalia flew low and fast. The Stingray soared forty feet above the ground. She arched and dipped over trees and housetops like a rollercoaster. It was easier to follow the roads of the community than GPS from the sky.

When she'd received LeBeau's frantic calls, she was almost at the parking garage on the far end of the island. LeBeau had cried that "federal troops" had him surrounded. Those words gave Dalia a sinking feeling in her gut. Was it just overzealous security guards —or real troops like he'd described? Would the feds risk sending troops in a Cat-5?

The Stingray hurdled over a tall house and back down to just feet above the road. Fighting the wind shear, she reached the cul-de-sac leading to the diamond house. She flew straight for the house, and then arced high over its roof, keeping an eye out for LeBeau's flare.

As she reached the pinnacle, she stopped abruptly.

"*Madre de Dios!*" Dalia shouted. Moving in her path was an immense MH-47 Chinook double-rotor helicopter. It was dark with no markings. The 100-foot aircraft hovered awkwardly in her path like a battleship.

In that instant, five years of Coast Guard avionics flooded her memories. The Chinook was one of the largest helicopters in the world and faster than most attack choppers. Dalia knew Chinooks were used for troop deployment –*and* the vehicle of choice for Special Forces.

Her instincts took over. She swerved low, maneuvering *under* the massive craft. The Stingray nearly skimmed the pool before it lifted back up, almost vertically to arch beyond the property. Over Biscayne Bay, she turned to observe the battlefield below.

Catching her breath, she had to think. With all the clutter, she hadn't seen the Chinook approach –ironically the same ploy the crashers used. On her Doppler the Chinook looked like a blob the size of a small raincloud. When she calibrated the radar to identify similar signatures, she gasped. Two more *blobs* were rapidly approaching from the opposite direction of Tiberius.

Crouching behind shrubs, Lex, Curt and Pitch gazed up to see their Stingray zip over their heads.

"Thank you, beautiful Dalia!" Pitch shouted.

Dalia's voice crackled through their headsets, "I can't go down there!"

When Curt looked up, his face was illuminated from the heavens. When Lex and Pitch looked up, they froze with wide eyes. Above them, the monstrous double-rotor Chinook ignited its floodlights. The entire yard was suddenly lit like a football field.

The three men sprung back into the vegetation like cockroaches escaping light. Pitch shouted the obvious, "They can see now!"

Troops were entering the yard from the house. Lex, Curt and Pitch crouched lower to the ground. *Splats* of bullets sprayed the branches above them. With the churning bay behind them, they couldn't retreat any farther. In front of them, a dozen troops were charging.

"Where's LeBeau?" Curt shouted. He fired erratically towards the troops. In doing so, he revealed their position. The soldiers returned fire with more precision. A mini ground war commenced.

Lighting the entire scene, the Chinook loomed fifty feet above them, creating additional cyclones of wind. With Lex unarmed, it was two and a half men against teams of lethally-trained experts.

In his panicked state, LeBeau struggled to climb higher on the slick, tiled roof. He wanted to be at the highest point before igniting his flare.

"Dalia, come in! Dalia!" LeBeau repeated as he arduously climbed on his belly. His boots slipped on the tiles. His gear was heavy; his hands couldn't keep a grip. "Dalia!"

As he strained to pull himself up the 45 degree incline, his vest became snagged on a vent. He tugged with impatience until his vest ripped. He pounded the tiles in frustration. He removed the vest, throwing it aside before resuming his climb. Behind him was a trail of lost gear: his knife, a puke saber, handgun and several tools.

At the roof's crest, LeBeau curled himself in a fetal position behind another small chimney. He held a hand to his headset, having to shout, "Dalia! I've reached the summit!" He looked at the Chinook hovering over the yard. He knew it was powerful, but Dalia's Stingray was sleek and nimble. He had faith she was planning his escape.

LeBeau curled tighter behind the chimney to hide from the lights. As the spotlights swirled to search for his teammates, his breathing became labored with anxiety. He watched his team being attacked by the troops as if watching an arena from nosebleed seats. *Better them than me.*

On LeBeau's headset he could hear Pitch shouting, *"Wind's too strong —I can't throw my grenades!"*

Grenades! LeBeau perked up at the word. Where were his E-PIGS? With a queasy feeling, he looked lower on the roof. *My Vest!* The E-PIGS were in his discarded vest.

LeBeau's entire body flinched as a wooden plank landed beside him, hurled by the wind. The four-foot board became wedged between the chimney and the roof tiles. After catching his breath, LeBeau guessed the winds were near sixty miles per hour, blowing from a high altitude towards the lawn below.

That's when he saw it: from his discarded vest, twenty feet away, an E-PIG began to roll down the roof. LeBeau's eyes bugged; he was too petrified to scream. He saw the grenade teeter on a shingle, about to drop six inches to the next tile. He squeezed his eyes closed with his hands over his head. *No...!*

When there was no explosion, he cracked open an eye. The grenade began bouncing down the roof. LeBeau smiled, *there's not enough force!* The E-PIG's sensors were designed to only detonate at impacts over thirty miles per hour. This protected the user if he accidentally dropped a grenade. When Pitch used them, his throws were well over eighty miles per hour.

With a smirk, LeBeau watched the E-PIG hop down the tiles like a Slinky walking down stairs. When the grenade bounced off the roof's last shingle, a sudden squall hurled it towards the backyard like an invisible force. LeBeau knew what would happen next.

With sixty mile-per-hour winds blowing *towards* the battlefield below, the E-PIG exploded with brilliant blue light amidst a cluster of armed troops. They had no idea what had hit them.

From his vest, LeBeau could see two more grenades bouncing down the roof like rubber balls. Gripping the chimney with one arm like King Kong, LeBeau laughed.

Curt, Pitch and Lex couldn't believe their eyes. Like God punishing the federal heathens, they watched the troops being torn apart by blinding explosions. Even through the drone of the Chinook, they could hear the soldiers' screams. The remaining men scurried to the sidelines like villagers escaping napalm. The Chinook teetered — probably due to electrical hiccups— and rose a hundred feet higher.

"It was LeBeau!" Pitch declared in disbelief. "He threw the grenades from the roof!"

"He saved us!" Curt shouted. They located LeBeau squatting behind a chimney. "Froggy's our hero!"

LeBeau blossomed with a sneer. He couldn't believe his ears. His team's headsets were still working, magnetically shielded from the blasts. He heard them add, "LeBeau, you're a genius!"

"Yes..." LeBeau replied into his radio, "I...was lying in wait, planning my attack." He nearly chuckled to himself. Blue-collar idiots.

"Come down. We'll call Dalia," Pitch shouted.

LeBeau paused. With the hovering Chinook, there was no way Dalia would approach the ground. His best hope for a pick-up was the roof. There was no way to get the three men up to the roof in time. He knew what he had to do. *Sorry boys, this is a one-man show.*

LeBeau grasped the wooden plank that was wedged on the roof. With both hands, he held it at one end. It wavered in the stream of wind. The board was blowing diagonally towards the ground below. He gripped it with all of his strength.

He'd heard accounts of storms blowing projectiles at unbelievable speeds. Broom handles have pierced telephone poles. And now, Tiberius's winds were aiming at his teammates.

"Pitch," LeBeau shouted into his headset. "You have more grenades?"

In the lawn below, he could see a man step into the open. It was Pitch. "Affirmative!" Pitch patted his vest, "Four more!"

Clutching the board with both hands, LeBeau struggled to aim. He let go of the plank and it flew from his hands like a guided missile. It soared diagonally towards the ground at over sixty miles per hour.

"See me?" Pitch gazed up at the roof with wide arms. The oncoming projectile was too fast to comprehend. Before he could utter another word, the plank hit his grenade-laden torso. Pitch exploded, red and black through blinding blue light.

Lex and Curt dropped to the ground with hands over their heads. With such a close blast, their goggles were disabled. Their radios crackled with static. Retreating into shrubbery, Curt shouted, "I think *LeBeau* just killed Pitch!"

Lex glared in disbelief. They froze as light encircled them like a prison spotlight. The men looked up to see the giant Chinook descending to just thirty feet. Ropes dropped from both sides of the chopper, twirling in the winds like whips. Countless geared troops began repelling down the cords.

With no radios or goggles, Curt and Lex were deaf, speechless and blind.

63. Brass Huevos

"Onboard electronics resuming," Onyx pilot Giovino announced from the cockpit of the Chinook. "Systems had a temporary glitch. Probably lightning. Over."

"If your men are a go, then drop 'em!" Sturges' voice ordered.

"Repelling now over target. Over."

Onyx Officer Giovino, a former pilot with the Special Ops Regiment of the U. S. Army, had received his orders from Onyx's headquarters in North Carolina only ten hours earlier. Normally their missions required weeks of planning and drills, using replica targets built in the Carolina forests. But they'd had no such luxury with this mission. Their superiors had remarked, "How tough can it be to stop half a dozen home burglars?"

Giovino had flown to countless hostile environments around the globe, but never into a hurricane. His cargo of so many men, summoned from around the country, was also a first. Onboard the Chinook were a mix of former Army Rangers and Delta Force troops. Giovino privately wondered if there was a national security threat –

but during a Cat-5 storm?

Fortunately, Giovino's orders seemed simple: deploy the troops and exit before Tiberius's landfall. He was then to proceed to the Air Reserve Base in Homestead, south of Miami. After the storm passed, he was to return to the site at first daylight, 06:00. He presumed that meant to collect however many men survived the storm.

"Watch that shear from the north!" Co-pilot Malone warned Giovino as the craft banked hard to the port side. Officer Malone was a flight engineer assigned to the mission, and a former Ranger. Giovino and Malone, from two different Onyx branches, had met for the first time while flying to Miami. They'd taken off from Avon Park, an auxiliary field used by MacDill, but discreetly located ninety miles away from the prying eyes of Tampa's base. Avon Park had a limited airfield, perfect for vertical take-off craft. Having chugged two Red Bulls before departing, Malone was chatty. According to him, Colonel Sturges had said, "History was being made."

"History?" Giovino scoffed, "Suicide by hurricane?"

"No," Malone replied. "Sturges specifically requested a mix of former Rangers..." He paused for drama, "*And* Navy SEALS, *and* Marine Anti-Terror troops. A grand slam of Ops."

With a burst of wind, Giovino focused on stabilizing the aircraft. They had to shout into their headsets. "Why multi-branch? We're finally taking Cuba —in a storm?"

"Unknown." Malone paused to speculate. "I don't buy the cover. My guess is a terror cell, maybe ISIL." He pointed to the radar, "Our help's almost here."

"Affirmative," Giovino saw the two Blackhawks approaching. "General Lindsey hired our entire fleet?"

"Negative," Malone corrected. "The General's out of the country. It's Sturges. As officer on duty, he's calling the shots."

Giovino coughed a chuckle, "Deploying Onyx *during* a Cat-5 — while the boss is gone? That's some serious *cajónes!*"

Before Malone could reply, he pointed at the house, "Look there — at three o'clock! Is that a man on the roof? Aim lights at the center chimney!"

64. Flight or Fight

The spotlights hit LeBeau like he was onstage. No matter how small he crouched, he was still visible curled behind the chimney.

"Dalia! Where are you...?" LeBeau's voice quivered.

Curt's unexpected voice boomed in his headset. "Dalia: don't listen to him! He *killed* Pitch!"

LeBeau was shocked. *Curt's alive? Their radios resumed..?* He'd assumed Lex and Curt were killed or injured in the blasts. LeBeau darted his head. The spotlight settled directly on him. The wind from the rotors grew almost unbearable as the chopper drifted closer. LeBeau gasped as he saw the Chinook's .50 caliber machine guns aiming at him.

He dropped onto his belly on the roof. Attempting to crawl downslope towards the front of the house, he began to skid. He stumbled and rolled to the edge of the roof. He tried to grab a gutter to halt his fall, but tumbled too fast, the shingles were too slippery. LeBeau fell twenty feet into a bougainvillea bush.

Without padding or gear, he panted, facing up. Directly above, he saw the Chinook's spotlights zigzagging. They were looking for him –

which meant he'd temporarily escaped. LeBeau painfully crawled out of the thorns. His left ankle felt like it was sprained. With no vest, his ripped fatigues revealed numerous cuts from the bougainvillea.

A voice crackled in his head, "Forget LeBeau —we need pick-up!" It was Lex. LeBeau's headset was still intact. *Lex and Curt know I killed Pitch!* They would tell Dalia everything. LeBeau's anxiety flooded back.

With a slithering spear of lightening, LeBeau saw the path before him. He began running into the street, limping blindly through the wind and rain.

Dalia shouted, "Lex: exit east —the adjoining property!"

"We don't have eyes!" Curt replied.

"I can track your GPS through your vest tags," Dalia said. "East, 100 yards. The brush clears to a small beach." She could hear the sounds of trudging and heavy breathing.

"How many on our tail?" Lex shouted.

Dalia hovered a hundred yards away. "Maybe twenty —forming a perimeter. They don't know which way you've gone."

"We're over the fence!" Curt huffed. "Get us outta' here!"

Curt and Lex tumbled and slid through mud and vegetation. The land was like a natural preserve, thick and almost impassable, the type of place where a machete would be useful. Without night vision, they had to rely on the pulses of lightning.

"Forty yards ahead," Dalia's voice continued. "I'm watching your back."

The men could hear gunshots advancing from behind. The snapping of twigs grew closer. With another flash of lightning, they could see the reflection of sand through the trees. It was a small clearing beside the bay.

Branches splintered as bullets sprayed through the trees. Curt and Lex huddled through gnarled mangroves. The clearing was fifty more feet.

Sudden blasts came from above. Lex looked up to see the flashing of fire from a weapon in the sky. It was the M60 machine gun from their beloved Stingray. Dalia was firing at the troops behind them.

"They're closing in," Dalia shouted. "Look for the clearing...thirty feet..."

Curt and Lex exited the woods to see a rocky beach the size of a convenience store. As the storm whipped in from the bay, a new gust blew from above. It was the Stingray.

"Get in!" Dalia screamed. She descended to four feet from the ground. As the men sprinted towards the chopper, its M60's armor-piercing bullets ripped through the trees. She aimed above the troops' heads, not at them. *Let's go..!"*

Troops fired from the dark, narrowly missing the invisible Stingray. Dalia continued to fire shots long enough for the men to board. She then pulled hard on the cyclic and the Stingray climbed almost straight up into the sky.

LeBeau whimpered as he ran with a limp. His teammates' voices echoed in his head, *"LeBeau killed Pitch...!"* He ran harder towards Rickenbacker Causeway, the only road that led to the mainland.

Hysterical, LeBeau had no strategy. He knew he had to flee an area crawling with troops. He had zero plans for shelter. In retrospect, he could've broken into another house for refuge. But he was too far away now, and there were no other structures before the bridge. The only semblance of a goal was to reach the mainland before the brunt of Tiberius came ashore. But the bridge was nearly a mile long.

Miraculously, the twinkling lights of Miami were still visible. LeBeau used the skyline as his nebulous goal. Unprotected and unarmed, it was at least a glimmer of hope at the end of his long, dark path.

Lex strapped himself into his seat and removed his helmet. He held on tight as the Stingray bucked in the screaming winds. He looked at Curt as if he'd lost his mind.

Rather than strapping in, Curt unfolded a tripod and attached an

M240 machine gun.

He slid open the cabin's door. Wind and rain howled into the chopper.

"What are you doing?" Dalia shouted.

With an insane grin, Curt began firing the gun out the door.

"Forget them!" Lex shouted. His words were lost within the gunfire.

Curt laughed as he fired out the chopper, like the so many visions of maniacal troops firing on villages in Vietnam.

"We have company!" Dalia's voice boomed through their headsets.

Lex looked back towards the Chinook. Like a whale, the large aircraft slowly turned to pursue the Stingray. He then gasped when he saw them: soaring from behind the Chinook were two Blackhawks.

Chinook pilot Giovino shouted, "They're not showing on radar!"

"I have a visual —but not good," Malone replied. "Follow the tracers from their fire!"

Giovino sped towards the Stingray. "Do we evac our troops, or pursue the targets?"

"Orders are to pursue the Stingray."

"This is Wasp-1," the Blackhawk pilot announced in their headsets. "We have a lock on the Stingray —follow our lead. Over."

LeBeau's ankle throbbed as he labored to run. The bridge's ramp was less than a block ahead. Without his mask, he sporadically choked on the rain.

With a monstrous drone approaching from behind, he looked back to see the Stingray fleeing the Chinook. On its tail were two Blackhawks in pursuit. The choppers were firing at each other. The crisscrossing tracers from their guns lit the sky like a scene out of *Star Wars*.

With a surge of energy —or fear— LeBeau ran faster towards the bridge. Peeking back, he saw the Chinook firing. He knew it was equipped with weapons much larger than Dalia's.

Maybe they'll destroy the Stingray! LeBeau hoped. As he ran through a puddle, his foot got caught in a pothole. He staggered and fell with a splash. Over his shoulder, the Stingray seemed to be coming straight at him. On its tail were the Chinook and two Blackhawks. *They're coming after me!* LeBeau curled into a ball with his hands over his face. The chopper buzzed within feet of his head. Its wind trail nearly rolled him ten feet. When the Chinook passed over LeBeau's head, its roar rattled his teeth. The choppers continued towards the lights of Miami.

LeBeau stood to resume his jog. The road became dryer as the bridge's ramp inclined. He suddenly flinched at a sound-barrier-breaking explosion. Over Biscayne Bay, a fireball appeared from the Chinook's rear rotor. The Stingray had made a direct hit. The blast reflected a brilliant orange in the bay.

The Chinook's front blades labored to keep the craft in the sky. With the destroyed rear rotors, the back half of the chopper began to dip. The enormous aircraft paused and slowly sank in the sky —rear first— like an airborne Titanic. After a mechanical moan, a second explosion lit the clouds as the aircraft hit the bay, hurling fiery debris in every direction.

"Ah ha haaa!" Curt laughed like a child. "I killed that fuckin' whale!"

Lex looked back at the debris from the blazing Chinook. Though the feds were now the *enemy*, he couldn't erase from his conscience that men had just died.

Dalia also seemed dazed at the sobering loss of life. She paused, reminded of their predicament. "The 'Hawks are closing!" The Stingray bucked in the sky like a bronco.

"Close the door!" Lex shouted. The opening was causing drag, sucking wind and rain into the cabin.

"I can fly twenty knots faster if you close that door!" Dalia shouted.

Astonishingly, Curt seemed to listen. Like a child getting the last word, he fired off several more rounds before securing the door.

Dalia engaged the throttle and pushed the cyclic creating instant thrust. Struggling to negotiate the winds, they were drifting towards the lit Miami skyline. "I have an idea."

Lex frowned. He saw Dalia flying directly towards the skyscrapers of downtown.

Curt grinned knowingly. "I get it! They'd be insane to follow!"

The Blackhawks were approaching to within a hundred yards. Dalia shouted into her radio, "Blackhawk at my six: *disengage!*" With no response, she shook her head at their apathy. Dalia sped towards the tallest building, the sixty-four story Four Seasons Hotel. The tower flickered with faltering electricity. She raced straight for it.

Lex squeezed his eyes closed as Dalia came within fifty feet of the building. With a Blackhawk on her tail, she dove, straight down and to the left. Unable to turn with equal precision, the Blackhawk's blades skimmed the building's windows, throwing the craft off balance. The chopper descended fast with rotor damage. It'd have to make a hard landing in the streets of Miami. The maneuver gained Dalia a hundred-yard lead from the second Blackhawk.

Lex had to trust Dalia's skills. Gripping his seat, with dips and thrusts like a theme park ride, he was about to vomit. Curt held on like a bull rider, laughing all the way.

The second Blackhawk moved fast into her trail. Its gunshots shattered into buildings around them. Dalia pulled back on the cyclic and rose again, this time towards the Marquis building. The sixty-three story tower was the tallest residential building in the southeastern U.S. —and Dalia was aiming directly for its center.

Is this a suicide flight? Lex gnashed his teeth. *Please let her have a plan...* The Blackhawk converged to within fifty yards. Their bullets getting closer.

By luck or divine intervention —from whatever God protects the wicked— Miami's power flickered out. For Dalia, an expert of night-vision navigation, the blackout was a miracle. With her unlit aircraft, they were invisible —heading straight for a black, unlit tower of glass and steel. She counted down, "...five...four...three..." She pushed the cyclic hard to the port side. The Stingray twisted to the left, within *feet* of the tower.

Utterly helpless, the Blackhawk smashed into the thirty-seventh floor of the unseen building. Its crew would never know what they'd hit. Blazing steel and glass lit the edifice as the pieces fell to the streets.

Dalia cruised west-northwest and dropped low to avoid the upper airstream. She panted and announced, "Hangar ETA: twenty-seven minutes."

LeBeau saw fire over the Miami skyline. *Was the Stingray destroyed?* The wind was rushing towards LeBeau as he labored to hike the bridge's ramp. He felt like a mime pretending to run in the wind, moving only four feet per second. Tiberius was blowing too hard.

He hadn't even reached the actual bridge yet. Behind him, it was nearly a mile to any other structure. The wind would soon immobilize him completely. He could drown in the rain alone. *Drowning,* his ultimate nightmare. *And I have no gear or tools...*

He perked up as he remembered. He reached for the small of his back. Tucked in his waistband was Pitch's new *Blister Tent.* He pulled out the circle of nylon. He moved near a cement guardrail, hoping it would block any flying debris. The elevated ramp was free of any puddles. The three-foot diameter tent unfolded automatically before him. He shoved it towards the ground before the wind could pull it away. He scurried inside the igloo-like tent to engage the CO-2 triggers. With abrupt *thumps,* steel barbs shot into the concrete forming permanent anchors. He tucked his legs inside and squatted into a tight ball. He closed the self-sealing zipper behind him. The fasteners were designed with an epoxy that no wind could rip. One-way vents allowed oxygen in from the sides. Though curled uncomfortably, he'd be protected from the wind and rain just like the Antarctic scientists who'd invented it.

Sealed in a locked cocoon on the bridge, LeBeau suddenly twinged with a new fear: could the waters rise above the guardrail? Antarctic scientists never had to worry about flooding. *Oh God, what have I done..?*

The tent seemed increasingly miniscule as the colossal Tiberius moved ashore.

Dalia, Lex and Curt sighed as they escaped the clutches of Tiberius. The Stingray was stabilizing west of Miami. After a moment, Curt unbuckled to stretch within the cabin.

Lex wondered about LeBeau. He had to be dead –killed either by troops *or* the storm. What was the future of this *team?* Was there any way to convince Dalia to escape with him, away from this insane Curt?

"ETA: fifteen," Dalia announced with increasing relief in her voice.

Standing beside Lex, Curt's voice boomed, "–I don't think so."

When Lex looked up, a chill shot through his body. Curt was holding a Glock 17 to Dalia's head.

"We're taking this bird to Naples," Curt declared. Before Lex could react, he aimed a second handgun to Lex's eyes. "There's someone I need to take care of."

65. Saved by the Orange and White

"Abort!" Colonel Sturges ordered into his mic. "Conditions too hostile!"

"Roger," an Onyx commander replied. "We'll seek shelter in local structures. Over."

"Hostile conditions? Riker scowled at the Colonel, "Would that be the storm or the suspects who slaughtered most of your hired guns?"

The commander's weary voice added, "Many assets are down, sir. Over."

The Colonel glared at Riker as he replied into the mic, "Leave the casualties. Take cover. We'll catch the fallen at daybreak. Over."

"In the morning?" Riker asked. "The storm will wash the men away!"

"You run your show; I'll run mine!"

"I tried that," Riker retorted. "And I lost my informant in the process –all for you to get your deserters back. Pretty ironic we lost more men in the process!"

Agent Capell appeared uneasy. "Colonel, you did say we had consent to employ Onyx on our own soil..?" She looked at Riker, "Maybe we should advise–"

"–This isn't the time or place!" Sturges erupted. He honed his eyes at Riker and jerked his head to the right, as in *not in front of them.* "Step outside!"

Riker and Sturges exited to the hall and closed the door. If Riker was intimidated by the Colonel, he didn't show it. "I abandoned an informant that took *years* to cultivate!"

"Stand down!" Sturges growled.

"Did you just say *stand down*?" Riker laughed. "I'm not one of your military grunts! *My* agents have law degrees!" He stepped closer to Sturges, "How are you going to explain *mass* casualties of federally-funded assets to the General? And this little massacre was stateside, not in some third-world warzone."

For the first time, the Colonel was silent. He opened his mouth and then closed it. He paused before replying, "My report will state... I received a tip about a national threat, possibly triggered during the storm. I had the *duty* to contain the threat using any means necessary." His eyes skimmed across the hall as he devised his yarn. "A possible...suitcase nuke, smuggled from Cuba to the Port of Miami..." His voice trailed with uncertainty.

"Pathetic," Riker turned to reenter the mission room.

Sturges added almost desperately, "We haven't heard from the Blackhawks. We lost contact –they were in pursuit." He placed a hand on Riker's shoulder as they entered the room. "Does your *law degree* have a better idea?"

Riker inhaled, ready to reply, but stopped when he saw Jenkins' look of astonishment. "What's up?"

Jenkins asked, "Who invited the Coast Guard?"

Against the black night, the orange and white helicopters stood out like neon Dreamsicles. Four Coast Guard HH-6oJ Jayhawk rescue helicopters landed on the bloodied and scorched "diamond house" lawn.

Randall Andris, Resident Agent in Charge, was the first to step out of a Jayhawk. He shouted over the wind, "Round up any men! *Fast!*"

His officers huddled into the yard aiming high-beam spotlights.

Figures materialized from the shadows. As Andris's eyes adjusted, he lowered his gun, startled to see a weary mix of injured troops. Though some uniforms had patches for the National Guard, something seemed wrong. They had advanced gear and night vision. More significantly, they carried massive rifles and MP5's, not the smaller carbines that were standard issue with the National Guard.

A man in amphibious gear approached. He spoke fast, "I'm Colonel McNair, here on orders from SOCOM. I got National Guard with us. Are you equipped with Medevac? We got heavy casualties!"

"Yes sir!" Andris pointed, "Each chopper can treat six!" It was clear these were off-the-book troops, and Andris didn't care. Any identity concerns would be sorted out later. These men were wounded and the storm was escalating.

Andris and his men spread out to usher twenty-three men to the choppers. A bruised, waterlogged mix of advanced troops. Andris looked into the men's eyes and they reflected something they were never supposed to feel: panic. The Coast Guard officers helped the men to their seats and stretchers, with each chopper fully-equipped as air ambulances.

As the last man was secured, the four orange Jayhawks lifted. Accustomed to air-sea search and rescue, the pilots were trained for flying in harsh conditions. Their NAVSTAR Global Positioning System used eighteen satellites to navigate, easing travel in zero visibility. Orders were to fly north, beyond Tiberius's path, to Palm Beach Mariner's Hospital.

Randy Andris cursed that he'd been forty-five minutes too late. Still, they were able to save almost two dozen men within minutes of the storm's full landfall.

Knowing the Coast Guard had no official "special forces," Randy gave a melancholy smile at how his team had just helped save three teams of *someone's* tier-one troops. He needed to thank Dan Holms, whose bizarre tip turned out to be perilously true. Being under the umbrella of Homeland Security, Randy had a duty to pursue Dan's allegations. *I'll submit Dan for a civilian bravery medal,* Randy decided.

But Randy wondered if he also had another obligation. These were *someone's* advanced troops –heavily armed and on U.S. soil. He was curious if he might have a duty to make certain other inquiries.

Riker motioned to Agent Jenkins to step into the hall. After the door closed, Riker looked over his shoulder and whispered, "Did you send Lex the address for the safe house where they're hiding Larriott?"

"Of course, yesterday," Jenkins replied. "But is Lex still...an asset?"

Riker paused to craft his words, "FBI Special Agent 'Lex' is no longer in our service. He was *eliminated* by the suspects, and/or Hurricane Tiberius." He narrowed his eyes, "Understood?"

"Yes sir," Jenkins replied without pause. "Does that impair our plans?"

Riker sighed with his back against the wall, "We've lost an asset to the CAT team before. I guess their brand of danger's too enticing."

Jenkins' eyes widened. "You've had a mole on the team before?"

Riker raised a brow playfully, "Perhaps." Switching gears, he mused, "I wonder if Lex had an opportunity to share Ms. Larriott's address with Curt?"

Jenkins cocked his head, unsure of his inference. "You think they still might...?"

"The Colonel and his rent-a-cops had a chance and they blew it." Riker grinned, "It's our play now."

66. Naples Rendezvous

From the Stingray's overhead racks, Curt pulled out every gun and hurled them out the door. "Give me your weapons!" Curt shouted, aiming his Glock at both Dalia and Lex. "Everything; puke sabers, Tasers, PIGS..."

Soaring over the Everglades, Dalia gave Curt an icy glare. "What if I fly us straight into the ground?"

Lex's eyes widened at the thought.

"Do it, you fucking *puta*," Curt laughed. "I dare you!" His sweaty face had a jagged grin. He pressed his gun hard against Dalia's cheek as he slid his left hand over her body to search for weapons.

Lex made fists, helpless. Despite all of his combat training, there was nothing he could do. Curt was armed and within a confined space. One stray bullet could either kill Dalia or damage the aircraft —then they'd all die. He had no choice but to surrender his weapons and remain calm. He shouted at Curt, "All this to find your wife?"

Curt ignored the question as he shoved a duffle bag towards Lex. "Put everything you took in this. Don't skimp; I saw everything!"

Lex grudgingly reached into his thigh pouches to remove cash and jewelry. As he stuffed it into Curt's bag, he asked, "What's your plan?

Kill your wife and take your daughter?" He gave a brazen smile, "Raise her out in the Everglades? A real father of the year!"

With his padded knuckles, Curt punched Lex in the jaw with all of his force. Lex's cheekbone made a gravelly *crunch*. His head fell back, unresponsive.

Dalia recoiled at the sound. She saw the streetlamp for their hangar pass below. Over the ink-black Everglades, she began to see the glow from Florida's west coast on the horizon.

Her pulse raced. Not from fear, but from an absolute loathing of Curt. For a second she actually considered flying –full speed– into the earth. Their chopper and all computer information of their exploits wouldn't be found for a decade. But Curt was right; she wouldn't do it. She loved the danger, money and power too much. And Dalia had to confess she had a growing desire for Lex.

"Follow my orders!" Curt shouted, "Lights off!" He handed her a folded printout.

She turned off all remaining lights on the Stingray. In the cockpit's dim light she looked at the folded paper. It was the coordinates for the *Ladies in Distress* safe house where they were hiding Curt's wife.

"There's a park two blocks east of this address," Curt said, his hot breath lapping at her neck. "You're going to land there. Can you *comprendo* all that?"

She gnashed her teeth. As the lights of suburban Naples came into view, she faintly announced, "ETA: five."

Lex slowly began to stir. He squinted a blood-shot eye towards Curt, who was checking his gear and loading his guns. Curt cracked his neck and slid open the cabin door. He inhaled the wind, "*Ahhh...* I can smell her!"

Dalia descended towards a new-construction neighborhood east of Naples. The small homes practically bordered the Everglades. Unaffected by the storm –so far– the neighborhood was well lit. On the east side of the community was a small park with a playground and a natural habitat of trees adjoining the Big Cypress Natural Preserve.

"Land there!" Curt ordered. "At the base of those trees."

Dalia landed near a hammock of cypress trees. The foliage would dampen the sound of the chopper. The closest house was over three blocks away.

"You going to kill us now?" Dalia asked with no hint of alarm.

Curt looked at her like she was insane. "I need you to fly this bird." He put on his helmet. "Tiberius is a comin.' I need you to get me the hell outta' here." He turned to Lex. "As for computer boy, you seem to like him, so I'll keep hurting him to make you cooperate."

Dalia said nothing. Curt handcuffed her ankle to her seat and her right hand to Lex's hand, seated behind her. Curt hopped out of the chopper. He pulled a thick bungee rope out of the cabin and coiled it around a cypress stump. He looked at Dalia. "Now give me your key!"

Dalia scoffed, "Stingrays don't have keys."

He narrowed his eyes and aimed his gun at Lex's temple.

She was caught. When the CAT team customized the chopper, Butch designed a key that'd be needed to start the primary engines as a safeguard. Cuffed to Lex, Dalia pulled her right hand below the cyclic and removed a standard-looking key. She flicked it towards Curt. He caught it, grinned, and ran off towards the cookie-cutter neighborhood.

Curt approached 228 Anita Drive. It was a pink, zero-lot-line home with a single-car garage. It looked like something newlyweds or the newly-retired would buy. With the abundant streetlamps, he had no need for night vision.

Holding his helmet under one arm, he slicked-over his damp hair with the other. He approached the door and cleared his throat. A TV-dinner smell emanated from the house. *This is too easy,* he almost laughed. He rang the doorbell.

Without the clomping of any footsteps, a tinny intercom blared, "Who is it?" It sounded like a mean old woman.

"Naples Police, ma'am," Curt announced. Knowing the door had a peephole, he hoped his black uniform looked similar to SWAT gear. "Please open the door. We need to speak with the homeowner."

After a minute, the door cracked open four inches. From behind a security chain, a gruff older woman frowned. "How can I help you?" She eyed him head to toe.

"Ma'am, is there an 'Alexandra Larriott' at this address?" Curt asked with meager authority. "We believe she might be in danger."

The woman furled her brows warily. "*Sir,* this is a house of healing. Let me see a badge."

Her response instantly confirmed he had the right house. Curt grinned, reached into his vest and pulled an object up to eye level. He moved it towards the door.

The woman moved closer to inspect what she presumed to be a badge.

Curt fired his electroshock weapon sideways into her face. 300,000 volts pulsed into her cheek. The woman fell to the ground, convulsing.

Curt kicked open the door. "Angel..? Daddy's home!"

67. Family Reunion

From under pink covers, she flinched at the crashing sound. "Hilda, is everything okay?" She then regretted shouting from the bedroom. *Is it him?* Even though she'd anticipated Curt's arrival, her heart still pounded.

"Where are you?" Curt's voice thundered from across the house.

She knew the bedroom's windows were reinforced and locked. The door was the only way in or out. She huddled under the covers, her brain spiraling with anxiety.

Curt's voice was closer, "Don't worry, I won't kill Cassie!"

Curt stepped over the old woman who was foaming from her mouth. Scanning the room, he saw a breaker box near the hallway. He opened it and shut off all power. "You still scared of the dark, punkin'?" Curt smiled and put on his helmet.

He kicked open the first bedroom door. He aimed his gun and scanned the room with night vision. All he saw was a vacant room with packing boxes.

"*Alex-an-dra...*" Curt sang in a mechanical voice. "Is that your name now?" He stepped to the second bedroom and kicked open the door.

He stopped —without any ability to hide, there she was. Lying in bed, she was covered by only a blanket like a child playing hide-and-seek. In the clarity of infrared, her body heat made her visible. She was heavily panting. *You idiot...* Curt grinned when he saw it: like an imbecile, she didn't realize her dark hair was protruding from the covers.

With his prey trapped before him, Curt reached for the blanket.

"What are we going to do?" Dalia began to tear, cuffed to her seat. For the first time in Lex's recollection, Dalia was losing her cool. "Maybe we finally call for help?"

"*What*?" Lex cringed. He shuffled into the cockpit, his left hand still cuffed to her right. "You have no idea what the feds would do!"

"I have *some* idea," she retorted. "I'm not an idiot!"

He paused. Lex knew the federal consequences because he *was* a fed. He had to be careful to explain. "Since I'm former Army, I know they could execute us as terrorists."

"*Terrorists?*" She frowned, "We steal things from houses that are covered by insurance!"

"No," Lex interrupted. "You're AWOL soldiers, with stolen weapons and technology. They might think we're some...sleeper cell."

"So what do we do?"

"We can't escape and Curt has the key to the engine." He shook his head, "We'll wait until he gets back, then hope for an opportunity to overpower him."

Lex gripped her hand. Though she gave a slight nod of trust, he couldn't reveal his true fear: his FBI handlers *knew* he'd leaked the safe house address to Curt. They'd expected him to go there —which meant the feds were on the way. He and Dalia could be shot or arrested under the harshest charges imaginable.

Before snatching the blanket off his trembling wife, Curt ran his hand across her covered form. She was an utter captive. He was al-

most orgasmic as he felt her nose and lips. He felt her body quiver –
but he knew it was from fear and not arousal. He cooed, "Baby, you
been gone a long time..." He tugged the blanket away like a magician.
"Surprise!"

The room filled with a light beam, and then an explosion. A gunshot –but not from his ex-wife. With a *thwack,* the bullet hit Curt
square in his back. He fell to the ground, motionless.

68. A Moth to a Flame

Dan Holms gripped his smoking Glock with one hand and a flashlight with the other.

"You got him!" Nadine tossed the covers aside and sprang out of the bed. She pulled off the brunette wig. "Is he dead?"

"I don't see any blood." Using his flashlight, Dan observed Curt, face down on the floor. He paused at what he was seeing —one of the fabled *mystery soldiers.* "He's wearing armor."

Nadine pulled out her firearm and also aimed it at Curt. He was unconscious, face down and surrounded by two guns. She couldn't contain a smile. "Hold the light, I'll cuff him and call back-up."

An hour earlier, Nadine and Dan had arrived at the safe house with an emailed court order from Assistant State's Attorney Negrin. Having his office number, cell number, email, and home number, Nadine knew she could reach him. She knew the importance of making key contacts when she'd moved to Florida.

A man of his word, Alberto Negrin dropped the case. He agreed that, with photographic evidence of three intruders standing in Larriott's home on the night of the shooting, it would've been an impossible case to pursue. A jury would never convict a sympathetic single mother threatened by at least three uninvited persons in her home during a storm.

Bypassing her superiors, however, Nadine had taken it upon herself to pick-up Alexandra and Cassie. If questioned about her actions, she'd state that she'd received credible information about a threat against Alexandra, and she was unable to reach Rodka or Coffey. With the storm on the way, she had to make an "executive decision during a time of crisis."

Nadine then asked her favorite AV tech, Toby, to drive Alexandra and Cassie to Dan's hotel in Marco. Mother and daughter would be able to rest, safe and anonymous, out of Tiberius's path. Toby cheerfully accepted the assignment to help Nadine. When they'd arrived in Marco, Toby confirmed by phone that Alexandra and Cassie had been safely delivered.

At the safe house, Nadine and Dan informed the house matron, Hilda, that there was a threat of a visit from Alexandra's abusive ex-husband. Hilda said she liked Alexandra and Cassie, and would be honored to help apprehend "the scumbag."

Nadine and Dan —armed and with the help of a thrift store wig— were ready in the remote chance that Curt would try anything so foolish. Hilda's role was to make visual ID of anyone who might come to the door. If anyone matched Curt's description, she was to call the police and flee. Nadine would wait under the bedroom covers as Dan hid in the closet with his loaded Glock.

On the floor, Curt was facedown and motionless —but he could hear every word his assailants were saying. He struggled to calm his breathing as if he were dead. The bullet had hit him in the center of his back armor. Though the slug couldn't pierce the vest, the blow felt like he'd been hit with a sledgehammer. A small price to pay.

The woman above him said, "Hold the light, I'll cuff him..." She sounded like a cop. *A pig.* Curt guessed there were two guns aimed at him. If so, he would need to act *very* fast.

He heard the names "Nadine" and "Dan." Knowing Nadine would have to stoop to cuff him, he could use the pause to his advantage. Curt still had one gun in his hand and another in his holster. He heard the ruffle of the woman crouching. *It's now or never!*

In one swift move, Curt rolled under the bed that was one foot to his left. He pulled the second gun from his belt and began wildly shooting from under the bed. He laughed as he aimed for Dan and Nadine's feet.

Dropping his flashlight, Dan hopped on the floor like a cowboy being ordered to *dance!* Nadine leaped onto the bed. Bullets ricocheted off brass fixtures and furniture. The gun's blasts in the small room were deafening. Curt couldn't stop his mechanical laugh, echoing through his helmet.

"Try to shoot him!" Nadine screamed.

"I can't see him!"

Knowing the woman was on the bed above him, Curt began shooting upwards through the mattress. "You dumb bitch!" He shouted through his mask, "Where you gonna go?"

"*Ahh..!*" Nadine shrieked in pain, "I'm hit!"

Dalia and Lex waited in the cockpit. Her eyes darted with anxiety.

Lex finally spoke, "Curt will have a weak moment." He looked at Dalia, "The alternative is getting killed or caught. If we got caught, we'd be charged with using weapons on domestic troops. *Then*, we'd be charged with interstate theft, laundering or murder. Indicted on charges of treason–"

"–I get it!" Dalia snapped. "How are you such an expert on the fed's legal process?"

It was too late in the game to reveal he was an expert because he *was* a fed.

With paranoia creeping into their despair, she reached towards his face. She dragged her black fingernail across his neck. "How long have you had those tattoos?"

He recoiled, "What are you talking about..?"

"Those spider web tattoos around your neck. How long?"

"Ten years..?"

Unpredictably, a corner of her lips curled into a grin. "You can't have visible tattoos above the neckline in the Army." She leaned closer with a sinister smile, "Especially ten years ago." She cocked her head, "Aren't you supposedly an ex-Ranger..?"

Lex froze. Was his cover blown? Could she still have a gun? "I got a waiver in the Army. I was used for undercover."

Dalia arched a brow, "I bet you were used undercover..." She smirked and ran her tongue around her lips. "Did you ever meet my old boss?"

"Who?" Lex blurted in frustration. "Butch..?"

"No," Dalia moved closer. "My first boss, FBI Special Agent Hugh Riker."

Curt's laughter echoed from under the bed as he fired in all directions. With Nadine trapped on the bed, Dan refused to flee.

When Nadine screamed that she'd been shot, Dan lunged to grasp her. With that opportune diversion, Curt rolled out from the other side of the bed. His footsteps could be heard running out of the room.

Dan's priority was Nadine. He held her tight, "Where are you hit?"

"My calf —my *fat* calf," she scoffed through tears. "I'll live —go after him!"

Dan picked up the flashlight. "I'm staying with you."

"No!" Nadine shouted. "I'll call for back-up —*you* catch Curt!"

Even with his flashlight, Dan found it difficult to run through the unfamiliar home. When something blocked his path, he jolted as he looked down. It was the matron, Hilda, flat on the floor. He was relieved to see she was still breathing.

The front door was hanging open, Curt had already exited. Dan ran out the door with his gun in front of him. Curt had a fifty-yard lead —and night vision.

In the pale streetlight, Dan looked to the left and to the right. The neighborhood was quiet. There was no indication which way Curt could've gone. Dan sighed at the reality that Curt had escaped.

"Which way'd he go?" Nadine shouted from the door. Dan turned to see her limping out of the house. She had a pillowcase tied around her calf and was gripping her gun.

Dan jogged over to support her. "He's gone." He groaned in defeat, "Maybe your back-up can set a one-mile perimeter. Unless they came by air..."

She rested her head on his shoulder, looking like she was about to cry. With a low rumble of faraway thunder, she looked up. "*And* the storm's on the way..."

They both sprung back like cats at sudden tires screeching. A black van abruptly pull up beside them. Its side door flew open.

Dan and Nadine gasped as four armored soldiers exited. They had helmets, body armor, goggles and massive guns. Four clones of Curt —were these his teammates?

They were petrified at their never-ending nightmare —but then Dan saw him.

Nadine didn't know if she was furious or relieved to see the man.

69. Red Rain

From behind the four armed troops, FBI Agent Riker step out of the van.

As the troops ran off into the night, Dan and Nadine could see the white letters "FBI" prominently displayed on their backs. They were the FBI's counterterrorism SWAT team known as the Hostage Rescue Team −HRT− or *Hurt* team. They were the good guys.

Agent Riker slicked over his hair. "Is *everyone* as predictable as children?" Another man in a suit, Agent Jenkins, joined him at his side.

Dan scowled at Riker, "You *knew* Curt would be here." His eyes widened as he concluded, "Your people *leaked* this address to them..!"

Riker shrugged, "*Real* cops know how to bait a hook."

Nadine exclaimed, "You would've *purposely* endangered Alexandra and a child?"

Riker gazed at Nadine with no concern for her injury. "Your presence endangered them. We *ordered* you to stay away. You failed. You now have to come with us."

Dan and Nadine looked down in utter defeat —then all four of their heads snapped towards the sound of heavy gunfire.

Curt ran through suburban lawns and leaped over fences. He smiled inside his humid mask when he heard the gunshots behind him. Somehow the threat of a good fight fueled his stamina. *Come and get me..!*

Glancing back, he saw at least four men following in his path. But it was easy math: the troops were a hundred yards behind him; the park was fifty yards in front of him. He had more than enough time. He might even have time to taunt and kill a few of them.

The troops' aim was poor since they were shooting while running. Curt located the park. Beyond the playground were the trees concealing the Stingray.

"Dalia! Have the chopper ready!" he shouted into his headset.

"You have the key, dipshit!" she replied.

Curt's voice over the speakers made Lex cringe. It had interrupted their intense discussion about Dalia's past.

"He's approaching," Dalia turned to the radar. "The storm's outer bands are an hour away."

Lex was still staggered at her confession. "So you *are* AWOL —not from the Coast Guard, but from the FBI?"

"I'm no different than you," Dalia glared. "It's why Riker has a bug up his ass to catch us. He keeps losing his top agents to this ridiculous team."

Lex shook his head, bewildered. "I had *infallible* intelligence that you were Coast Guard!"

She huffed, "I'd love to discuss this over coffee, but..." Her voice trailed when she looked at his face. She rolled her eyes and spoke faster, "Butch was in the market for a chopper when Riker began watching him. They put me undercover to seek him out and *mesmerize* him. I was placed in the Coast Guard as a supposed transfer. My character came off the *Spool*, just like yours."

"Why'd you run?" Lex lifted his hands, pulling her cuffed hand with his. "I'm here because they deserted me in a Cat-5!"

"Call me unimaginative, but adventure, danger and cash seemed a tad cooler than a government job. All from victimless crimes."

"*Victimless?* Your team's killed people!"

"That wasn't the plan, *Lex!*" She looked at him with sudden sincerity. "I was going to flee after this *diamond* score. No one was supposed to get hurt. I'd escape Tiberius and retire in New Orleans in a French Quarter loft." She looked into his eyes, "I researched your background; I had a hunch about you. I even covered for you..." She paused, "I was hoping you'd fly away with me."

He didn't know how to respond. As he opened his mouth, a bullet ricocheted off the tail. She reached to engage a secondary power supply. "I thought you needed a key!" Dan shouted.

"The key is to fly." She gripped the controls. "I have auxiliary –just for guns." With that, the Stingray's M60 machine gun sprang to life. On the radar she saw a cluster of troops approaching. "Curt's got company."

Dalia fired towards the four troops. Her goal was to spook them, not to kill anyone. "I'd rather take my chances escaping with Curt than guaranteed arrests!" Lex didn't argue.

Avoiding her line of fire, Curt approached, running zigzag from the side.

Dalia saw the troops drop to the ground to dodge her fire. Outside the cabin door, she could see Curt approaching. "Throw me the key!" she shouted.

Ten feet from the cockpit, Curt threw the key towards Dalia. It clanged into the cabin, falling to the dark floor. Dalia growled, "Moron!"

Lex dropped to the deck to feel for the key with one hand. After a few aggravated grunts, he exclaimed, "I got it!" He handed it to Dalia.

She started the engines which began to hum. "It takes a few minutes!" Dalia shouted. With her other hand, she continued to fire the M60 towards the troops.

Curt stood at the cabin door to reload his two pistols. "Get this bird going!"

The rotor blades started to slowly turn. Dalia lifted a mic and an external bullhorn blared, "Drop your weapons!" Her voice echoed through the trees.

Four FBI troops appeared in the darkness. Dalia fired deafening warning shots above their heads. Knowing the M60 would mow them down like a weed-wacker, they halted. "Drop your arms!" Dalia's bullhorn warned again.

Fifty feet away, the troops looked at each other. After another burst, they reluctantly dropped their weapons. Curt sprinted over to hurl their guns far into the brush. He laughed, "That was the worst plan I ever saw!" The men said nothing.

The Stingray's rotors began to pick up speed. Curt ripped off his mask and threw it aside. With an idiotic grin across his face, he untied the bungee cable from the stump and clipped it to his vest. He shouted into his headset, "Dalia: rise −*now!*"

Dalia grasped the collective lever and the chopper began to lift. She and Lex weren't surprised that Curt was staying on the ground a few extra seconds to taunt the troops.

Lex asked, "What if we cut the cord and leave him here?" He turned to see the bungee cord bolted to the winch, two feet out of his reach. Without any tools, it was impossible to sever the cord. Lex looked outside to see the cord attached to Curt's uniform. As expected, Curt was going to remain on the ground to gloat. He would ultimately spring himself up to the chopper, using his remote to wench himself in. Agent Riker was right: Curt was recklessly predictable.

"Don't worry so much..." Dalia cooed. "Let me do what I do best." She winked.

On the ground, Curt waved at the troops, "Goodbye, assholes! See ya' next season!"

The Stingray was rising beyond fifty feet. Curt shouted into his radio, "Keep going, I'm about to release!" He wanted to wait until the last second to launch himself to the chopper.

"It's too tight —it won't stretch any further!" Lex's voice warned.

Curt knew if the cord snapped, he'd be stuck on the ground with the troops. He hit the cable's release clip. It didn't work. *What happened?* He looked down and saw the cord tangled on a gnarled cypress stump. Without delay, he pulled a knife from his belt and began sawing the cord. "I'm cutting it! Keep rising —*HIGHER!*"

Dalia lifted the Stingray to seventy-five feet. The cord was stretching to its limit.

Before slicing the last fibers of the bungee, Curt gave a snide grin to the troops. "Ever see a man fly?" He shouted, "Up, up and away..!" He severed the cord and Curt miraculously launched into the sky.

The FBI troops gazed up in amazement —and then shock.

Curt looked up to see the Stingray's belly approaching fast —too fast. In that millisecond, he could envision Dalia's smirk as she suddenly dropped the chopper twenty feet.

Curt's eyes bulged when his deficient brain grasped what was happening. As if in slow motion, he reached the chopper —then continued upwards, *into* the spinning blades. The razor-like titanium — reinforced to slice through branches and debris— hacked through Curt's armor, exposing his pink flesh to the swirling rotors. His infuriated face and body were instantly hacked into a thousand pieces. His carcass, tossed like a ragdoll to each circling blade. Blood rained down onto the horrified troops below.

The Stingray's wench pulled up a bloody frayed cord. Lex looked soberly at Dalia. "Get us outta' here."

She nodded and sped inland.

"You're heading *towards* Tiberius!" Lex exclaimed.

"You might want to strap yourself in."

70. And to All a Good Night

LeBeau's shrieks for oxygen echoed within the claustrophobic Blister Tent.

The tent remained anchored to the causeway. Ten-foot waves poured over the seawall, flooding the roads with four feet of churning water. Within minutes, the waves covered the final inch of the tent's peak.

LeBeau had no knife to cut the indestructible fabric. His deep, panicked crying was ironically depleting his oxygen. His fingernails clawed at the walls, being crushed by the weight of four feet of seawater above him. In his crouched position, he had no room to move. The pressure was piercing his eardrums.

Before his dying eyes, his strained neurons twinged with visions: him fleeing his country; his inept struggles for power; abandoning Butch and leaving Tag for dead. And his final sin: murdering Pitch.

"I'm sorryyy...!" he bellowed with his lung's last scorching gasp.

Alexandra held her daughter tight. They spooned in bed in the Marco Island Inn. The room had ice-cold air conditioning and Dan stocked the fridge with Cokes and frozen Snicker bars. The television had 120 channels. To Alexandra and Cassie, it was paradise.

Initially unable to sleep, Alexandra had left the blinds open to watch the palms sway outside. According to the news, Tiberius's northwestern path wouldn't affect Marco beyond a few showers. Things were going to get better.

The rain patter on the aluminum awnings lulled her into an overdue slumber. As she embraced Cassie, inhaling her shampooed hair, Alexandra smiled.

Unfortunately, the alarm was set for 5:00 a.m. Alexandra had laid out their clothes for the morning. Dan and Detective Stratton would be disappointed, but she and Cassie had a plane to catch. After retrieving their *other* passports, she knew they couldn't leave any trail. Her plan wasn't over.

Within the Stingray, Dalia and Lex had a romantic front-row view of Tiberius's fury. The parking garage was built with four-foot-thick concrete. Even in the worst of the storm, the Stingray would be dry and protected.

Dalia landed the chopper at the entrance to the garage. By parking on the first-floor ramp, she'd avoid any flooding. She'd positioned the Stingray facing out, protected on three sides by solid columns. When she turned off the engines, she and Lex unbuckled and sighed in liberation. They gazed out at the street as the storm whipped through.

Dalia smiled at the escalating howl of wind. The gusts made a high-pitch wail like wolves at a full moon. She looked at Lex, "Listen to that. Incredible..."

Lex's eyes agreed. They sat side by side like watching a movie. Lightning and exploding transformers created a light show.

"Look!" Dalia pointed like a child. Dumpsters were rebounding down the street like pinballs.

Lex clutched her arm and gasped as an entire car came tumbling, end over end, down the street. "My God..!"

Dalia's eyes blinked faster. "I've never seen the *inside* of a storm..." She pulled Lex's cuffed hand and pressed it to her inner thigh. "The eye won't be over us for nearly an hour."

Lex looked at her. She shuffled over to straddle his lap. She leaned in to slide her tongue over the tattoos running up his neck. "*Mmm...*" she moaned as if the ink had flavor. She then placed her lips over his, delivering a passionate kiss.

He slid his free hand under her black fatigues, surprised to see a soft-pink bra underneath. She soon had little on above the waist other than a dog tag jingling between her breasts. His cuffed hand moved to her pants –pulling her hand with it.

Like an animal, Dalia simply ripped Lex's pants off, shredding the supposedly-indestructible fabric. Cuffed and half naked, she sat in his lap. She clutched his black hair and pulled his face tighter into hers.

Their vibrant and entwined bodies fogged the Stingray's windshield as the storm raged around them. Screaming cyclones swirled down the street forty feet away. Glass, debris and explosions couldn't drown out their passion. More cars tumbled down the street. In their ecstasy, they were oblivious to the destruction around them.

Agent Riker approached his dismayed troops who were ordered to stay-put. The soldiers' uniforms were splattered with Curt's blood.

From behind Riker, Dan Holms walked up, assisting a limping Nadine. Dan gazed into the horizon, "Their chopper flew *into* the storm? That's suicide!"

Nadine covered her mouth at the bloody scene. "This is your fault!" She growled at Riker, "You endangered *everyone* –and they still just flew away!"

Agent Jenkins recoiled with disgust as he observed the ground covered with flesh and bone. He shouted at the paralyzed troops, "*Do not* move until a HazMat team can spray you down!" The men were not pleased.

Agent Riker rubbed his face with uncharacteristic distress. He muttered to himself, "Okay, okay...How do I spin this..?" He noticed Dan and Nadine looking at him with revulsion.

"What's your plan now, *real-cop* Riker?" Dan sneered.

Riker brushed off his tie and cleared his throat. He installed a phony smile and looked at them, "How can I be confident that you two never saw that chopper get away?"

Nadine's eyebrow went up, "I can think of a couple of things."

71. Commendations and Catastrophes

It was standing room only in the Fort Myers Civic Auditorium. The art deco performance hall was filled with hundreds of Lee County Sheriff's deputies. On the sidelines were citizens, local politicians and the press with flashing cameras.

At the stage's podium stood Detective Al Rodka. He'd shaved and actually dressed nice, though his suit had graduated to the mid-80s. He spoke with sincerity, "Not only am I honored to welcome back my partner after her injury," Rodka produced a real smile at Stratton, seated beside him. "I am proud to be the first to call her *Sergeant*." Applause erupted from their law enforcement peers.

A smiling Sergeant Nadine Stratton sat beside the podium. She was in uniform with her flowing blonde hair on her shoulders. Beside her sat the Sheriff of Lee County, Scott Dunn.

"Great job, Sergeant," Sheriff Dunn whispered and smiled. With her calf in a soft cast, he'd helped with her crutches when they'd entered.

"But first," Rodka glanced at his boss. "We have a very special word from our own Lieutenant Dale Coffey."

Lieutenant Coffey stood and patted his helmet of hair. He shuffled down the line of guests and shook Nadine's hand. He cleared his throat into the microphone, "Our prayers go out to the overwhelmed victims of Tiberius from Miami to Tampa. Like the resilient folks of our own coast, they *will* rebuild –stronger than before."

The audience applauded. A few shook their heads at the destruction they'd witnessed.

Coffey looked at Nadine. "Seldom do we have an opportunity to assist our federal partners in ensuring our nation's security. When I'd learned that our own Nadine Stratton provided vital information to authorities, I could not have been more proud."

Nadine smiled at Coffey's unexpected sentiment.

He smiled, "Her exceptional work helped authorities identify and eliminate a cell of lethal *terrorists* preying on our citizens." He smiled at the press, "Lee County Sheriffs *encourage* the sharing of information with federal authorities, in the name of national security."

Nadine knew he was full of shit and didn't care. She accepted he was using poetic license to gain as much good press as possible. *Whatever*, she shrugged. *I got my promotion.*

Nadine was confident her promotion was earned and not merely bestowed as part of some backroom deal between Riker and Coffey. If a person's true character is determined by their actions and how they're perceived, then Nadine knew she deserved her rank. For nearly twenty-four hours, her coworkers had lined up to shower her with praise. Their acceptance of her was greater than any pay raise.

Coffey's voice snapped her back to the moment, "Sergeant Stratton, we most certainly need more officers like you. Your entire police family should be proud."

The crowd erupted into applause. Things had happened so fast, it was impossible to get her father or brothers to Florida for the ceremony. They were thrilled on the phone and she would indeed have a story for them at the Thanksgiving table.

The thought of loved ones made her gaze at the audience. There, in the front row, was his empty seat. Dan Holms was gone. He'd arrived late, and was there for only a few minutes before vanishing. Dan had missed her big moment.

Two hours before Nadine's induction, Dan had been packing his bags at his hotel. Though his storm duty was far from over, Insurex's HR department had ordered him on administrative leave. There were a slew of human resource issues including: unapproved assisting of law enforcement, possession of a firearm on duty –and not returning customers' phone calls. Dan was outraged. It was like a poor 7-Eleven clerk getting fired for defending himself during a robbery.

But there was another reason Dan was incensed: this case was not over. He was shocked to discover Alexandra and Cassie gone from his room with no explanation. Scotty at the front desk said Alexandra took coffee, juice and Pop-Tarts from the continental breakfast, and then left in a cab before 6:00 a.m. *That's a nice way to thank me for saving their lives –twice!*

Compounding the mystery, Dan checked his messages to see that Alexandra's former gun instructor had called twice, stating it was "urgent." In addition, the *Island Life* magazine photographer finally called back. For a case that Dan would love to consider closed, he desperately wanted to tie the last few loose ends into a neat bow before heading home.

Dan looked at his watch. It would take ninety minutes to get to the auditorium to see Nadine. That gave him a half-hour to shower and put on the shirt and blazer he bought at Target. He calculated he had five minutes to call the gun instructor.

"Hello, Mike Burrs?" Dan said. "This is Dan Holms with Insurex. I believe you were the instructor hired by Alexandra Larriott before she applied for a concealed-weapons permit?" Dan doodled on a pad. "I originally called because she claimed a gun lost in the storm," Dan lied. "I was confirming she hired you when she purchased her weapon."

"Yep, it was me," replied Burrs. "I can confirm she owned at least one firearm."

"Okay, great. By the way, why'd you say it was 'urgent' when you called?"

"Is it the same *Alexandra Larriott* who's on all the news for shooting an intruder?"

"Sure is." Dan poured a cardboard cup of coffee. "The poor woman's had a string of tragedies. Why do you ask?"

Burrs chuckled, "Those burglars didn't' stand a chance."

Dan paused sipping his coffee, "What do you mean?"

After Burrs explained, Dan accidentally dropped his coffee into his open suitcase.

Dan sped to Nadine's ceremony, but still arrived late. She'd reserved him a seat in the front row, which only emphasized his tardiness. As Rodka rambled on about his own illustrious career, Dan's eyes darted around the auditorium. What did this new information mean? *I have to tell Nadine!* He knew he couldn't interrupt Nadine's moment. He fidgeted in his seat with nervous energy.

Dan nearly leaped out of his seat when his phone vibrated in his pocket. Deputies on both sides of him frowned at the interruption. The caller ID said it was the *Island Life* photographer –again. Dan stepped on several cops' toes as he exited the row to take the call.

"Mr. Castillo, sorry for playing phone tag," Dan whispered in the corridor. "I have an odd question about a layout you photographed several months ago. You might not remember it."

"Who was it?" Castillo replied. He sounded early-20s and overly chipper.

"The subject was a Ms. *Alexandra Larriott*. She lives in Captiva. She's an art–"

"–How can I forget her!" Castillo exclaimed.

"Why do you say that?"

"Well for one, she was very attractive." Castillo laughed, "But she also had some very bizarre requests."

Dan raised a brow, "Such as..?" He almost didn't want Castillo to reply. Could it be remotely possible that one of his farfetched theories might have some merit? *Please, let me be wrong,* Dan prayed.

Within thirty seconds, Castillo confirmed Dan's ill-fated theory was true. Combined with the comments from the gun instructor. Dan felt like he'd been played like a smitten teenager, fooled by the Prom Queen into doing her homework.

In the humid night, Nadine Stratton stood with her superiors in a receiving line outside the auditorium. They shook hands and chit-chatted with exiting officers. The compliments helped her forget that Dan −the man she thought she loved− was absent.

As Toby −her last admirer−shook her hand, Dan appeared before her like magic. He was handsome in his white dress shirt and Navy blazer. He still had stubble and his buccaneer grin. Like a romance novel, his face glistened with perspiration as if he'd run across a vast field to find her. But his smile seemed somehow...false.

"Congratulations Nadine." He stepped forward and kissed her. "Sorry I was late."

Nadine melted. "Oh, it's okay. I know how traffic is−"

"−No," Dan interrupted. "It wasn't traffic." He leaned closer as if delivering another kiss. When she smiled and closed her eyes, he whispered. "We need to talk −now!"

Nadine hobbled with her crutches as Dan ushered her from the crowd. Rodka and Coffey glared at him like disapproving uncles.

"Let's go over here," Dan said as he steered her to a vacant court-yard.

"What is it?" Nadine asked. "You're scaring me."

After assuring they were alone, he looked at her. "I know it's bad timing− but do you know where Alexandra went?"

"No." Nadine frowned, "When she was freed, she had no duty to report her whereabouts...?"

"I just heard from Nadine's gun instructor."

Nadine lifted her hands, confused. "She told us about her gun training −for protection from her insane ex-husband."

Dan placed his hands on her shoulders. His words were clear and succinct, "Her instructor described her as an expert marksman. She could hit a centimeter bull's-eye at fifty yards. Alexandra was his best student in twenty years."

Nadine shook her head trying to grasp the significance. "This upsets you, why?"

"There's more: the photographer from *Island Life* called me. He vividly remembers visiting her house." He leaned in, "He said Alexandra *insisted* that every room be displayed in the magazine, saying she'd renovated the place."

Nadine was growing impatient. "Why should we care?"

"When he took her photograph, Alexandra kept insisting that her art be clearly visible in the background." Dan pulled from his pocket a folded printout and handed it to Nadine.

She unfolded the paper to see a copy of the issue's cover. The title read, "Captiva's Newest Art Collector." In the photo, Alexandra – smiling and beautiful– was standing on her staircase with the Jean-Luc Brulé paintings in plain view over her shoulder. Nadine narrowed her eyes at the image. After a pause, she mused, "Why would she be so adamant in showing the paintings –*especially* if she was hiding from Curt?" After a second, she looked at Dan. "Unless–"

"–She *wanted* to be found," Dan finished her thought. "She knew her husband's team used magazine articles." He pointed to the picture, "Her face is clearly visible." He paused before delivering the only conclusion. "Alexandra Larriott wanted Curt to find her. She lured her abusive husband to her house as a trap."

Nadine's mouth opened but nothing came out. She blinked faster as her mind computed the implications. Gazing up at the moon and at a royal palm rustling in the breeze, it reminded her of Larriott's house.

As if turning on a movie projector, memories began to flicker before her eyes. Just days before, when they were researching, she'd mentioned the magazine to Dan, *"Look: in the background you can see the art. She's even wearing all her jewelry... The photos even show the layout of the rooms."*

Dan had replied, *"Doing this cover was Larriott's biggest mistake."*

It wasn't Alexandra's biggest mistake. It was her most genius plan.

Dan's voice regained her attention. "I did research: only half the U. S. states have some sort of 'Make My Day" law which allows citizens to meet 'force with force' without fear of prosecution. Out of *those* states, only Florida and Hawaii are tropical states –more storms hit Florida than any other state."

Her eyes widened at the inference, "She *purposely* moved to a hurricane zone..."

Dan nodded, "The magazine was published before the height of the storm season. Captiva is a barrier island. *Any* storm targeting *anywhere* on the west coast would warrant an evacuation. Or, if Curt was impatient, he'd just come for her anyway. Alexandra had a security system and she was armed. All she had to do was wait."

Nadine exclaimed the obvious, "Shooting her violent ex-husband as an *intruder* wouldn't be murder."

"She meticulously set the trap, and was armed and deadly. Selina aimed at the west coast, and she banked on Curt's predictability."

"–Except she shot the wrong man," Nadine retorted. "In the chaos of the storm, she accidentally shot Curt's brother. That infuriated him even more..." Nadine turned in a slow circle, gazing across the courtyard as she retraced her memories.

Another vision raced back. It was Detective Rodka on the dunes when he'd examined the dead soldier's wound. He'd said to Larriott, *"You're quite the sharpshooter. You hit the only inch of exposed neck."*

Standing over the corpse, Alexandra had replied, *"They were burglarizing my home, endangering my daughter...I had the right to shoot!"*

Nadine's gruff –but more experienced– senior partner had been correct. She suddenly felt guilty for hating Rodka. She'd even laughed when attorney King ripped him apart. Nadine looked down in shame; she could've learned from the man.

Nadine felt humiliated for believing a cold-blooded liar playing the part of a shattered, single mother. *She looked in my eyes and cried...*

She sighed with a poignant smile, "Rodka was right all along: Larriott is a first-degree murderer."

"But..." Dan lifted a finger. "She knew if she got caught, she could never use any 'abused-wife' defense. Her plan was too elaborately premeditated, including the staged photos and publicizing her own whereabouts. She's too smart for any insanity defense."

Nadine felt a wave of nausea at the only solution. "She used *us* for her defense. You and I fought to free her. We worked day and night, risking our lives. And we succeeded."

"And now she's gone," Dan added. He stepped towards Nadine and opened his arms. She hugged him, but her posture was a wilted version of her former, triumphant self.

Men's voices suddenly called out from behind them. "Look –there she is!"

Dan and Nadine turned to see a half-dozen uniformed deputies. A bald deputy smiled and shouted, "The lady of the hour!" The men approached and the friendly cop patted Nadine on her shoulder, "We want to buy you a drink!"

Nadine and Dan locked eyes. The happy spirits from the men were infectious. Nadine couldn't help but smile, "That sounds great, guys."

Nadine and Dan sat in the back of one of the men's SUVs. They drove to the newly-reopened Key Lime Bistro on Captiva Island. *Poetic,* Dan thought. *The island where it all began...* The bar was just blocks from Alexandra's estate. No more visits to that house. He could use a stiff drink

Dan put his arm around Nadine. As she and her peers exchanged war stories, Dan quietly contemplated. Did he have any further duty to investigate Larriott? *Nope, I'm not a real cop,* he chuckled. If the truth was ever revealed, it could strip Nadine of her honors. He would never let that happen.

If *Alexandra Larriott* –or whatever her name was– wanted to vanish, she could do so. It would be useless to check outgoing passports or credit card activity. Alexandra would have those bases covered. Maybe, with Curt now dead, she'd just retire with Cassie, far away.

At the café's Tiki bar, Nadine was surrounded by colleagues asking what it was like to stop "terrorists." Dan smiled that she was being praised for her impeccable police work.

After three hand-shaken *Patrón* margaritas, Dan confessed to Nadine that Insurex was thinking hard about firing him. Nadine gave a mischievous grin and whispered, "If the truth leaks, I'll just quit and we can open our own agency."

"That'd be paradise," Dan smiled.

Epilogue, for Now

Tampa was mopping up Tiberius's trail. After the storm tore into Miami, it proceeded northwest, across the Everglades, and out through Tampa Bay. Thanks to prepared residents —and almost no humans in the 4,300 square miles of the Everglades— there were few casualties other than "gators, snakes and storm crashers," as Agent Riker had joked.

The impenetrable Special Ops Command at MacDill had been unscathed. Colonel Sturges leaned forward at his desk. His hand visibly shook as he poured water from a pitcher. "How can we be sure this is...concluded?"

Riker sat in a leather wingchair with his legs tightly crossed. "The storm destroyed their hangar. We found weapons and priceless artifacts strewn across the swamp, but their systems were destroyed. Jenkins believes an E.M. pulse wiped all hard drives."

"But that's bad!" Sturges barked. "We can't decipher their accounts!"

Riker leaned forward and hissed, "No, that's good! There's no evidence of our operation. They never existed. It was a bad dream. No harm, no fowl."

"A bad dream?" Sturges exclaimed. "Tell that to the families of troops that were lost!"

"That's the nature of high-risk contract work!" Riker's tone shifted to that of a press agent, "The unfortunate loss of life was due to a credible threat against our nation. That part is fact. We can manufacture evidence to suggest a probable, impending hazard. The condition was further thwarted by an untimely natural catastrophe." He concluded with, "The men will be artistically submitted as heroes, and the contracts will compensate the families."

Sturges paused at the notion. "Are we sure there are no surviving suspects?"

"Four bodies have been confirmed," Riker was smug. "We ID'd the leader, *Christian LeBeau*. Kids found his bloated body in a tent when the water receded. He'd sealed himself in some sort of *suicide tent*." Riker chuckled, "Considering the *ripe* corpse, we'll provide the kids with some sort of counseling."

"And the rest?"

"First, we had Butch Hulett, the dead mystery soldier. His body's still missing. Lex reported they buried him in the swamp."

"And his brother, the wife-beater?"

"We confirmed Curt's body. He was hacked into so many pieces, we had to match the DNA with his mother's."

"The old woman you arrested with the art."

Riker nodded, "She's all over Curt's cell records. Agent Capell is ecstatic with all the art."

Sturges relaxed, increasingly content.

"And Army dental records confirmed the corpse of Earl "Pitch" Snipes. He evidently detonated himself at the diamond house."

"And Tag, our last living suspect. He was shipped far away with a new life?"

Riker looked at his watch, "For about twenty more hours... He'll then be arrested for underage sex and hauled off to a lovely Thai prison for a few decades."

Sturges squinted, "That's five —what about your two runaway

agents, Lex and the pilot?"

Riker shifted to re-cross his legs. "Our troops witnessed the pilot, Dalia Covarrubias —a former undercover— purposely flying *into* the storm." He spoke as if to a grand jury, "My report will reflect that she realized she couldn't outrun the storm. She chose to fly *into* it as a suicide tactic to kill the *extremist* traitor, Lex, sacrificing herself as a hero."

Sturges leaned back in his chair, "Is there any further evidence of this operation?"

"Trucks from Onyx collected the Blackhawk debris from Miami before any witnesses. Other than that—"

The door burst open. Riker leaped out of his chair like a tightly-wound spring. The Colonel bolted upright.

Standing in the threshold was General Eric Lindsey, the Commander of the Special Operations Command. The lanky and handsome sixty year-old officer was in his dress blue uniform. He focused his dark eyes at Sturges.

Sturges saluted and stammered, "General. How was your honeymoon, sir?"

Flanking the General were two Air Force Security Officers in their tiger-stripe camouflage, carrying M9 Berettas.

General Lindsey motioned to his men, "Handcuff Colonel Sturges and FBI Agent Riker. They are under arrest." The men proceeded with their guns drawn. One guard began reading the Miranda rights to Riker. The other recited the military Article 31 rights to Sturges.

"We need to debrief you!" Sturges exclaimed as he was cuffed. "This is a mistake!"

Riker stood tall with feeble authority. "General, there was a need to shield you. To afford credible deniability. There are no witnesses—"

"—*No witnesses*?" The General screamed. His face displayed pure rage. "Residents who remained in Key Biscayne witnessed 'World War III' in their neighbor's backyard! People in high-rises watched the shootout in the sky! Men were killed! An old woman was shot in the face with a Taser!"

The General turned to glare at Sturges, "Your *fusion team* had zero authority to dispatch *any* troops for your scavenger hunt!"

Sturges brazenly replied, "Sir, with any threat of terrorism, I *did* have the authority!"

Lindsey cocked his head, "How do you *assume* you had *any* authority?"

"Sir," Sturges stood tall. "You were 7,000 miles away in Fiji. As Lieutenant Colonel, I was the officer on duty. It was impossible to contact you for anything less than a verified nuke. I was 'in charge while the rest sleeps.' With a credible threat against our citizens – with an impending storm– I had to pull the trigger."

General Lindsey eyeballed Sturges like an inquisitive animal. "That's not why you didn't have authority..." He turned to Riker. "You're the attorney here –tell me: why didn't he have authority to deploy *any* troops."

Riker froze with rigid shoulders. "We...believed it to be a genuine threat, sir..."

Lindsey sighed at their idiocy. He turned towards the hall. Standing in the corridor were Agents Jenkins, Louise Capell and the Navy analyst, Engel.

Riker's eyes widened at the three as he understood –they were the whistle blowers. He scowled at his protégé Jenkins.

General Lindsey asked the three informants like a game show host, "Who can tell me about the *posse comitatus*?"

Sturges interjected, "Sir, the *posse comitatus* has language allowing exceptions for emergencies on U.S. soil!" His face twisted with resentment. "I'm smart enough to employ contractors and not use our own men! It was way off the books."

"*Way off the books*?" Lindsey's face reddened, "You left a trail of bodies! Kids finding weapons on their lawns! And whose idea was it to give them National Guard patches?"

"–Mine sir," Riker spoke up as if proud. "The National Guard are prevalent during storms. Their presence wouldn't raise any suspicions."

"One little problem," Lyndsey snarled at the neat fool in a suit.

"Brad Snyder's a friend of mine. You know who he is? He's the Adjutant General of our National Guard. He *knows* those aren't his men!" His shout echoed within the small room. "Obviously the uniforms are fake! So that's *another* charge —you directed men to *impersonate* armed forces." He shook his head like a disappointed parent. "You dispatched armed men during a hurricane to stop *cat burglars*." He jabbed with sarcasm, "What's next? Launch nukes at hackers?"

"General," Agent Louise Capell spoke up with a raised hand, "If the troops were deployed unlawfully, does that mean any evidence and recovered art were obtained without proper cause? Could I legally lose it?"

"No." Lindsey cracked a bittersweet smile at Capell. "All evidence —including your precious art— were recovered legally." He paused, "Thanks to the Coast Guard."

"The *Coast Guard*?" Riker blurted, "They weren't part of our team!"

"Exactly!" Lindsey snapped his head towards Riker. "Somehow the Coast Guard received the same terror tip. As part of Homeland, they *legally* responded. They're not under Defense, so the *posse comitatus* didn't apply." He looked at Sturges. "Thank God! The Coast Guard swooped-in and saved your ass! Any good press for this fiasco will go to them!"

Agent Jenkins asked, "Sir, do you know who tipped-off the Coast Guard?"

"No. But they're a hero in my book."

Riker and Sturges said nothing as they were led out of the room.

It was a bright morning at the Miami International Airport. Alexandra Larriott wore dark sunglasses. She wasn't hiding per se, but was cloaked by an open newspaper. Beside her, Cassie wore headphones plugged to a pink iPhone.

From her seat at the departure gate, Alexandra —or Elizabeth Louise Hulett— could see two different televisions. The channels were consumed with the devastation of Tiberius. Meteorologists rambled on about two storms hitting back to back. *I say it's only going to get worse, Phil…*

The *Miami Herald* touched on the story of the foiled "terrorists." They used words like "rogue soldiers" and "possible stolen weapons." There was a story about a "fiery aircraft battle" reported over the city. The military denied any knowledge, suggesting it was "ball lightning" from the storm.

One story applauded Lee County Sergeant Nadine Stratton for un-covering the threat. The story made Alexandra smile. She liked Nadine, and was truly upset that she had to lie to her. The insurance guy, Dan Holms, wasn't mentioned in any story, but she liked him too. Nadine and Dan worked hard to exonerate her, and they risked their lives doing so. Alexandra wasn't proud of that, but knew it was necessary in destroying Curt.

But how'd my plan go so wrong? Alexandra had planned her strategy with a year of meticulous research. When Canada issued her a new identity for testifying against Curt, she knew he and his team-mates were clever enough to obtain the name. Then, all she had to do was publicize her new name in any public record.

But she couldn't do it blatantly like obtaining a driver's license. That'd be too conspicuous. Alexandra presumed Curt's team had search programs that combed the web for her new name. So she bought a house. Florida –the most hurricane-prone state– had property records available to the public. Her new name, Alexandra Larriott, would flag a response.

Second, publications like *Island Life* relished stories of wealthy new residents. The magazine was mostly stories of pretentious residents. When she contacted the magazine, introducing herself as a new art collector, they promised a cover story.

Since *Island Life* was also published online, Alexandra would have her name and face beamed around the globe. Combined with her property records, it created a virtual roadmap for Curt to her front door. Like dropping filet mignon in front of a starving tiger.

But it all went wrong! Alexandra fumed. She'd waited through eighteen named storms until Selina created the perfect opportunity. Her guns were loaded. Her safe room was ready to protect Cassie.

Alexandra even wore her robe in case police responded to the scene immediately. *I should've worn shoes!* Her security cameras watched every door.

My cameras, she repeated to herself. It was the damn security cameras that were supposed to prove her innocence. If she had intruders, she'd have a legal right to shoot the men. She even located brash attorney Sheldon King, who'd saved clients before using the state's self-defense laws. It was supposed to be an open-and-shut case.

But then she saw the face of the man she'd shot. In the swaying palms and blinding rain, she'd killed the wrong man. She'd hit his neck perfectly, but when she saw Butch's face instead of Curt's, she knew she'd made her first fatal mistake.

Mistake number two: not killing the rest of the team. In the chaos of her bedroom, the men fled into the night. She knew Curt's evil teammates, and she knew they'd come back for her. Especially with Curt leading the charge.

The third and most significant mistake had been beyond her control. Believing the security cameras' recorder was safe in the attic, she hadn't anticipated roof damage destroying the system. When Rodka told her the video had been ruined, the evidence of her "innocence" was gone. They whisked her and Cassie off to the station like hardened criminals. Until Detective Stratton saved the day.

Alexandra looked at the television. The news was repeating the story, currently dubbed, "Tropical Terrorists." They now stated only four "terrorists" were rumored to be killed. She knew Curt's team had at least six men. *Some are still out there.* If anyone could survive, it could be Curt, she thought. If he was alive, he would be back.

Panic began to creep into her brain. She could never enter a dark room or sleep soundly again until she *knew* Curt was dead. He would travel the globe to slaughter her and take Cassie. And Curt would destroy other women along his path. Alexandra would *have* to see his dead face for herself before she could ever rest.

Alexandra checked her and Cassie's new passports. They were now "Carolyn" and "Diane Humphries." She'd already rehearsed the names with Cassie, making it a game of "pretend."

She looked at Cassie, "Sweetie, we're getting on the airplane soon. Get your bag ready."

As Cassie packed away her phone, a hand touched her from behind. She turned to see a five year-old boy in a Miami Heat cap peeking through the seats. Knowing she was never supposed to speak to anyone, Cassie looked to see her mom occupied with the newspaper.

"Where's your airplane going?" the boy asked.

Cassie whispered, "We're moving to pretty Hawaii."

The boy wiped his nose. "Why?"

Cassie looked over her shoulder again, "My mommy says she wants to wait and hide for something called a..." She paused to recall the strange word, "A *typhoon*..."

Handcuffed, Riker and Sturges walked five paces behind the security officers.

Sturges leaned toward Riker with a whisper, "Do they know that chopper got away?"

Riker shook his head, irritated, "There's no way they could've survived!"

"How can you assume that?"

"You think their Stingray just flew off into the eye of the storm?"

Seventeen hours earlier, the Stingray had indeed flown off into the eye of the storm.

The rain had trickled to a stop over the Stingray. Gazing straight up, Dalia and Lex could actually see stars. But the clear eye of Tiberius was only twenty miles in diameter. They had to move fast.

"You called it 'riding the eye...'" Lex said like a kid buckling-up for a Disney coaster.

"We're just hitching a ride." Dalia raised the Stingray to two hundred feet. "We'll fly in the center of this donut until the next safe structure."

They followed the vast storm within its comparatively tiny eye.

Watching the ground terrain radar, Lex gasped when he realized their path. "We're heading over the Gulf!"

Dalia raised a cool eyebrow as in *so?*

He pointed at their fuel gauge. "The Gulf's 600,000 square miles!" His voice grew louder, "There are no *safe structures!*"

Dalia stroked a finger erotically across his lips. "You worry too much..."

The dawn's light cast a violet hue on the immense storm wall encircling them. Below them, the Gulf was churning with whitecaps, and indeed appeared endless.

Lex sat back, striving to appear cool. But as Tiberius led them over the sea, it only emphasized his sense of despair.

Then, in the morning light, he saw them. They appeared on the horizon like buildings on the surface of the sea.

Dalia grinned when she knew he saw them.

"Oil rigs..."

"Just a pit stop," Dalia replied. "How does New Orleans sound when this whole thing blows over?"

The End

Author's Notes and Acknowledgements

Though most of the technology in this story is real, all characters and situations are an invention of my overactive imagination. *However...*

Years ago I stayed in a hotel on the west coast of Florida. The waterfront hotel went out of business shortly thereafter. I would've never thought of the place again if it hadn't been mentioned by one of my police contacts. I discovered, in the wake of 2004's Hurricane Charley, officials had used the hotel as a temporary morgue. I remembered the place vividly, and it gave me chills envisioning corpses lying where I'd slept.

After that storm, when rumors about the derelict hotel swept through the community, officials had to admit using the location for the dead. The Director of Emergency Management refused to acknowledge how many corpses were there, but promised the bodies would be moved to refrigerated trucks. (Even more unsettling is the fact the hotel subsequently reopened!)

After that same hurricane, residents of Sanibel and Captiva Islands were denied reentry to their homes. Access was delayed due to the lack of sewage, electricity and damaged bridges. Abandoned mansions sat exposed for days. Police couldn't get to some of the homes even if they'd wanted to. Numerous burglaries were reported during that period.

Thieves stole over $100,000.00 worth of prescription drugs from a pharmacy during the same storm. When the hurricane crossed Florida, jewelry and art gallery heists occurred in the storm's path. During evacuations for Hurricanes Jeanne and Wilma, a Palm Beach community experienced record burglaries. Police were astounded that thieves could apply their trade during 100 mph winds and without electricity.

Burglaries of evacuated properties are not limited to Florida. Harris County Texas recorded 201 burglaries from Hurricane Rita's evacuation in 2005. In Houston, police arrested seventy-four burglary suspects. Police arrested a dozen suspects burglarizing homes evacuated for Hurricane Gustav, and later a suspect tied to ten burglaries during an evacuation for Hurricane Ike. For Hurricane Sandy that devastated the northeastern U.S., police for the Rockaways of Queens, NY reported a 500% increase in burglaries after evacuations (compared to the same period, 2012.)

You never heard any media reports about burglaries during hurricanes? No need for alarm; the insurance companies paid for it all.

I'd like to thank the following people during this project's unusual journey: Dan Jevons with DJ2 in Santa Monica, who read my proposal and realized what a great movie and game Storm Crashers could be. Thanks to Rich Liebowitz with Union Entertainment in L.A. who agreed, and successfully sold an option to a "big six" movie studio. To attorneys Tom Collier and Howard Bliss who helped me navigate that fun ride. I'd like to thank the following experts who endured my odd what-if questions: Lee Malone, a former Loadmaster for the U.S. Air Force; Lieutenant Nancy Alvarez, Monroe County Sheriff's Office and Homeland Security; Randal Thompson, Resident Agent in Charge, U.S. Coast Guard Investigative Service; Special Agent Ralph Garcia, NICB and Brad Snyder for his knowledge of Special Operations.

Last but not least, to my wife Anthea and my daughter Cassie for their undying support. And to sons Jack and Rich for their brainstorms on action and ideas for really cool weapons.

Richard Wickliffe – January 2, 2016, Somewhere over the Atlantic

If you enjoyed this book, please leave a review on Amazon.com, or, email your comments to Publisher@oaktreebooks.com if that is more convenient.

Available on Amazon and at Publisher's online bookstore: www. ShopOTPBooks.com

About the Author

This is Richard Wickliffe's third novel, which was inspired by actual crimes and was originally optioned by a major film studio. Rich enjoys speaking about creative and unique crimes, including twice at the FBI's InfraGard Counterterrorism conferences, to the U.S, Coast Guard, and on panels at seminars in Las Vegas dedicated to accuracy in crime writing. Rich's writing borrows from the unique (scandalous, criminal or satirical) environments of South Florida where he resides with his family.

Please visit RichWickliffe.com to see more.